Chocolate Flava

Also by Zane

Addicted
The Heat Seekers
The Sex Chronicles: Shattering the Myth
Gettin' Buck Wild: Sex Chronicles II
Shame on It All
The Sisters of APF: The Indoctrination of Soror Ride Dick
Nervous
Skyscraper

Zane Presents

Chocolate Flava

The Eroticanoir.com
Anthology

ATRIA BOOKS

New York London Toronto Sydney

ATRIA
BOOKS

1230 Avenue of the Americas
New York, NY 10020

ISBN-13: 978-0-7434-8238-7
ISBN-10:   0-7434-8238-7

First Atria Books trade paperback edition January 2004

20

ATRIA BOOKS is a trademark of Simon & Schuster, Inc.

Manufactured in the United States of America

For information regarding special discounts for bulk purchases, please contact
Simon & Schuster Special Sales at 1-800-456-6798 or business@simonandschuster.com

Copyright Notices

*This book is dedicated to Pamela Crockett and Destiny Wood.
Thanks for always being there.*

*This book is also dedicated to all the people in the world
who believe in sexual freedom.
Live life to the fullest
while you still have a life to live.*

Contents

Introduction

       I first decided to edit this collection several years ago, when I established Eroticanoir.com. Since then, writing, publishing, and living life in general have delayed the process but I was determined to bring it to fruition. A lot of other erotica anthologies, particularly African American ones, have come onto the scene since I first started writing erotica underground in late 1997. I am glad to see that people are finally embracing their sexuality.

With this book, I was not searching for big-name authors to participate because I don't believe everyone can write erotica. It is a special niche. So I went to those people who I knew could write it. Most of the people in this book write only erotica. It is their passion. I will admit there are a ton of pseudonyms in this book, including my own. We do this for the love of the craft and not for the attention.

Erotica has been defined in many different ways. Some believe it is borderline pornographic, and some of the stuff that comes out probably is just that. To me, erotica is mentally stimulating. It deals with more than just sex but also circumstances, passion, and feelings. It is true that some stories are just meant to make people horny. You can't knock that hustle. However, I reached for something much deeper when I made the selections for this book.

I wanted stories that took risks, that explored unique situations, that were creative beyond compare. I had hundreds of submissions and narrowed it down to the ones contained within these pages. Why? Because they all turned me on. It is as simple as that. I write erotic books for a living so I figure that if a story turns me on, and I am practically immune to them, then the story will more than likely turn other people on also. I also wanted to show that men and women can equally express themselves when it comes to erotic fiction. There are no limitations to the mind.

I could sit here and go on and on about what this book is about and why I decided to edit it, but that would be criminal. You should be getting turned on. So get to it already. I hope you enjoy.

Peace and Blessings,
Zane

LADIES FIRST

The Reunion

Ife Ayodele

It was nearly night in the city they both loved. He stood at the window of the luxurious hotel room she'd arranged for in celebration of his return, the curtains drawn back, open to the sight of the lighted Capitol dome.

Over two years had passed since they last made love. I can't believe that I'm home and that she waited for me, he thought. He was so lost in his thoughts of deep joy and anticipation that he was unaware the woman he had loved for so long stood silently behind him. Two years ago he would have bet any amount of money that this day would never come.

In 1995, Carrie had no time in her life for a relationship. Work—designing her line of hand-painted scarves—and small business development classes occupied most of her time. There was little energy left, even for her love of reading. On many nights, a book would slide from her hand to the floor with a thud, startling her awake with just enough energy to turn off the light and pull the covers closer.

"How you doing this morning?" Nasir smiled. He was a recent regular passenger at the Metrobus stop on Fourteenth and Missouri avenues in Northwest Washington, D.C.

3

Smiling back, she returned his greeting. "Freezing, and waiting for June."

It was a cold, cloudy morning in late January and the streets were dotted with mounds of dirt-flecked slush, remnants of a huge snowfall that had unexpectedly hit the city. D.C. had been virtually shut down for nearly a week and was finally getting back to a semblance of its normal workday routine. Carrie and Nasir traveled the same route daily: up Connecticut Avenue, around Chevy Chase Circle, and then on to Bethesda. They often exchanged small talk that was part of the camaraderie of the daily commute.

"Man, I'll be glad when I don't have to work for anyone but myself. Nothing beats owning a business and doing it for yourself. I know it'll be harder than clocking in and clocking out, but there's nothing like it. At least, not for me." Nasir spoke with great feeling and expressed the same thoughts that ran through her mind each day. In her opinion, too many of the attorneys in the firm where she worked as a legal assistant invoked the law of "divine right of kings" when it came to dealing with anyone whose office wall was not decorated with a framed law school diploma.

"I know what you mean. One day I'm going to work and tell them all 'Massah day done! Beulah done lef' de buildin'.'" Nasir laughed out loud in surprise at her perfectly exaggerated mammy imitation. That was the beginning of their friendship, and they made sure to share a seat on the fifteen-minute ride to work each day. On some mornings, they took an earlier bus and shared breakfast at Bethesda's Metro Center, enjoying its early morning quiet. The realization that there was a mutual attraction both pleased and frightened her.

He was witty and curious, both articulate and streetwise. Handsome and intensely masculine, his features were an unusual combination of smooth dark skin and curly, wavy hair that was completely natural. Long lashes graced his brown eyes and the shadow of a beard enhanced his good looks. It amused her greatly to see the reaction his looks caused in both men and women.

"Ooh, girl, he looks like Rick Fox, only darker," stage-whispered one of two young women who slowed and stared on their way out through the glass doors leading to the subway near the Uno's where they were having lunch.

"He must be some kind of foreigner. Ain't too many homegrown brothers looking like that!" exclaimed her friend.

Laughing at his obvious embarrassment, Carrie spoke. "You must be used to it by now. I'll bet it started when you were about eleven years old."

Ducking his head in embarrassment, he told her, "Yeah, but I get tired of it; especially that 'good hair' shit. A woman damn near rubbed her ass on me yesterday on the bus, talking 'bout 'Where you from? Can you take me wit' you?' I ain't got time for that bullshit. I'm on a mission."

"And what might that be?" she asked in amusement.

"One part of my mission is to open my own business. I took classes in gemology from a school in Georgetown and I want to explore what I can do with that knowledge. The other is finding out when I can take you to dinner. And the third is to tell you some more information about myself that may or may not affect how you feel about me."

"Go on, I'm listening," she replied. There was no anxiety in her tone. She'd been in a lot of places and originating from the country, had seen more than she ever expected to see. Thus, she felt no real apprehension concerning what Nasir was about to reveal.

"You know where I work but what you don't know is that I live on North Capitol Street in a halfway house. I was released from Lorton earlier this month where I did time, more for harming myself than anyone else. I'm a recovering crack addict and got my ass in trouble trying to feed that habit. I wasn't violent, though, just very, very stupid." He hesitated, waiting to see if she would offer him the standard "Be strong, brother, you can do it," while making a very hasty retreat.

"I don't know anybody who doesn't know somebody who went to jail for one reason or another. If they say it's not true, they're lying. I've even got some relatives who I think prefer to be guests of the state than free men at home. My godfather was convicted, rightly so, I might add, for armed robbery. He did it all but gave up that life after doing his time. So I don't hold that against you. You know that old saying 'There but for the grace of God . . . I know you know the rest."

He grinned and sighed with relief, returning the conversation to part two of his mission. "Now, when can I take you to dinner?"

His words and the tone with which he spoke were both a question and an acknowledgment of their growing mutual attraction. She hadn't missed his genuine smile of pleasure as he greeted her each morning and the way his eyes sometimes swept her from head to toe with a slow, simmering gaze.

Carrie was also keenly aware of whose image came to mind during the times when "the sap would rise" as she referred to the desire that often flooded her body. At those times, she would stand at the mirror and stroke her nipples; first through the fabric of her blouse, watching them harden under the brush of her thumbs, completely immersed in the exquisite sensation. Next to her clitoris, they were the most sexually sensitive part of her body and even the thought of how good it felt would arouse her. Opening each button slowly in anticipation, she would then drop the garment and marvel at the soft sheen of her skin and the sexually charged sight of her full breasts with their erect nipples centered in their large brown areolae. Not bad for over forty, she often thought as she cupped each naked breast, her palms making circles around each nipple. "Ohhh," she would breathe softly. "Oh, *damn,* that feels good!"

The sweet sensation traveled like live wires down to her center, already wet with the excitement she'd created. Leaning against the sink, legs spread apart, she'd slide her forefinger slowly through the damp hair and then in and out of herself, enjoying the slick, wet sound. "Oh, yeah—I guess everything's still working 'cause I'm wet like the rainy season." She often laughed as she talked to herself. Imagining her finger to be the tongue of her lover, she would roll her hips against it, feeling the pleasure build and tighten. Looking down, she was even more aroused at the instinctive motion that existed from memory, and thrust faster and faster until sweet release broke over her like a tidal wave. "Mm, mm, *mm!* Every time I explore myself, I'm creating a pleasure map for the man who's going to become my lover." And lately the face that came to her mind's eye at the height of that pleasure was that of Nasir.

"Is there a special place you would like to eat?" he asked. The Friday lunchtime line was long for pizza at Uno's on Wisconsin Avenue and they stood talking, making plans for the much-anticipated first date that was to take place later that evening. They were finally seated, and over seafood pizza, the planning continued.

"I guess it depends on what time you have to be back on North Capitol," she replied with concern, realizing that he probably had a curfew at the halfway house. "Do you think we should just find a place close by and go directly from work? You know we're right near Bethesda's Restaurant Row."

"I pulled a rabbit out of the hat and arranged to be back by ten, so that we wouldn't end up at McDonald's." He laughed.

"I also saved up a good piece of change just for tonight, so don't hold back."

"Well, then, how about F. Scott's? I had dinner there years ago and loved the place!" That it was elegant and romantic was something she wanted him to find out for himself.

Too quickly, lunch was over, and as they passed through the still-crowded restaurant, she caught a glimpse of some of her female co-workers craning their necks. They had rarely seen her with a man, and never with one so handsome and attentive.

Because it was Friday, time seemed to pass as slowly as molasses in January. At five on the dot, Carrie rushed out onto Georgetown Road to catch the subway back into the District. The Bethesda station was a couple of blocks from her office and was never crowded. She arrived home filled with sweet anticipation of the night ahead of them. Instinctively, she knew that they would make love and prepared herself accordingly.

Filling the tub, she added bath oil scented with vanilla and sandalwood and sipped a glass of white zinfandel. The CD was loaded with the mood-enhancing music of Al Jarreau, Dakota Staton, and Etta James. In excited anticipation, she laid silky sheer stockings and undergarments on the bed. Carrie was tall, brown-skinned, and curvy. She had a head full of light-brown, shoulder-length locs, and full lips. Her "big pretty legs" were one of her best features and she intended for him to notice them immediately. A deep-rose knit dress hung outside her mirrored closet door. One day, when she wore a pink sweater, he told her that the color was beautiful against her skin. It reminded her of Janie in Zora Neale Hurston's book *Their Eyes Were Watching God*. Janie tells a woman why she is wearing blue. "Tea Cake love me in blue, so Ah wears it." Carrie was certain Nasir would be aware of why she chose pink for tonight.

While enjoying her luxurious, fragrant bath, a tiny ache began to nag at her right temple. Blaming it on the wine she'd drunk too quickly, she eased her body farther into the warm, oil-silkened water, hoping for relief. When it did not come, she left the tub and took two Excedrin washed down with Coke, hoping for relief from the extra boost of caffeine. Intending to lie down for just a few minutes, she awoke to a knock on the door.

"Oh, shit!" she exclaimed, looking at the clock. "It's seven fuckin' o'clock and I was supposed to be dressed and ready to step out of the door!" She grabbed her robe, ran her fingers through her locs, and ran to pull open the door.

"Oh, my God, I'm sorry." An apology rushed and stumbled from her lips. Nasir stood smiling at the fact that she was obviously flustered, then he stepped inside.

"Don't be—actually you look and smell beautiful." The scents of vanilla and sandalwood still filled the apartment and the oil's fragrance clung to her body, as did the satin robe she wore. Oh, shit again, she thought. I went and grabbed the wrong robe. If this doesn't look like a come-on, I don't know what the fuck else does.

Stammering on, she explained, "I developed the beginning of a migraine headache and took some medicine to ward it off. I guess it worked too well. I'm *so* sorry. I know you have a time constraint, and here I am, nowhere near ready."

"I've got a better idea. You know, Allah is the best of planners. Maybe this is what we were supposed to do—get some food delivered, listen to some very good music, and talk. We've never had enough time to really enjoy knowing each other, so let's make the best of it."

Since D.C. was undergoing major urban renewal with an influx of different kinds of city dwellers, many businesses had cropped up to cater to busy, single, urban pioneers. One such enterprise was a food delivery service that boasted an extensive menu of American and international foods. Nasir ordered Tex-Mex because he loved salsa, which he referred to as "the red stuff," and Carrie chose Tom Yum Soup, one of her Thai food favorites, full of spicy noodles, chicken, and lemongrass in a spicy fish broth. Hope I have some Big Red gum, she thought.

Over food, drink, and wonderful music, they talked about their pasts and their future aspirations. He had become a Muslim many years ago and spoke reverently and earnestly about his faith. Answering her questions about the role of women in Islam, he clarified many popular misconceptions and piqued her interest in a religion that came close to her philosophy of the God of many prophets but no offspring. They spoke of each other's families and his keen desire to have children.

"At last," Etta James sung low and sweet. "My love has come along . . ." Their eyes met at the moment created by the music and their unspoken desire for each other was obvious.

"I want you," he said simply.

Opening his arms to her and drawing her face to his, he kissed her, deeply and tenderly. Wrapping her arms around him, she caressed him, holding him as if she had finally found the one thing she needed to make her life complete.

He lifted his sweater over his head, revealing a chest softly covered by a curly mat of hair. Her eyes traveled down to the waist of his pants and she breathed in quickly at the sight of his navel and the thicker thatch of hair just below. As they held each other, she said to him, "I know this was supposed to happen. I know it in my heart, instead of just in my body.

You've been in my heart for a long time. I just had to find you."

"And now we have found each other. But before we go any further, I need you to know this. Some people automatically think that if a brother is in prison, he must be having sex with a man and lying about it. When the urge hit me, I would masturbate and believe me, I learned to do it good. If a man cares for a woman enough to make love to her, part of that caring is to protect her. So I brought protection for us both, to accommodate any kind of love we want to make; just in case this was in fact the right time."

Wordlessly, they removed their clothes and stood skin to skin, her nipples brushing his chest. Guiding him over the same trail she took during her explorations in self-pleasure, they began a discovery of their own. The scents of sandalwood and vanilla again filled the room as he poured a thin stream of the fragrant oil onto the middle of her back. His fingers caressed her, and were soon followed by strokes from his erect penis. Sliding up and down her back with the circular motion of his hips, he stroked her, moaning, "Mmm . . . mmm, baby, baby."

She reached back and parted herself as he slid into the slick crease of her behind.

"Let me look at you," he said. She turned onto her back as he gently spread her legs and then the center of her that opened up like a dark wet rose at his touch. "Ahh, right there," she gasped, as he made sweet hot circles with his finger. He plunged his finger deep inside her, then out again, as she worked her hips furiously in rhythm with him. Remembering the times she could only touch herself, she thought, There could be *nothing* I could do that is as good as this. . . .

He paused to give her a deep soul kiss. "You're so sweet to

me. I would love to taste us together, but that will come in time."

"I want that, too, but right now I want you in me up to the hilt, deep and hard."

Eager to please, he rode her like a beautiful stallion, muscles flexing, in and out, both of them gasping at the sweet hot center of pleasure they had created. "Give it to me, baby! Ohh, that is so good! Do it to me, do it to me, baby! Damn, you're so sweet and so tight. So sweet . . ."

Their words gasped in passion, the scent of sex and the sounds the union of their bodies made together fueled their senses until they were lost to everything but each other.

"Wait, please, baby," she gasped, and drew him up to her face. He kneeled over her and she took him deep into her mouth, the flavor of the condom now mixed with her own juice. "Now give it to me here like you gave it to me there." She sucked him deep and sweet until he came with a shuddering explosion; a "tongue-lashing" of the finest order.

Full, complete, and content, they lay wrapped in each other's arms until the reality of his curfew caused them to reluctantly part at the last possible minute.

"Can't go back smelling like pussy," he joked as he washed off quickly. "Although some brothers have come back like that, deliberately. They just want to let everybody know they got some. I ain't on that kind of time—all I need is for you and me to have the memory of how good we were together."

Because Carrie had no knowledge of the true nature of addiction, she was unaware of the signs of his relapse although she began to see differences in the man she first knew. What began as inconsistencies and erratic behavior came to a head one cool spring night when Nasir appeared at her door, sweating, wild-eyed, and disheveled.

"I know there's a warrant out against me," he spoke breathlessly, rapidly stepping from one foot to the other. "I walked away from the halfway house yesterday." Sticky white foam caked in the corners of his mouth as he spoke and she was deeply shocked at his appearance.

"Oh, no!" she cried, reaching out to hold him. "Can't you just go back and make the best of it? Won't it matter if you just turn yourself in?"

"It don't matter what I do now. They still gonna send me back. But I just wanted to see you one more time, even though I realize I disappointed you badly. I want to tell you, in spite of what you may believe, that I love you."

Sobbing, trying to retain some kind of control over her emotions, she cried softly, "I love you, too. Please, if there's anything I can do to help you, tell me!"

"I have to go, baby. Please take care of yourself! I just want you to believe me. I'm sorry. I just fell weak—again," he cried, as he sped down the steps and into the darkness of Fourteenth Street.

Heartsick from the losses of both his freedom and their beginning love for each other, she immersed herself in work and study. One night while she was working on a new design, the phone rang. "This is AT&T with a collect call from . . ." The recording hesitated and she heard Nasir speak his name in its pause. "An inmate in the District of Columbia Department of Corrections. If you accept this call, dial one now." She pressed one and waited. She heard his voice, tentative and unsure. "Hi, baby . . ."

"Where *are* you? I was so worried, I didn't know what to do or who to call. I had no idea where you would be sent—"

"Baby, it's okay. I'm right here in the D.C. jail. I have to wait until they decide what to do with me. I may be sent back to Lorton."

"Lorton? Isn't that somewhere in Virginia? How far away is it?"

Laughing at her rush of words, he cut in. "Slow down, baby. It's not far, right outside D.C., and there are buses and vans that bring visitors, if you want to see me. I'll write you and let you know what to do, because I don't want to run up your phone bill. We only have ten minutes and I just want to tell you that I have never been happier than when I was with you. If I ever can, I promise I will make it up to both of us. Love you, baby. 'Bye."

This is surely going to be an experience, she thought. Carrie was amazed at the number of people congregated between Eleventh and Twelfth streets. I have no idea what to do and who to ask, but I'm about to find out.

Vans, cars, women, and children lined the street in front of Woodies, between F and G streets in downtown D.C. One of D.C.'s landmark department stores, it was also transportation central for wives, girlfriends, mothers, children, and other relatives of inmates at D.C.'s correctional facility in Lorton, VA. Some came dressed casually and comfortably while others dressed in a manner that expressed the importance of looking good for the men in their lives.

One young woman, resplendent in gold chains hung with charms, designer jeans, shoes, and a fresh hairdo, bragged to her girlfriend. "Yeah, girl, I just sent my baby two cards for our one-month anniversary and some Timberlands. When them guards turn they heads, I'm gonna give him one a these chains."

"What the fuck you talkin' 'bout?" her friend exploded. "He ain't away at college. His ass in *jail!* What do he need wit' all that shit anyhow? To show off for the rest of them jailbird assholes? So he can profile in jail? Y'all make me sick—acting like just 'cause they black and in jail they some kind of political prisoner! That muthafucka ain't Nelson Mandela or Robin Hood—he a straight-up thug and yo' ass know it. And on top of everything else, who was he robbin', cheatin', and stealin' from—other black folks! Shit, if he want a gold chain, gold watch, or gold teeth, his ass ought to get a job like the rest of us. You know what—I'm tired of bringin' your butt down here every week, but that shit gon' stop! Catch the fuckin' bus!" Still cussing as she reached into her purse for keys, she angrily looked back at her friend who was by then running to get a place in a van, oblivious to the sense behind her friend's tirade.

"Excuse me . . ." Carrie approached a sister who looked less likely to explode and asked how the transportation system worked. She decided to ride in a van. Even though the cost for riding in a van was higher, it was less crowded with a more flexible schedule. Missing a van meant boarding the long bus that she referred to as the "stretch Metro" with its accordion-pleated center that literally bent around corners on its route through the city.

Paying her fare, Carrie boarded a van whose driver operated his vehicle like a conductor and talked nonstop.

"Yeah, I was in Lorton years ago, for child support. But now I got my own business and I'm doing well. Look at me, I'm sixty-five years old and I got me a forty-year-old girl-friend. I know what to *do*, y'all. She told me she can't get enough. . . ."

Oh, shit, Carrie thought. Come on, Dick Tiger, just drive your van and get us there. I hope he doesn't have anymore "my ding-a-ling" stories. Dick Tiger was a Nigerian boxer who had won the world middleweight championship in the sixties. Although she had never seen him, the name was perfect for the image that came to mind whenever an older man boasted of his virility.

Just then, a woman took over the conversation, which swirled around one of the many rumors surrounding the jail and its prisoners, apparently always rampant. Today the story centered around a female corrections officer involved with an inmate, apparently a regular part of prison life. The sister spoke angrily about her own situation. She had recently married her longtime boyfriend at the prison, and was incensed.

"Every time I would come down for a visit, that bitch would grit on me. One day I got tired of that shit and I told her 'That is my man! I know where you live and I will come to your house and beat your ass if I ever hear of you tryin' to fuck with him.' "

Adding her two cents' worth, another traveler spoke in dry amusement. "Some of them *po-lice* bitches ain't thinking 'bout no *co-rrection*. They thinkin' 'bout *e-rection*. Now don't get me wrong—most of them sisters is cool. They let you slide on the pat-down and everybody need a job, but some of them took that job so they could wear them tight-ass pants around a bunch a dudes!"

Well, well, take me to school, Carrie thought. If I ain't getting an education *today* . . .

The van wound its way through the entrance to the prison. The maximum facility, its first stop, loomed like a ruined medieval castle.

All it needs is a moat with some alligators and archers at the turrets, she thought in amazement.

The central facility, also known as Big Lorton, was where Nasir was housed. Men milled around dressed in blue pants, light blue shirts, and jackets, and were housed in dorms as if they belonged to Uncle Sam. In fact, the facility had been a military installation before being taken over as the District's prison.

In the gym-like visitors' room, she waited with anticipation, not knowing what to expect. Her heart stopped and started again when she saw him come through the door, his eyes never leaving her face. She stood as he beckoned her, and walked to meet him. Reaching for her hand, he found seats for them.

"I know you told me you would come, but I was afraid to believe it, even after they called my name, until I saw you when I came through that door."

Facing each other in the seating arrangement mandated by the prison, they embraced and kissed deeply, sharing as much love as could be had under the watchful eyes of the corrections officers.

"I feel like I'm being chaperoned at a high school dance," she remarked, as correctional officers stood around and sometimes walked up and down between the rows of couples.

"You'd be surprised at how creative some of these brothers and sisters can get." He laughed as he pointed out an officer walking toward a pair who were about to get too close for his comfort.

That was the first of many visits for the two years that followed. She came for the religious celebration of Eid, which celebrates the end of the holy month of Ramadan. She traveled to the prison for family days, holidays, and most weekends. In spite of its limitations, prison was the forge that fired, molded, and shaped their relationship and strengthened rather than diminished the love that others dismissed as temporary and ill-advised. They grew stronger together, in spite of never-ending unwanted advice. "Girl, you got to get you some. You can do better than a man in prison. He's just using you."

Nasir and Carrie also discovered the whole of each other, not just the romantic ideal that existed at the beginning of their relationship. He had a volatile temper and she found him at times to be harsh and abrasive. To him, she was overly sensitive and too quick to "get all in her feelings" as he described her emotional reactions.

And too often huge phone bills threatened their communication and their delicious, erotic phone sex play. He would sit at the phone, wrapped in a blanket, while she lay on her bed, each whispering and stroking themselves to orgasm.

"Hold it in your hand and look at it, baby," she breathed. "See that line underneath going to the head of your dick? That's the spot I like and the spot I'm going to lick when I have you in my bed—when I lay you down, straddle you, and wet you with my honey from top to bottom. I wish you could see my pussy now, baby. I wish you could feel my pussy muscles put a hold on your dick and suck it dry. It's wet and juicy and my finger is going in and out and it's making that sound that drives you crazy and you know you like how it smells when I'm hot. Just waiting for you to suck it and lick it, baby. Just waiting for you to lap it up like cream."

He heard her make a soft, hissing sound. He knew she was about to come and whispered, "Come on, baby. . . ." The sound of her pleasure caused his seed to shoot out into the tissue he held in his hand under the blanket. "Whew . . . mm, mm, mm," he breathed. "Can't wait for another bedtime story, baby."

Her love sustained him in prison and his love supported her wait for him. She listened to Al Jarreau a lot. His songs were soothing to her in the middle of the night when she especially missed Nasir, and these words were their anthem: "The love that heals the wound after the war is through." Their pledge to each other was that nothing and no one could break the circle they created for themselves. They would be together "forever and a day."

True to their word, two years later, they stood together.

"Don't turn around," she whispered softly, standing close enough for him to feel her warmth and again smell the vanilla and sandalwood scent he had used on her body that first time. Soft hands gently covered each side of his chest, her fingers stroking his nipples through the down of hair covering his torso. A deep sigh escaped his lips, turning to soft gasps of pleasure as her tongue flicked in and out of his ear, a particular point of pleasure for him. Her travels took her from the nape of his neck to the curve of his behind, while stroking him into an iron-hard erection.

Standing before him again, she slowly removed her rose-colored robe, followed by each item of pastel pink lingerie, which made a pool of silk before him on the floor. She remembered that he liked her in pink, and in preparation for this day had made a special-order selection from a sister-owned adult fantasy boutique in the city.

He bent to pick the garments up, bringing them to his face, inhaling her scent. His eyes devoured her beauty as he spoke. "Forever and a day is how long we said we'd be together. But while I was away, I would lie awake at night, replaying in my mind the times we were together, aching with wanting you and stroking myself thinking of you. I was imagining how it could be again and tried to rid myself of the thoughts of another man loving you, touching and tasting you instead of me."

Her words reassured him as her touch continued to arouse

him. "I want a man that I can depend on, a man who won't make me hold my breath and wonder what's next. I have always believed that man was you and never gave away what I always felt was yours. If there were someone else, I would have told you. If there were someone else, this room with you and me together would not happen. You have always been the man for me."

Following a deep and passionate kiss, he began to take his tongue down the center of her body. Remembering how sexually sensitive they were, he left a heated trail across each of her swollen nipples, licking circles around them and stroking each with the pads of his thumbs. "Oh . . . my . . . God!" she gasped, each word punctuated with pleasure. Reaching between her legs, he searched for and found her wet, diamond-hard clitoris. Encircling it with his finger, he began to slide it back and forth, in and out of her "sweet spot" as he loved to call it. She worked her hips in time with his touch, and with her eyes closed, completely abandoned herself to the pleasure building at her center.

His tongue found its way to that same spot, exploring, encircling, and inserting itself wherever he could give her the most pleasure. Gently trembling at first, she began to shudder and cry out softly, "Oh, oh, baby, I'm coming . . ." Raising herself to a half-seated position, hands gripping his hair to ensure that his tongue stayed on target, she worked her hips in rhythm with him until the sensation took her over the edge and she fell into an erupting, explosive climax.

Weak from pleasure but aroused again by her lover's scent, she rested her cheek against the thick, soft hair at the base of his penis and ran her fingers through his thatch, up to caress his stomach and down to his waiting erection. He laid himself on her tongue and she took him in small swallows until he was completely encircled by her warm, wet mouth. As she slowly released him, his breathing quickened and his hands drew her mouth back for more.

Holding his slick erection in one hand, she slowly licked the length of him, lifting his penis and then sliding her tongue down to his testicles. One by one, she sucked them into her mouth, in and out, loving them with her tongue. Leaning into his own pleasure, he cried out, "Give it to me, baby!" as he made love to her mouth. Eyes closed in ecstasy, the roll of his hips quickened as he thrust deeper into her mouth. "Ah, ah, *ah!* Give it to me, baby!" he gasped. She didn't lose the rhythm or a drop as he exploded deep into her throat.

Entwined, they kissed each other's taste onto their lips, happy in the knowledge that the chemistry that had always created such passion was still there and would always be for years to come. Their "forever and a day" had just begun.

Grocery Gettin'

Eileen M. Johnson

" 'Yester-me, yester-you, yester-daaa-aaa-aay!' "
Singing along with Stevie Wonder, I swung into the parking
lot of Albertsons. Gene left a message saying that when he got
back to New Orleans tonight, he wanted to go out for surf 'n'
turf. After a day of unsuccessfully trying to adjust to my new
work schedule, the last thing I felt like doing was getting
dressed, driving across town, waiting for a table, and then
waiting for our food.

Instead, I decided to stop at Albertsons on my way home.
Gene would get his surf 'n turf wish fulfilled but it would be
served much more cheaply and in the comfort of my own
home.

Temporarily telling Stevie good-bye, I turned off the ignition and got out of the car. The university had recently
adopted a dressy casual policy for faculty and although I was
comfortable, I was hot! My khakis stuck to my thighs as the
late afternoon heat engulfed the city.

Walking into the welcoming, artificial coolness of the supermarket, I dropped my purse into a basket and listlessly
pushed it toward the meat department. Stopping in front of

22

the beef cooler, I picked over the New York strips. Finding a suitable pair for a decent price, I tossed them into the basket. Moving on to the seafood department, I planned on quickly picking up two lobsters and hurrying back home.

Gene and I had only been seeing each other for two months but I had already grown weary of his finicky appetite. The only things he seemed to like were things that I either detested or hated to prepare. For years, I'd watched my mother, her mother, and my great-granny cook everything from quiche to consommé to pigs' feet to portabellas. There was no doubt that I knew my way around the kitchen, but Gene found flaws in everything that I set in front of him. Jokingly, I sometimes wondered to myself if he found my pussy to be bland and undercooked when he ate it.

Giggling to myself, I stopped in front of the lobster tank. Bending down, I tried to spot two that looked large enough for me to pay nine dollars a pound.

"Let me have him, him, and her," a smooth male voice on the other side of the tank was saying. "I'm going to grill the tails so I need really plump ones."

Smiling like a man who was satisfied with himself, the man watched as the clerk used tongs to extract three lobsters from the tank. He was dark brown, tall, and lanky. A little too thin for my tastes, but his smile was intriguing the hell out of me.

"Did I take the ones you wanted?" he asked, his voice thick with amusement.

"No. I am going to take these two," I said as I motioned toward a pair that were playfully clawing at each other.

"Just checking. I have the habit of *taking* what I want," he said in a voice filled with innuendo. Eyeing me openly, he slowly ran his tongue along his top lip.

"Is that so?" I asked, playing along. "How can you take what is being given to you willingly?"

"Well, sometimes people insist that they want to give it to me but they renege and I wind up having to take it."

His words oozed out with a strong, lascivious force. The icy cold air of the supermarket had caused my nipples to strain against the fabric of my bra and my black cotton blouse. Aiming his gaze directly at them, he again gave his lips a slow lick.

"Are you a giver? Or do you prefer to be taken?" he drawled.

Embarrassed, the seafood clerk slinked away to weigh and wrap his lobsters.

"Well," I began thoughtfully, my eyes wide and full of innocence. "I never give and refuse to be taken."

"Oh, yeah? Is that so?" he replied jauntily as the clerk handed him the wrapped lobsters. "Write down a way that I can get in contact with you and I'll teach you the rules of give and take."

Scribbling down my name and number on a receipt that I extracted from my purse, I handed it over to him. Reading it, he smiled.

"Okay, *Miss* Adu. I look forward to talking," he said saucily before walking away.

Turning toward the waiting clerk who had a silly smile on his face, I pointed impatiently to the two I wanted.

"I'll *take* those two," I indicated right before he burst out laughing.

Closing the oven, I reached for the pan on the stove and poured the clarified butter into two ceramic cups.

"It doesn't look separated enough," Gene said from his perch at the bar.

"I've seen and done this a million times. It's separated enough," I retorted with a bit of an edge.

Shrugging his shoulders, he went back to reading the

Times-Picayune. Ever since he'd arrived, he'd picked at my nerves. It was wonderful having a man present in my bed and to curb my loneliness, but Gene had something to say about everything. In his mind, he was an expert at everything. He'd already made comments about the type of foundation I used on my face, the way I wrapped the foil around the potatoes before I put them in the oven, and the way I was grilling the steaks. Taking the lobster tails out of the steam tray, I decided that I was simply going to agree with everything he said. Hopefully, my humbleness would get on his nerves and he would see how it felt to be aggravated.

Opening the oven, I tested the baked potatoes with a fork. Taking them out, I set them on plates along with the steak and lobster tails and brought them over to the table. I walked back to the refrigerator and brought out the condiments. Sitting down, I bowed my head in prayer before digging in and dipping a chunk of the lobster tail into the "not-separated-enough" clarified butter. It was delicious. Cutting off a small piece of the steak, I popped it into my mouth and savored the taste as it melted away. I had really outdone myself.

Looking across the table at Gene, I saw from his facial expression that he was enjoying the food. But I also knew that in a second or two, he would find fault with something. He wanted fucking surf 'n' turf and I'd made it to the best of my ability. Still, not good enough for him. To test him, I silently began to count. *One. Two. Three. Four. Fi—*

"If you would've wet the potatoes and made a slit in the foil, they would've baked easier and been moist," he said, scraping some of the flesh from the skin.

I knew it! I didn't even get to complete the count of five and he was complaining. What really burned me was the fact that he had yet to stop chewing. He was handsome and educated but he had such an immature, small mind.

"So, which courses are you teaching this semester? I'm scheduled to instruct an African-American lit class that you would be great at teaching," I said brightly, changing the subject to something that would allow peace between us. "Can you believe the semester begins in just a few days?" Putting down my wineglass, I braced myself to listen to yet another of Gene's antic stories about his job. *Oh well, no one can ever call me a lousy listener.*

The shrill ring of the telephone shook me from my soft field of sleep. Beside me, Gene snored lightly and wasn't awakened by the ringing.

"Hello?" I queried sleepily.

"My, don't we turn in early," a male voice joked.

Looking at the alarm clock, I saw the face read 10:30. Gene and I had come upstairs after dinner and I had been disappointed to learn that instead of sex, he merely wanted to sleep. I still had on my day clothes but felt like it was morning.

"Sometimes we do. Who is this?" I asked.

"This is Larron. You met me earlier at Albertsons."

"Oh!" Sitting up, I walked with the phone into the bathroom and shut the door behind me. "How are you?"

"I'm fine. Didn't think I was gonna call, did you?" he asked with a laugh.

"I *knew* you were going to call sooner or later. I think I left a lasting impression on you."

"Confident aren't we, Miss Adu?" he said.

"Sure I am. So to what do I owe the pleasure of this call?"

"I was wondering if you wanted to go for a ride."

"Well . . ." I hesitated, peeping out of the bathroom door at Gene's sleeping form. "Why not?"

Laughing like the cat that swallowed the canary and a double serving of cream, he gave me directions to his house, which was only an exit away from mine. Hanging up the phone, I padded lightly back into the bedroom and took off the jeans and tank top that I'd fallen asleep in and put on a simple cotton shift. Slipping my feet into black slides, I grabbed my keys and tiptoed downstairs and out of the house.

"So how long have you been on the air?" I asked Larron as he sped over the Crescent City connection.

"I've been in radio about six years altogether, but I started out in production. I've been a club and party deejay for about eleven years, but I've been doing it on the air for the past two," he answered.

"Okay. I've never listened to WKJI. What genre of music does it feature?"

Looking at me with a deliciously crooked grin, he let a throaty laugh escape his lips. "At WKJI, we feature gospel and spiritual."

"Well, alrighty then!" I answered, turning straight in my seat and looking out the front windshield. Goodness, I needed to change the subject. Here I was, at eleven o'clock, wearing a dress and no panties, riding with a gospel music deejay. "So how long have you had this car?"

"Only about six months."

"Snazzy," I said as I sniffed the leather of his Montreal blue BMW Z-3 convertible.

"It is, if I must say so myself," he said, smiling at the compliment I'd just given his car. "Can you drive a stick?"

"Sure I can," I replied eagerly.

"Shit. That's usually the excuse I use for not letting anyone else drive. Most women don't. Wanna give her a run?" he asked me.

"Hell, yeah!"

Exiting the expressway, he drove until we approached a hospital parking tower. He drove up the winding tower, shifting gears, until we reached the twelfth level. He turned the car around, pulled up the parking brake, and got out of the driver's seat. Getting up to take the wheel, my dress was rumpled around my hips, giving him a clear peep of my pussy and ass. I quickly pulled it down, knowing the impression had been made.

"Why a parking tower?" I asked, hoping he wouldn't soon forget about the sight I'd just treated him to.

"I figured we could start here, just in case you aren't good at driving a *stick*," he said in the same lascivious tone that he'd used at the supermarket. "On second thought, maybe I should drive?"

Immediately kicking into bad girl mode, I lifted the hem of my shift up so he could see my hairy pussy.

"Why don't we *both* drive?" I asked.

"Now how on earth can we both drive?" he questioned.

"Watch," I answered, getting out of the car.

I moved the seat as far back as it could go. Motioning for him to sit down, I lowered his zipper and reached over him to my purse. I took out a Trojan, pulled out his already stiff cock, and rolled the rubber down over it. With my back toward his almost prone body, I lowered myself onto his dick. I shut the door, pulled up the parking brake, shifted the car into first gear, and slowly drove the car down the first ramp while I rode his big, hard dick. Hearing him moan from his position under me turned me on so much that I hit the gas and shifted straight into third. After letting go of the clutch, I began bouncing up and down on his dick while turning down onto the eleventh level. Squeezing down on his dick with my wet pussy muscles, my mind raced with excitement. Trying to navigate the sharp downward turns of the garage while fucking his brains out was very interesting. By the time we reached the third level, the car was in overdrive and so was my body. Speeding down the curves of the tower, I was about to have one of the biggest orgasms of my life.

"Don't wreck my car. Oh shit, baby, please don't wreck my car. Oh yeah, girl, fuck me. Fuck the shit out of me," he mumbled as he brought his hips up to meet my wet and rotating pussy.

As we flew down the ramp of the second level, two nurses who had probably just gotten off duty stopped in their tracks and gave us curious looks while I used one hand to steer and one to shift. While I drove and fucked, Larron's arms reached around me, his hands busily rubbing my nipples. My dress was hiked up over my tits and I was bouncing up and down on Larron's juicy dick. Banging my fist on the horn, I greeted the shocked nurses as I came closer and closer to exploding. We sailed down to the first level as I pressed my left foot on the clutch and used my right hand to throw the shift into neutral. Letting the car roll down onto solid ground, I bucked away as I felt myself coming, my pussy muscles contracting and squeezing every drop of come from Larron's dick. I heard him shout out in ecstasy as my mind exploded with a million colors. Steering the now slow-moving car into a parking space, I tapped the brake lightly to get it to stop. I lifted myself slowly off Larron's dick as he held the spent rubber in place, then I opened the door and stepped out of the car onto my wobbly legs. Standing in the parking lot, I pulled my dress down to cover my breasts and then my hips and my behind. Across the bottom parking level, I noticed three maintenance men staring at me with unmasked curiosity. Smiling and giving them a thumbs-up sign, I walked over to the passenger side and got in.

I looked over at Larron, who was breathing heavier than a horse and hanging his head over the side of the headrest. I couldn't help but smile. He looked absolutely drained. Reaching over to rub his knees, I let out a light laugh. *I am going to have to get groceries more often. Where else can I find more excitement?*

"You must *take* me driving again! I found give and take to be very interesting," I said with my voice full of energy.

Larron looked at me and seemed baffled about why I still had energy. A frown spread over his face.

"Girl, you put something awful on me. But, um . . . yeah. We can go driving again very soon." Tossing the used rubber out onto the ground, he zipped up his pants and sped away toward his house.

I took off my slides and tiptoed back upstairs. Gene's car was still parked on the other side of the garage. Pushing open the bedroom door, I fumbled in the dark to my closet and tossed my shoes inside, then placed my keys down on the dresser. I was about to step into the bathroom for a quick shower before bed when the lights flew on. Gene was sitting, fully dressed, on the edge of the bed.

"Do you always go gallivanting into the night when your tricks call?" he asked in a rough tone.

"You don't know where I've been. I could've gone out for a pint of ice cream."

"Is that why you smell like the whore of Babylon?"

"Look, Gene, I'm not going to argue with you, especially not in my house," I said as I snapped on the bathroom light and took off my shift.

"Look, if you wanted to fuck so bad, why didn't you just wake me up?" he asked, walking in the bathroom behind me.

"Gene, I didn't go and fuck anyone. I had a craving for a shake so I went to Rally's. That's it," I said, turning to look at him with tears forming in my eyes. *Gee, I sure hope this works,* I thought.

"I believe you. Don't cry, Adu. I believe you," he said as I began to bawl.

I deserve an Emmy, I thought, as Gene dropped to his knees in front of me and began to lick away the traces of Larron from my pussy.

Do I really want someone who pretends to be tough on the outside but is actually this soft? I thought, as I watched him get busy with his task. Shaking my head and letting out a sigh, I decided Gene would do . . . for a while, at least.

White Heat

Marilyn Lee

I woke in the middle of the night to the totally delightful sensation of Steve's naked body sliding up mine, his rock-hard cock nestled between the lips of my pussy. His warm lips nibbled at that special spot on my neck just below my left ear. That never failed to infuse my entire body with heat and need for him.

"Oh, Steve . . ." I wrapped my arms around his neck, rubbing my mound against his throbbing dick.

"Yeah, girl?" His deep voice held a question.

He never took my acquiescence for granted, even after twelve years of marriage. Even when I was clinging to his neck, a trembling mass of need for his big, sleek, ebony cock.

"Yes," I pleaded, lovingly massaging the hard muscles of his rump. "Oh, yes, lover. Yes."

"Yeah, Tasha, girl." He settled his hips firmly on mine, slowly sliding the big head of his dick into my waiting, wet body. I shuddered and nearly came. There was nothing in the world half as exquisite as the first electric touch of his big honeyed cock. Moaning in anticipation of the pleasure I knew was coming, I thrust my hips upward, greedily enveloping his

3 2

sweet meat in my clenching body. I knew he loved to have me wrap my legs around his waist and undulate my body against his like a wave breaking against the shore as he pumped his hard, pulsating length deep inside my quivering pussy.

Sex that night was particularly hot and explosive. I lost track of how many times we pushed and pumped and pounded each other into sweet, searing bliss. He came in me again and again. When we finally parted, I felt his sticky cum leak out of my sated pussy and drip down my thigh.

"Damn, girl, that was good!"

"It was de-*licious,* Detective Long," I countered.

He was gone when I woke the next morning. I sat up and looked at my night table. When Steve left for work before I woke, he often left a note.

"Last night was the bomb, girl. Keep that tight wet pussy of yours ready for me."

Smiling, I sank back against the pillow and continued reading. "Jake and I will be part of an undercover sting, so I probably won't see you until tomorrow. But don't worry. Jake's got my back. Love you, girl. Steve."

I lay there smiling as I remembered our early morning lovemaking, until I heard JR's bedroom door open. "Mom! Mom, you awake?" JR was a healthy ten year old with an excellent pair of lungs.

I glanced at my bedside clock and groaned. It was barely seven o'clock. Steve and I almost needed a crane to get JR out of bed at seven on school mornings.

"Be there in a sec," I called and scrambled out of bed. Later that morning when JR was heading to the Poconos on a trip with his Scout troop, I was in the living room ironing with the radio tuned to the local news station when I heard the beeping sound that signaled a special bulletin.

"This just in," the newscaster announced. "A police officer

was seriously wounded this afternoon in a shootout in the East Park section of the city. The officer's name is being withheld until his next of kin can be notified."

With a pounding heart, I set the iron down and looked around for the cordless phone. It was on the sideboard. During the ten years Steve had been on the force, we'd developed a system. Whenever he heard about a police officer getting hurt or killed, either he or Jake would call me ASAP to let me know they were okay. They'd never taken more than an hour to call, even when they were on a stakeout.

Two hours later, as I was getting really scared, the doorbell rang. He'd come instead of calling. "Thank you, Lord," I whispered and ran through the house and threw open the door. "Steve! I—"

But it was Steve's partner, Jake Diamond. One look at his pale face and I started shaking. "Jake! I heard about the shooting. Steve was shot, wasn't he?"

He swallowed several times and nodded.

I grabbed his shirt. "Oh, God, Jake! How bad is he? What hospital have they taken him to?"

"Honey, I—"

I looked past him and saw his car, a dark sedan, parked haphazardly at the curb.

"I'll just get my purse and we can go to him. Please, God, let him be okay."

Feeling more afraid than I'd ever felt before, I started away. I'd only reached the living room door before Jake grabbed me and turned me to face him. "Honey, I don't know how to say this, but—"

I tried to pull away. "Jake, we can talk later! I just need to get to him now."

His grip on my arms tightened and part of me died as I

saw the tears welling in his eyes. "Honey, honey he didn't make it."

"What!"

"I'm so sorry, but he . . . he died at the scene."

"No! You liar!" I tore myself away from him and began hitting his face with my fists. "You lying bastard! He's not dead! He can't be! He said you had his back! Why are you still alive when he's dead? Why are you still alive? You bastard!"

He made no effort to stop me from hitting him and I continued pummeling his face until I collapsed, sobbing hysterically. Then he was on his knees beside me, crying with me and trying to hold me in his arms.

"Take your hands off me!" I screamed. "How could you let him get killed? Where were you when he needed you?"

He stared at me, tears mixing with the blood I'd drawn on his face. "Honey, honey, please——"

"Don't you 'honey' me! Don't you ever call me that again! You get out! I never want to see your white behind again!"

"You don't mean that! You can't mean that!"

"I do! I do! Get out! Now!"

The following days passed in a blur. The house was filled with family, friends, and police officers offering condolences and just sitting with me and JR. I couldn't feel anything. I'd seen Steve's body, but I couldn't accept that he really was dead until I saw Jake again. Then it all came back. I felt a wave of hate wash over me that he was alive while my lover was dead.

"Get out of here!"

He spread his hands helplessly. "Honey, please, I would have died to save him. You know that!"

"Then why aren't you dead, too?"

I heard the gasps of the others gathered and knew they were shocked, but I couldn't help hating the sight of Jake.

"Tasha, baby, you don't mean that." Mom squeezed my shoulders and looked at Jake. "She's upset. She doesn't mean—"

"I do mean it!" I pulled away from Mom and stormed over to stare up at Jake.

His face still bore the traces of bruising from where I'd battered him. I had to clench my hands into fists to keep from clawing my nails down his face. "Get out and don't come back! JR and I don't ever want to see you again."

"Mom!" JR grabbed my hand in protest. "Mom, we need Uncle Jake."

"He's not your uncle, JR. He's the man who let your father get killed!"

Jake blanched, then turned and walked out of the house. I didn't see him again until the funeral. I allowed him to be a pallbearer because I knew that's what Steve would have wanted, but I refused to allow him to come back to the house afterward.

The months following Steve's funeral were horrible. I fell asleep every night reliving our last night together. I savored the memory of the feel of his thick, heated cock repeatedly torpedoing into my slick, pulsing pussy, sending delicious chills and shivers of bliss and lust through every nerve ending in my body. Knowing I'd never experience that joy again was almost more than I could bear.

Jake called often, but I couldn't talk to him.

"Girl, you know that man would have died for Steve," my best friend Tia said one night after I'd again refused to take Jake's call.

"Because of that man, my Steve is dead!" I said bitterly.

"You know Steve trusted him with his life."

"And look where it got him! I don't want him anywhere near me or JR ever again."

She gave me an angry pat. "Oh, so it's all about what *you* want. Well, what about what JR wants and needs?"

"JR doesn't want to see him either."

"Girl, you are talking foolish and you know it. You know how JR feels about him and you know how Steve felt about him. I'm not going to sit here listening to this. You know in your heart that if there was anything that man could have done to save Steve, he would have. Or have you conveniently forgotten that he got shot three years ago because he jumped in front of a bullet meant for Steve?"

"So what? It was just a scratch."

"He was in the hospital a week!"

I stared at her with angry tears streaming down my cheeks. "Fine! But this time he let him get killed!"

"Girl, get a grip! Remember he and Steve were friends since high school. How do you think he's feeling?"

I knew she was right, but I needed someone to hate. And at six-two and roughly 190 pounds, Jake made a nice-sized target. "So?"

She hugged me. "So? You know you and JR are all he has. He needs to be with you."

I shook my head. "No."

"Yes." She gripped my hands. "You've kept him away for over four months. You think that's what Steve would have wanted?"

That shook me because I knew it wasn't. Steve had often told me that Jake was like the brother he'd never had. "I don't know."

"Tash, do the right thing." Tia sighed, shaking her head. "If you'd talked to him just now, you would have heard how . . . I'm afraid for him. Call him to make sure he's all right."

"So now I'm supposed to be his keeper?"

"No. Just a friend. As he's been yours and Steve's for years. Don't you think he needs a friend?"

"He has other friends."

"None as close as you and Steve. You know that. Tash, the man sounded as if . . . you'd better call him. Tonight. Now."

I shook my head. "I wouldn't know what to say to him. The breach between us is too wide now."

"Narrow it. Go see him."

I thought of the things I'd said to him. Things I couldn't take back. Things I didn't want to take back. "I can't leave JR alone."

"Alone? So I'm nobody now?" She pulled me up from the sofa. "Go see him. Stay the night if you have to. I'll stay with JR."

Jake had a small rancher on the other side of town. I knew he was home when I arrived because his car was in the driveway and his house lights were on. But he didn't respond to the bell.

I wanted to go home, but deep in my heart, I knew I'd treated him badly. And I did miss him. During the past six years, he'd had dinner with us at least twice a week. He'd stood in for Steve at any father-son event with JR that Steve couldn't make. He'd sent me a dozen red roses on my birthday and sometimes for no reason at all. And he'd always provided a shoulder to cry on whenever Steve and I were fighting.

In fact, I'd once told Steve that when I needed to hear an endearment, I went to Jake. Steve's idea of an endearment had been to call me "girl" in that deep, honeyed voice of his that I'd loved so much. Steve had often joked that Jake called me "honey" so often, he must think it's my name.

I rang the bell again. When he still didn't answer the door, I walked around the house and peeked in the window of his

living room and nearly screamed. Jake was sprawled in a re-
cliner with his gun in his hand, pointing toward his body.

With a pounding heart, I ran back around to the front of
the house, digging in my handbag for the key to his front
door. I was shaking so hard, I couldn't get the key in the lock.
"God, please! Help me!" I prayed, then stepped back from the
door and took several deep breaths. When my hand was
steadier, I opened the door and ran down the hall to the living
room.

"Jake! Oh, God, Jake, what are you doing?!"

He didn't answer, but lifted the gun higher.

"No!" I screamed and ran across the room to his chair.
"No!" I grabbed his arm and tried to wrestle the gun away.

He resisted and lifted his free hand to push me away. I
stumbled back and nearly lost my balance. "Jake! Jake, what
are you doing?"

When he turned to look at me, the anguished look in his
eyes made me realize how badly I'd hurt him. He'd loved
Steve like a brother and I'd treated him like dirt and kicked
him to the curb and beat him down. Tia had been right. He
needed comforting, too. "Jake . . . what are you doing?"

"Cleaning my gun."

I'd never heard him sound so miserable and defeated. I
glanced wildly around. I saw none of the paraphernalia I knew
was necessary for gun cleaning. "Jake . . ." I bit my lip and
inched forward. "What are you doing?"

He pointed a finger at me. "I'm thinking of taking care of
your little problem."

"What . . . what problem?"

He shrugged and took a deep sobbing breath that made me
ache for him. "Of my being alive when Steve is dead."

My eyes filled with tears and terror filled me as I realized that I'd driven him to the brink of despair. "No! No! I didn't mean that, Jake!"

He shook a fist at me. "Oh, yes you did! Don't you stand there lying to me! We both know you meant it! You want me dead! Well, damn you, if that's what it takes to get your forgiveness, I'll give you what you want!"

"No! No!" I stumbled over to the chair, grabbing his arm. "No! You selfish bastard! You put that gun down! How much grief do you think JR and I can bear? We can't lose you, too! You put that gun down now!"

He pushed me away again and I scrambled to my knees, fear clutching at my heart. When I realized how close he was to shooting himself, I think that's the first time I realized how much he meant to me. How much emptier I'd feel if he were dead.

"No! No! God, Jake, no! No! Oh, God, don't!"

He stared at me, his eyes filling with tears. "Damn you, Tasha! How could you shut me out of your life? How could you think for a single moment that I wouldn't have died to protect Steve? You think I would have allowed anyone to take him from you and JR if I could have prevented it? I tried, damn it, but I couldn't reach him in time! It happened so fast. I heard the shot and when I got there . . . he was lying on the ground. When I picked him up and knew he was dead, part of me died, too!"

He put his free hand over his face and sobs shook his body. I was used to Jake being strong. Strong for Steve, strong for me, and strong for JR. To see him sobbing like that was more than I could stand.

"Don't! Please!" I rushed to him and wrapped my arms around him. "I'm sorry, Jake! So sorry!" I reached for the gun and this time he allowed me to remove it from his hand. I put the safety on, placed it on the table out of his reach, and wrapped my arms around him. "Oh, Jake! Jake, I'm so sorry for hurting you."

His arms went around me and he buried his face against my breasts. "Oh, God, I can't stand the pain anymore! I failed you and JR. I let Steve get killed!"

"No! No!" I pulled away and cupped his face in my hands. "No! You didn't fail us. You've never failed us! It wasn't your fault, Jake! I know that. Part of me has always known that. I was just hurting so badly . . . I needed someone to blame."

He stared up at me. "I feel empty. I have nothing and no one."

"That's not true." I stroked his damp cheeks. "You have me and JR. We need you, Jake."

"I would have died to protect him. If I could, I would have taken that bullet. I just couldn't get there in time."

"I know that. I always have." I stroked my fingers through his dark, silky hair. It was longer than he usually wore it and he looked as if he hadn't shaved in days. I sighed. "I'm just so . . . sorry I made this so much harder for you. Forgive me, Jake."

He stared up at me, his eyes filled with sorrow. "I'm the one who needs to be forgiven." He pulled me down onto his lap and pressed his cheek against mine. "I thought I'd die when you wouldn't let me be there for you and JR. I need to be with you both." His arms tightened around my waist. "Oh, honey, I've missed you!"

"We've missed you too, Jake!" When I turned to face him, he leaned forward and devoured my lips with his mouth. At the contact, a series of electric charges sizzled through my body, making my pussy clench and throb.

It wasn't the first time he'd kissed me on the mouth. When Jake's parents had been killed in a plane crash two years earlier, he'd been so distraught that Steve had asked me to spend the weekend with him. "He needs a woman's touch, and right now, girl, you're the only woman in his life."

The first night, I'd held him in my arms, kissing his hair and rocking him. When he lifted his head, his blue eyes wide, looking like a little lost boy, I'd done what I did when JR looked like that: I leaned down and kissed him gently. He'd responded by kissing me back. We'd traded a few gentle, healing kisses that had no trace of passion. And although I'd been vaguely aware that he was slightly aroused, he'd made no move on me.

So it was strange to feel the rush of desire that surged through me when he kissed me now. Maybe it was sitting in his lap while he held on to me like he'd never let me go again. Or maybe I'd missed him so much. I don't know. I just know one moment, I wanted to comfort him, the next, I'd wrapped by arms around his neck and I was eagerly returning his kiss, conscious of a mounting need to feel his cock inside me.

His lips were warm and sweet against mine. He kissed me slowly, as if savoring the taste and feel of my mouth. With a gentle tenderness that took my breath away, he encouraged me to part my lips. When I did, I felt his tongue, warm and moist, searching for mine.

I leaned into him and he deepened the kiss. Within moments, I could feel him hardening under my buns. When I felt his big hands brushing against my breasts, I shivered and dragged my mouth away from his. I pressed my face against his shoulder, aware I'd already reached the point where I was ready to slam my pussy down onto his hard dick.

Just as Steve always did, he lifted my face and looked up at me, asking for permission to continue. "Honey . . . ?"

My mind screamed that I needed to stop this now, but I felt limp and needy. I wanted, I needed to be made love to. I needed to feel a cock inside my aching, empty pussy. And who better to fill that need than Jake, the man who'd always been sweet and gentle and who'd called me "honey" from day one?

"Yes," I whispered and lowered my face for his kiss.

He lifted me in his arms and carried me upstairs to his bedroom. Once there, he undressed me slowly, kissing each part of my dark body he exposed. He lingered a long time over my breasts, sucking and licking me until I felt my pussy dripping and my body shaking with cock lust.

When he undressed, a fresh surge of dampness oozed from my body as I stared at him. He had an absolutely beautiful body with broad shoulders, flat abs, narrow hips, and a surprisingly large cock with a thick, pink head. He slipped between my parted thighs, rubbed his dick against my pussy, against my clit, and then finally, slowly, he pushed the enormous head into my aching, hungry twat. It had been so long and I was so horny that I moaned, shuddered, and came when he bottomed out in me.

"Oh!! Oh, God! Jake! Jake! Please! Oh, more! More!"

The feel of his big dick moving inside me in slow, measured strokes was mind-numbing. As I lay on my back, I lifted my head and looked down our bodies. The sight of his pale, thick cock sinking balls deep into my dark pussy was enough to send me to the brink of another orgasm. I fell back against the bed, pushing my hips up to meet his downward thrusts, loving the feel of his hot meat cleaving through my wet twat.

"Please! Jake, please. I'm almost there again! Please!"

He suddenly cupped my bottom in his big hands, lifted my hips, and ground his down against mine. Then he thrust his hard length deep in me at the same time his hot devouring mouth found that sensitive spot below my left ear.

I moaned and shuddered and sobbed with delight and shattered into a million pieces as my body was flooded with delicious wave after wave of blistering pleasure. He stopped to soothe me before following me over the edge into pure paradise, pumping my unprotected pussy full of cum.

Afterward, he held me in his arms, kissing me gently, and cupping my breasts in his warm, caressing palms. I loved having my breasts held and my nipples tweaked. And I liked to be talked to after sex.

"Honey? Are you all right?"

I felt safe, loved, and happy. I rubbed my body against his and smiled when he shuddered in response. "I'm . . . fine."

He pressed a tender kiss against my forehead. "Did I . . . please you, honey?"

"Yes. Oh, yes, Jake! Yes!"

He sighed and hugged me against him. I fell asleep feeling warm and content for the first time since Steve's death.

He woke me in the night, wanting me again. "Honey?"

I felt him hard and throbbing against my leg and a jolt of desire shot through me. I turned willingly into his arms and moaned when he slid into me with a slow steady movement that left me gasping with wanting him.

"Oh, honey, you're so sweet." He rained soft, heated kisses on my breasts. His hot hands were everywhere: stroking my breasts, my thighs, cupping and massaging my rump, rubbing my clit.

My body burned everywhere he touched it. I found myself wanting him as much as I'd wanted Steve. "Jake . . ." I gasped. "Jake . . . oh, Jake!"

"Honey, you feel so good. You smell so good. I need this. I need you. Oh, honey. Honey."

His whispered words of delight fueled my passion and hunger for him. I clung to him and we kept at each other until, exhausted and sexually sated, we fell asleep in a tangle of arms and legs, his slowly deflating dick still in my pussy.

In the morning, I couldn't believe what I'd done. Steve was barely cold in his grave and there I was jumping in bed with his partner. His white partner.

"Honey . . . about last night . . . I don't want you to think that I . . . I . . ." He ran a hand through his dark hair and looked at me with a helpless look in his eyes.

I stared at him, wondering why I'd never noticed how blue his eyes were or how handsome he was. I shrugged with a nonchalance I didn't feel. Having him call me honey reminded me of the night before, when he'd groaned the word in my ear as he'd repeatedly plunged into me like an out-of-control jackhammer. And I'd happily accepted and welcomed him in my arms and deep into my body.

"Last night was something we both needed," I said as we shared coffee in the kitchen the next morning. "It was . . . therapeutic. We don't need to apologize for it or analyze it to death. We needed it and it happened."

He sighed, leaning against the counter. "Honey . . ."

I put down my coffee cup and went over to him. I leaned up and kissed his cheek. "It's all right, Jake." I drew back and looked at him, amazed I could look him in the eye. That last time we'd made love, I'd responded to him like an alley cat in heat, demanding that he fuck me. And he had, driving me into a frenzy until my whole world centered around his conquering cock.

"Just promise me that you won't clean your gun like you were going to do last night."

He sighed. "There didn't seem to be much point to anything. Steve was dead and you'd tossed me out of your life."

"And now?"

He licked his lips. My stomach muscles tightened as I recalled how pleasant his lips had felt sucking my breasts. Why had I never noticed how full and sensual his bottom lip was? Come to that, how had I never noticed how sexy he was or what a big cock he was packing?

"Honey . . . I don't know how to say this."

I shrugged. "Just say it."

"Last night was very special for me. I've been . . . wanting you for a very long time."

I stared at him. "What? You've wanted . . . but . . . you were Steve's best friend! He trusted you with me!"

He flushed. "And I never stepped out of line with you. Never! I never let you see how I felt, but Steve knew."

"I don't believe you! If he'd known, he wouldn't have let you anywhere near me!"

He shook his head. "He did know, but he also knew I would never act on those feelings. Not only because we were best friends, but because I'd never do anything to hurt you."

I thought of all the times Jake had greeted me by locking me in a bear hug and felt betrayed. When I thought he was being friendly, he'd wanted to sleep with me. And now that Steve was dead, he thought I was going to be his woman? Just for a moment, I wondered if he'd allowed Steve to be shot so he could have me, but quickly dismissed the thought. No matter how he felt about me, he'd loved Steve.

"I can't handle this, Jake. Last night is not going to happen again. If you need sex, you'd better—"

"I don't need sex. I want *you*. I *love* you."

I backed away from him. "Well, I don't love you." I remembered that gun in his hand the night before and rushed on. "I do love you, Jake. You know I do. Just not like *that*. But JR and I miss you and need you back in our lives. As my friend."

He ran a hand through his hair. "Just a friend, honey?"

I nodded. "We both needed last night, but I don't need or want you as a lover, Jake."

He sighed and sagged back against the counter. "Fine. I'll be your . . . friend, Tasha."

I nodded. "Come see JR soon."

He came the following night. When JR rushed at him and burst into tears, I felt awful for having kept them apart for so long. Jake and I avoided looking at each other and only spoke to each other when necessary. But after three weeks, it became easier to be in the same room with Jake and behave as if we'd never spent a lustful night together. Until . . .

. . . I started having erotic dreams about him. I'd want him in the middle of the day. And when he came to see JR, I began visualizing him naked, aroused, and wanting me. It got so bad I could barely look at him without feeling a rush of dampness between my thighs.

He never alluded to our night together and he'd stopped calling me honey. And I missed that. After six weeks, I wanted him so badly, I didn't care what people would say about my sleeping with Steve's ex-partner who also happened to be white.

He'd said he loved me and I wasn't so sure anymore that I didn't love him in the same way. I was certainly consumed with desire for him and his big, thick cock.

One Friday night, I sent JR to spend the weekend with my parents. I chilled some wine and asked Jake to come over. The look in his eyes when I opened the door wearing nothing but a red teddy and matching heels made me ache for him.

"Oh, honey," he whispered and drew me into his arms. There, in the doorway, we kissed with wild abandonment, uncaring of what the neighbors would say. Within moments, he was aroused and I was ready for him. He lifted me in his arms and carried me upstairs.

Holding me in his arms over my bed, he hesitated. I saw a look of concern in his eyes. "Here, honey? Are you sure?"

I didn't know how I was going to feel in the morning about sleeping with Jake in the same bed I'd shared with Steve. I didn't know what the future held for me and Jake; or even if we had a future together. I knew my parents wouldn't be pleased. But I didn't care. I just wanted him. I'd loved Steve with all my heart and soul. But he'd been dead for nearly six months. I was alive. I had needs and wants and they all centered around Jake and his cock. I meant to spend the entire night with him buried to the hilt in my pussy, while I shuddered under him like a shameless hussy.

"Yes," I whispered.

He laid me gently on the bed and settled his big body between my trembling thighs. "Oh, honey, I need to be inside your sweet, sweet pussy."

"Funny you should mention that," I murmured, reaching down to part the lips of my twat for him. "Because I've been dreaming about that big, pussy-pleasing dick of yours. I need it inside me. Now, Jake! Now. Shove it in! Shove it in!"

Cupping my breasts in trembling hands, he kissed me and thrust into me with a maddening slowness that made my toes curl. I closed my eyes and shut the world out. Tonight there was just me and Jake in a world filled with luscious, illicit pleasure.

What If?

reese williams

You ever notice that most black colleges are either in the ghetto or somewhere out in the fuckin' sticks? Well, my college was a mix of both. We were in the sticks surrounded by a poor-ass town. Remembering back to when I was a freshman, I would like to say that I wasn't typical, but I was. I was wide-eyed, dick-hungry, and majoring in meeting my future *husssben*. That's *husband* to all you proper tricks. It wasn't even a guess where I was going when I graduated from my bama-ass high school. Shoot, I spent eighteen years of my life living less than a mile away from Wheatley College.

After dropping off my one suitcase at the freshman girls' dorm, I met up with some of my homegirls and headed over to Assembly Hall for a meet-and-greet with the president of Wheatley, Dr. McGregor. The only fucking thing I remember about freshman orientation was when cue-ball-head McGregor said, "Look to the left of you and the right of you. One of you will not be here to see the grass turn green in spring semester." Did I know he was talking about me? No, I was too busy cutting the fool with my girls.

On the way out of orientation, I noticed all these fine-ass

49

brothers standing under a big tree right in front of Assembly Hall. You know my hot ass had to boom strut right over there to get a closer peek.

"Yo, fresh meat!"

This dope brotha stepped up. He was 6'5" with skin the color of cinnamon, a jet-black corkscrew curly afro, and a real thin frame, which my girls said meant he had a long, lean dick.

I tried to play the role. "Ill, boy, is you talking to me?"

"Yeah, shorty. My name is Mare."

I'm thinking they named him right with that pretty-ass hair. He was looking like the Pretty Pony doll I had when I was growing up.

"My brothers and I are choosing this year's little sisters and I want you to be down."

"Listen, I ain't washing none of your drawers or typing no damn papers. I'm slick to y'all. I ain't no dumb chick."

"No, it ain't even like that! The men of Beta aren't like these other knucklehead fraternities on campus. We treat our young ladies just like they were our little sisters, nothing more. So, shorty, what's your name?"

"Tiffany."

"Oh, Tiffany, is it? That's a pretty name. You got any brothers at home?"

"No, but I got cousins."

"Tiff, it's just like that! I wouldn't ask you to do anything that they wouldn't ask you to do."

I thought about it and the worst thing my cousin Roscoe had asked me to do was eat a mud pie.

"Tiff Money, you gotta let me know what's going on in that pretty mind of yours. You think you might be interested? If so, I need to know, now!"

I peaked at them eager beavers salivating over my beaver under the Beta tree. I guess Mare peeped what I was thinking.

"Naw, Tiff, you would just be my little sis. Ignore them nuts!" Mare placed his hand on my cheek, forcing our eyes to meet. He lowered his voice to a raspy whisper. "Listen, meet me at Miller Hall at nine on the dot, if you want to be down."

He pulled out a dope leather Beta organizer from his Phat Farm messenger bag, ripped out a clean sheet of paper, and wrote down his room number.

"Tiff, the frat is known for community service. It'll look great on your transcripts. Plus, everybody knows, Beta only selects dimes to be their little sisters."

I snatched the paper. "Whatever. I might be able to help you out."

Mare winked at me and walked back under the Beta tree. His fraternity brothers surrounded him, giving him dap and yelling, "Player! Player!"

I tried to be calm and maintain as my girls begged me for information about Mare. Shit, I had to go sit on the steps of Assembly Hall so that my knees would stop shaking so much. Even though I was a freshman, I knew Beta ran Wheatley's yard. Even old head McGregor was a Beta. I heard his seventy-year-old ass would be still trying to step if he hadn't thrown his back out last homecoming. I opened the paper and under Mare's room number, he'd scribbled, "Come alone!"

You know where my fast ass was at the appointed hour, knocking on Mare's door. I had to step over all these miscellaneous dudes looking punked out in the hallway, marking a trail to his room. Mare opened the door so damn fast, I almost fell into his room. He yelled at the guys in the hall, "Yo, keep it down! Beta business going on!" Since most of them tricks wanted to pledge Beta, they shut the fuck up quick.

His room was laced with black-and-silver paraphernalia from floor to ceiling. Mare was blasting jazz out of these big-ass speakers and his room smelled like African queen incense.

"Whoa, who is this?" There was some chickenhead chilling on Mare's bed. Yeah, I recognized that stuck-up bitch. Her name was Lauren. "Mare, I ain't down with the threesome!"

"Tiffany, it's not even like that. But you should know that it's between you and Chi-town here for the lil' sis position. I just want to ask you both a few questions."

Damn, a test? I hadn't been spending no time with the books! Not one to be clowned, I stared Lauren up and down, with her fly-ass Coach backpack and name-brand gear, took one step forward, and said, "What's the first question?"

Mare gave me this Chiclets smile, looking like he was gonna pat me on the head like a puppy. "That's the attitude Beta needs!" He glared at Lauren. "Chi-town, would you do anything for Beta?"

Stuck-up stammered, "Li . . . li . . . like, what?"

"Like what? What kind of fucking answer is that, Lauren?" Mare was heated. "I'll tell you what kind, a wrong fucking answer!"

I saw the opening and went for it. "I'll be down for Beta."

Mare looked down at his dick. "Well, Tiff Money, then get down."

I walked over to Mare and unbuttoned his camouflage pants, pulling them down real slow as I did a deep-knee bend. Mare had on these tight black cotton CK briefs and was about the hairiest motherfucker I had ever seen. I guess he felt me pause 'cause he got this real pissed-off look on his face. It kind of reminded me of the last time I babysat for my two-year-old cousin and he threw my favorite shoes in the toilet to see if they could float.

"I guess you ain't the one, Tiff."

Mare started to bend down and pull up his pants, when our eyes met. "Don't rush me!" I rolled my eyes while sticking my fingers down the sides of his briefs, pulling them down around his ankles. I looked up and was introduced to disappointment a.k.a. his dick. It was no longer than my hand! I wasn't even going to dignify it and try to hold it with two. A fucking one-hander! I looked up at him and he looked damned pleased with himself. I chuckled. "Beta for life, right?" I took the whole dick and nuts into my wet mouth.

Well, little Miss Chi-town went screaming out of the room. I figured since I was down there with the door wide open to the hallway, I would finish the job. The pledges, who now had full view of Tiffany's World Famous House of Blow, were hollering while Mare was trying to knock my top teeth out with his Peter Rabbit buck and hop moves. Mare was moaning, "Oh, sis . . . yeah, sis . . . make it good for Beta. Make it good for America."

America? I'm just as patriotic as any other sister, but "make it good for America?" That's when I looked up at the fraternity paddle on his wall (I was that bored) and saw his line name was, get this, Mr. America! What a joke! I stroked the tiny space between his nut sack and asshole with my pinky and Mare came with the quickness, damn near pulling out my hair the entire time. Mare pulled up his pants, while I did a quick tooth count to see if I was missing any of my fronts. I then found out the source of Mare's line name, when he started talking just like a Miss America contestant—for a long time, about himself, and boring the hell out of me!

"My real name is Phillip and my father and his father are Beta men."

Phillip closed the door and the pledges in the hall groaned, fearing they would miss something. Phillip, alias Mare, pulled his tight "Bleed Beta" T-shirt off, exposing a sandy-colored Beta brand on his left arm.

"The reason why I copped this phat single is 'cause I'm president of the chapter."

He stripped off the rest of his clothes, put on his shower shoes, and threw a towel around his waist. Before he left the room, he looked back and said, "Tiffany, you are so lucky to be with me."

Ouch, Mare hurt me with that comment! But being down with big head (and you know which head I am talking about) did increase my popularity on campus. In return, I fucked Mare every day, every way, for the rest of the fall semester. Pledges carried my books to class, I went to all the Beta parties, and I was even crowned Miss Freshman.

When I went home for spring break, I got a letter from the college asking my ass not to return. I had flunked out. I called Mare, who was back home in Lake Vista, Louisiana, to see if he could talk to "Super Beta" McGregor. Even though it was one o'clock in the afternoon, Mare knocked the receiver off the phone and was pissed because I woke him up. After I read the letter, Mare yawned and gave me this long-ass speech about how "Beta stands for books" and how I apparently couldn't hang. Then he tells me that he has to go because his girlfriend, Lauren, had to use the phone.

I damn near dropped the phone. "Chi-town?"

He whimpered in the receiver, "Yeah."

All I heard after that was the dial tone.

• • •

It's now three years later and I'm starting off at Wheatley College all over again, as a twenty-year-old off-campus freshman. I attend classes in the morning and then jet across town where I work the late-afternoon-until-dinner shift as a waitress at Delight's Diner. Every evening, weekend, and free moment is spent with my son PJ. This time, I was ready to get my diploma. I was doing well too, until I had chemistry. The lab was kicking my ass! I knew I was in trouble when the lab assistant pulled me to the side one day after class.

Beaker, the assistant, was a thick, sturdy brother. He had a closely cropped afro, bushy black eyebrows, and juicy lips that you just wanted to suck like a dick. The girls in the lab didn't even try to step to Beak. The word on campus was unless you were a chemistry formula, Beaker wasn't a bit interested.

"Dini Brewster, right?"

So I wouldn't get associated with Phillip or that Beta drama, I now went by my middle name on campus.

"Dini, you're close to failing chem lab. Do you need some help? If you do, let me know. I tutor students under the Beta Community Service Project."

"Hold up, Beaker, you down with Beta?" I just couldn't see it, with him always sporting that corny white lab coat all over campus.

"Shh, I'm pledging now."

Beaker held up one finger to his beautiful mocha lips. He looked around on some Secret Service shit.

"I really don't even wanna be down but my pops, gramps, and big brother are Bleed Beta."

I'd heard this shit before. "Beak, what's your last name?"

"DuBois, why?"

"Oh, shit!"

• • •

Weeks went by, I played the game like I didn't know he was Phillips's baby brother, and Beaker tutored me and earned points with Beta. I even managed to pull a C out of chemistry. Later, my boy Beak would ask me for a favor.

I'd bumped into him in the student union. "Damn, Beak, your face is fucked up!"

I guess his future Beta brothers didn't care if he was related to Mr. America, 'cause it looked like my boy Beak had taken three the hard way. Back when I was associated with Mare, I used to get my rocks off on all the attention. Pledges would approach me on campus begging me to keep Mare busy all night. Seeing Beaker scared, face shot to hell, and paranoid just didn't give me that same rush anymore.

"Dini, can you meet me later in Miller Hall?"

"Hell, no! Whatever you got to tell me you can do it right here!"

Beaker started looking around like a crackhead getting ready to sell you some hot shit, and let out a deep breath.

"Listen, Dini, I'm still a virgin. I dated the same girl all through high school. I just knew this girl was going to be my future wife. We decided to lose our virginities on our prom night and . . . I'm sorry, Dini, I've been practicing this in my head all day. I didn't realize it was . . . this is just so hard."

I snickered. "Yeah, yeah, yeah. Look, Beak, I don't mean to interrupt *As the World Turns,* but I got to roll out."

"Wait, Dini!"

He grabbed my arm and I gave myself mad props. Why? Because if a motherfucker had done that a year ago, I would have broke my foot off in their ass. Beaker was different, though, and he looked so hurt.

"Here we go again! Beak, you got five minutes to plead your case."

He took my hand and led me to a table. I sat on the bench and he straddled it so that he was facing me. I glanced down at his lap. I know, bad habit. Damn, was Beaker smuggling socks, or what?

"On prom night, we made it to the hotel room and she asked me to undress for her. So I did this mean striptease for her. I had the Luther Vandross CD, the candles lit, and er'thang! I took off my jacket, then my tie, my cummerbund, my shirt, and finally . . ."

"Damn, what?"

"When I took off my pants, Dini, her eyes got big. When I pulled down my boxers, she grabbed her purse and ran out of the room. I still don't know what I did wrong. She never spoke to me after that day. I been living like a monk ever since."

Beak looked like a weight had been lifted off his shoulders. He started fiddling with the hem of his lab coat. He took another deep breath and started talking at warp speed.

"The big brothers told us we have to start choosing little sisters and the whole campus knows the pledge picks the girl they get down with and I ain't trying to put myself out there again. I thought I would ask you."

Damn, I must have a Beta magnet implanted in my ass. "Listen, I don't do virgins."

He took my hand. "The other day you left some papers in the chemistry lab and I got your address from the registrar's office. I drove to your house, Dini, and I saw you outside playing with a little boy who I am going to assume is your son, right?" Beaker turned over my hand. "I don't see a ring on your finger."

I know nerd boy wasn't going to blast me for being a single mom! I tried to snatch my hand away, but he tightened his grip, leaned in close, and smiled.

"I admire you, Dini. I like the way you keep your head up. You're beautiful, you seem like a caring mom, and I know you're smart. I guess I just wanted to ask for your help and let you know that I understand that some of us hide life's scars well."

Was he Dr. Phil? Am I Oprah? Were we supposed to be sharing a moment?

"If you need a place to hang when the brothers are beating your ass, just let me know."

I grabbed my backpack and started to walk away. Delight ain't playing with the lateness! He had the prettiest smile just like his brother, damn him! Beaker followed me out and opened the door for me.

"So, Beak, what is your real name?"

"Huh? Oh, my name is Xavier."

Things were pretty uneventful on campus until Hell Week, when the Betas tried to break the pledges' will and make them drop line. Xavier met me after my last class and begged me to sneak him off campus.

"Please, Dini. I'll sleep on the sofa."

I was not having it. I finally had a weekend free of my parents and PJ. I planned to spend it soaking in my tub, Xavier-free. That was when I saw him—Mr. America, strutting around campus liked he owned the place. He was shaking hands, kissing babies—the whole nine. I instantly felt like "fresh meat." I hate admitting this, but I wanted revenge.

"Dini, please! That's my brother, Phillip. If he sees me . . . damn!"

Phillip the peacock, emphasis on the pea, came strolling over.

"Little brother, who is this?"

"This is my little sister, Dini. Dini, this is Phillip. He's visiting campus this weekend to take the new brothers over."

"Shut the fuck up, Xavier! You talk too much, just like a little bitch!"

Oh, it was on! Mare opened up that same tired Beta organizer and started writing. "Let me get your name again, shorty?"

I couldn't help it. I screamed at the top of my lungs, resembling one of them kids in the "Peanuts" cartoon, with the big blacked-out mouth. "My name is Dini, dumb ass! Maybe you would remember me by my first name, Tiffany?"

It registered. Phillip looked around with the "oh shit" face as the whole damn campus stopped to peep the drama.

Phillip snarled, "Tiffany! How could I forget the notorious Tiff Money?"

I could tell Phillip was nervous. He peeped some Betas walking toward us and took it as an opportunity to make his exit.

"Well, would you look at the time? I'm meeting my father-in-law for lunch. Glad to see you're still supporting Beta. Peace."

Luckily, Xavier was talking to one of his lab students while Mare was strolling down memory lane. By the time he turned around, Phillip was walking toward the president's house.

Xavier yelled at his brother's back. "Tell Lauren I said 'what's up'!"

"Lauren McGregor?"

"Actually Lauren DuBois now, my sister-in-law. She grew up in Chicago with her mom, but came to Wheatley to be near her dad. So you know Lauren. Small world, huh?"

Xavier kept on talking and I tuned him right out. I was

thinking about one thing. Revenge. It was going to be fun now!

Later that day, Xavier met me at the front gate of the college. He looked a mess. He was coated head to toe in dried mud. Apparently, the Betas thought it would be funny to pile into a Jeep and drag the pledges across a muddy field while they jogged behind it. Each pledge had a rope attached to his waist. One bad slip and that's all she wrote. Instant Roscoe mud cake. Xavier limped over to my car and spread a towel on the passenger seat before getting in and closing the door.

"Sorry about the mud, Dini."

"What did your brother say about me?" I tried not to catch his eye, hoping he wouldn't notice my knuckles turning white while I gripped the steering wheel.

"I haven't seen him since this afternoon. I hope you're not interested in him. Remember, he's married."

"Naw, he ain't my type."

On the drive home, I stopped at the supermarket and sent X in to buy the ingredients for dinner. I could tell he was embarrassed by his appearance, but I really wasn't in the mood to give a fuck. We got back to the house where he showered and then fixed dinner. Yes, him! He was a decent cook, too. It was getting late, so I told him to get some sleep in my son's room on his Tommy Tinker Big Boy bed. X didn't seem to care. He took the steps in twos, like they were having a government cheese giveaway upstairs.

"Shit! He better not use my mom's expensive-ass guest towels!" When I got to the bathroom to check on X, he was already in the shower blaspheming Prince's "Pink Cashmere" with the door wide open. Xavier shut off the water, rubbing the last trace of shampoo out of his eyes with my mom's precious white guest towel. That's when I saw it. At first I thought he had a growth on his thigh, but upon further inspection I realized it was his dick. It was a record breaker. It looked like one of those beige rulers you used to measure shit with in grade school. My mouth started salivating and I couldn't move. It was love at first sight. Not me and X, but me and the dick. I slowly examined his body, not wanting to miss one inch. With the exception of his pubic hair, he was hairless. We locked eyes and I could tell he was waiting to hear a verdict.

"Listen Xavier, don't be fucking up my good towels."

"Alright, Dini. Thanks again for letting me stay over." He looked disappointed, but he wouldn't be for long.

When he left the bathroom, I was standing right next to the doorway, completely naked. "X, every place got rules, and mine is you can't lay an ashy ass on my sheets. Shit, a strong wind blow through and you'll disappear right out my window."

I know I caught him off guard, but he regrouped quickly and laughed. I pushed him over to the bed and snatched his towel. "Lay down on your stomach!" He was still limp so it was manageable. I wanted a chance to see that ass, up close and personal. I straddled his back, rubbed my favorite frankincense oil on his neck, and then worked my way down his back. He had the same Georgia-clay skin as his brother. I rubbed his ass cheeks and I could feel him shudder. I spread them, paused, and asked him if he scrubbed real well like a good boy.

He just whispered, "Yeah, Dini."

I stuck my long tongue right into his asshole and Xavier let out this deep guttural moan. I licked all around his hole, gingerly tracing figure eights on that small area right above his sack. I started massaging his hairless ass cheeks and sucking on his nuts. First the left one and then the right, just like they were Jolly Ranchers, really gentle at first, like when you get that hit of the sour taste and then harder as it starts to melt in your mouth. "Flip over!"

"Dini, why are you being so mean?"

"Shut the fuck up! Just turn over!" Mare was right about one thing: Xavier was a chatterbox. He turned over, snatched the towel off the floor, and covered his johnson. "X, I got a two-year-old son. That means I see a naked dick on the regular. PJ ain't shy about his, so don't be shy about yours. It's a dick."

I threw the towel back on the floor and damn if I didn't hit the mother lode. It was long and thick. What to do? I played the role, like a sis sees a foot-long on the daily, put more oil on my hands, and started giving his freshly shaven "pledge head" a scalp massage. I wasn't going to promise not to call *Guinness Book of World Records,* but I sure as hell wasn't going to run like his prom date.

"Dini, did you breastfeed?"

"Damn, is it the Tommy Tinker bed? You breaking my flow, Xavier."

"Can I suck your breasts?"

I held my tits in my hand and fed one to him. He propped himself up on his elbows and put my entire C cup in his mouth. I'm thinking, he is just as stupid as his brother. He slowly took it out of his mouth and gently bit my hard nipple. "Ouch!" He started sucking on both nipples, trying to see how thick and stiff he could make them. He stuck his huge tongue out, making sure he lifted each tit with his hand and lapped underneath them. This went on until my breasts were covered with red marks. I could feel my pussy juices flowing all over his thigh. Fuck the foreplay! I wanted his dick inside of me now!

I led him by his rock hard dick to the dresser. I always loved PJ's dresser; I bought it at a yard sale because it had a huge mirror attached to it. I knocked all the shit that was on top of the dresser onto the floor in one swoop. I wanted to see his face without him peeping mine. That way if my eyes rolled back and I started foaming at the mouth, I wouldn't scare a brother. I never had a dick that big and thick inside of my pussy before—ever!

I stuck my ass out so that it brushed his dick and said, "Hit me from behind, X."

He placed his hands on my shoulders and squeezed. He traced his index fingers down along my spine and tickled my shoulder blades with his nose. He hugged my body and tickled me as his fingers found their way to my pierced belly button.

"Did it hurt?"

"Please, I didn't even feel it."

X kissed me on my back and whispered, "That's good to know."

Why did I scream when he put in the head?

"Do you want me to stop?"

"Naw, baby boy, keep it moving." He eased his shaft in slow, taste-testing the pussy, and then backed out, just leaving the head inside of me. After twenty minutes, I was in the groove! X was big and all, but I knew how to work it. "Pick up the pace, X. You ain't gonna hurt a girl or nothing!"

"D, I'm not completely inside of you yet."

"Um, okay."

I turned around and wrapped my legs around his waist. He carried me back to the "mini-me" bed and gently placed me on my back. X parted my thighs and placed one leg over each side of the bed so that I was straddling it. He squeezed my ass cheeks and inserted both of his middle fingers up its hole. As I gasped, X didn't finish there. He stuck both thumbs in my hot dripping pussy. Although I was trying to play it cool, my pussy juice was all over his hands. I grabbed the back of his neck and brought his face to it.

"No."

"No?" Just like his brother, don't eat the pussy!

He took his fingers out and sucked both thumbs and moaned, "Hmm, Dini taste good. But right now, I want you to make love to my mouth."

"What?"

He gave me a sly smile and positioned me so that I was straddling his mouth. I didn't know what to do, so I just started to gently lower my pussy onto his mouth. He parted my lips with his fingers and blew on my clit. He licked right inside each lip, moving his thick tongue up and down its seam. Damn, I thought I was going to melt! He forced his tongue into my pussy hole. He found my clit, flicked it, and then sucked on it. I jumped up and he had this frustrated look on his face.

"Dini, stop teasing me. Do you want this to happen or what?"

I started fucking the shit out of his face. I placed my left hand in a push-up position and gripped the headboard with my right hand. I tried to suffocate him. X's entire face was covered with my juice. I guess I got a little mack in me 'cause I started yelling, "You feel how I wanna be fucked? You feel it? You best drink this shit like water!"

X was in the zone. He was slurping it up. He licked me from the top of my ass crack all the way to the roof of my pussy. He rolled me over and pulled me down to the edge of the bed. He got on the floor and put my thighs on his shoulders. He was licking my clit and massaging my pussy lips with his index finger and thumb. I felt my pussy contract and I knew I was getting ready to cum. As I was having the ultimate orgasm, cum shot out of me and landed on Xavier's face.

"Damn, I ain't never came like that!" I screamed.

We caught some sleep and when I woke up, he was gone. "Oh, hell no!" I ran down the steps fastening my robe, wearing one slipper, ready to run his ass down in my car for hitting and quitting. I was gonna decide when this was over, not some knucklehead nineteen-year-old. I heard the microwave timer go off and I poked my head in the kitchen. "Xavier, what are you doing down here at three in the morning?"

"Damn, Dini. I just got hungry! I was going to wake you up but you were knocked out."

I unfastened my robe and sat on the kitchen table. "Why don't you just help yourself to some of me?" I know the line was tired, but I just had to take another go at the dick.

"Get on your tummy and let me make you feel good," he said.

I happily obliged. He got on top of me, making sure not to crush me with his weight. He wasn't built like his brother. He was squatty, thick, and felt like he weighed at least two hundred pounds. He gently parted my ass cheeks and slid his mammoth dick inside my still soaking-wet pussy. "Eww, work that shit, baby. . . ." Because we both knew the table was going to break if we went all out, X took it slow, filling me up inch by inch. He pulled my legs apart and kept his straight. The kitchen table started creaking as X started winding his hips. I started feeling it till I damn near blacked out. We were warping my parents' table until four in the morning. His thrusts started getting deeper and deeper. He grabbed my tits and licked the back of my neck.

Slipping in and out of consciousness, I could hear X whisper, "Dini, thank you . . . thank you, baby, for letting me inside of you. Damn, you feel so good. Shit, Dini, shit!"

Mama DuBois had taught the baby DuBois some good manners. He must have thanked me on every down stroke as he was pushing himself deeper and deeper inside of me. I placed my left arm around the back of his neck and rubbed his bald head. "Baby, I don't want you to cum like this. I want you to cum in my ass."

He got up slow and we went into the living room. He was looking around as if he was casing the joint. "X, what are you looking for?"

"Someplace you can't run."

He took my wrists and pulled me down onto the hardwood floor. He placed the top half of my body on the couch, facedown with my tits touching the cold leather seat cushions. He knelt down behind me and pushed the couch against the living room wall. He was right; there was no place to go. I had to take them inches right up the ass. He put his fingers in my pussy, but even with all that wetness coating my asshole, that big dick was not getting into my tight ass. Xavier told me he would be right back. He went into the kitchen and brought back some olive oil. He poured it all over my lower back and watched with excitement as the oil ran into my ass crack. I felt like an experiment in his chemistry lab. He emptied the rest of the bottle on his dick.

"Yo, X, I'm tired of the bullshit. Will you come on?"

"Oh, you think just 'cause a young buck is a little inexperienced, he ain't got no flow? I guess I'm just going to have to own this ass tonight!"

He entered my ass hard and slow. He was forceful but he didn't hurt me. I didn't realize I was bilingual until Xavier DuBois had me speaking Swahili, biting the sofa cushions in my parents' living room. As his thrusts got more forceful and he was losing control, he gently pulled his dick out.

Xavier wiped the sweat off his chest and rubbed it on my breasts and tummy. I turned around and Xavier was licking those beautiful lips. He brought his face close to mine and lightly bit my bottom lip. He whispered in my ear.

"I want to shoot my load in you so bad, Dini, but I can't figure out who wants my hot cum more. Is it Dini's wet pussy or Dini's pretty mouth?"

Oh, he was switching up on me. With that big dick, go right ahead! I know it was tacky, but I started to throw a fit like a two year old. "X, I don't give a fuck! I just want it now!"

"D, you got to let a brother know——"

"Dini's pussy wants your cum, baby. I can't wait anymore. Please baby, can I have it? I promise to take every drop."

Xavier flipped me over and jammed his dick inside of me. I could hear my ass slapping against his six-pack. I tried to change positions, so I could see his face when he came inside of me. I guess X took it the wrong way because he started talking smack.

"Dini, you've been dissing me with this pussy all semester. Every time I try to get close to it, you just straight flag me. Shit, I even tried to get in good tutoring the pussy! You know what I got out of it? A C! Damn, a C, Dini? You just gonna have to do some extra credit work taking this dick tonight! Xave is going to take all semester out on this pussy tonight!"

I didn't even have to tighten my muscles like I did with my other lovers. His shit was so thick, it totally filled my pussy. All you could hear was Xavier's shit-talking and the juice in my pussy trying to escape what little bit of room X's dick was willing to give it. X leaned against my back, grabbed my clit between his two fingers, and started tugging on it.

"Damn, baby boy, work Dini's pussy. Yeah, that's my spot. *Shit, X, you da man!*" Did I just say that?

After I came again, he whispered in my ear, "Now that I gave you yours, can I get mine?"

All I could mutter was "Umm mmm."

He grabbed both my ass cheeks and started pumping into me harder and harder until I thought we were gonna drill a hole in the wall. He was holding on to my hips like they were handles and his dick was a joystick. He moved his hips so that he wasn't just hitting it straight on; he was tapping all sides. He scooped both arms inside my inner thighs and lifted me off the floor so that he could have full access. My ass slapped against his chest until I thought I felt his dick hitting my rib cage. X finally exploded inside of me. Cum escaped my pussy and ran down my legs onto the floor. Xavier lay on top of me until I felt his sweat turn cold.

X and I hung out a few times after that night. He finally got his precious Greek letters, too. His line name was "X marks the spot." I just wanted to know who was in charge of the line names! The last time I spoke to Xavier was Thanksgiving weekend of my sophomore year, when he flew me to Lake Vista to meet his family. You should have seen Phillip's face when he walked in and saw me eating cornbread at his parents' table!

The dinner came to a quick end when I finally had enough courage, after four apple martinis, to announce to the DuBois family that they had a grandson, my son, Phillip DuBois, Jr. I think I remember saying it right before I asked Lauren to pass me the cranberry sauce. While the turkey flew, I managed to grab my overnight bag and take a Greyhound bus back to Wheatley. Revenge ain't always sweet.

After graduation, I married a nice "safe guy" who works as

a bank manager in Wheatley. I just got tired of the drama, the lies, and the bullshit. My husband respects me and is a good father to PJ. Every year we drive PJ to Lake Vista to spend the summer with his dad. On the long drive back to Wheatley, I always look out the car window, think about Xavier, and wonder, what if?

Discovery

Sha'ron

Watching him in the shower was making her reconsider waiting. He'd been a perfect gentleman with her—wining and dining her and treating her with the utmost respect. But the sight of his enormous dick brought on an orgasmic tingle throughout her body. It was huge! The tightness of his body confirmed that with each thrust, she'd reach new heights of pleasure. With this thought, her hand unknowingly found the center of her throbbing excitement. She was reluctant to move it away, but did so out of fear he would notice she was there.

As he turned in full view of her, she caught sight of what this fine, virile man had to offer. A gasp escaped her at her discovery. She was caught. He turned to her with a look of shock and seduction. He didn't acknowledge her right away, but instead began to stroke his manhood to tease her.

She couldn't believe what he was doing. She could not believe her virgin eyes. He slowly stepped out of the shower and walked past her to his room. He knew she was watching him with her mouth wide open. He knew she wanted him. She wanted him to fuck her, but didn't know how to tell him. He would continue the game just a little while longer. Hell, she'd made him wait almost three months.

When she finally came in the room behind him, the Prince CD was still playing softly in the background. The seductive voice singing "Do Me Baby" made her blush. A mischievous grin crossed his face. Damn!

She looked *so* sexy. She had showered before him. Now she wore these skimpy ass shorts and a tank top. He didn't think he was going to be able to play this game with her any longer. She was making his dick hard.

Shit! He couldn't hide what he was feeling.

By the time he turned around to walk over to her, she was lying there watching him. She was bold at this point, and didn't turn her head away in embarrassment. Instead she slowly crawled to the end of the bed and met his manhood, mouth to skin. A moan escaped him. He didn't realize how much tension he had built up. He wanted her *so* bad. Three long months he'd watched her erotic walk, listened to the seductive way she read her poems to him. He wanted her.

She started by sucking the tip, but as she became more comfortable, she took it whole. Oh, my God! He couldn't stand it any longer. He bent over, grabbed her by the waist, and flipped her over onto her stomach. He sensed she wanted to say something, so he quickly covered her mouth with the fullness of his lips.

Dag, this brotha has some sexy-ass lips, she thought.

Her breasts were very subtle. He took care to suck each one just the same. With this, she felt the throbbing begin again between her legs. He worked his way down to her clit. He began by teasing it with his tongue, which made her moan uncontrollably. Shit, if I would've known he could eat pussy like this, I would've surrendered a long time ago.

As if he'd heard her thoughts, he began a more forceful

sucking motion. He came up and looked her in those beautiful eyes, which attracted him to her since day one, and slowly glided himself into her soft, wet flesh. "Ahhhhh!" came a loud moan from the both of them. He had never made love to a virgin before. The tightness just overwhelmed his big, massive dick. She thought she was going to faint as he became more in tune with her pussy, thrusting in and out with long, slow, and easy strokes. "International Lover" was playing now. The song was at the end, the part where the song comes to a climax.

He didn't want to stop. He wanted to come with her. He wanted to bring her as much pleasure as she had brought him in these past three months. If she only knew how much he enjoyed her being around.

Shit, I can't hold it any longer.

Just as he was about to explode into her womanhood, he felt the initial sporadic contractions of her walls against his dick. She screamed his name and dug deep into his back, and he let go of what he was waiting for for too long. They caressed each other well into the night. The only communication was through the explorations of their bodies and from moans of pleasure.

He woke early the next morning with a sense of excitement. He had the sensation of being aroused. His hand found its way down to his penis. Damn, it was hard as a rock. At the shock of this discovery, he opened his eyes to find out that she had beat him to it.

She was now working her tongue down his thigh. She felt that he had awakened; she knew this technique would do the trick. She looked up at him and just smiled as she continued to tease him with her tongue, making her mouth very familiar with the anatomy of his dick. When she sensed he'd reached the point of eruption, and she was at the point where she could no longer contain herself, she rose and lowered herself onto his dick. She believed she had gotten the hang of it. After all, they did go at it all night.

When he glanced at her, he had a slight grin on his face. He knew he had her with the first stroke he gave her last night. It turned him on that she liked it so much that she would just take it. That's the kind of woman he liked. The kind that wasn't afraid to go for the dick. He was a little reluctant to admit that she had whipped it on him also.

The tightness of her pussy was all the reassurance that he needed to know that this woman was his. No one had sampled the sweet juices that came almost instantaneously with just a touch from his tongue. No one had nursed from the hardness of her nipples. No man had shown her how capable a man could be in pleasing a woman or the many discoveries of pleasure.

The Fourth of July

Jai

Tonight was the big night, the party of summer. It was our annual Fourth of July BBQ. We had about twenty guests on the list for that day, and in all likelihood, every last one of the greedy bastards would be there. Every year it was off the hook. The party normally lasted into the wee hours of the night. Hell, half the time we ended up having to kick people out with our famous saying, "You don't have to go home, but you have to get the fuck outta here."

"Yo, Jay. Dammit, nigga, I know you hear me calling your deaf ass."

Nikki was calling my name at the top of her lungs, making ignoring her damn near impossible.

I walked around the corner to where she was standing half-dressed. "Why in the hell are you yelling like you don't have an ounce of sense?"

"Well, hell, if you'd answered me when I was calling your name like a normal person, then I wouldn't have to yell for your ass in this big-ass house."

I looked at Nikki like she was crazy. "Anyway, what do or did you want?"

Nikki had this blank look on her face, like she had forgotten her question. "What you doing?"

"Now I know damn well you wasn't calling my name like that 'cause you wanted to know what I was doing."

"Yep."

All I could do was smile, 'cause she was serious as hell.

"Fuck you, Nikki."

Nikki was five-eight, 150 pounds, light-skinned, with matching light-brown eyes. Nikki thought she was God's gift to the femme world. She had a short fade haircut, which brought out the Indian side of her family (her grandmother was full-blooded Apache). I must say that if I myself were not butch, I would be on her jock, too. We had been friends at UC Berkeley when we came out to each other by pure accident. We saw each other at one of the gay clubs, then again in a math class. Nikki and I became best friends fast and in our sophomore year, we got an apartment off-campus. After graduation, both of us ended up in the computer field. Nikki moved to the east coast for a few years to work, but moved back to California to work at Cisco, a large computer company, while I went on to work for Sun Micro.

I already had a house that my father bought for me as part of the "you graduate from college, you get a house" deal. What other incentive does one need? It was a four-bedroom, three-bath, split-level home that I'd spent two years renovating; much at the expense of my dad, who happened to own a real estate company in L.A. I put a pool in the backyard, put in a BBQ pit from hell, and a Jacuzzi. Things were definitely looking up.

Nikki moved in about two years ago. Her lease was up on her apartment so it just made sense for her to take the other master bedroom. Hell, we ruled shit in college, and now we had our own private funhouse to rule.

"Hey, Nikki!" I was at the top of the stairs yelling down to her. She talked about me. Shit, she could be just as deaf.

Nikki came to the bottom of the landing, wearing some boxers and a sports bra.

"Wassup?"

"Hey, did you invite Kim?"

"Which Kim? We know two different Kims."

"Yeah, but only one has been on my jock since Tanya and I broke up."

"But, Jay, I don't think you know this but the other Kim, the one with the short haircut and green eyes, told Lisa that she wanted to holla at you, too."

"Damn, well, is she coming?" This party was going to be off the hook.

"Now, Jay, don't be in here starting no shit. Which one are you trying to get with?"

"Well, hell, if I'm lucky, both of them." I smiled and walked back to my room. As my boy Ice Cube would say, "Today was a good day."

Nikki yelled back up the stairs. "Play on, playa!"

The sun was blazing hot, the pool and Jacuzzi had been cleaned the day before, the grill was heating up, and our guests would be arriving soon. Oh, I forgot we are talking about black people. Even when there is food on the table, we still manage to be late.

Nikki came out of her room and knocked on my bedroom door.

"Hey, Jay, you dressed?"

"Nope, but you can come in."

Nikki walked in wearing some FUBU shorts with a matching jersey, and some Nikes that she'd bought the day before when we were out shopping. I was sitting on the side of my king-sized bed, wearing some black silk boxers and a T-shirt.

"Wassup?"

"Hey, before you get dressed, can you come and clip the back of my nugget?"

"What, your arms too short to reach back that far?" I said with a wide smirk on my face. "What you trying to get all dressed up for? Is Stacy gonna be here?"

"Fuck you, man. You know I like to keep my shit tight, and plus you know we're going to have mad honies up in this house. You know this playa will not let the night go by without getting some pussy. That's my mission, and should I choose to accept it, and you know I do, I will get lucky with a capital L."

All I could do was laugh at her silly ass, 'cause I knew when she was serious about getting her some pussy.

"Yeah, I will fade your nugget."

"Aight, cool, lemme know when you're ready. By the way, what are you wearing today?"

I pointed to a pair of CK shorts and a matching shirt, with a CK hat to match.

"You and your damn hats. Do you ever go without something on your head? Why don't you let me cut your hair? Let me hook you up with a fade like me?"

I looked at Nikki like she had just lost her dayum mind. My hair had grown. It fell in between my shoulder blades. "Are you out your fucking mind? Have you been sniffing glue again?"

"Well, hell, stop covering up all that nice-ass hair."

"Damn, Nikki, how long have you known me? Why do you think they call me LL Cool J, Jr.?"

"Yeah, I know. You got that shit down; even the lip thing."

I flashed her a big sexy grin. "And you know this . . . *mannnnn.*"

Nikki was laughing her ass off as she walked out of my room.

• • •

The invitations went out with 3 P.M. being the start time, but you know black people. They always feel the need to be on CP time. So the majority, if not all, didn't show up till after four. Any other time, I would have been pissed, but today I was cool. I was nowhere near ready, and neither was the food. I cut Nikki's hair and then got hung up on the phone with my mother. She felt the need to lecture me on alcohol usage and the being responsible tip. I indulged her for a little while before telling her that people were starting to arrive. I lied.

Nikki was downstairs greeting everyone that was arriving. I was out in the backyard slaving over the damn grill. We hired a DJ to set it off. This was the only party of the year that Nikki and I went overboard with as far as food, drinks, and music. That's why no one ever scheduled their parties around the time we had ours. It was the bomb every year. It was strictly a lesbian party; no men allowed.

It was about seven and the house was packed. We had wall-to-wall women. We had invited about twenty-five people, but we had at least thirty-five to forty beautiful women wandering around the house. Some in swimsuits, some in less than swimsuits. I was about to have the time of my young life. Nothing but pussy everywhere I looked.

I was done with the cooking, had taken another shower, had on my gear, and now it was time to circulate the crowd. Nikki was already making headway with Stacy. I caught them over in the corner by the kitchen, all hugged up and kissing like there was no tomorrow. All I could do was smile.

"Hey, sexy," I heard someone say from across the room.

I looked around to see who had spoken and whether they were talking to me.

"Hey, sexy," I heard again, but this time she was right behind me. I turned around to see that it was Kim, the one with the green eyes.

Kim was wearing a two-piece bathing suit with a towel wrapped around her waist, hiding most of her beautiful legs. Kim was light-skinned, five-six, and was thick in all the right places, especially the chest. She was a healthy 38DD, and had no fat in those titties. Hell, it was all Kim.

"Wassup, cutie?" I asked.

"You."

"Umm, me, and why you say that?"

"Damn, Jay, why you keep playing like you don't know wassup?"

Kim had this serious look on her face that said she had a purpose.

"I'm just asking you wassup. Are you having a good time?" I asked.

Kim looked at me with this seductive grin. "It could be better."

"How is that?"

"Oh, so now you wanna act like you don't know wassup. You're a trip, Jay."

I smiled at her, because it was apparent that she was getting frustrated with me. I decided to play along with her to see where she was going.

"Okay, so tell me, baby. What's really going on? Do you really think that you can truly fuck with this?"

Kim walked up on me real close, till we were only inches apart. "To be honest . . ."

"Yes, please do."

Kim leaned over and whispered in my ear, "Right about now, I want you to invade my entire body with your tongue, then I want you let me ride you till I can't ride anymore. Are you game?"

I had to admit it. She had a girl speechless and curious. It took a lot to keep my cool. With her whispering in my ear like that, it making a sista horny.

I stepped back to evaluate her to see if she was serious. She was dead serious.

I smiled back at her and thought, let the games begin.

I took Kim by the hand and led her to one of the downstairs bedrooms. Nikki and I had a rule: never take them to the master suite. If we play, we play downstairs. Our rooms were our sanctuaries. She had her own playroom with her toys, and I had mine. I led her into the room and locked the door, so we were not to be interrupted.

I walked over to where she was standing and asked her, "You ready to play, or have you changed your mind?"

She walked up on me and looked me square in the eyes. "I've been waiting to get next to you for quite some time."

"Is that right?"

"Yes. Now are we going to stand here and chat all night or did we come in here to do something?"

I saw it was time to stop playing with her. She had an agenda and now was the time to see if she could back up all this shit she was talking. I walked up on her till I could feel her breath on my neck. I placed an arm around her waist and pulled her closer to me as if to try and blend her body with mine. I took the other hand and placed it behind her neck and brought her into me for a kiss.

The first one was actually a series of short kisses. I wanted to taste her lips and tongue, trying to see if she had skills in the kissing department. She did not disappoint me at all. We shared a long, deep, soul-searching kiss. She did not miss a beat. My hands began to roam up and down her back, till I was able to find the string to the top half of her bikini.

Within seconds, it was on the floor along with the towel

she'd had on. Now, being that I'm someone that loves breasts, I had to step back and admire them, as if I was an artist studying their subject. I took the right breast and began to let my tongue flicker across her nipple until it became nice and firm in my mouth. Proceeding to do the same for the left one, I continued until they were both standing at attention. Kim was letting out soft moans to let me know she was pleased. Her perfectly manicured hands were running through my hair, which for me was a definite turn on.

I led Kim over to the bed and laid her down. I let my hands roam to each side of her hips and pulled down her bikini bottom. She lifted her hips so it could slide off more easily.

"Umm Jay, you have no idea how long I've waited for you to touch me, to taste me, to fuck me."

I looked down at her and could only smile.

"Well, love. It's no longer a waiting game. I'm here to give it all to you."

"Oh, baby, umm, give it to me right now. I can't wait. I feel like I'm getting ready to cum right now. Please take me! Take me now!"

I walked over to the table and retrieved "Spanky," strapped him on, and headed back over to her.

Kim looked at me. "Aw, dayum! It's on!"

Kim grabbed me by the shirt and pulled me down to her. I gave her a long deep kiss. She was right; it was *on*.

I started sucking on her titties, and it didn't take much to get her nipples hard again. My tongue began to trace down the center of her chest. I let it stop and nestle itself in the crack and crevices of her navel. Kim was squirming on the bed. I could tell she was using every bit of energy to contain herself. I could feel the heat between her legs. She was on fire.

"Oh, yes, baby, yes! Oh, Jay, that feels so good! Please don't stop! Hmm, it feels so good!"

I started my journey to find her treasure, and her pussy was like a lighthouse guiding my way. The minute my tongue touched her pussy, I thought she was going to lose her mind. I let my fingers spread her lips apart and my tongue found her clit. Kim started squirming again, this time too much. I grabbed her around her hips so that I could keep her stationary. I wasn't in the mood to chase her all around the bed tonight. So I got a tight grip and went back to the task at hand. I started to gently suck, lick, and massage her clit. I could feel Kim's body begin to shake, letting me know that she was ready to explode. She did not disappoint me. She came and came and came.

When Kim finally opened her eyes, I was back on top of her.

"Damn, baby, you and that tongue are quite talented," she said.

"Well, thank you. You ready for another ride?" I asked.

"Umm, yes. Now lay on your back. I'm ready for a little ride of my own."

I smiled and did as she said. I reached over to the drawer and pulled out a condom and gave it to her. Kim smiled. "You think of everything, don't you?"

"Always."

Kim took the condom and put it in her mouth, then went down on me and put it on. That was enough right there to drive me crazy.

Kim slid her sexy self on top of me and let Spanky enter, like she was a pro. Her motions were slow and deliberate. I laid on my back in total bliss. I wrapped my hands around her hips and began to go with her motion. We were moving together in sync, as one. I opened my eyes long enough to see Kim looking down at me. She was smiling hard.

"What are you smiling for?"

"Umm, 'cause you got some skills, baby."

Kim started to pick up the pace. The visual I got from watching her ride me was getting me hotter and wetter with each thrust. She was riding me with everything she had, like it was the last time for her. I felt Kim's body begin to shake. I knew she was ready to cum, ready to release all that she had.

"Oh, baby, Jay, oh shit! Hmm, I'm getting ready to cum."

Kim's body began to shake as she exploded on top of me. With that visual, I came shortly after her. She laid herself on top of me, the sweat from her dripping down on me. Our breathing started to return to normal. This was turning out to be more than just a fuck. It was better than that. Then that all-too-familiar phrase came back to mind. *Don't get caught up, it's just a fuck.*

It didn't take Nikki long to find me. She was on me like white on rice.

"Where the hell you been?"

All I could do was grin. I started to tell her, but decided to let her suffer a little bit longer.

"Aw, nigga, who did you have in the playroom? Why you playing, muthafucka? Which Kim did you have in there?"

Nikki was shooting questions at me like a cannon.

"Aw, so now you wanna—" Nikki stopped in mid-sentence and looked over my shoulder to see Kim come out of the room. Nikki looked back at me with this big-ass grin. "Was it good?"

I tried but couldn't hold it in any longer. "Whew, it was the bomb! Baby has got some serious skills. I might have to give it another run."

Nikki gave me a high-five. "Play on, playa, but remember

what we say. Don't get caught up, it's just a fuck. Unless you see something else in her. Do you?"

I couldn't deny it. I did feel something, but I quickly dismissed it.

"Naw, she knows wassup." I looked over my shoulder to see Kim looking directly at me, smiling. Another satisfied customer.

Later on that evening I tried to avoid Kim, but I had to admit she had me curious in more than one way. I saw Nikki go into her playroom with Stacy. *Play on, playa.* It was 3 A.M. when the last few people left, or better yet, when we kicked them out.

Nikki and I sat on the sofa and looked around the house, checking out the big-ass mess that awaited us in the morning.

"So, Jay, you gonna see Kim again or was this a one-time thing?"

"I don't know, maybe. I talked to her for a bit before she left. I may hook up with her soon. What about you and Stacy? I saw the two of you go into your playroom."

"We're talking. Earlier was just a fuck and she knew it. We'll see. Well, I'm heading up to bed. I'll see you in the morning."

"Okay," I said.

I sat on the couch for a little while after Nikki went upstairs. Another slamming-ass party was in the box. Yeah, I'm going to have to call Kim. I got up and went to the bottom part of the steps. I thought to myself, *If these walls could talk.* I clicked off the light and headed upstairs.

Copland

Ms. B. Haven

Keisha knew she was in trouble. The red and blue lights of the siren alerted her to that fact. Damn, she thought to herself as she placed the small bottle of Absolut between her thighs. She thought she could handle a drink and a car at the same time.

Keisha was on her way to the club. She was dressed in a black low-cut sweater that showed off her 42Ds and a skirt so short, a piece of her enormous ass showed. She knew that the other women at the club talked about her behind her back, but she didn't care. She was twenty-two, firm, and fully packed. Or, like my aunt would say, young, dumb, and full of cum. Keisha had an agenda, and the women at the club knew that if you didn't watch your man, he could end up on Keisha's "to do" list.

The cop walked over to the open driver's side window.

"Good evening, Ma'am."

"Good evening, Officer."

Keisha stuck out her chest, and hoped that her cleavage was visible. This cop wasn't bad looking. He was downright fine! The navy blue uniform barely contained his muscular build. His skin was the color of deep, dark chocolate, and his brown eyes were accentuated with flecks of gold.

The cop spied the empty bottle of Absolut between a pair of shapely caramel-colored thighs. Under his scrutiny, they parted slightly.

The cop cleared his throat. His dick was hardening.

Keisha saw the bulge forming in his pants. She immediately opened her thighs wider.

"Officer, I know I'm not supposed to be drinking and driving, and I know it's your duty to arrest me, but can't we work something out?" she purred.

The officer didn't comment. He just reached inside the window and placed his hand on Keisha's left nipple. She moaned and placed her hand atop his, encouraging him to continue. He played with the sensitive flesh until it was as hard as his dick.

"Officer . . ." Keisha looked at his name tag. "Williams. Do we have a deal?" Keisha reached out and massaged his dick through his pants.

Officer Williams moaned. "Bet. But we'd better get off the street," he said, huskily. "Park your car, and you can ride with me."

"Bet," Keisha replied. "But let me give you a little somethin' somethin' before we go." Keisha unzipped Officer Williams' pants. She reached inside and brought his hard penis out through the hole provided by his boxers. His size made her squirm in her seat in anticipation. Keisha jerked the erect flesh, bringing the foreskin over the head of his dick. She squeezed him so hard that pre-cum ebbed through his hole, saturating the swollen head. Keisha then took his dick into her mouth. She took him deep; the head of his penis touched the back of her throat. Keisha jerked and sucked him at the same time.

Officer Williams withdrew from her mouth. "Let's take this party to the park." He caressed her smooth, silky thighs.

Keisha started her engine and parked. She walked back to Officer Williams' car. When she was inside, she handed him a black lacy piece of cloth.

"I won't be needing these," Keisha said as Officer Williams unfolded the pair of French-cut panties, still warm from her body heat and wet from her cum.

The policeman held her panties up to his nose and inhaled deeply. The musty smell of Keisha's cunt almost sent him over the edge. He put the police cruiser into drive and sped off in the direction of the park.

As he drove, Keisha pulled up her skirt to reveal a cleanly shaven pussy. She turned in the seat so he could have a better vantage point. She licked her fingers and touched her enlarged clit. She ground her hips into her own hand. Keisha knew she was about to climax and was happy to feel Officer Williams' fingers probing her labia. He removed her hand and placed two fingers into her wet snatch. Keisha cried out as the officer finger-fucked her. He went slow at first, and then increased his speed. The smell and sound of wet pussy filled the car. Keisha grabbed the officer's wrist and her entire body began to shake as the orgasm claimed her. Officer Williams felt a flood of cum coat his hand. He brought his fingers to her lips, and Keisha eagerly cleaned her cunt juice from his hand with her tongue.

Lincoln Park was deserted. The police closed the park at dusk to keep drug dealers and users out. But the cops also used the park for their own pleasure. They brought prostitutes and other women in trouble with the law to the park so that they could fuck and suck their way out of paying fines or doing time. The park was so notorious for this that the cops affectionately called it "Pussy Park." Just a couple of nights ago, Officer Williams had brought another honey to the park. She'd been stopped because she was speeding. In order to keep her man from paying yet another ticket, the honey ended up facedown and ass up in the woods of Pussy Park.

Officer Williams pulled into a secluded, dark, wooded area. He cut the lights and the ignition. Keisha leaned over and undid his pants again. His erection was stronger than before, she noticed. She placed the long fat dick into her mouth as she played with his balls. Officer Williams leaned his head back and placed his hand on the back of Keisha's neck. She felt the slight pressure of his hand as he guided her up and down his pole. Keisha placed the officer's balls into her mouth one at a time. She chewed on the skin that covered his nut sack.

"That's enough head," Officer Williams hissed out.

He got out of the car and gently pulled Keisha from the front seat. They stood by the trunk of the car. The cop slid his hands beneath Keisha's sweater and removed it, along with her bra. Her D-cup titties swung in the air like two caramel-colored helium-filled balloons. Officer Williams bent down and took one chocolate-dipped nipple into his mouth. He sucked the hardening knob, all the while snaking his hand under her skirt and playing with her pulsating pussy.

Then the officer made his way to the other nipple when the first was sufficiently hard. He bit it, hard, and Keisha's scream of delight and pain filled the night air. Officer Williams felt the nipple discharge a liquid into his mouth. The cop released her and saw white liquid dripping out of her nipple, down her breast, and onto the flat plane of her stomach.

Officer Williams attacked the nipple with a vengeance. He sucked and swallowed her titty milk like an overly hungry baby. Then the cop turned Keisha around. She braced herself on the trunk of his car. Officer Williams took out his nightstick. He spread her legs. Keisha was sprawled out over the trunk like she was getting patted down. The officer then rammed the stick up her cunt until it hit her cervix. Keisha grabbed his powerful forearm and yelled like a stuck pig.

"You like that stick in you?" Officer Williams asked, ramming the stick in and out of her.

"Yeah, baby," Keisha replied as she moved on the stick, "but I'd rather have some dick."

Officer Williams pulled the stick out of her.

"Give me the stick," Keisha said.

Officer Williams handed her the stick, which was now white with liquid. Keisha placed the stick into her mouth and cleaned her juice off of it. She was having so much fun giving the stick a blow job, she hadn't realized that the officer had positioned himself behind her until she felt his dick bust through her pussy. He held on to her hips as he fucked her hard and fast. He then lifted her torso from the trunk and squeezed those tits. Once again, her milk began to run. Officer Williams collected some of the nectar onto his fingers and licked them clean, never slowing the pace at which he pumped his dick into her.

"Oh, shit, baby, I'm cumming!" the officer exclaimed. "This shit's going down your throat." He turned Keisha around and pushed her onto her knees. "Suck it and swallow, or the deal's off."

Keisha placed his meat back into her mouth, and started to suck harder than she had all night. The officer's thick cum filled her mouth. As Officer Williams recovered from his orgasm, Keisha opened her mouth wide and showed him his cum. She closed her mouth, and swallowed it down.

After replacing their clothes and fixing up a bit, Officer Williams drove Keisha back to her car.

"Drive home safely," Officer Williams offered as she opened the door of his car.

"Home?" Keisha replied. "Who's going home? I'm headed to the club. You were a delicious appetizer. Now, I'm ready for the main course."

Officer Williams just shook his head and smiled as he made sure she got into her car safely, and drove away.

1-800-HOT-TALK

Shonell Bacon

It was a typical day for Sharon. She worked as an administrative assistant at a busy real estate office. However, today it was quiet, and except for the occasional phone inquiry she spent her day surfing the 'Net, checking out two of her favorite places: Black Planet and Black Voices.

After returning from lunch, her bosses—two female realtors—informed her that they would be out the rest of the day for meetings and checking out sites, so she would be running things from this end. *Joy,* thought Sharon, *I can finally have a quiet day.* She slipped out of her chocolate-colored pumps, wiggled her toes, and took a deep breath, relaxing herself. She ran her left hand through her short, naturally curly 'do and smiled. Today was one of those workdays that employees rarely had. The ones where there was no slack and nothing but smiles, and that's exactly what Sharon did. Smiled.

She lazily surfed the 'Net while typing up some correspondence that wasn't really due out, but she wanted to keep ahead. When you want to 'Net, you learn how to multi-task *real* quick.

An hour before she was scheduled to head home, the

phone rang, interrupting Sharon's quiet space. She sighed. "Please don't let this be *too* complicated," she muttered to herself.

"B & D Realtors," Sharon chimed. "Sharon speaking."

"Hey." Instantly, Sharon's body perked up and a smile as big as a canyon floated across her lips.

"Hey, baby," she softly crooned into the phone after hearing her boo's voice through the phone line. "Wassup?"

"Nothing, boo," his dark, chocolaty voice whispered into her ear. "I'm still at work, and wanted to speak to my baby. Will I see you tonight?"

"I dunno. I have the gym, then I gotta go pick up Mom and have dinner with her and my cousin, and then I have a project I'm working on."

"A project, huh? Is this for your lil company?"

"Yep, yep. But I'm free tomorrow. How about I meet you at your place after work?"

"Sounds good, babygirl."

A silence fell across the lines, only broken by the sound of Sharon and her boo—Brian's—breathing.

"So tell me, babygirl," Brian began. "What are you wearing?"

Sharon laughed. "My monkey suit!"

"Come on, boo, play with me."

Sharon smiled. "I have on my chocolate business suit—jacket off, white silk tank top, knee-length skirt with slit on right thigh, my champagne-colored panties and bra, and my shoes off."

"Mmm." Sharon could hear Brian's voice struggling to maintain its professional tone. "Boo, I just locked my office door, and now I'm sitting here thinking about getting up under that desk of yours."

Sharon felt a flutter in her lower belly and a slight ache begin to form between her legs. "Oh, yeah?" she offered back.

"Oh, yeah," Brian answered. "I wish I could spread those smooth brown legs of yours apart and kneel between them . . . kissing up your thighs and dropping kisses on the crotch of your panties. . . ."

Sharon groaned. "Babe, what are you trying to do to me?"

"Anyone there?" Brian asked, ignoring Sharon's question.

"No," she whispered. "Out for the day."

"I want to make love to you with my tongue, Shar."

The slight ache had turned into a deep throbbing between Sharon's legs. She closed them tightly to try to keep the feelings inside, but the sound of Brian's voice was doing things to her.

"Tell me . . . can you *feel* me slip your panties to the side . . . letting my tongue hit that swollen button of yours? Swirling my tongue around it . . . sucking it into my mouth?"

"Mmm hmm," Sharon whimpered, now sitting languidly in her chair, her breathing deep and labored. "I can feel it, boo."

"I swear I can already smell your sweet juices and taste them on my tongue. Licking them up as I lick up and down your hot spot, babygirl . . . damn, I love when you purr in the back of your throat when I lick you *just* right."

"Boo," Sharon crooned into the phone. "You have me *soooooooooooo* wet right now. I can feel it against my panties."

"Damn, none of that should go to waste, baby," Brian answered. "I want it all, either on my lips, or . . ."

"Around that nice, stiff, thick pole of yours?" Sharon finished Brian's sentence. The phone beeped. Sharon sighed. "Sorry, hold on, baby."

"Uh, hello?" she answered, ever so unprofessionally.

"Sharon? This is Debra, are you okay?"

Shit, Sharon said to herself. It was one of her bosses. She cleared her throat and slipped back into her professional voice.

"Why do you ask, Deb?" Sharon chirped.

"Your voice . . . sounds funny."

"Oh, my throat's just dry, I think. What can I do you for?"

"Just calling in, making sure no calls came that were too important. I wanted to tell you to have a nice weekend."

Yeah, Sharon thought, *one very important call.*

"Nope, no calls, and you have a good one, too, Deb."

"Okay, later."

Sharon quickly clicked over and her voice flipped instantly into her "in need of her baby" voice. "Brian," she moaned into the phone.

Sharon could tell by Brian's voice that the little interruption hadn't halted any of his needs and desires.

"Tell me something good, babygirl," he whispered.

"Can I straddle you in your chair, baby?" she spoke, softly, in a girlish voice.

"Oh most definitely, boo," he groaned.

"I want to slip off my panties, hike up my skirt, and straddle you, feeling you press deeply inside me."

"Mmm, I'm so hard, baby. I would *have* to slip that shirt off you and the bra too . . . suck on those dark-brown, stiff nipples of yours. I know how you like it . . . suck those nipples nice and slow. When I let the tip of my tongue lightly stroke around your nipples before I nip at the tip of them and suck them into my mouth, they taste just like Hershey's Kisses."

"I love feeling your warm mouth on my nipples, licking and sucking and biting them, boo. They're hard right now just thinking about you doing that . . . and while you suck on my nipples, I would ride the hell out of you, pumping up and down, milking you of all your juices."

"Milk me, baby," Brian groaned, his voice strangled. "Milk it like you know how."

"Can you feel me gripping you, boo?"

"Yesssssssss."

"Can you feel yourself buried deep inside of me?"

"Yessssssssss . . . lemme lick up your neck, babygirl . . . hit that spot behind your right ear."

Sharon shivered as a sensation slivered from the bottom of her feet to the ends of her hair.

"Oh damn, boo," she cried out, oblivious to her surroundings. "You know that's my spot."

He smiled. "Yeah, and I know a few others, too. Like when I'm hitting you from the back . . . got my hands pressed against the small of your back . . . your ass up . . . and I swivel my hips and pop that spot . . . that spot that makes you cream and scream out my name and cum all over the place . . . know that spot?"

Sharon bit down on her bottom lip, but not fast enough to catch the cries of passion that were flowing from her mouth. "You know I do, boo," she cried. "When you start wiling, and slamming inside of me, and smacking my ass too? Oooh shit, boo, all I want to do is scream and cry out your name and beg you to do me harder . . . and you always come through."

"Babygirl?"

"Yessss, boo," Sharon replied, her voice quivering.

"I'm leaving now . . . you're off in ten minutes. I *will* be at your apartment when you get there. Love you."

"You too."

There was no need in protesting. It wasn't like Sharon wanted to anyway. She would just have Brian as her gym time, and Mom and her cousin? A late dinner never hurt anybody. Sharon slipped on her pumps, stacked her work, and took in deep breaths, anxiously waiting for the next ten minutes to pass so she could break the sound barrier on her way home.

"Baby?" Sharon called out as she unlocked her front door. She dropped her purse on the living room sofa and stepped out of her pumps. "I thought he said he was going to be here," she mumbled. The apartment was pitch-black. Sharon plopped her bottom on the back of the sofa as she ran her fingers through her hair.

Closing her eyes, Sharon let out a moan, gliding her fingertips along her cheeks and neck. "He better get here soon," she whispered, "or I'll have to start solo." A moment later, a smile made its way along her lips as she took in a whiff of Obsession for Men cologne. Sharon spun around, coming face-to-face with a smirking Brian.

"Thought you could sneak up on me, didn't you?" she asked, laughing.

"Thought I could hit it from the back," Brian answered, jumping onto the sofa and leaning over to kiss Sharon.

Once their tongues untangled from each other, Sharon added, "You don't have to sneak up to do that, baby."

Sharon raised her hands to Brian's chocolate face, gently stroking his bald head and trailing her fingertips down his neck to the front of his collar. "So," she whispered, unbuttoning his shirt, "hit anybody on the way here?"

With the last button unfastened, Sharon removed Brian's shirt with a rush, her hands hungry to feel the taut, dark skin that dwelled beneath the fabric.

"One or two pedestrians," he said, chuckling, before removing Sharon's jacket, letting it drop to the floor. "Raise your arms, boo," he whispered in that deep voice that left

Sharon's panties damp. As she raised her arms, Brian raised her silk tank top, kissing each newly exposed piece of heated flesh. Sharon cooed.

"How do your lips stay so warm?" she crooned.

Brian answered by stroking up and down her back, unsnapping her bra and removing it. His eyes raked over her full breasts, her nipples standing at attention. He watched the lust dance in Sharon's eyes as he nimbly played with her taut nipples, gently pinching them. He kissed her, once, quaintly, twice, gently, and thrice, sucking the life force from her very being.

Brian's moist, heated lips traipsed down her neck where he sucked a nice round hickey before he continued his journey down to her mocha brown slopes. There, he took turns ravishing her chocolate nipples, devouring them.

"Brian," she moaned, holding his slick head to her bosom, "I'm aching."

Their eyes connected, and he could feel the sexual pain emanating from her. In a flash, he jumped over the back of the sofa, pressing his body close to Sharon's. His hands trailed down her back, cupping her firm ass. Their lips connected, tongues danced, bodies grinded tightly together. With bated breath, Sharon broke the kiss. Her wet tongue began to sensually slope down his neck to his thick chest. She bit his nipples, causing a strangled cry.

"Shar, you know that's my spot," he groaned.

After much lip service, Sharon looked into Brian's face, smiling wickedly. "It's not the *only* one," she said.

Sharon's hands followed behind her tongue as she licked and kissed her way down to Brian's tight stomach. Quickly, she unbuckled his belt and unzipped his slacks, pushing them down to the floor. The only thing standing between her and her needed object were his Calvin Klein's. Her hands moved along the stiff terrain under his briefs, causing them both to moan.

On her knees, Sharon kissed up Brian's right leg, sucking his inner thigh. She could feel his thick member growing. She kissed along it through the fabric before kissing and sucking on his left inner thigh.

"Girl," he whispered, "you got me hurting."

"Let me make it feel better for you." Latching her fingers under Brian's waistband, she pulled the briefs over his magnificent parts and let them drop down with his slacks.

"Mm mm mm," she cooed, reaching her hands out, stroking his hips before moving to his groin. The silky feel of his dick always turned her on, especially when he would get so turned on that thick veins strained under the skin . . . like now.

Sharon stroked Brian, kissing his head. He shuddered. She licked down the length of him before rubbing her mouth along his balls, humming on them. She took her time, leaving no spot of his balls unattended. She sucked and kissed as her hands worked magic on his throbbing dick.

Sharon felt Brian's fingers slither into her short hair, silently begging her to take him into her mouth. Without hesitation, she did, taking him whole.

"Ahhh!" he cried, always amazed at how Sharon never went slow, always going straight for the gusto the first time out.

Her jaw worked his muscle like a pro. Brian had to look down, take in the sight of his baby's full lips wrapped tightly around him. Just the view made his hips pump toward her mouth, made his dick harder, made him feel lightheaded.

"Ooh shit!" His hands were firmly on Sharon's head, guiding her up and down his muscle as his hips pumped in unison. Almost angrily, he pushed her off him, watching her softly land on her bottom. She looked up at him questioningly. Brian gave her a devilish smile before yanking her up from the floor. He kissed her hard and deep before turning her, pressing her back tight against his front. Sharon could feel his dick against her ass and she felt faint.

Brian bent her over the back of the sofa. His hands moved to her skirt. He unzipped it and removed it with a swiftness before ripping her panties right off her ass. He knelt down, kissing each of her round brown ass cheeks before parting them, running his tongue down her crack to her wet, dripping center.

"Gawd," Sharon whimpered, bucking her ass back to Brian's face.

"So sweet," Brian whispered against her wetness.

"Take me, Bri!" Sharon yelled, turning her head back to him.

He looked to his right, seeing the fire glistening in her eyes, and without thinking a second longer, he stood, rubbing his hands from the nape of Sharon's neck to her ass. He stroked himself before letting the tip gently probe down Sharon's ass to the wetness that developed at Sharon's entrance.

"Umph," she grunted, as Brian gave three short pumps against her hot box before pushing soundly into her. She screamed. The initial full, long stroke always caused pain for her, but she quickly recovered, Brian fitting her like a glove.

Brian's hands gripped Sharon's shoulders as he swiveled his hips and long-stroked Sharon. She milked him with each stroke. "Harder," Sharon grunted out. "Harder, Bri . . . ooh, Gawd."

"Mm hmm," Brian whispered, giving her three short pumps for every long stroke. "You're on fire, baby . . . and I'm about to put this sweet pussy out."

Sharon's eyes rolled up into her head. She could feel Brian damn near tapping into her belly and she felt weak in the knees and overheated.

"Baby!" she yelled, bucking hard against him, "I'm coming! Shit!"

Brian moved with pistonlike precision in and out of Sharon until he felt he would rip from his skin. "Ahhh shit," he groaned. "Ahhh shit."

Deeply planted within Sharon's hot, throbbing pussy, Brian came, crying out. Their heavy breathing ricocheted off the living room walls as Brian's almost lifeless body lay on top of Sharon's.

The phone rang and they both glanced at it over on the coffee table. Their exhaustion didn't afford them the chance to get it before the machine clicked on.

"Girl!" It was Sharon's cousin. "Where you at? Your mother and I are waiting at the restaurant. Hit me on my cell, peace."

Sharon and Brian broke into laughter as soon as the beep sounded on the machine. "So, are you going to go?" Brian asked, rising from Sharon's back before giving her a little smack on the ass.

"After my *gym* time . . . and all this exercise?" she asked, slowly turning to face him. They kissed. "I'm famished!"

Midnight Letter to Fran

Tenille Brown

My sweet Frances,

I can't get two good hours of sleep without you creeping into my thoughts. You have invaded my mind once again, and I had to crawl quietly out of bed, sneaking away to jot down all these things your vision makes me feel. Night after night, I see you all around me, your face on these ivory walls dimly lit by the moon, your legs tangled with mine under this crisp white comforter, your hands in mine helping me touch you. Then, I jerk myself awake to the sound of your voice after coming hard in my sleep, and I find that it is only he, this unforgiving and unkind husband of mine, breathing his sourness into my face. This is my cold reality. This is the life I chose in spite of what we had together, in spite of myself.

Listen, honey, I know you told me not to even look your way until I had my shit figured out, but I think I've got it. Now, I don't claim to be coming with all the answers, but this is what I do know. My body experienced its awakening at the touch of your hand. My mind became open to experiences real and new and fantastic, and every year of the thirty-one we've shared as friends took on new meaning when our lips touched and parted and our tongues joined for a slow, sensual dance. And risking everything doesn't seem like such a bad idea at all, now that I'm thinking about it, now that I'm waking up in the middle of every night with my pussy and nipples throbbing and my tongue darting at the empty air and calling to you. My intent was to save face, to put my family life first, even if it was only a front to cover up the dual feelings I had for my husband and my lover. But four months, two weeks, and six days have passed me by and my life has proven to be the biggest comedy act to ever hit the center stage. But, you see, Fran, I'm the only one laughing. I mean, after the fallout, when he has finally won, the bastard doesn't even bother to touch me anymore. I remember back in the day (pre–you and me) when the two of us couldn't even walk a block without him reaching for my hand or stroking my back. Now this king-sized bed we've loved in, whispered in, argued in hushed tones in for thirteen years, has been distinctly divided into two halves, appropriately titled *his* and *hers*.

But I can't say that his no longer touching me is the problem really, and it's not like his touch has thrilled me that much lately anyway. I mean, a little tickle of the dick is good, but it's no more than what I can do with this trusty little machine of mine (I am grateful every day for that little gift from you). The problem may really be that he has never touched me and will never be able to touch me like you do. You have that marvelous way of sifting your fingers through my cropped waves of hair, touching the sharp nose I have despised since puberty, and tickling my chin like I'm your adorable little baby. What makes me the biggest fool of all is that I knew all this when I told you to go.

In the days when he made the effort to at least let the hair on his chest brush my bare back under the covers at night, I would imagine his heat was your heat, and that his bristled chest was the top of your head buried in my back. Now he has taken even these small, yet vital thrills from me, as he lies in the same space with me and jacks himself to ecstasy while I wait for the bed to stop rocking so that I can settle into my own naughty dreams of you. My favorite is you and me in the shower, sliding against each other's lathered bodies, or me and you in the closet at your mom and dad's fiftieth anniversary party, your fingers probing deep into me, rubbing my clit into oblivion. Damn, Fran, it's been hell. Do you forgive me yet?

I don't know when I began hiding in the bathroom past midnight with that wicked picture of you in my palm. Sitting on the edge of the toilet with my panties on at first, and then tossed into a frustrated pile in the corner on the cold gray tile, I like to stroke the shine reflected by your smooth caramel skin and kiss your cold, red, Polaroid lips. I know you're probably pissed that I didn't trash this picture after all, but it really helps me through these times, and let me tell you that your full, glossed lips and long, thick hair bring rhythm to my stale-ass life. I keep wishing you could feel me rubbing your quarter-sized nipples and darting my tongue in and out of your "innie." I keep trying to take back everything I told you that night when I forced you away from me and returned to my comfortable, married-with-children life, but I don't know how. I know too well, though, that it's damn hard to reach out and grab back those words I let foolishly fall from my lips and there's no way to soothe the hurt and confusion I put in your eyes. What can I say? I'm human and I fell for the hype. I believed everyone when they said that a woman's body was made to fit a man's and that it was unnatural to love a woman, when the truth is, this forty-two-year-old body fits none better than yours, Fran.

But I forced the fit with me and Gary and I chose to continue our lovely little charade. Then came the cold nights and the longing. See, Fran, as a strong, sexual black woman, I long to be touched and talked to and gazed at every once in a while, even if the rest of my life is just a show. I mean, humor me; but he won't even do that anymore. I'm sure it's because he's bitter and rage and jealousy has him all fucked up inside, and I try to tell him that I gave you up but he won't see past his man pride and machismo. I get accused of sneaking over and seeing you when all I'm trying to do is go to the fucking 7-Eleven. What he doesn't know is that an interlude between you and me would last much longer than it would take me to pick up a carton of milk.

Remember that time I saw him with the woman and the baby and I was so close to him I could smell the green beans on his breath and almost feel the flaky dryness of his skin? But he said it wasn't him, right? Said I must be losing my mind 'cause he's never been with anybody else and he only has three kids and they all look just like me, his wife of thirteen fucking years. And you and me, me and you on that big, soft canopy of yours just rolling over laughing 'cause that Negro had the nerve. I don't recall your lips ever being as soft as they were that day when my laughter turned to screams and then to un-controllable sobs and you kissed my tears away and told me, "Patricia, you don't need that shit." And I don't know if it was the hurt and betrayal running throughout my being that sent me running top speed to your arms, but at that moment, there was nowhere else I wanted to be. I wanted that kiss on my forehead and eyes and nose and then my lips. I wanted you gently sucking the chocolate sweetness from my tongue, while your long, slim fingers traced the four letters of your name across my chest. I wanted to be taken over by the or-gasm you provoked from me when you invisibly wrote an F on my left nipple and ended with an N on my right and traced it with your warm, wet tongue. I am nearing the edge right now thinking of your soft, tiny fingers and tongue going in and out of my center on that hot afternoon. That was the day I knew I was bound to you.

You were right that day and you would be right now if you told me what a fool I am for hiding up in this cold-ass bathroom in my own house pleasing my damn self. I know all this already, Fran, but we've been through this shit before. It's hard enough raising three hard-headed, potentially woman-hating boys without having to break it down to them that their mommy likes to eat pussy. You know it would take an act of Congress to prove that I am a fit mother, that my lifestyle ain't got shit to do with it. And when did love and pleasure become a fucking lifestyle anyway? You're probably laughing at my vulgarity right now, but you know I'm not bullshitting. This is what I've been reduced to since I can't get to you.

I tend to wonder, was it the complete and utter honesty I reluctantly gave him that turned him so cold, or was the front coming for some time before and this was just the clean break he needed? I mean, doesn't everybody tell us that men like that shit? And ain't he a man? (Don't go there.) But, no, he didn't go on about how fine you were ('cause we both know he's been watching you for quite some time) and he didn't tell me how happy he was that I was finally brave enough to explore my bisexual feelings. Hell, he didn't even want to know if he could he watch us sometime. He wanted to know why the hell I was still exploiting his dick if my gay-ass girlfriend was what I really wanted. If I wanted some dyke bitch to sit on my face and finger my pussy, what was I still doing with him? Honey, I was shocked to hear that come from even him. But, I wouldn't even give him the pleasure of an argument that would drive me to tears. I wouldn't even try to reason with him that yes, it is possible to feel equally attracted to a man and a woman without slapping some big political label on myself. No, the asshole wasn't grown enough to handle a conversation like that, so I just complied. "Yes, I'm gay. I'm such a nasty bitch. You're right, Gary, I've never liked men. All these years you've just been a front for my family and my straight friends. I never enjoyed one moment in bed with you. And those three kids, huh, they were just the icing on the cake, the perfect addition to our fairy-tale life." That one earned me a sound smack across the face. And so I wouldn't be selfish and try to have you both. I was ready and perfectly capable of making a decision. And after calling you at work and listening to your voice break and quiver on the phone, your naked picture and my own hands are all I'm left with.

I know you said you would forget me and I know that you wish that you could, but I also know that it is still me you smell on your sheets even when you've changed them and sprinkled them with powder a dozen times. The truth is, I found my way inside you even when you saw my crazy life and decided you didn't want me there. That's what I loved about you. You opened yourself up so completely and let me all the way in. You showed me your life's mistakes and imperfections and you were willing to accept mine. You loved every one of my 155 pounds of womanhood and you touched every gray strand of my hair as gently as if it were a baby's. You kissed every part of me that was beaten, scarred, and bruised, and told me I was still beautiful to you. You knew me when I was barely grown, celebrated with me when I legally was. You helped me rediscover myself when I felt I no longer recognized the woman in the mirror myself. I fucked it all up, and I know it, Fran, and, now I am looking for a way back home.

If, by chance, I am not the chickenshit that I am convinced I am and this letter just happens to fall into your beautiful, brown, manicured hands, call me and let me speak these exact words to you. Let us bring each other to sweet release over the phone and then come together at our spot in the Valley and really discuss this thing. What I'm trying to say is, I love you, Fran, and I don't give a fuck anymore.

Yours truly,
Pat

There's Always Hope for the Ride Home

Geneva Barnes

Feeling her disapproving eyes fixated on him, he just swallowed the last bit of vegetarian lasagna that he had been chewing on for at least five minutes out of anxiety and frustration. She had been quite unresponsive to all of his advances—sexual and otherwise—the entire evening, but she wouldn't leave. It was as if she enjoyed rejecting him.

Not knowing exactly what else to do and tired of her painfully castrating him with her espresso eyes, making him feel dickless, he said, "Okay, I'm going," as he tossed a fifty on the table to cover the price of dinner and a negligible tip.

As he rose from his seat, her eyes followed his ascent as if he were moving in slow motion. They followed him from his licorice hair, that was stiff and shiny with gel and glistening in the ambient light like ejaculate on skin in the moonlight; to his eyes, which were the color of midnight and full of rapture; to his clit-colored lips that were begging to be kissed; to his black silk shirt, unbuttoned at the collar, through which his shiny black hair peeked, his nipples emerged, and the outline of his biceps and abs rippled; to the zipper on his pewter gray wool slacks that bisected the picture frame his hips and thighs made for his grossly overgrown cucumber dick and balls that sat like peaches in his pants, all firm and round and ripe on either side of his zipper.

Mentally, she had been fucking him all night. She had climbed atop his lap and grinded her cunt against his dick through his slacks. She had sucked on his tongue until it had grown numb. She had pressed her tits against his chest until she could feel him feeling her through her nipples. She had licked his skin between his thighs, up to his balls until her lips stung from the taste of the salt on his skin and her mouth was full of his silky black hair.

She had strapped on a black plastic dildo, had him down on all fours and pumped the plastic dick in and out of his ass, fucking him like a man fucks a woman he never thought that he'd have—slow with a little hesitation at first, and then fast and furiously like only his orgasm matters—fucking him until his breathy, masculine moans and groans foretold that he was about to cum.

Throughout the evening she had felt her tits, underneath her baby blue one-size-too-small sleeveless cotton blouse whose buttons would've popped open with one deep exhalation, swell up longing for his touch. She had felt her nipples pushing out from the smooth lines her black bra was trying to make for her tits. Throughout the night, she tried to conceal her arousal by keeping her arms folded across her chest. She felt her juices ooze through her black lace thong, ooze down around her crotch, down her inner thighs, staining her jeans. She had become so excited by him from the moment when she first saw him that her pussy tingled with anticipation for his penis and her mouth watered for it.

All night, she had been trying to deny her attraction to

him. It was so strong that she feared, if he knew the size of her lust, she would somehow become his slut. She didn't want to give up her identity to become that. She hated that she was so affected by him. Who knew a blind date could turn out that way?

As he turned away to leave her, she was so excited by his tight, round ass that it caused her to rethink the negative stigma attached to kissing ass. She wanted to do more than kiss it. She wanted to pull on his pants until they came off. She wanted to pull on his underwear until his cock and balls spilled out, until his juicy ass was out, and stare at the bounty, at least initially. Her vagina began screaming at her, demanding that she get him inside of her any way that she could. Unable to deny its demands any longer, she had to follow him. Halfway uncertain as to what she should do to solicit him, and as she got close enough to him to speak to him in a conversational voice and be easily understood, she said, "Would you mind taking me home?"

Yes, I fucking would mind, he thought, but being the decent guy that he was, he said, "Where do you live?" as he opened the passenger's door, motioning for her to get inside his SUV.

"803 East Dickerson Avenue," she answered.

"Okay," he replied, as he walked behind his SUV and got in on the driver's side. He thought about trying to engage her in conversation, thinking maybe she wouldn't continue acting cold toward him, but he resolved that she'd probably turn bitchy so he didn't say anything else to her.

She watched him slide the key into the ignition, start the engine, and turn the steering wheel as they exited the parking lot of the restaurant. She stared at his hands clenched around the steering wheel. They were large and seemed soft,

smooth, and delicate enough to fit into any orifice. They
seemed honest enough to make his touch sincere, to make it
seem like he could touch her and it would feel like she was really touching herself. He took his right hand off the steering
wheel and placed it on his upper right thigh, drawing her eyes
to his crotch, causing her to fantasize about the bulge in his
pants, the promises his penis could make and keep.

She extended her left hand and rested it on his upper right
thigh. She squeezed his thigh and ran her hands up to his
crotch, over his groin, up from his balls, to his shaft, to his
hips, and up to his navel. She could feel him flinch in surprise
upon feeling her touch, and he jerked the steering wheel
slightly.

Why is she doing this now? he wondered, instantly excus-
ing the coldness that she had exhibited toward him the entire
night, noticing that they were approaching the bridge. Sus-
pecting where this was going, he berated himself for not taking another route to her house, so that he could pull over and
enjoy her. Upon realizing that the most important thing is to
get laid and that it doesn't matter where, he encouraged her
to continue by releasing a barely audible "Thank you."

Consumed by the possibilities of the moment, she unbuttoned her blouse. He took his eyes off the road and looked
down at her, absolutely titillated by her reversal in character.
She pulled her blouse down over her right shoulder. Her right
bra strap fell off her shoulder as if it were commanded to do
so. She arched her back and took her blouse off and dropped
it on the seat behind her ass, then reached behind her back to
unfasten her black lace demi-cup bra. She pulled it from her
chest and slid it over her arms. He looked at her tits, these
perfectly round melons four or five times the size of his balls,
that could easily be made to squeeze his dick so tight that he'd

feel like his dick was breaking through a virgin's hole. They were firm, but bounced and dangled a bit with the vibrations of the SUV, like they would when a woman straddles a man, cradling his dick between her legs, as she rises and falls on him, taking his dick in and taking it out, slowly, right before she knows he's going to cum.

He took one hand off the steering wheel and cupped her left tit, squeezing it up from the base, up to her purple nipple, squirting the nipple out through his hands until it became erect with the same animalistic fervor as if he had used his mouth, to suck her tit like he really wanted to do. He was beginning to feel his dick respond through his pants. She was beginning to get wet.

She leaned over into his lap, beneath the steering wheel, as he released her tit. She smelled his fluid beneath his cologne, like he must've jerked off before their date that night. Becoming more turned on by his smell, becoming more turned on by his lust, she unbuttoned and unzipped his pants. She slid her fingers into the dick slot to his plain white cotton briefs, pulling out his grossly overgrown cucumber dick that instantly became all stiff once out of his pants and pointed in her direction.

As they were now approaching the top of the bridge, traffic began to build. He had to stop the SUV. She hadn't noticed. He started wondering if anyone would notice what she was doing to him. That thought was rapidly chased away as she rubbed her face against his dick, sliding her face up and down, over and around, holding on to it as if she had just gotten what she needed, feeling it heat up. She drew herself into his lap even more. He was now no longer certain that he could keep his foot on the brake as he waited for the traffic jam to ease.

She held his dick with her fingers and kissed its mushroom head. She licked the tip. He slid his hand down her back, between her skin and her thong, down the crack, to her hole, while rubbing his dick with his left hand. Realizing that her jeans were too tight for him to work his hand into her ass anymore, he said, "You've got to help me."

She let go of him, unbuttoned, and wiggled out of her jeans.

He continued to slide his hand down her naked back, moved aside her thong, and tickled her around her hole. He took his hand away from her ass and licked his fingers to ease their entry into her ass. He considerately and slowly placed finger number one, finger number two, and finger number three into her hole, fucking her ass with his fingers. New at this, his fingers felt like a dick in her ass, fucking her with the same force and sensitivity.

She reached down between her legs, balling up her hands she pressed on her cunt, coaxing herself to cum, marching her fingers into her clit, up her hole, manipulating her hand against, around, and in her cunt like a directionless dick stumbling to find its way.

Now craving his dick even more, she capped the tip of his dick with her mouth and began taking his shaft in slowly, a half-inch at a time, feeling him with her tongue, sliding it around his creases, lubing him up with her saliva, and feeling her own lips becoming even slicker with her fluids. She started rocking toward him and away, taking his dick in more and more and then less and less as she rocked. She continued rubbing her clit with her fingers. He was pushing his fingers into her ass even more.

She felt her cunt spasm uncontrollably, felt herself orgasm, as she was taking his penis more and more into her mouth each time, as his fingers were pulsating in her ass, in the same rhythm as she was sucking him off. It felt like his fingers were about to shoot and then his dick did, in her mouth. All down her throat.

There is always hope for the ride home.

The Merry Widow

Rosalyn Davis

    To say that I was shocked when I found out my husband was dead is an understatement. We had only been married for five years and were both still relatively young— Robert was only thirty-one and I was twenty-seven. We both worked out religiously and he was a vegetarian, so I knew it wasn't his health that got the best of him. I had to make the state trooper repeat himself when he said that Robert had died in a car accident on the interstate. Apparently he had been trying to ease off the highway to change a flat tire and was broadsided by an eighteen-wheeler. I was immensely depressed over the next few days and had to leave all the arrangements to his family. My mother was flying in the day before the funeral so I still had three days to myself to deal with things. I planned on immersing myself in the tragedy and never having an intimate relationship again. I knew that I was probably being dramatic but at the time it seemed fitting. I could at least carry on that way for a few years; then I would get on with my life. And that was my plan until the funeral. At the funeral, everything changed forever.

    There I was on a beautiful Saturday afternoon, flanked by

my mother and Robert's family. The pastor who had married us was saying how the Lord only calls us home when he needs us for other work. I was not in the mood to hear this and began to glance around at the other people there. I saw a lot of Robert's friends from work and a number of his fraternity brothers but other than them, there were no men in the church full of people.

There had to be nearly a hundred people in that church and only fifteen of them, tops, were men. I started to wonder who all these women were and why they were at this funeral. I figured that maybe a couple handfuls could be from the office, but that only eliminated ten of them. And as I was starting to turn back around to face the pastor, partially to hide the growing jealousy in my face and partially so I wouldn't have to see all these women, I caught sight of five of the most beautiful women I have ever seen. They were the kind of girls that made you nauseous in high school because their breasts were always perky, their waists were tiny, and their hair was always flowing past their shoulders. I knew I had seen one of them before. She was the immediate ex before me, but the rest just made me want to jump up screaming, which is what I did.

"Okay, you all know me. I'm the widow, but I know I don't know most of you from anywhere. Why are you here and how do you know my husband?"

The church grew eerily quiet and everyone stared at me.

"Well I'm not sitting down until someone tells me something, so let's hear it."

That's when the row of beautiful women all stood up. Tanya, the ex, spoke up first. "Well, you know who I am. I'm here because I was in love with your husband; even though he never deluded me into thinking he was in love with me. I was sleeping with him, though, and I'm sorry for that. But you know how loving and caring he was and I couldn't bear to turn him away when he came by."

"Neither could I," was almost shouted from over half the women in the room, including the row of women with Tanya. I couldn't believe that I was standing at my husband's funeral finding out that he was not only cheating on me but doing it with nearly everyone he met.

"Well, I asked a stupid question now, didn't I? I should have realized that when I looked at all of you the first time, but a wife doesn't want to see these things. And lest we all forget, I was his wife. But now that I have an answer, I'll excuse myself. Robert can rot in hell without me."

I heard my mother calling my name as I walked out of the church. I was sure that she was following me, but at the time, it didn't matter. I made it to the car before she could get out of the door and then I raced home and locked myself in. I didn't answer the door or the phone for almost a week and the first time I picked up, I wished I hadn't.

"Hello?"

"Yes, is this Chelsea Duncan?"

"Yes, who is this?"

"It's Tanya."

"What can I help you with, Tanya, or do you prefer your given name, slut?"

"Okay, I deserved that, but I think you'll want to hear what I have to say. What we all have to say."

"We all who?"

"Me and the women that were sitting with me at the funeral. You left before I had a chance to tell you—"

"I think you told me quite enough already. What else could you possibly have to say?"

"Chelsea, please. We won't take up more than an hour of your time and I'm sure that what we have to say will make you feel better about your husband."

"That's a tall task, but what the hell. I can't feel any worse."

"Okay, well, meet us at the Cliff Side Inn in an hour."

"I'd rather not. Just come out to the house. I'm sure you know where it is."

"Actually, I don't, but I have the address and I can find directions on the Internet. See you in forty-five minutes?"

"Fine." I got up and showered and changed into this lounging set that Robert had bought for me right before he died. It was a dark blue, our favorite color, and for some reason that soothed me. I twisted my hair up into a bun, the way he always liked, and then poured myself a drink. I curled up into the big wicker chair that had the comfy cushion in it and watched the only thing I'd allowed myself to look at since the funeral, our wedding tape. It seemed like I knew very little about my husband in retrospect, but I know that I loved him, which is why this was hurting so much.

Forty-five minutes after we hung up, Tanya was at the door with the other women in tow. "Can we make this quick? I have a bottle of wine to finish before bed."

They all looked at me for a second and then introduced themselves.

"My name is Denise," said a tall, light-skinned woman who was about twenty-five. Janet and Nicole followed; they looked like twins but weren't related. Both were chestnut brown with dark hair in the short Toni Braxton cuts. The last woman was Jasmine. God, I hated her. She was the embodiment of that mythical brick house. Except that she was mixed, maybe half-Asian. Regardless, I suddenly felt even less attractive than I did five minutes ago.

She began speaking first. "I don't want to make this any harder on you, but we all loved Robert, too." They all shook their heads in agreement. "It would have been strange if we hadn't showed up for the funeral, even though we could have probably come by the graveside later. We all knew each other and had been comforting each other, so we decided to take the risk and come together. If we had known about the others, we wouldn't have come. I promise." Once again with the nodding.

"So why are you here and what do you mean, comforting each other?"

That's when one of the Doublemint twins spoke up. "I'm sure that it would be hard to make you think any less of us. We were sleeping with your husband and all—"

"Do we have to keep saying that?" Jasmine's voice was sort of hypnotic, though. Very pleasant. Maybe that's why I didn't notice that she had moved closer into my personal space than I normally like women to be.

"Anyway, the only reason that all of us knew Robert is that all of us were sleeping together, too."

I'm sure the dumbfounded look on my face said a lot, but since I didn't kick them out the other twin, Janet, started talking.

"I know you're probably wondering why five very attractive women are sleeping together instead of with men. Well, we do sleep with men but we have more fun together. And before you ask how, let me just say that we had all left really bad relationships before we were initiated, so to speak. But every woman in this room had the right to stay in our little sorority or leave after we comforted her."

"What in the hell does this have to do with me?"

Denise spoke up then. "We all loved Robert. He was very good to us and despite the fact that he loved you dearly, he loved the hunt even more. That's what we were. Part of his hunt. We entered that role willingly but realize that you were never given a heads up on his outside activities. We know how much this hurts. Believe me, we've been there."

"Yeah, right, and monkeys are going to fly out of my butt soon."

"Well, we all better duck and your ass is going to hurt."

I started cracking up then and moved back into the living room. "Would you ladies like a drink? And then someone can explain what you are doing here, because I still haven't heard the reason."

Denise and Janet nodded that they wanted some wine, but everyone else just sat down.

"Let me continue. Chelsea, we are here to initiate you. We figured that anyone that Robert loved could be someone we love. If nothing else, it could help you hold on to a piece of him."

"Look, I have all the pieces of him I want. I have the house, the car, and all the things we filled this house up with. I have my memories and I have just enough anger to not dwell on the fact that he isn't going to make any new ones with me."

Tanya walked over to me and put my wineglass down. She led me over to my wicker chair and proceeded to untie my bun.

"Don't you like it better when your hair is flowing around your face?"

"I like it when strange women don't fondle my hair."

But she didn't stop. She kept running her fingers through my hair and over my cheeks. I don't know if it was the wine or my general sense of exhaustion, but I just gave in to the sensation. It felt nice to have someone touching me again. Before I knew it, the others descended on me. I guess my lack of resistance was their cue because I felt my slippers and pants being gently removed. I felt hands making circular motions over different parts of my thighs before someone reached for my panties. They were off before I even thought to object. Tanya straddled me and pulled off her top, then mine. She leaned in and for the first time, I felt my naked breasts touching another set of naked breasts. It felt strange but nice. I couldn't believe I was doing this but I had no intention of turning back now.

"Do you mind if I kiss you?"

I just shook my head no and then it happened. I kissed Tanya. I was kissing my husband's mistress and, for some reason, that thought made my kiss more urgent. I thought about all the times he must have kissed all of them and then I felt my tongue seeking hers out. She wrapped me in her arms and started grinding her hips on top of me, and then I felt a tongue snake up the thighs that had been continuously stroked since they were bared. Suddenly it hit home. There was no hesitation or clumsiness. It probed into me so hard and fast that all I could do was moan.

"Shh, you don't want to disturb the neighbors," Tanya said.

She popped her left nipple into my mouth and told me to suck, which I did like an obedient puppy while she stroked my head. She let out a contented sigh and turned to look at who was between my legs. Jasmine was the one orally delighting me. The pseudo twins were sucking on each of her breasts and Denise was sitting in my line of vision, buck naked and masturbating with a vibrator.

Somewhere in the back of my mind, I was thinking I shouldn't be doing this. I should be very angry with these women. But they were right, in a way. I was getting my own piece of Robert back. When I felt my orgasm rushing on me, I had to push Tanya away. I wrapped one leg around Jasmine's neck, draped the free leg over the arm of the chair, and bucked for dear life. Everyone in the room stopped and looked at us and when my final shudder eked out of me, they started applauding.

Jasmine stood up, licking her lips. "Very nice. Can't say why that man was roaming, but I can't be too mad he led us to you after all. But your initiation isn't done. You have to worship before each of us, then join us in the circle before we can call you sister."

I said, "Just know that I don't know what I'm doing here, so don't be afraid to tell me what you want."

They all giggled and walked over to the long sectional sofa. When they were all situated, they started kissing and stroking each other before I could move close to them. Hands were traveling over clits and nipples at breakneck speed. They all looked so inviting that I couldn't decide where to go first, but Denise spread her legs over the others' thighs and beckoned me to come close.

"Come on, darling, have a lick."

I crawled between her thighs and closed my eyes. My tongue eased out of my mouth and then I felt her hand on the back of my head. Before I could blink again, I was tasting my first pussy. She was wet already from the masturbation, but she seemed to get wetter each time my tongue made a pass over her folds. When I finally made it up to suck on her clit, her hips had started rotating. I licked at her nub gently and stuck two fingers inside her as I increased the pressure. I got to make about five pumps before she slammed my tongue back into her pussy and started to shake. She let out a low roar and then gushed all her honey onto my tongue. She pulled me up to her and kissed me, tasting a bit of herself in the process.

"Round one is over. Who's next?"

I went over to Tanya then because something had caught

my eye when I saw her playing with her pussy. Her clit was pierced and this fascinated me. "Did that hurt?" I asked as I leaned in to suckle her nipple again.

"Not at all. But it's not time to ask questions. Be a good girl and lick mommy dry. But brace yourself first."

"Brace for what?" Before the thought became reality, I felt something probing my pussy. It was almost the size of Robert and damn, it felt good. I looked behind me to see that Denise had strapped on a dildo and was going to fuck me while I ate out Tanya.

"Don't worry, honey. I won't hurt ya," she said as she slapped me on the ass. "Now get to work."

I pushed myself back onto the artificial dick and then proceeded to lick around Tanya's piercing before I started sucking on her clit. She wrapped her thighs around my neck and kept me locked into place with my tongue lodged deep in her pussy. With each stroke from Denise, I bounced further into Tanya's pussy. I managed to snake an arm near her waist and then let my thumb play with her clit while my tongue found her weak spot. We both started screaming together; only my screams were muffled in her wetness. She started shuddering and then squeezed her thighs around my face one last time before pushing me away.

"Umm, maybe we should have come and gotten you earlier. Oh, well, I think it's time you played with Jasmine. She was the first one to get a lick at your sweet spot, so return the favor."

"Wait, Tanya, I'm not done yet," growled Denise.

"It's okay, I'll move for ya, Nisey," Jasmine said as she slid into Tanya's recently vacated spot.

"Thanks, baby. Give me a kiss before you start."

I heard them kissing above me and felt Denise's dick buried firmly inside me. Jasmine sat back and Denise grabbed a handful of my hair and force fed Jasmine's pussy to me while she long-stroked me. I had finally found a nice rhythm when I felt a tongue start caressing my clit and breasts against my thighs. I opened my eyes and saw Janet and Nicole licking on Jasmine's ample, honey-colored 38Ds, so that only left Tanya.

"See, you making Tanya get all freaky and you still haven't bucked that ass back on me yet," Denise said. "Well, you are gonna come for me, bitch, or you're never getting up."

Now, any other time I hear the word "bitch" from a woman's lips, it's a fighting word, but I was in a sexual haze, so I only licked and bucked harder. Each tongue flick from Tanya made me gyrate harder against Denise, which made me fly further into Jasmine's bare cunt. It was all I could do from collapsing right there but, instead, my body started shaking. I licked Jasmine harder and faster as I felt a supreme orgasm approaching. Denise giggled and then began pounding my pussy. When we started resembling a piston on overdrive, my body convulsed and Jasmine clamped down on my tongue like a vise. We were one big connected orgasm. Jasmine and me coming hard got Denise off, and Tanya had been playing with the vibrator while we were going at it so she was rushing over her own orgasm beneath me.

We all fell apart laughing, but my break was short-lived. Janet and Nicole formed a little daisy chain with me and we started probing and licking each other with whatever was handy. I could feel the others watching me as I shoved the double-headed dildo further into Nicole and bucked against Janet's tongue. All that anticipation must have worked them up because they both came quickly and we separated to sprawl out on the floor.

"Okay, ladies, just one more thing to do and then our new initiate will be a full member of the group. Everyone locate the cunt you find the sweetest and grab hold. It's time for the circle."

With that, I felt Jasmine slide between my legs again as I reached out for Tanya. Denise started sucking on Jasmine's clit, while Janet pulled up to dine on Denise and Nicole to munch on Janet. When Tanya snaked over to Nicole, the circle was complete. Fingers and tongues made deep long explorations of the pussy in front of them. Moans started escalating as one body shook after another somewhere in the circle. Finally screams filled the air as the sensations became too much and pieces of the circle broke up. I was left to dine on Tanya as the other ladies watched. When I rolled over on my back, she lowered her pussy over my tongue and rocked on top of it. She ended up riding my tongue and when she came, she covered my entire face in her juices.

Denise stood up on wobbly legs then and started speaking. "Well, it's been a most productive night and, as usual, we've lost track of time. But I'd like to thank our host for being so gracious and to welcome our newest member, Chelsea, here-after to be known as the Merry Widow."

The kissing and probing started again and went on well into the next morning, but that's a story for another time. For now, the Merry Widow has an initiation to plan. Good-bye.

GENTLEMEN NEXT

The Hot Maid

blk_man4u

Walt Lafitte dropped the leather briefcase down on the sofa and threw the stack of unread newspapers on the kitchen counter. The grueling morning at the office had taken its toll on him and he had taken the afternoon off just to get some needed rest. But as he stumbled through the clutter in his condo, he saw that the place was a mess. Dishes were piled in the sink, magazines and newspapers were scattered across the coffee table, and books were stacked in a pile along the wall. His plans to build a bookcase had given in to the demands of the job that kept him working twelve-hour days on a regular basis.

As he walked into the master suite, he noticed several dress shirts strewn across the bed and chair. Slacks and belts were also draped across the arm of the chair. Over ten pairs of shoes were in disarray and strewn throughout the spacious bedroom. The unmade bed was just a reminder of how little time he actually spent sleeping in it. Some nights, he had even stayed over at his office working on various proposals. It was now clear to him that it was pathetic to earn a six-figure salary as an investment broker, live in a $400,000 condo, and yet have the place looking like a pigsty. He realized what the condo needed was a woman's touch. But he could forget about trying to get any of the women that he dated to help. Not today's modern black woman; most could hardly keep their own places clean. What he needed was a maid.

Walt picked up the phone book and flipped through the yellow pages. He found an employment service and asked them to send over some applicants for housekeepers. He told the lady at the agency that it didn't matter who they sent as long as they were competent. The lady told him he would have to come down and fill out some paperwork before they could send out a housekeeper.

Walt hopped in his BMW and sped over to the agency, which was a few miles from his place. Just as he finished filling out the necessary paperwork and giving them adequate references, he was interrupted by a call on his pager. Checking his message, he saw that it was a client whom he had been trying to meet with in order to close a major deal. He informed the lady that he had to leave and asked if they could get someone over there today. The lady stated that they could and Walt left her the directions and a spare set of keys to his condo.

Later that night, after a long and successful dinner meeting with his client, Walt arrived home about midnight and was stunned to see a freshly cleaned and neat apartment. After stripping his clothes off, he plopped down in his freshly made bed and was soon sound asleep.

The light from the window awakened him and he heard footsteps approaching his bedroom. He sprung from the bed just as the door pushed open. Fearing that he was being robbed, he looked around for the baseball bat he used as protection, but he was totally surprised to see a brown-skinned young woman walking in with a basket of folded clothes. He stood there frozen, totally unaware that he was buck naked until the woman blushed as she glanced at his groin area. Walt grabbed for the covers to hide his nakedness.

"I'm so sorry," the woman said with a Spanish accent. "I thought you were still asleep and I was going to put these in your dresser."

"Who are you?" Walt asked, sounding very alarmed.

"I'm your housekeeper, Conchata. You hired me yesterday."

"I did?" he said, wiping the sleep from his eyes. "Oh, yeah, the cleaning agency. Damn, I forgot all about that. You did a great job on the place."

"Sorry that I awakened you," she said, sitting the basket down. "Let me leave this so you can get dressed."

Walt watched her as she turned to leave. She must have been no older than twenty-two or twenty-three. He noticed that she had a body that wouldn't stop. Nice large breasts, shapely brown legs, and an ass that jutted out for days. He wasn't sure if she was Mexican, Puerto Rican, or what, yet she had some African features as well. Regardless of her heritage, he thought, the woman was fine.

Once Walt got dressed, he went in to formally meet Conchata. She was bending over dusting and Walt noticed that her outfit, which consisted of a snug-fitting blouse and cutoff jeans, could barely hide her curvaceous figure. Walt chatted with her for several minutes, inquiring about her background. He soon found out that she was a student from Panama who had been living in the United States for several years. She was attending classes in the afternoons to become a physical therapist.

She and Walt hit it off well and he learned that she was hoping to make enough money to move out of her parents' home and get her own apartment. With six brothers and sisters, the place was very crowded and she couldn't always find the ideal environment to study.

Walt thought about it for a while, then offered her the use of one of the extra bedrooms in his condo. "Since there's ample room in the condo and I work long hours, it would give you a place to stay and a quieter place to study." He saw the look of surprise come across her face and he added, grinning, "Besides, I had hoped that you could do some cooking, too."

"Mr. Lafitte, that is so nice of you, but how much would I have to pay for the rent?" she asked.

He saw that she was very sincere. "No problem. I'll pay you what you normally get for cleaning and an additional amount to cook. Your room and board will be a part of the agreement."

"Oh, Mr. Lafitte, you are so nice. Wait till I tell my *madre*," she said, slipping back into a bit of Spanish.

"And by the way, Conchata, you can call me Walt. You make me feel like I'm an old man. I'm only thirty-two."

"Okay, Mr. La— er, I mean, Walt. Thank you very, very much."

She walked into the next room to call her mother and Walt was happy that she accepted the job. It would be nice to have some company there as well.

Walt thought about Conchata's voluptuous body as he worked out in his gym. He hadn't used the equipment that he had installed in the third bedroom of his 2000-square-foot condo in weeks. The unit on the tenth floor had spectacular views of the bay and the mountains in the distance. Between thoughts of her and the strenuous workout, he was totally whipped after a ninety-minute workout. It had been weeks since he'd had a chance to use the gym and the equipment usually sat idle. Now that he had closed his big deal, he was going to work some reasonable hours.

He was stretched out on the bench resting when he noticed that Conchata was peeking in from the hallway.

"I'm sorry," she said. "I was walking by and noticed that you were resting. Can I get you anything?"

"Just some water," he said.

Walt was already starting to like this kind of treatment. He wondered why he hadn't done this sooner.

Conchata returned with a glass of water and she stood there watching as he downed it quickly. She noticed that the sweat made his tank top cling to his chest muscles and she could see his washboard stomach. She continued her slow assessment of his tall, brown, muscular frame. Tree-trunk legs and a tight butt complemented the bulge in his shorts.

"Can I give you a rub down?" she asked. Walt was a little surprised. She noticed his quizzical look and said, "It's one of the subjects that I'm studying. It's one of the first steps in becoming a therapist."

Walt relented. "Well, if you say so. If your massage technique is as good as your cleaning skills, then I'll be a lucky guy."

Motioning for him to lie back down on the bench, she said, "Okay, remove all your clothes."

She walked over to the rack to retrieve a fresh towel. Walt slowly removed his shirt and gym shorts until he was down to the thong-like jockstrap.

"C'mon, that, too," she said as she stood there with her hands on her hips.

Walt was hesitant. He wasn't quite sure about getting totally naked.

"Come on, I've already seen you naked," she said with a

stern look on her face. She shook her finger at him and said something in Spanish. She really didn't need for him to get completely naked, but she wanted to check out his body again and this was a good excuse.

Walt, realizing he was getting aroused by her demanding behavior, turned his back and slowly removed the jockstrap. Her hard stare at his body made his penis start to react to the situation and he quickly lay on his stomach to hide the hardening erection from her view.

Her hands felt soft and firm as she worked the muscles of his back and shoulders. She knew what she was doing, and Walt soon relaxed and let her work out the stress in his neck, shoulders, and back. When she reached the lower back, he wondered how much farther she would go. She kneaded his buttocks and thighs and worked his legs from his calves to his feet. The sensations were heavenly and Walt could feel his prick bulging beneath his stomach. Usually *he* would be giving the massage to some woman as part of foreplay. But Conchata was all business as she worked his tired muscles and he was able to get his mind off her body and sex.

Finally, she gave him a playful slap on his backside and told him to "hit the showers," sounding like his old high school coach. Walt got up slowly and grabbed the towel to cover his still rigid erection. He thanked her and headed for the bathroom. Conchata watched as he padded out of the room. She noticed that his large erection bulged out prominently, even with the towel wrapped around his torso.

The following week, Conchata had moved her things into his place and soon had Walt's home in tip-top shape. It looked like the home of a successful black executive bachelor.

However, despite enjoying her presence, Walt had trouble sleeping at night. His thoughts and dreams were usually about the fine specimen that was asleep down the hall. He hadn't even gone out with any of his old girlfriends since she'd started working for him. Conchata would tease him about the lack of dates and he would play it off, saying that work kept him too busy at the moment.

Walt enjoyed the Latin-influenced dishes that Conchata cooked and he even showed off by cooking some of his specialties for her. He looked forward to her surprising him with a new dish every so often. He was very surprised at her maturity, intelligence, and grasp of current events. He'd never before spent as much time talking politics with a female as he did with her. Despite her young age, Conchata had matured rapidly due to being the oldest and living a hard existence in Panama. Things were much better for her and her family now that they had moved to America.

One night a thunderstorm awakened Walt. The loud claps of thunder rattled the entire building and lightning flashed through the window as if a fireworks show was just outside the window. Suddenly, a loud bang occurred and it even scared Walt. Without warning, the power went out and it was totally black in the room. Walt heard a knock on the door and before he could answer, Conchata bolted through the doorway into his room. Walt could hear her whimpering and he got out of the bed and stumbled in the darkness toward her sobs to see what was wrong.

"Are you okay?" he called out. He motioned in the darkness, trying to find the wall or the door. Suddenly he felt something soft and warm and he realized that he had grabbed Conchata's breast.

"Oh, I'm sorry. I couldn't see you standing there."

She fell into his arms, sobbing at this point.

"What's wrong?" he asked. "Don't tell me you're scared of thunder."

He chuckled at the thought of her being afraid of the lightning, or maybe it was the pitch-black darkness of the place.

"I am," she said, sniffling. "It reminds me of the bombing in Panama during the Noreiga capture. I was a young girl when it happened and the bombs were all over the place."

Walt felt bad for making fun of her and he tried to soothe her by telling her that he was there to protect her. They just stood there for minutes holding each other. Soon her sobbing subsided and Walt told her she could stay with him until the storm was over.

"You lie down on the bed and I'll sit here in the chair," he said as he released her. But she clasped him even tighter. "No, please don't leave me. Please hold me till it's over."

Walt decided not to argue. He got on the bed and they snuggled together. The warmth of her body and the faint scent of her perfume felt intoxicating to Walt. He could see from the occasional flashes of lightning that she was wearing only panties and a bra. The lacy bra was a low-cut model that revealed a lot of her ample cleavage. He tried to get his mind off that, and soon they both drifted off into a catnap.

Walt drifted in and out of consciousness. He dreamed that there were hands stroking his chest. But it was not a dream. Conchata slowly reached over and grabbed Walt's hand and placed it on her backside. She continued rubbing his chest and playing with his nipples. He was now wide awake as he felt her descending to his stomach and navel area. By now, Walt was sporting a throbbing erection, and if her hand went any further south, she was bound to collide with it. He wasn't sure where this activity would lead, but he was enjoying every moment of it. He stroked her soft behind and slipped his hand beneath the waistband to feel her soft butt in the flesh.

She began to kiss his chin and neck softly. Her hands had

moved farther down and found his penis pulsating with excitement. He moved up to unclasp the back of her bra and at that precise moment, the lights came on. The sudden brightness in the room from the hallway blinded them momentarily, but soon he could see her breasts, which had spilled out from her bra. The beautiful brown nipples had very large and dark aureoles surrounding them. She looked at his huge veined penis protruding upward from his shorts. They both hesitated for a moment, unsure of what to do next, but Conchata reached up to kiss him and soon their tongues were working feverishly against each other.

They continued their deep kiss for a few minutes, then Walt moved down to tackle the beautiful brown titties. They were even more immense than he had realized, as his eyes had now adjusted. He cupped her titties in his hands as he worked his tongue over the firm buds. Her nipples had become more erect and they felt like extra-large raisins in his mouth.

Conchata had a firm grip on his penis and was stroking it up and down.

"Oh, papi, your *pene'* is so huge," she said, referring to his penis in Spanish once she had gotten a good view of it in the light.

Walt knew that every woman had been either in awe of or repulsed by his nine-inch penis. Some could not accommodate something that huge. Thick as a Polish sausage, the width presented even more of a problem.

Conchata moved down to rub the head of it, which was oozing pre-cum, over her nipples. The texture of her nipples sent a surge through Walt's body. She then placed the huge dong between her tits and Walt moved it up and down between the valley of her luscious jugs.

"How big are those tatas?" he asked, pretending he knew the Spanish word for *titties*.

"I wear a 38DD cup," she said. "I was always the biggest in my class."

"They feel so *gooood*," he said, letting the word *good* languish on his tongue.

She motioned for Walt to hover over her as she pushed the melons tighter together to give him more pleasure. She flicked her tongue as the huge rod slid between her breasts. Walt moved over her face as she began to lick his penis around the head and down the sides. Placing it in her mouth, she coated it with saliva and started sucking feverishly. Walt started pumping it in and out and Conchata took it deeper and deeper each time.

Walt watched in fascination as she expertly deep-throated his member and he felt his balls up against her chin. She held it in her throat for a minute and slowly pulled it out. It glistened with saliva in the lamplight and she took the head in her mouth again. She continued her work on it and Walt leaned back to slide his hand in her panties. Her mound was covered with soft hair and he soon found her inflamed clit. He stuck a finger in her vagina, which by now was sopping wet. He eased two, then three fingers in her burning hole. She moaned with his penis in her mouth as he continued his manual stimulation.

They continued their mutual activities and finally Walt pulled out before he lost control of his actions. He kissed her lips, then each breast, her navel, and the insides of both thighs before finally plunging his tongue deep into her womanhood. The hotness of it and the wetness made him more active as he nibbled at her clitoris and caused her to have her first orgasm. Conchata screamed out and arched her body so high that Walt lost his grip on her thighs. She repeated several words in Spanish, over and over. It was such a turn on to hear her moans of ecstasy in another language.

He got up on his knees and placed his penis at the entrance

of her vagina. Moving it up and down along the slit, he coated it with her secretions and pushed it slowly in, inch by inch. Then he drew it out slowly and repeated the process several times. Conchata started begging him to put it in deeper. Finally, he thrust forcefully until the entire nine inches were buried deeply in her raging inferno.

Conchata grabbed Walt by his firm buttocks and helped him pick up a rhythm that had her thrashing about as he continued to plow into her. She loved Walt's way of pressing up against her clit each time he plunged in. She leaned up as both of them watched it pull out and then back in. He pistoned in and out with such fervor that he surprised even himself. Walt pulled out and rolled her over and entered from the rear. He grabbed her large soft backside as he stroked in and out. She clenched his penis as it went in deeper and deeper. She reached under and grabbed his large testicles and caressed them.

After several minutes of doggy-style, Conchata then pushed him back and told him to lie down. She straddled his thighs and slowly lowered herself on his mammoth rod, which looked thick and menacing. She moaned as he plunged deep inside her. She began to bounce up and down on him and ride him like a horse. He rubbed her buttocks and fingered her anus as she bucked violently. He eased a finger in slightly and she called out in Spanish and he could tell she was having another orgasm. He rolled her over on their sides, not breaking the connection, and started to pump into her harder than he had done any woman. He built up a rhythm so furious and fast that he felt like he was almost a blur. She continued to scream out in passion and her shouts caused him to erupt. He felt the semen pulse into her and he pulled out quickly, shooting jets of cum on her backside. She quickly rolled over to take his still-hard prick into her mouth, licking the cum from the tip. By now he was starting to get soft, but she kept her tongue-lashing going. She sucked up and down on his dong like it was a lollipop.

Soon it was hard again and she started to work it down her throat again. In and out . . . in and out . . . in and out. Walt played with her tits, molding and pinching and rolling the pliable flesh in his hands. He felt himself about to blow again and tried to pull out but she grabbed his butt and held him firmly in her throat. Walt grunted like a bear as he felt the cum spurt down her throat. She milked him dry and after a few minutes she pulled his limp penis out. Walt realized that this woman was amazing and had many talents. He was looking forward to a great working relationship with his wonderful "hot" maid.

At Peace

Tatu

"Buenos días." The old Spanish painter smiled and greeted us as we made our way carefully through the maze of small houses along the century-old street, trying to avoid the rain. The day had started out normal enough, with breakfast in bed, lovemaking amid crumbs of croissants, and then a swim in the warm waters of the Caribbean. This was our first trip to the Bahamas and we'd purposely decided to avoid the tourist crowds associated with Nassau and travel to Freeport instead. We had not seen one another for nearly fourteen years and knew we needed some uninterrupted time to really catch up. We'd been more than lovers all those years ago. We were friends. We always seemed to get each other's jokes, and each of us always knew what the other was thinking. Yes, Freeport was our one chance to see if our love had endured, if we were in fact meant to be together.

"Bwenis deeass," came your wholly un-Spanish-sounding reply. The old painter smiled again. Either he smiled at your attempt at being respectful by replying to him in his native tongue, or he was smiling because your white sundress was now soaked and sticking to your body. Having removed your bikini top while we sunned in a perfectly isolated stretch of beach, your hardened nipples were now standing at attention and prominently showing through your dress. Even though the heavy rain had stopped and the sun was peering out, the streets were still very empty, save for this gentle old painter. The now sun-drenched oils we had used were creating an even stronger erotic aroma in the air between us. As we stood pressed together in some stranger's doorway, I wondered if you still wanted to visit the bath and body shop across the street since we were both soaking wet. Even more, however, I didn't want to walk through the streets with the erection I now had after being pressed up against you. Ever the impulsive one, you insisted that we continue on. "I'm not ashamed of my man," you add devilishly, looking down at my dick bulge beneath my soaking white pants.

The young attendant in Heavenly Scents must have thought you were a movie star because she was so in awe of your beauty. Several times I noticed her taking quick glances at your body. She even became visibly embarrassed when I caught her looking as you bent down to pick up some fragrances and your perfect right breast emerged slightly from your half-unbuttoned shirt.

You had me carry the basket. We made sure to get several scented candles and some spiced body oils. We also picked out some massage soaking pads and some tropical bath oils made from natural substances. As we paid the young cashier for our basket of love goodies, I playfully massaged your butt and kissed your neck while you giggled like you used to when we were teenagers.

Just before leaving, you turned to the cashier and said, "Sweetie, when love comes knocking, grab it. Savor it. Drink it. Don't let it go."

The girl was so moved that she broke into a huge appreciative smile and said, "Thank you, ma'am. I will. I really will."

Outside, the sun had returned and the air smelled of dried and re-hydrated flowers mixed with tropical spices and foods. The city had come alive again and people began going to and fro. You insisted we stop by the open-air market to buy some fresh fruits before returning to our secluded villa. As we walked through the old streets, I kept glancing over at you. I was so content right at that very moment. You were here with me holding my hand and you were smiling. You looked more beautiful at that moment than I ever remembered. I wondered silently why I had ever let our love go unfed. All those years ago, you had been totally dedicated to what we had. Yet, I didn't understand that we could have built a foundation for a solid life together.

A voice in my head told me, "It's never too late."

I watched you dance as we walked down the street. The music from the open-air bars along the old street seemed to mesmerize you and in turn, you completely captivated me. As you spun around and shook your hips, the peach hibiscus in your lone French braid seemed to dance right along with you. Its petals were gently caressed by the soft breeze your moves created and with each movement, the scent of our sun oils mixed with the aroma of your body aroused me more and more. This has to be what life is all about.

When we got back to our villa, the housekeeping staff of two old Bahamian ladies was just leaving. The way they smiled told me that they knew we were deeply in love but perhaps we were still denying it. They reminded me of old grandmothers filled with wisdom and I knew you couldn't get anything past them.

"Enjoy yuurselves, chihrehn!" they yelled, smiling as they drove away in their Jeep.

Without thinking, you replied, "Thanks, mum."

Inside, our house maids had laid fresh fruits out on the living room table and on a small table in front of the large bay window overlooking the ocean. They had opened the window so that a nice gentle breeze blew all through the house. They had also left two bottles of wine we'd previously bought chilling in separate ice containers. Spectacular floral arrangements were left in the dining room, kitchen, on the back patio, and in our bedroom. In the bedroom, they had pulled back the white cotton sheets halfway and littered the bed with tropical roses. There were his and hers matching robes draped over the back of a chair in the room. The bathroom had been prepared as if the housekeepers knew exactly when we would be returning. There was hot water already sitting in the huge tub made for two. A slightly gold-tinted oil was already in the water and giving off a heavenly scent that grabbed at your senses, dragging you in deeper and deeper. A bowl of grapes, strawberries, and peeled mangoes sat on the side ledge of the tub with a small saucer of cream for dipping the fruit. Finally, two extremely thick and fluffy towels sat on a small chair along with a medium-sized bottle of some local tropical lotion. We both simply stood there smiling for a couple of minutes, wondering how we could have ever been so blessed to receive all this.

Since we were fully three miles away from the city, I decided to strip out of my damp clothes right there at the front door. As I walked to the back patio, I could feel your eyes on my butt and I could imagine you smiling devilishly. As I sat down on one of the oversized fluffy pillows in front of the back bay window, I noticed you had decided to join me. In like manner, you had completely disrobed and you now gently lay down beside me. We gazed out to the ocean for what seemed like hours. We took turns feeding each other some of the fruit left for us and the fruit we had purchased. You decided to get more comfortable so you moved over and reclined between my legs with the back of your head on my chest. I reached down and poured us both some wine and then slowly began to undo your French braid. When I removed the hibiscus, I used it to gently caress your neck, your breasts, and your stomach. Your nipples seemed to reach up toward the flower petals as they hardened each time the petals glided past. You shifted your weight, not wanting to hurt me as you felt me harden beneath your back. When we finished the bottle of wine and the fruit, we decided it was time to go and wash the day away.

As we walked to the bathroom, I was no longer embarrassed about my now fully erect cock, which caused me to look like it was leading me around. We stepped into the warm water of the tub and you leaned over to me and kissed me deeply.

As you reclined, you looked at me and said, "You are my love."

"And you are mine, sweetheart," came my reply.

Somehow we knew any further words would be completely unnecessary. With that, I told you to close your eyes and I removed the massage pads from our bag of goodies. I poured some of the water and warm oil onto the pad and began to rub your chest. I stood up fully in the tub so that I could get access to your back. As I bent over you to caress your back with the pad, my warm and throbbing cock seemed to play games with your forehead and temple. You reached out and began to stroke my thighs while you kept your eyes closed. I washed your neck and arms and gently washed every finger. The tub was large enough for me to have you turn onto your stomach so that I could wash and rub your back. With your eyes still closed, I rubbed and washed your back and the backs of your thighs. I could see that contented smile still registering on your face as I gently washed your feet and toes. When I had you sit up, I began to softly kiss you on different points on your body. I kissed just below your chin and then the sides of your neck, the insides of your elbows, the back of your knees, and inside your thighs.

I did not realize that the housekeepers had also set the timer on the stereo, but just as I whispered in your ear, "Now do me," Will Downing began crooning at a perfect level that was neither too soft nor too loud. With another smile, you reached out your hand to me and ran your perfectly manicured fingernails down my chest.

"Lay back, lovely man," you told me.

With a washcloth, you cleansed my entire body. You playfully licked my nipples as if to ensure they got really clean. You had me extend my leg over the side of the tub so that you could rub and wash my feet. As you played with my toes, you fondled my cock with your free hand. I started to breathe fast a bit and you laughingly reminded me to pace myself. It's amazing how little you notice about your surroundings when you're totally focused on someone else. Throughout our little love play, I had not noticed that the housekeepers had also lit a few candles in the bathroom and throughout the rest of the small house. As we stepped out of the tub, the glow of candlelight against our bodies made the entire scene even more sensual. You decided that we should not dry off, but return to our spot in front of the bay window and air-dry. I knew what you really had in mind. We always did think alike.

My cock still remained defiantly erect. A soft warm breeze blew through the open bay window, causing our white curtains to slightly ruffle. Under the glow of the setting sun, the waves had an interesting orange hue to them. As we retook our positions, we decided to try out the products we had purchased. I had you roll onto your stomach, facing the window so that you could continue to watch the sunset. As you lay there, the sun's reflection off the skin on your butt made me want to just bury my tongue in you right then and there. Instead, I poured a healthy amount of the spice oil onto my hands and rubbed it into your back. As I rubbed, I noticed the oils becoming warmer. I sat with my knees under me, straddling the back of your knees with my cock resting on your left thigh. As I rubbed the oil into your skin, you moaned approvingly as if every single stressful moment or thought you'd had in your entire life was oozing away. Using my fingers and the heel of my hand, I rubbed oil into your butt, paying special attention to that area where the back of your thighs meets the beginning of your butt. I moved down and rubbed more oil into your calves and onto your feet. As I pampered your feet, I kissed and licked each toe. While I was down there, I happened to glance up and realized that my upward glance caused me to look right into your pussy. From my vantage point, I could see it glistening as you had become extremely wet. I wondered what you were thinking at that moment. Funny thing is, the tip of my cock was dripping pre-cum, signaling how much we both wanted each other.

"Roll over now," I whispered.

With your eyes closed now, you followed my directions. While I had seen you totally naked many times before, your body lying before me with the newly arrived moon casting a glow against your caramel skin caused me to silently gasp at your beauty. Your dark and raised nipples looked like two chocolate kisses sitting atop a moon-drenched, caramel-coated hill. Your aroused breathing made your breasts shake ever so lightly and you were now beginning to move your hips

in small circular paths. I concentrated on your navel and decided to begin by gently kissing you there. I placed my lips
softly against your stomach, allowing my lips and tongue to
slowly caress the soft and tiny pubic hairs that almost unno-
ticeably ran to your navel. I ran my tongue and lips up between your breasts and kissed your chin before I resumed my
massage. This time, I decided to warm the oils slightly more
by placing some in a glass and warming that over a candle.
When I rubbed the pre-warmed oil onto your body, you
shuddered and let out a satisfied groan. After rubbing oil all
over your front, I placed my hands on the ground at your sides
and lowered myself to just above your body as if I were doing
push-ups. I used my body to rub the oil into you even more.
As I moved back and forth above you, my cock poked at your
navel and pubic hair. You began to arch your back and parted
your legs but I kissed you and said, "Not yet, love."

I got up and went into the bathroom for the remaining
fruit and cream. As you lay there, I took a slice of mango and
used it to spread cream on your breasts, in your navel, and on
top of your thighs. I then gently licked up the cream. When
all the cream was gone, I inserted the mango slice into your
pussy and ate it from there. I took another mango and placed
it in a glass of wine where it soaked up some of the wine, then
took the mango slice and began to kiss you in the mouth while
keeping the slice between us. As we kissed and sucked on the
mango, you reached down and grabbed hold of my cock. You
started rubbing the shaft with both hands and teasing my testicles with your fingernails. I was getting too excited so I
stood up and beckoned you to come with me. We stepped out
onto the back patio. Now fully outside and unclothed, we sat
together in one of the long reclining chairs on the patio. You
sat on top of me facing me and we began to kiss deeply. My
cock was pressed up against your pussy but not going inside.

You moved back and forth to allow your pussy to massage and caress my cock as we kissed.

You then stood up and placed your right leg on my shoulder. "Hungry, mister?" you playfully asked me.

Seeing no need for an answer, I dove right in. I ran my tongue from the top front of your pussy to the very back where that little flap of skin separates your vagina from your ass. I ran my tongue back and forth along that area and lapped at your pussy opening. As I licked, you reached down and poured some oil onto your left hand and began to masturbate me. I licked and nibbled on your clit and when you asked, I would insert my tongue deep into you. Knowing your leg was getting heavier, I lifted you up and laid you down before me as I got up, repositioned myself, and buried my face in your pussy again.

By now you were pumping against my tongue and moaning louder. With my right hand, I lifted your butt to me so that I could stick my tongue deeper inside. With my left hand, I fondled and squeezed your breasts. You grabbed my left hand and placed two of my fingers in your mouth and began sucking them. I came up and kissed you hard.

Even more aroused by your own taste in my mouth, you said, "Make love to me now, Michael."

You took hold of my continually throbbing cock and guided me into your warmth. As the head of my manhood entered you, you arched your back and raised your hips to meet me. You felt so wet that I slid right in, despite the tightness. Our bodies immediately created suction, as if your pussy now refused to let my cock exit. I placed my right hand under the small of your back to support your desire to keep your back arched. Balancing on my knees, I placed my left hand beneath your right butt cheek and with my fingers, I spread your love even wider. I began with slow long strokes in and out. I wanted us to concentrate on the feeling of my dick shaft radiating against your inner pussy walls. Each time I came out, I would pull my cock all the way to the tip to allow you to feel the head once again as I drove it into you. By now you had your right hand on my butt and your left hand on my neck. Your eyes were closed and I even thought I noticed a tear rolling down your left cheek. In spite of the nice oceanic breeze that continually greeted us, both our bodies glistened with tiny beads of perspiration. Noticing the beauty of the glow of the moon on our wet bodies, you stuck out your tongue and took a long lick of my chest. This was more than I could handle. I had to change up.

When I started pumping in slow circular movements, you bit your bottom lip and grabbed my butt with both hands. You raised your legs higher into the air and gently rested your heels on my butt. I could see the muscles in your shoulders flex as you grabbed harder and harder at my butt. After each full circular movement, I would quickly and deeply thrust into you, causing you to make a short high-pitched moan. Then you took your hands and began to push me on my chest. I realized you wanted me to kneel straight up and pump into you that way. What I didn't immediately realize was that you also wanted to be able to reach your own clit while I pumped in and out. As my circular motions continued, you began rubbing your clit with one hand. This was an amazing sight for me. With your other hand, you reached for my balls and started gently fondling them as I glided in and out.

"Turn over, sweetie," I told you.

Your expressionless face told me that you were too caught in the moment to verbally respond. You simply turned over and placed your glorious ass at my stomach level. I had to admire your form for a moment. Your butt was perfectly round and the color of slightly darkened caramel. As I knelt there admiring you, my cock continued to throb impatiently. Similarly, you moved your hips up and down and around and around, still apparently feeling me inside you.

With both hands, I steadied your hips as I entered you from the back. I knew immediately that I was positioned rather well against your G-spot because I could feel myself rub against the wall as I pushed into you. I reached over and under with my right hand to rub your clit while I placed my left hand on the ground to balance myself. Before I even began to move, you began pumping back into me. I decided to stay very still because I knew if I moved too much, I would definitely cum and I didn't want to just yet. Your hips moved around and up and down on my dick like a well-oiled machine. Throes of pre-orgasmic waves were beginning to take over me. I could never handle doggie-style all that well. As I pushed in and out, you once again reached under to cup my balls with one hand. Sensing that I was about to cum, you quickly got out from under me, flipped me over and climbed on top. Facing me, you rested your chest on mine and buried your face in my neck. Only moving your hips, you squeezed your pussy muscles and began to expertly fuck me. I wrapped my arms around you and with all my might concentrated on making my dick as hard as possible. I held on tight. You held on tighter. Suddenly we both began to jerk and buck. I knew you were cumming and I was, too. As I shot my load into you, you yelled with each spurt but you kept pumping. Your thighs quivered so strongly as you came that my knees were knocked together. You kept pumping until the very last drop of cum was sucked from my dick. We both collapsed, breathing hard.

We lay there still and quiet; simply holding each other. I

loved the way I felt inside you. I loved the way my chest muscles shivered, causing your entire body to shake in return. We lay there letting our senses roam. With massage oils, tropical breezes, and the afterglow of lovemaking permeating the air, I knew, my every sense knew, we belonged together.

I'll Be Invisible

V. Anthony Rivers

There have been moments in my life recently that have made me sit back and wonder why I am who I am. I mean, sometimes the decisions I make are a real trip. I'm a fool sometimes, always trying to discover new opportunities and taking chances with my direction in life. Hell, I'm married to a beautiful woman and we have one child on the way. My wife's name is Porsia Marie Gordon, standing about five-nine and a half, weighing about 155 pounds, light-skinned, and proportioned in all the lovely places. Hell, when she comes to bring me lunch sometimes on my job, the fellas and even the women notice how beautiful she is.

"Yo, man, is that you?" one of my co-workers asked me one time.

"Yeah, that's my wife," I responded nonchalantly.

Dude just started shaking my hand excitedly while looking at my wife with that universal "Damn, she fine!" expression written all over his face. Strangely enough, I didn't care if he looked, and that's been my problem lately. I've just been in a "ho hum" state of mind recently about everything. I'm working here in dot-com heaven, thinking that sitting in front of a computer eight hours a day is gonna make me a rich man. Then as I said, I have my wife, a new baby on the way, and I'm considering going to graduate school. All that sounds positive to anyone listening but I'm just feeling bored with it all. I thought that buying that new PlayStation would get me excited about life, but even that failed. I took up playing basketball with the fellas at work on the weekends but, again, I would just end up yawning my way through that experience. I was feeling like I needed something to spruce up my life and return me to being a man who was passionate about everything he touched. I mean, I used to walk around with my chest sticking out all the time, acting like every word I said should have an exclamation point behind it. A true brotha with the appearance of a playa, but at the same time, one that should be featured prominently on the front page of some black gentleman weekly magazine. I'm remembering a time when I definitely had it going on and believe you me, my motivation back then had me smiling for days. Plain and simple, the fuel I needed and got was S-E-X. I got me some all the time and it was that pursuit that led me to my wife.

I met Porsia four years ago when our company hired her consulting firm. I was kind of pissed to hear that they were having someone come in to tell us what we needed so that our company could run and operate more efficiently. That kind of shit only brings about the conclusion that people should be laid off and more work should be given to those that remain. Yeah, I was definitely walking around with a serious attitude and looking like some new-generation militant with my multi-colored beret, and a Microsoft necktie on. I'm only kidding about the beret, but a brotha did have attitude, initially. Then on the second day that the firm was going through files and meeting folks around the office, they introduced one of three consultants that would be working closely with us.

"Everyone, this is Porsia Turner. She'll be with us for the next couple of months, so make her feel welcome!" our boss announced. Everybody in the office let out a simultaneous "Hey Porsia!" and I was looking at her like "Shit, I need to get with her real quick!" I started to walk toward her but others who admired this gorgeous new consultant intercepted my efforts.

"Dude, I'm 'bout to mess up some paperwork so they can have her come over and investigate my ass, ya heard me!" my friend Keith whispered to me.

"I know what you mean, she is fine," I said while keeping my eyes focused on Porsia.

My imagination was working overtime as everyone around disappeared from my focus and I could only envision myself nibbling on her lobes and working my way down until I reached her hot spot. For some strange reason, I was having a craving for caramel syrup. I started licking my lips and imagining how sweet that would taste right about now. That alone inspired a lovely vision of Porsia sitting on my desk, leaning back and wearing only the bottom half of that black mini-skirt suit she's wearing right now. I could see myself pouring the syrup on her nipples and just licking and sucking and licking. Damn, I would just be devouring that lady and I know she'd love it!

"Yo, dude, you think she'll go to lunch with me?" Keith asked.

His question interrupted my caramel dreams.

"Huh?" I responded.

"Me and homegirl! You think she'd go to lunch with me?"

"I don't know, Keith. I guess you're gonna have to try and see. You might have to stand in line behind a brotha like me, though!"

"Oh it's like that, huh?"

"Yeah, it's like that!"

Well, a couple weeks went by before I finally approached Porsia. She was sitting in the break room, looking over some paperwork and eating her lunch. When I saw her, I got all happy but I sat down at another table and watched her for a moment. She had me feeling slightly nervous but I just looked around, saw that nobody was in the room but us, and figured that this was my best chance to approach. I walked slowly toward her and before I knew it, she stood up and turned around. Our eyes met instantly and she gave me a somewhat innocent smile.

"Hey," I said softly.

"Hi," she responded.

Again we smiled and just from this innocent moment, I began to get aroused. Porsia and I were standing so close to each other, and the way her eyes were roaming from the floor to my lips and back to my eyes again, it felt like she wanted to kiss. I know I did but of course I didn't take that chance, being that she didn't even know my name at this point. It was time to fix that and let the sista know whom she was admiring so closely.

"My name is Michael Gordon," I told her.

"Nice to meet you."

"Of course, I remember your name, Porsia. I haven't been able to erase it from my mind since you were introduced to all of us."

"Why is that?" she asked.

"Because I find you to be one beautiful woman. I guess I'm taking a chance speaking with you this way in the workplace and all, but if they gonna lock a brotha up for expressing himself, then let it be known first that I am crazy about you, lady!"

"Oh, really? And do you always come on this strong?"

"I've never approached a woman in this way or chosen these words before that I've expressed to you, if that's what you mean."

I could tell she was flattered, even though she made attempts to hide the fact that she was blushing and maybe even becoming aroused by this moment, too. It was like I could feel her body temperature rising. As for me, my body was on fire. I was feeling all warm inside, like I wanted to romance her and then at the same time, I basically wanted to fuck right then and there. Once again, it was too soon for me to express certain desires to her. It was best to leave that for the next time.

That next time didn't come soon enough for me, because I was battling boredom along with just being horny all the time. I'm not saying that I wasn't getting any back then, but I probably was enjoying a little too much self-pleasuring for my own good. One day I was sitting in the break room enjoying some leftover rib roast that I'd made over the weekend. I can throw down in the kitchen and even my leftovers are the bomb! Then, all of a sudden Porsia walked into the room, and I started to get a hard-on because I remembered the last time we stood face to face. This time it was me using my peripheral vision and wondering if she was gonna approach. I started adjusting myself in my chair 'cause I was literally sitting there aroused and erect while at the same time frantically wiping the juice from my lips. I was nervous and trying to cover my food up when Porsia walked over to me from behind.

"Hey, Michael, I hope I'm not disturbing you," she said.

"No, not at all," I said while still wiping my mouth.

Seconds later I stood up to greet her and then I noticed her eyes began to look downward.

Oh shit, she noticed! I thought to myself.

Porsia just smiled, moistened her lips, and moved closer to

me. I could feel that body heat between us even stronger than the last time. All this energy had to be recognized and I wasn't gonna let this moment pass me by. That's when something different began to happen to me. I found a way to be "invisible" and lose all inhibitions. I imagined myself as someone without fear. Someone that could seize the moment and make it hot! My right eyebrow began to rise and my smile turned devious.

"What's on your mind, Michael?" Porsia asked.

"Hmm, would you prefer that I tell you or show you?"

"Take charge, baby!"

The real me might run from that last statement, but the real me was not standing before this beautiful woman. I was someone else as I leaned forward and began kissing Porsia softly on her lips. Then I used the tip of my tongue as I made a trail from the side of her mouth to beneath her right ear. She moaned and that let me know that Porsia was very sensitive to a light yet sensual touch, but I wasn't here to be soft and sensual. I pulled her close to me and began kissing her very passionately. My own moans and heavy breathing seemed to get Porsia very excited, and I was turned on by the fact that I could see someone peeking through the window at us. It was a lady co-worker of mine named Brenda who didn't look at all embarrassed by what she was seeing. In fact, I think she was turned on and maybe even a little envious, though I'm not sure if she wanted to change places with me or with Porsia. Brenda watched closely as my hand caressed Porsia's behind. She seemed to smile a lot when I raised Porsia's dress only to reveal that she wasn't wearing anything underneath. Hell, that had me smiling too, and I couldn't wait to see what other surprises I might find.

"I like the way you take charge, Michael," Porsia whispered.

After she complimented me with more affectionate moans and sweet words from her lips, I dropped my pants and sat down on the hard plastic chair. Porsia quickly climbed on top of me and eased her way down. I could see Brenda still watching, and she appeared to be clutching one of her breasts as she watched Porsia slowly ride me. I couldn't believe that all this was happening in the break room at work but every time I hit that special spot, I was convinced without a doubt that this was truly happening.

"And I thought you were too sweet to do something like this, Michael," Porsia said softly before she leaned her head back and enjoyed an intense orgasm.

Well, in between that incredible moment in the break room and a few years of marriage, Porsia and I have had some very passionate moments. Besides my continuing to practice my personal art of being "invisible," my sexual fire would also become fueled by a friendship that I developed with my co-worker Brenda. She approached me not long after she witnessed that moment of passion in the break room. She applauded me and told me how much she admired my risk-taking. But lately she's also been the source of my inspiration. No, I haven't indulged with her. Porsia is indeed the only woman I've been intimate with since we were married. However, Brenda and I do talk about sex a lot and interestingly enough, she's been the one to help me become "invisible" and thus bring Porsia to the height of ecstasy. Brenda likes to school me on various things relating to satisfying a woman, and so far she's been right on the money each time. Porsia's been smiling a lot throughout our marriage and it ain't just because I do the cooking or because she's about to become a mother. Nah, I've been hitting that spot and doing amazing things with my tongue, which give her the greatest orgasms. I keep her body shivering and it ain't because it's

cold. Brenda showed me that keeping Porsia satisfied could
definitely be beneficial for me. Just go in our kitchen and look
to your left as soon as you walk in. You'll find none other than
a brand-new George Foreman grill that I only had to ask for
once! Then look in our closet and you'll find a few new ties,
shirts, and pants in there. Hell, she even hooked a brotha up
with some new Karl Kani jeans that I like to wear on the
weekends. Oh yeah, great sex has had its benefits.

Recently I've been feeling strange about it all. The many
times that I've been "invisible" are starting to get old and
telling Brenda about each experience has lost its magic for
me. Well actually, telling Brenda about everything can be
arousing, but not so much with regards to Porsia any more.
Now I'm wondering what's up with Brenda and what does she
get out of telling me how to please my lady and then hearing
the results later.

"You writing a book or something?" I asked her one day.

"No, Michael, I'm not writing a book."

"You, uh, maybe using the info for personal reasons?"

"What do you mean?"

"You know!"

"No, Michael, what do you mean?"

"Maybe a little masturbation when you think about what
I've told you?"

"Umm, yes, I touch myself sometimes when I imagine or
think about the things you've said."

"Really?"

"Yes, does that shock you?"

"No, I think it's nice."

"Does it arouse you, Michael, to hear me say that?"

"Yes, very much so! You got a brotha wishing he could
watch!"

"Then maybe you should fantasize about that tonight when you're intimate with Porsia."

"Maybe I will."

Well, that night I tried fantasizing about Brenda touching herself and it worked. I was very passionate with Porsia and she could feel the power of my thrusts like never before. She had to wrap her legs around me to try to slow me down but I was lost within my passionate imagination and Porsia reaped the benefits by cumming so loud that she woke up the next morning embarrassed.

"Baby, why didn't you cover my mouth last night?" she asked me.

"What do you mean?"

"My ass was so loud!"

"Oh!" I started to laugh. "No you weren't," I told her.

She was kind of loud but for a man that is not a problem, and in fact a woman getting uncontrollably loud is the greatest compliment of all. Still, that morning my mind kept drifting as I continued to imagine Brenda. This time the inspiration didn't make me want to become "invisible" and experience my wife. Instead, I wanted to experience Brenda in some way and to do it as me, Michael Gordon.

I shared my thoughts and desires with Brenda soon after that but she just brushed them off and took it as a compliment. After a while I sort of took exception to her refusal to take me seriously, and I stopped sharing my sexual escapades and intimate stories with her. When we would talk, it would be strictly about work-related issues. She was definitely bothered by that. Actually I probably suffered more than she did because that's when things became "ho hum" with the sex life. As the sex life became boring, so went my zest and passion for life. That certain spark that I've always carried seems to have disappeared. Now I just kiss, cuddle, missionary position, and then kiss and cuddle some more before drifting off to sleep. Luckily, since Porsia is pregnant, I can just use that familiar excuse of "I'm afraid to do anything because you're pregnant, sweetheart," and she buys it and tells me how sweet I am for always being concerned.

Well, a couple days ago Brenda confronted me about the disappearance of our sexual discussions. I was kind of surprised when she brought it up but, to be honest, I was gonna mention it to her myself pretty soon.

"Hmm, so when you don't get what you want you just cut things off completely, huh?" Brenda asked.

"Cut things off?" I responded innocently.

"Yep, because we never talk about intimate pleasures anymore. It seems to have stopped ever since I denied your request of watching me."

"I guess I'm a little spoiled."

"A little, Michael?"

"Okay, a lot, but can you blame me for being aroused by the thought of watching you?"

"I can't really answer that."

"Well, Brenda, after all our discussions, memories of that time when you watched Porsia and me in the break room, not to mention you occasionally wearing something that makes me want to see more, my curiosity is heightened!"

"Your curiosity?"

"Well, yes! My curiosity for you," I said cautiously.

"Oh, well, I think you value your marriage to the point where you wouldn't want to chance losing it. Am I right?"

"Yes, you're right but—"

"Let me ask you something, Michael."

"Okay."

"Now I know you requested to watch me pleasure myself."

"Yes, I did."

"Would you perhaps settle for simply listening to me?"

"You mean phone sex?"

"Yes."

"I wouldn't mind a little phone sex."

"Okay, but with one condition, Michael."

"What's that?"

"When we have it, you have to describe an intimate moment between you and your wife."

"Okay, you have a deal!"

Well, the day for Brenda and me to indulge in a little phone play is today. My wife was taking forever to leave this morning but I guess that's because I was anxious to call Brenda. I keep imagining how good she probably sounds and I hope she does something freaky like put the phone up to her wet pussy and let me listen to possibly a dildo going in and out. Thinking about that keeps me aroused. I know this is gonna be good. In fact, I fear I'm gonna end up being a two-minute brotha over the phone because I'll be so excited right away. Brenda asked me to call her around 10:00 A.M. and as I looked at the clock, it was about three minutes till. That was just enough time to go get that jar of Vaseline and a towel. My three minutes were up when I walked into the bedroom and spread my towel on the bed. I called Brenda exactly at the top of the hour.

"Good morning, Michael, you are right on time!"

"Oh, you know it!"

"Anxious, huh?" Brenda asked.

"Yeah, I am."

"I'm flattered."

I got kind of quiet at first but I was already aroused by the mere fact that I was gonna indulge with Brenda over the phone.

"Okay, tell me something sexy, Michael. Remember the deal, 'cause I want to hear something delicious about you and your wife."

"Okay, let me tell you about the time I had her literally climbing the walls!"

"Ooh, sounds good already!"

"This actually happened at her mother's house."

"What?"

"Yeah, for whatever reason Porsia was so horny that day. There I was trying to set up her mother's computer and Porsia kept wanting to play with my dick. Actually she had me aroused with all the touching she was doing."

"Oh, really?"

As I began telling Brenda this story, I found myself getting lost in the memory as if I were living it all over again. I remembered how Porsia's mother kept walking by the computer room and each time I would remove Porsia's hand from my crotch.

" 'Would you stop!' I'd tell her.

" 'But I wanna play with it,' she'd speak in a child's voice.

"At one point, I just stood there and allowed Porsia to remove my dick from inside my pants, all the while keeping an eye out for any shadows or footsteps coming down the hallway. Porsia put me in her mouth and it felt incredible. She was sucking and moaning and making my dick get so fat with arousal. She was making it hard for me to continue standing. My knees were definitely getting weak."

"Umm, she sucked it that good?" Brenda moaned as I continued the story.

"Hell, yes! Porsia kept playing with me and I wanted my turn to play with her. 'You keep your eye out for your mother,' I told her. Porsia said okay, but I noticed that as soon as I started using my tongue to draw circles around her clit, she would close her eyes and moan with pleasure. My lady was unable to keep watch but somehow I didn't mind because I enjoyed pleasing her very much. She raised her legs up and rested them on my shoulders while burying my face deeper into her pussy. I could feel her hands massaging the back of my neck and pushing my head closer. Her moans grew louder and her body shivered a couple times as though I'd hit her most sensitive spot."

"Ooh, uh huh, what else happened?"

"Porsia then turned around, put her knees on the floor and placed her elbows in the chair. She was ready for me to hit it from behind, although at first I teased her a little bit by licking her asshole and rubbing my manhood against her flesh. She was pushing against me and that alone could've made me cum because it got so hot and heavy but I wanted to be inside of her before I did that. I wanted her to feel every inch of me. I wanted to explode and fill her up inside with every last drop."

"Damn, baby, that sounds so good! Please keep going!"

"Porsia lifted her ass slightly and that was a welcome invitation for me to enter her from behind. Her pussy was already dripping with her own juices so that made for an easy entry. She felt incredible inside and I just knew that was where I truly belonged. I didn't care who walked in on us, including her mother, though that would've been pretty embarrassing. But I just started grinding and pushing against her. Porsia would grind and push back against me. Our rhythms complemented each other perfectly until she whispered to me to go faster and eventually she told me to cum inside of her. Once she said those magical words, that's exactly what happened and I couldn't prevent myself if I tried. I came and she arched and dipped her back in a way that drove me to an even more intense orgasm. My moans and groans seemed to cause a chain reaction, because she came too and she didn't hold back."

"Oh yes . . . yes . . . yes, baby! Ooh yes! That's exactly how it was!"

Damn, for some strange reason Brenda just sounded like Porsia. Maybe I was just too deeply involved in the memory I was reliving.

"Ooh!"

"Wait a minute! Porsia, is that you?"

"Yes, baby, it's me."

"Damn, ain't that something," I said with a sense of discovery and delight.

"I can't believe you remember that special moment, sweetheart," Porsia whispered.

Not only did I remember but I also discovered that I no longer had to be "invisible" when thinking of my wife in an intimate way. Brenda's little trick showed me just how blessed I was to be married to such an incredible woman. Having phone sex with my wife cured my "ho-hum" state of mind completely and right now, I ain't invisible.

"Ooh, Michael!"

"That's me, Porsia. Come back home, baby!"

"Okay, sweetheart."

The Shower

Reginald Harris

Another gray-tinged morning. Again his eyes open ten minutes before the alarm goes off, as he is awakened by . . . what? Anticipation? Workday dread? Sounds from the TV set, still on from the night before when he and his partner had fallen asleep watching the Olympics? On the screen now is the inevitable early morning infomercial, a gaggle of actors crazed with admiration for some inane product, some New Thing, the One Great Innovation No One Can Live Without. He rubs his eyes and groans.

He rises slowly from the bed. The movement does not cause his sleeping partner to even stir. The exhaustion caused by repeated twelve-hour shifts ties the sleeper to the bed as if by silken threads. Even the sharp buzz of the alarm has no effect. Turning off its drone, the still-drowsy early riser makes a mental note to try to wake his other half before leaving the apartment for work.

He goes into the bathroom, turns on the radio, pisses away the first hard-on of the day. Goes to the kitchen, winces in pleasure over a glass of grapefruit juice, and starts a pot of coffee on its way to perking. Returning to the bathroom, he sits, shits, stands, shaves. Turns on the water in the tub, measuring its temperature with a quick sweep of the hand, then turns a dial upright, changing the origin of the flood from faucet to showerhead. Another check to make sure the first bracing coldness from the pipes has subsided. He steps inside and begins to wash the previous evening from his skin.

The rush of water beats a counter-rhythm to the laid-back jazz of his favorite morning radio station. He runs a soapy hand across his chest and smiles, remembering the most recent episode of a cable TV show with an all-black cast he'd seen. It had begun with one of the male actors getting caught beating off in the shower. All of the men on the show were fine, but to him, this one seemed better looking than the rest. He was not sure why. Perhaps it was his thick but muscular body—so like his sleeping partner's—or his mocha skin and smoothly shaven head. Or maybe it was the character he played, the image he projected: a solid, stable black man, hard-working, devoted to his family. All so very attractive and still so very rare to see on television. Perhaps, too, it was the all-too-quick shot of a bare, fat brown ass beamed across the cable wires for the entire nation to see that convinced him to give the actor his props.

He leans a shoulder against the wall of the shower and closes his eyes. *I am the guy from the TV show beating off in the shower (a blur of water bouncing off a bald brown head). I am beating off in the shower with the guy from the TV show (a curving arm around bare wet shoulders, pulling close). I am in the shower beating off the guy from the TV show (warm drops of water licked from the neck, lips pressed together in a kiss).*

His right hand pauses, slowly curls around his rising dick. How long has it been since he and his partner made love? A shared shower almost a month ago, each soaping the other's familiar back before dammed-up passion overtook them. He hates their current mismatched schedules—one working early shifts, the other late—the overtime, the few hours in the evening when they are both in the apartment together and awake. They long for some kind of break, a vacation, but they have goals in mind: a newer car, a house. So they must work and save. All that's understood, but still . . .

Each time he closes his eyes to avoid a spray of water in his face he sees another image: A pen and ink cartoon, two lovers cavorting in the rain. *(He grabs his filling meat.)* An X-rated video, a pair of honey-drenched Brazilians in dappled sunlight making acrobatic love beside a waterfall *(a long slow squeeze).* Showering years before with a guy tall enough to be a basketball star *(a quickening pulse),* who had leaned against the soap-filmed tiles *(pull),* bent over *(up),* and spread his caramel-colored ass cheeks *(slide down),* yearning. *(He's slowly stroking now.)* The freshly cleaned hole inside had winked *(move up),* flexed like a begging mouth *(down),* urging him to fill it with his manhood. *(Faster, he's beating faster now.)* Later, his well-fucked but still insatiable partner had turned him around in the tiny stall *(no, not yet, almost there),* and tried by force of will to shove his soap-slicked tube of black steel deep into his ass. *(Better stop for now.)*

He covers the showerhead with his left hand to slow the water down. It trickles through his splaying fingers in a steady stream. He sticks out his tongue, imagines lapping at liquid gold from a heavy, midnight-black cock, warm piss spreading through the velvet down of his hairy chest. *("Always knew you was a freak,"* his partner had teased him when he'd confessed some of his youthful sins.) His dick leaps, a dolphin breaching from the curling mass of pubic hair. He reaches out to soothe it back down under the waves.

He removes his hand from the nozzle, and the water returns in force. He can twist the showerhead until it pulses sharp needles of water, thousands of tiny pinpricks on his skin. He turns to face the rear wall of the stall, spreading arms and legs. Can almost feel clamps forming around his wrists and ankles. He sticks out his furry butt. The water's bite is the lash of a cat-o'-nine-tails wielded by a hooded, harnessed S and M master. (*"Yeah, but you like that I'm a freak. I'm your freak,"* he'd said, diving again between his lover's legs.) Mounted, on display as part of a demonstration on a festival-crowded public street, he can feel all eyes on him, the crowd sensing his craving, wanting either to wield the whip themselves or to feel its sting on their own skin. From somewhere a growl comes up as if the song of a pride of panthers prowling a twilit veldt had been brought to him on a gust of wind. He coughs, regains his composure. Realizes the sound was coming from him. He goes back to scrubbing torso, legs, and ass with shower gel.

Again he closes his eyes, again steps into a dream: Two athletes in an otherwise deserted locker room. He's seen them before, saw them run earlier this Olympic week, imagined them lovers competing against each other in a race, the 100, or 200. Or was it last night, and not even track, but something else—boxers from rival countries sharing an embrace after their match; sun-darkened beach volleyball players brushing a thin skin of sand from each other's arms; mahogany swimmers, sleek as otters, rising from the pool, chlorine spilling from their pores. Soccer players tossing off their shirts in celebration, wrestlers shimmying from one-piece suits, decathletes sliding out of nylon shorts . . .

One man is sculpted ebony, the other hammered bronze. Sweaty from their contest, they take to the showers. Blunt fingers of water drum against their skins, replaying the first music of the world, the call of rain singing against dark bodies. The two watch each other warily, soaping up, massaging tired muscles under the steady stream of water.

A casual touch. An "it means nothing" bump. A half-joking slap on the ass. Make it all seem playful, just a game, just like kids in school. Don't let on how intensely a fire burns inside each one for the other. No, not yet. For now, it's all a joke. The two dark towers rising from their crotches, however, prove this joke is real.

A slightly longer touch. A deeper stare. Soon they cannot contain themselves, are in each other's arms, touching, tasting, kissing, holding. The hairy chest of the lighter man scratches across the other's smooth dark skin like a hundred scrabbling fingernails. Each reaches for the other's hardness. The chatter of the shower is like the repeated crashing of waves against the shore, or the cheering of a million rapt onlookers. They begin to beat each other off.

(Faster, he's beating faster. One hand curls up to brush against the tender aureole of his nipples. He pinches it erect. His eyes close tighter, concentrating. He sees his destination dead ahead.)

A slightly graying older man, their coach, joins the others in the shower. No words of approbation, no complaints, he simply strips and joins them. *("I'm into older men,"* a young guy had whispered to him and his partner once, offering his body as filling in a lover sandwich. *You know—that Daddy thing.")* His head spins, imagining himself to be the darkest of the three athletes at play *(slowly)*, lying on the cool damp floor of the shower *(there)*, intently sucking the coach's heavy, cum-filled balls *(squeeze)*, his tongue flicking across the low-slung nut sack like a flame, willing it to catch fire, burn, drain. *(His hand beats faster.)* His mouth fills with water *(beats)*. He spits it out *(his hand)*. The third man's close-cropped head bobs at his crotch *(squeeze)*. A hungry mouth gobbles up his meat *(faster)*.

The coach's massive hand comes down to caress his face *(pulse)*. He pumps his hips into the sucking mouth *(there)*, urging it to take more, swallow all *(his hand. up)*. Hears a moan of satisfaction and looks down *(beats. slides down)*. The vision of a shirtless track star's blazing smile and wave to the crowd during his victory lap fills his blurring sight *(pull. faster)*. Sees those full dark lips around his meat *(no, not yet)*.

He slides against the tile wall of the shower. *(His hand beats faster.)* Feels his lover's velvet skin against him every night, seductive as rainforest mist *(almost)*. Even the alarm has no effect *(there)*. Wince of grapefruit juice *(better)*. Framed shot of fat brown ass *(stop now)*. Rain-rhythm, first music, the distant sound of jazz *(move up)*. Mismatched schedules *(stroke down)*. Pen and ink cartoons. Magazines. X-rated videos *(beating faster now)*. Soap-slicked tube of black steel up his ass *(beat)*. Sharp liquids warm and spreading. *(His hand beats faster.)* *You like that I'm your freak (his hand)*. Chattering cheering onlookers *(beats faster)*. Sharp needles *(his heart)* of the shower *(beat faster)*. Bodies thick so like his sleeping partner *(faster)*. *You know, that Daddy Thing (almost)*. Chocolate mocha skin *(there)*. *I am the TV show. (Hishandbeatsfaster.)* That velvet fat brown velvet ass fat against him fat velvet brown every night *(stroking)*. Skin *(almost there)* A shot—

He cries out—cannot help it, has to scream—grunts and growls and cries. He cums. Blurts out *Damn, Shit, Gawddamn it* as he pulses *(gawd. shit. aww, damn)*, exhaling all the air from his heaving lungs. Thick juice continues to spill, keeps on flowing, pumping from his dick as if from a hose. His spinning head slowly slows, returns to earth. He notices for the first time the milky film of night on his unbrushed teeth, the goosebumps on his arms, how cold the water of the shower has become, the blare of news from the radio *("Mind if I join you?")*, the nutty scent of burning coffee walking through the door, his partner pulling back the shower curtain to unveil him standing there *("Guess I moved too slow . . .")*, deflating cock still in his hand, dripping water, dripping cum, his familiar cough, smile and raised eyebrow, raspy first-thing-in-the-morning voice asking, *"Aren't you going to be late for work?"* as all the week's released frustrations, desires and dreams, a sticky goo between his fingers, splashed onto the shower's walls, spelled out in wriggling letters on the flowered plastic curtain, or sliding down his legs, get calmly washed away, eddying, pooling in the water at his feet, swirling slowly, oh so slowly, down the drain . . .

What's Real

Bootney Farnsworth

I first saw Tanisha as I was walking through the mall on a Sunday afternoon. I was there scooping up a few housewares. I found the mall a lot less hectic on Sunday afternoons. I don't know if it's because folks were sleeping off the partying from Saturday night or they were getting their eat on at their parents' houses. I'd usually be at home watching "NFL Sunday Ticket," but I had to get the crib ready for inspection. That's what I call it when mom comes over for dinner. As I made my way to the mall exit, I spotted her trying on shoes (what else). She was dressed as if she had just gotten out of church, a nice dress with stockings, blue I think. Anyway, I was down the hall before my flirtatious nature as well as my curiosity sent me back in her direction.

As I turned the corner into the shoe store she was taking off the shoe she was trying on. I feasted on the sight of her sexy-ass legs underneath her stockings. While she was taking off the shoe, I could see up the back of her thigh. I closed my mouth before she saw me standing there dumbfounded. I gathered myself and sat down next to her. "Shouldn't you be in church passing out blessings?" I asked.

"Excuse me?" her lips released in response. I watched every syllable fall off them.

"I mean, you're an angel, right? You should be passing out blessings, then."

She responded to the corny-ass line as I expected, with the "yeah right" look and a smack of the lips.

"My bad, that was corny as hell, but I couldn't think of anything else to say."

"How about 'Hello, how are you? My name is . . . ' "

I stood up. "Hello, how are you? My name is Anthony." I extended my hand.

"Oh, it's too late for that now. You have been filed under ghetto-ass, playa wannabes." She laughed.

A sexy-ass woman with a sense of humor, that's my Tanisha. We've been going out for a few months now, five to be exact. Funny thing is, for as long as we've been together we've never gotten down to it, if you catch my drift. Not that I wasn't trying; heaven knows I was. However, Tanisha and I had a serious discussion about her attitude toward sexual relationships. She told me that she was different from other females. I thought she was running that tired-ass game everyone uses to try to distinguish themselves from all the exes and the nexts. But as she delved into her past and told me things I would have never even begun to guess about her, I became convinced that she was very different. She went on to say that the act of sex itself was nothing. "I mean, dogs hump each other" is how she illustrated her point. "Real sex, lovemaking, is done with every ounce of your being. Making yourself a slave to each other's wishes, desires, and pleasures." A lot of the things she shared with me about her past bothered me. As a man, it was hard to deal with the fact that my woman was "worldly." Nonetheless, these are the experiences that made her who she was. The following months gave me time to deal with those issues, as well as spend time focusing on the person rather than her body. So for the first time in a while, I had actually gotten to know the lady I was with before we did the damn thang.

Now I'm on my way to see Tan. She left a message on my machine asking me to come over after I came home from work. I have a key to her place and she has a key to mine, so if she isn't home, I'll let myself in. It's starting to rain. Damn, it's coming down in buckets. I hope that I can find a parking spot in front of her apartment building. As I turn the corner onto her street, of course there are no spots. I walk, well, more like run, a whole block from the car to her building in this maelstrom. Out of breath and uttering obscenities, I make my way up to Tan's apartment. She doesn't appear to be home. Great. I drive over here and run through the rains that floated Noah's ark and she isn't here. Oh, well, enough self-pitying thoughts. I have to get out of these wet clothes.

After putting my clothes in the dryer and running off a few sets of push-ups, I fall asleep watching "Sportscenter." Drifting off into dreamland, I can already feel the horny dog in me shedding his leash. Since Tan and I have not had sex yet, this is where I get off. A grown man having wet dreams sounds pretty sad, but that's the situation. I usually dream of Tan, living out fantasies. Using my imagination and experiences to create erotic scenarios that always end with ejaculation. Now I have to be real—I did not say I always dream of her. In the last couple of months I've been with Janet Jackson, Jada Pinkett Smith, Jenny Lopez, Salma Hayek, and Angela Bassett, in the champagne room dream. And uh, don't believe Chris Rock. There is sex in the champagne room.

What the—? I didn't think I had drifted off to sleep, but I can feel warm wet lips on my nipples. Damn, that always equals instant erection for me. I smell Tan's perfume. Is she here? Am I having one of my freaky dreams? I sit up quickly, as if I have awakened from a nightmare. Panting frantically, I scope the room for Tanisha. No one. Funny thing is, I can still smell her perfume, but her place always smells like this. Doesn't it? Either way, I'm sitting here with a dick hard enough to slice diamonds like wheat bread. I ain't up for punching the clown right now, so I go out to the kitchen and get a drink of papaya juice. "Well, well, what have we here?" I say to myself. "Half a blunt." I forgot I had taken that out of my wet clothes. It's dried out too. This'll help me relax, because right now I'm wondering where the hell Tan is.

"Mmmmmm . . . Suck this dick dry, Janet." I moan as I figure the sensations are another one of my wet dreams.

"Who the fuck is Janet?!!"

Damn, that's Tanisha's voice! I sit up with a quickness and sure enough there's Tan, kneeling between my legs. With my dick in her hand, I better get to explaining and I best do a damn good job!

"Well, I thought I was dreaming. I mean that's the only sex that I've been having for a few months. Besides, what's with you and the blowjob? I thought we were holding off on sexual relations."

She tells me how sexy I looked lying in her bed in my boxer briefs and she couldn't help herself. "Besides, it's time," she says with a look in her eyes I've never seen before. She pushes me back down and flattens her tongue on the underside of my dick. She slowly slides her tongue up and down the shaft. It's been so long that I feel like I'm going to bust off already. The head is magnificent. She swirls her tongue around like she's trying to taste every inch of it. Then she reaches over to the dresser and grabs a small cup. She has warmed up some scented oil and she is massaging my scrotum with it. At the same time she has the length of dick in her mouth, moving her tongue around frantically.

I sit up and hesitantly ask her to stop. After all, this is a special event, our first time together. I stand her up and kiss her deeply. Our tongues do the rhythmic dance that they have done so many times before, but it is much more intense now. I help her out of her clothes, down to her underwear. I stand there and visually feast on the sight of my Tan's lovely body. It was like I had met the *Jet* beauty of the millennium! She leaves me speechless, so I'll express myself through my actions.

Circling her like a vulture, I decide to caress her from behind. I kiss and lick her neck as I stimulate her breasts through her silk bra. I run my tongue down the center of her back as I undo her bra. Down to the small of her back, sliding her panties off. Now I'm kneeling down behind her, her picture-perfect ass right in my face. Her perfume fills my nose while I skim my tongue over her ass. I spread her cheeks and give her ass a little lick. I can tell she's down when I hear the deep moan she lets out. She's leaning forward to let me know to lick harder, faster. Soon she's ready for me to move to more erotic areas because Tan opens her legs and takes a step back. Now I have full access to the pussy.

Her pussy isn't totally shaved; it's nicely trimmed though. I can smell a mixture of bath oils and her natural juices. As I grip both cheeks of her heart-shaped ass, I plunge my tongue deep inside her. I have this thing I like to do. I start out by spelling my name, then running through the alphabet, upper- and lowercase. The swirls and turns that are involved are usually more than enough to send women over the edge. Tan is no exception. Right around lowercase *l* I hear her breathing pause. She finally lets out a heavy animal-like growl and cums all over my face. I thought I might drown. I had heard of women with an orgasmic release but I had never been with one. It turns me on to feel her hot love running down either side of my face as I try to swallow as much of it as I can. It is running down my neck as Tan bends all the way over and starts to suck my dick again. But I interrupt her. "As gifted as you are orally, baby, I'm ready to fuck."

I lay her on the edge of the bed, with her feet on the floor. I stand next to the bed and I slide her closer to me. Her ass is off the edge of the bed. This position gives me total control. I control the tempo, the depth, and direction of every stroke. I also want to look into her eyes as we cross into the next phase of our relationship. I start with slow circular motions and work my way into deep strokes. She doesn't seem to mind that I am dictating the pace of things. Hell, she doesn't care if the building is on fire and I don't either. I am in ecstasy.

Clasping my hands together underneath her, I lift her pelvis up a bit.

"Oooh, damn, Tony. You seem to know a little something, something, huh?"

"I know a thing or two, or three. . . ." I smile.

I can feel the ridges of her G-spot rubbing lightly against the head of my rod. She is impressed with my skills. "Well I know a thing or two also, mister," Tan says seductively. Right then I feel her vaginal walls contract. *"Damn!"* It's all I can do to keep stroking. The grip she's putting on is almost enough to push me out, but she backs off enough to make it pleasurable. While I am holding back a big-ass nut, we switch to the doggy-style position. I slide in easily into her hot wet box. She starts to squeeze me again. "I think I can, I think I can." I am so close to cumming, it's insane. I push and push and push.

Tan is letting out screams of passion. I can feel my leg starting to shake. I slow down the pace and Tan looks back and asks, "What's the matter? Can't hang?" Feeling up to the challenge, I grab her around the waist and go drilling for oil. Sweaty, sex-covered skin-slapping echoes throughout the room. I slap her on the ass and she screams at a high pitch. "Yeah, nigga, that's what I'm talking about!" She's pushing back and the slapping is louder, faster. I keep smackin' that ass, pulling her with the other hand. We made love a position ago; we're fucking now. "Oh, shit!" she yells out and I feel the hot rush of her cumming all over my dick. She got hers, I can get mine now. I lean over and put my arms under her arms and my hands up onto her shoulders. I feel the sweat from her back along my chest and stomach. I am beating it up now, short hard strokes. Bang, bang, bang. "I'm . . . shhhh . . . I'm . . . cuuh, cum . . . ahhhhhhhhhh!!!!!" I thrust into Tan as far as I can go. My back is arched and my face is buried into the nape of her neck. This is the biggest orgasm I have ever had. It feels as if I am never going to stop cumming. I relax for a moment and push right back in.

I am totally drained. I fall asleep almost immediately. After drifting off for what seemed like a minute or two, I realize how inconsiderate that was. I spring up to see if Tan is still awake, only to find I am alone in the bed, boxer briefs soaked in cum. I have been asleep for four hours. I don't know if it's the chronic or the sex, but whichever it is, it has me dog-ass tired. Wait a minute, the TV is on in the living room. As I turn the corner in a bit of a daze, I am embarrassed to see Tanisha pointing and laughing at the wet spot in my briefs.

"I thought you stopped wetting the bed around twenty-five years ago?" she jokes.

"Ha, ha. I did, but I thought you would remember how it

got here. Besides, it's not piss, it's cum," I said, slightly annoyed.

What the hell is going on here? Was I having another one
of my sexually starved, horny-ass dreams?

"I have no idea why you're having wet dreams. Maybe you
should ask Janet."

Selena the Sexual Healer

Victor DeVanardo

Part I

"What we need is a master of sex," the man said.

"A master of sex and finesse," the woman added.

"That's good, Margaret," the man agreed. "Sex and finesse. Someone who can fight in the hot arena of passion but remain cool. Someone who can wield the sizzling instruments of eroticism with the sure, dispassionate hands of a surgeon, who can walk over the flaming, red-hot coals of sexual intrigue without the slightest singe to her littlest toe. Someone . . ."

". . . who can fuck the yolk out of an egg without cracking the shell," Margaret said.

"You do have a way with words, Margaret," the man said.

"Yes I do, Ted," Margaret replied.

Ted sat behind a large oak desk, piled high with files, ledgers, and books. Margaret stood by his side, hands folded in front of her. They wore identical gray flannel business suits, white shirts, black ties, gold wire-rimmed glasses, and prim, business-like facial expressions.

Their office was small, austere, and decorated plainly and in black and white.

"I'm your man—woman—person," Selena said. She sat in a high-backed leather armchair across from them. She wore a Burberry trench coat, a black fedora pulled low over one eye, and polished, high-heeled black leather boots. She sat with her big fine legs crossed. The bottom coat buttons were unfastened, revealing a sleek, brown, sexy thigh.

"You came highly recommended," Ted said, fiddling with some folders, eyes riveted to that luscious expanse of thigh. Selena idly kicked her foot. As she did, her trench coat opened and more and more of her leg was exposed. Ted swallowed hard; despite himself he felt warm stirrings in his crotch.

"But we have to be sure!" Margaret said, slamming a fist down on the desk. "You must not fail. How do we know you have the right stuff?"

Without a word Selena stood up, unbuttoned her coat, and opened it wide.

Ted and Margaret gasped. Selena was totally nude. She let the coat fall slowly to the floor, threw back her shoulders and her head, and let them get a load of all her sexy assets: her firm, flawless breasts, her flat tummy, the hot, dark, triangular woman patch of her loins, her lush hips.

Slowly she turned and as she did she seemed to glow, to throw off an aura of sexual heat, as though her skin was the warm, living, metal surface of the statue of an African-American hoodoo goddess of love and sensuality.

Ted gasped. The stirring in his loins exploded tight against his trousers. His vision blurred. His heart pounded and sweat trickled down his back.

"Well? Whatchoo think?" Selena asked.

Ted gulped. "You got my vote."

"I don't know," Margaret said. "We are dealing with a smart, dangerous, and slippery character here. Suppose you should be talking to him, minding your own business, and somebody slips up behind you and does this!"

Margaret suddenly grabbed Selena by her waist, pulled her close, cupped one of her shapely breasts in one hand and stuck her tongue in Selena's ear.

Selena giggled. "I'd just parry that thrust like this!" and she flicked her tongue like a hot whip across Margaret's.

Margaret jumped like she'd tongue-fucked a thousand-volt electric cable. She stood there trembling. Her eyes were moist and her mouth was a wet O.

"That's enough!" Ted shouted. Any more and he was sure he was going to shoot a big wad in his pants. He didn't want to have to walk around the rest of the day with cum stains at his crotch. Any more of this briefing and he was sure he'd starch his briefs.

Margaret walked stiffly back to Ted's side. She laid a hand on his shoulder, smiling dreamily.

That'll show them they ain't dealing with no buster, Selena thought. She picked up her coat, put it back on, buttoned it up, and sat cool as a cucumber.

Ted shook his head to clear it, then reached into a file and took out a photo. He passed it to Selena.

"You know him?" Ted asked.

"Yes. William G. Gaddys. Ex–pro football player. Businessman. Pillar of the community. Anti-porn crusader—"

"Hypocrite!" Ted shouted. "He hides behind a mask of propriety while engaging in behavior that he condemns himself! Look at this."

Ted got a remote control and clicked on a VCR. Margaret softly stroked his shoulders and whispered to him.

It was a tape of William G. Gaddys speaking to a woman's group about the dangers of dirty literature.

Selena saw a bald, square-jawed man, handsome and serious looking. Even now, years after retiring from the gridiron, his shoulders and neck were massive and muscular. The cloth of his expensive suit jacket bulged with his biceps.

Not bad, Selena thought, licking her full lips. She wondered if those arms and shoulders were as firm as they looked. She imagined kneading them like dough under her strong fingers until he begged her not to stop.

She was gonna like this job.

"Quit it!" she heard Ted say. Margaret was straightening back up, but not fast enough. Selena could see that she had leaned over and nipped Ted on his ear. He was trying to act irritated, but Ray Charles could've seen that Ted was likin' it.

"His kind is dangerous," Margaret said. "Even when they are sincere. But they are especially so when they are fakes. We aren't perverts or libertines, Selena. We're for free, healthy expression and discussion of sex, and against any attempts by anyone to make it unnatural and nasty."

"Those people—the bluenoses, the self-appointed censors, the anti-sex people—they are just trying to control everybody," Ted said. "And what better way to control people than to dictate what they should do in private, behind closed doors, in their own bedrooms. Where would it all end? Why—"

"I'm a big girl and totally aware of what is at stake," Selena said. "Say no more! I'll help you!"

"Good!" Margaret said. "Bring him down! Neutralize him! Get him by the *balls!*" She made a squeezing motion. Ted involuntarily winced and clapped his knees together. Margaret put her hand back on his shoulder, then slid it lower and rubbed his chest. Ted's knees opened again.

Yes, by the balls, Selena thought. She wondered about Gaddys' balls. Was he packing cannonballs or sweet peas? She wondered what he would do when she had them in her hand, when her fingers closed around them, whether he liked them gripped soft and tender, or whether he liked 'em grabbed rough. She had a special trick—she could tickle and prick a man's balls lightly, oh so lightly, with long red fingernails until he screamed with ecstasy.

Whatever. Soon she'd know what floated William G. Gaddys' boat.

"Now the hard part," Ted said. "You have only seven days. In seven days, Gaddys is supposed to address a Congressional Committee on Regulation of Adult Entertainment. He will make a most impressive witness."

"He must not testify," Margaret said.

"You can count on me," she told them.

Selena wasn't even out of the room good before her mojo kicked in. Margaret slid her hand down into Ted's lap. She was giggling. Ted was already breathing hard. Selena tipped out of their office and closed the door behind her. She stood outside in the hall a minute, listening.

Shortly there came from within the sound of folders, files, and ledgers being swept off the desk onto the floor, and then jagged gasps and whispers as their clothes came off and were cast aside, and then the groans and bumping sounds of Ted and Margaret fucking and humping on the desk.

Selena smiled and strode away down the hall.

Part II

Later Selena took a long hot herbal bath, ate a light vegetarian meal, and meditated for an hour alone in her sanctum sanctorum, a spacious wood-paneled room bare of furniture and decorated in earth tones. The only light came from several aromatic candles placed here and there around it.

When she came out of her trance she mentally checked her mind, body, and soul. She ran her hands over her arms, her legs, she stroked her neck, and then she tenderly stroked herself between the legs, vulva, clitoris, assuring herself that all was well, well lubricated and in working order.

She also knew what she was going to do.

Selena was no ho or skeezer, oh no. She had studied the works of sexual researchers at the finest universities and traded information with hardened ancient putanas who had worked in the cathouses of Havana before Castro, with Japanese geishas who knew a thousand ways of pleasing a man, with sex professionals of Bangkok who knew of the secret sacred G-spots, and with phone sex magicians who could talk a person into orgasm—in short, with people and folk from all over who knew the secrets of sex.

Selena was a professor, a high priestess of sex. If she had known as much about karate as she did about sex she would have had a hundred degree black belt.

In her body, her mind, her hands was the power of the Big Bang, the first orgasm that conceived the Universe.

She was Venus, Erzuli, Foxy Lady, Da Bomb.

She was the devil with the blue dress on.

She was a ninja of sex, a countess of cum, an O.G. of orgasm, from the top of her head, to her cunt and cute wiggling ass, down to her succulent toes. She made Masters and Johnson look like shade tree jackleg mechanics.

She was strong, confident, healthy and ready, ready, ready to rock 'n' roll a regiment, if need be; fuck them high and dry and make them beg her for more!

Let's do this, she thought.

Part III

William G. Gaddys was a predator, crafty and cagey like the crabs that camouflage themselves as rocks or plants on the ocean floor and lie in wait for their unwary prey to swim along unknowingly so they can pounce on it.

His game was tight.

Selena's game was tighter.

His bait was the Shalimar Club which wasn't especially on the wild side; just your usual chrome-and-glass, dance, suck-up-watered-drinks-in-a-stylish-setting, buppie-pick-up kind of joint.

He was a silent partner in that club. He selected his prey from among the single, attractive, inexperienced young ladies who wandered in. He never set foot in the place himself. He had his partner, Rance States, the club manager, select promising "talent" for him.

Selena went there that very night. She was dressed like a square schoolteacher or secretary from Podunk in town for a vacation—bulky sweater, long skirt, running shoes, thick glasses. She ordered club soda, didn't dance with anyone, shyly brushed off the guys who tried to pick her up.

States didn't make a move on her. Cool. Selena had banked on that. She would, like the Terminator, be back. Then she would flush the cock out of the fly.

The next night she showed up looking loaded for bear, like her biological clock had exploded, like the world was gonna end in the morning and she had to do the wild thang one mo' time!

She was wearing a see-through halter top, her round, fine, fat titties spilling out and her rock-hard nipples poking through; a black leather mini that hugged her luscious ass and was slit up the side almost to her waist; fishnet stockings; and stiletto pumps with five-inch heels and cum-fuck-me straps across the ankles.

Oh, heads turned, eyes bulged, tongues lolled, crotches

were massaged as she switched 'n' sashayed, her buns squirming like two pigs screwing in a burlap bag.

She tossed down three scotches fast, one behind the other, then leaned against the bar, arms stretched across it, legs wide like a sexual gunfighter ready for a shootout with Mr. Goodick, and waited for the right moment.

It came when the DJ threw Mystikal's "Shake Ya Ass" on the box.

Showtime, she thought.

She was up on the floor like a shot. She waved all potential partners off—she had to fly solo, didn't need no slew foot cramping her style—and she got *down*.

She flipped through her mental Rolodex of hot dances and finally decided on a medley.

She started with a hip grind that had been cooked up by the priestesses of Ishtar, the Babylonian fertility goddess, that had gotten Hammurabi so hot he left his legislating and hit the streets of ancient Babylon for some tomcattin'.

Then she did a little Yoruba Oshun river goddess move where her whole body rippled like ocean waves, and her breasts spun in separate directions like fleshy whirlpools.

Then she threw her hands up in the air, shouted, and did an ol'-time New Orleans shimmy that made her ass shake like a bowl of jelly and wouldn't have been out of place with Satchmo blowin' at the Funky Butt Cafe.

Then, she vaulted up on a table, did a Voodoo spin that would have made Marie Leveau proud, and did the Dog the Slop and the Slow Drag so down and dirty she'd have made a hoochie mama in a rap video look like Miss Muffet.

She was rolling her ass, flicking her tongue out like a dick-sucking lizard, and rubbing her hands all over her tits and belly and hips, and then she did a deep-knee bend.

She wasn't wearing any drawers.

That did it. Several spectators who were standing too close were bowled over like tenpins.

She wound up doing a little move all her own, an impossible thang where she traced figure eights with her swiveling hips and grinding crotch, running her hands up and down and up her skirt while trembling like she was getting off with multiple, machinegun, jackhammer orgasms.

Everybody else had long since stopped dancing to watch her, a sexy hot fireball flaming across the stratosphere.

Then the song ended. For a New York minute, it was dead quiet.

There were audible gasps, moans, and sighs from the crowd, a release like a mass orgasm. Several couples hurriedly headed for the exits and cars and alleys and homes where they could do the nasty. Other couples fell to necking and groping right there. Some guys who came stag broke for the men's room, from which soon came the loud sounds of frantic whacking off.

Other people sat stunned at the bar, pouring down drink after drink like they were trying to quench fires of desire, fires that no drink ever poured could put out.

That oughta hold 'em a minute, Selena thought, quietly satisfied.

"I hope y'all brung some protection!" she yelled at them and laughed like a wild woman.

As she started to get down off the table, a tall, tanned, and terrific young man in a red silk T-shirt and tight black pants who had been enjoying the show gallantly offered her a hand.

She nodded to him, all ladylike, and quickly pulled a card with her phone number from her stocking top and slipped it in his hand before he was shoved out of the way and she was surrounded by several big beefy bouncers who escorted her to a table in the corner.

A man was sitting there who looked like a big ugly ol' bullfrog. It was Rance States, the club manager.

"Well, that was some show," he said, clapping his large fat hands.

"Fair to middlin'," Selena snapped. "If yo' fat ass had any class you'd hire me to put some life up in this dead-ass joint." She laughed like she was out of control.

"What are you drinking?" he asked.

"Scotch," she said. "And don't bring me none of that ol' watered-down shit. I want the real deal!"

He made a sign to a waitress. She brought Selena a tall glass. She swooped it up and downed it with one gulp. Even she would have been drunk on her ass had she not coated her stomach with a special preparation beforehand that neutralized the alcohol. She leered boozily at States.

"I know someone who'd like to meet you," Frog Face said.

"Who? You?" She wondered if she'd have to do him as part of the bargain. She wasn't knocked out at the prospect but if duty called . . .

"Not me," he said. "A friend and associate. A discreet gentleman who likes to meet quality ladies."

I bet I know what quality he likes, Selena thought. "I like men who like quality," she said as nasty as she could. "How do I get in touch with Mr. Deescreet Gennelman?"

"You don't," said Frog Face, pushing a napkin and a pen toward her. "Write your number down there, beautiful. You don't call him. He'll call you."

"Bet," she said as she wrote. "Hey! Whose ass I got to kick to git me another drank up in this heah mothafucka?"

Part IV

Margaret called her after she got home.

"Red alert!" she said. "We don't have seven days anymore. The hearing's been moved up. Gaddys is scheduled to testify within a few days in Washington unless you can stop him."

Oh, great, Selena thought. A rush job. What if the mother decided to hold off calling her until he got back? Might just be easier to go by his house, knock him over the head, and kidnap him.

She had a restless night, and went out jogging in the morning.

When she got back there was a message on her answering machine. It was from Gaddys.

"My little mojo," she said to herself, patting herself on the butt. "How could I ever have doubted you?"

At about two that afternoon she was sitting on a bench in the park near her condo as instructed, when a tall, dark-skinned man with long dreadlocks and a beard, dressed in coveralls and sunglasses and toting a backpack, sat down next to her.

"Ms. Epperson?" the man said, extending his hand. She knew that voice! It was William Gaddys, wearing a disguise. She tried not to show surprise.

"Yes?" she said.

"I am the gentleman Mr. States told you about," he said. "You look surprised."

Shit! "Well, I was expecting someone who looked a little more . . ."

"Like someone who owned a nightclub?" He chuckled. "I'm wearing a wig and false whiskers," he explained. "I have enemies. Business competitors. I must take precautions when I move about."

So you ain't seen picking up chippies in the park, Selena thought.

"I hear you're quite a dancer," Gaddys said.

He was peering at her intently.

Selena was back in her fresh-meat bag, wearing a long-sleeved, high-collared white blouse that was buttoned up to the neck, a long black dress that reached down to the tops of her very sensible, clunky shoes, no jewelry or makeup, and a bashful, rueful expression.

"I'm so ashamed," Selena stammered. "I can imagine what you've heard. You must think I'm a—trollop or something. Please believe me! I—I don't usually act that way in public. It's just that I—I'm so . . ."

"Lonely?" Gaddys said.

Selena bit her lip and looked away, playing the role to the hilt.

"It's no fun, being alone, getting older," she said, sniffling back a fake tear. "It makes you do desperate things Mr., Mr. . . ."

"Gaddys. William G. Gaddys," he said. "You may have heard of me."

She purposely showed surprise this time. "You? But—"

"Ms. Epperson, we don't have much time," Gaddys said. "I am prepared to walk out of your life right now, and you can go your way and there will be no hard feelings. Your loss of self-control last night will never be mentioned to anybody." He leaned close to her and said it as though it might be. "But I sense that you are a woman in search of new horizons. Knowledge. That you are a woman who wants to . . . learn. I can teach you, Ms. Epperson. I can be your guide. I can guide you to new vistas, new horizons where you can discover your true potential."

Are you pushing Amway distributorships? Selena thought.

I bet I know what kind of new horizons he means. Horizontal horizons.

Gaddys pulled a flat brown envelope out of his backpack and handed it to her.

She started to open it.

"Not now," he said. "Wait till you're home. Alone. Then peruse the contents. If you are intrigued, if you want to go further, call this number."

He handed her a card. Oh, he was good. A cagey bastard. But Selena had more moves than a Russian chess master.

"If you don't, it's been nice meeting you."

As he stood up, Gaddys "accidentally" brushed her knee. She made herself jump skittishly. It was the reaction he wanted to see.

"Have a nice day," he said. And then he was gone.

Back home, Selena opened the package and found it contained a document of several pages and a book. The title of the document was "Agreement between Pupil and Instructor" but it was your standard B&D master and slave contract. Probably changed the "hereinafter referred to's" out of deference to African-American sensibilities—even the most masochistic sistah ain't gon' let nobody call her no slave!

The book was a copy of *The Story of O.* Oh brother. Not only had she read it, but she'd written three or four under her pen name, "Whippi" Goldberg, that made it look like Mother Goose.

So we like to play rough, do we? She laughed to herself. Well, baby, I hope you got your kneepads on!

Part V

"Well, Ms. Smartypants," Selena whispered to herself. "Here's another fine mess you've gotten yourself into."

It was the next evening. She was naked, spread-eagle, and tied to a bed in Gaddys' house.

Well, she wasn't really tied down. Her "bonds" were red silk ribbons with cute little bows in the knots. Not very tight. She could have ripped loose anytime she wanted to.

Her surroundings were rather pleasant, really. She was in a bedroom with ornate pink-white-and-gold-inlaid wallpaper. There was a mirrored ceiling, of course. The comfortable, king-sized bed was made up with scented black silk sheets. Soothing music played on the box, romantic stuff. The air was thick with sweet perfume and incense. Several cut crystal vases holding red roses sat around the stuffed room.

Earlier she and Gaddys dined on pheasant under glass and had sipped expensive Cristal champagne in a sumptuous dining room, using gold plates and flatware.

He had then led her to a luxurious bathroom with a huge marble sunken tub, where she had stripped and bathed alone in warm, herbal-scented mineral waters.

After that they'd necked a little in his spacious living room, and then he'd led her to the bedroom and asked had she read *The Story of O.*

"Yes," she'd replied.

Did she want to go further, he'd asked. You can leave now with no questions asked. No hard feelings.

She had nodded. Only then did he have her sign the contract.

Oh, he was good!

He'd then gently peeled away her bathrobe, then lifted her

up and laid her down, naked, on the bed and fastened her wrists and ankles to the bedposts with the red silk ribbons.

He was good, all right. A sistah could get to love her some of this B&D, 'cuz this was the shizzat! Maybe he was too good. She was so comfortable, full, and warm, she felt a little like taking a nap.

No time for that.

Gaddys was standing at the foot of the bed, naked but for a black silk Japanese kimono, and sipping from an expensive antique crystal brandy snifter full of vintage cognac. He was looking all debonair with one eyebrow raised like he was B'wana Dick or somebody. If she fell asleep on him now, he'd get so miffed he probably wouldn't be able to get his little peter stiff.

C'mon, Selena, gurl! Try to tremble with fearful expectation a little! You got to make him miss that plane to Chocolate City!

"Well, Ms. Epperson, my pupil," he whispered. "Are you ready to walk through the joyful gates of wisdom?"

Ready when you are, buster, she thought. "Yes, master," she whispered fiercely.

"No no, Ms. Epperson, my darling pupil," he chided her gently. "None of that vulgar 'master-slave' action here. No doubt you have heard many things about our discipline. Our life. Many ugly rumors. Superstitions. "Like that book *The Story of O.* I gave you that only to test the limits of your commitment. Look about you! You see no whips, no branding irons! No instruments of torture!"

Only your corny-ass rap, she thought.

"Your bonds are merely symbolic. It is the voluntary surrender of your will I desire. Your unforced submission."

"Will it hurt bad?" Selena forced herself to whimper.

"Pain? No! By no means! We will not make you trod the

paths of pain, we will trace for you the thin, white-hot line between pleasure and pain that leads to ultimate wisdom."

We? Who the fuck else is up in here? What a cornball!

She sighed audibly and trembled as though it was the thing she wished for most in the world.

"Are you ready, Ms. Epperson, my little star pupil?"

"Oh, yes, teacher! Yes! Yes!"

He took off his kimono and dropped it on the floor.

I hope he don't expect me to pick up after him, too, she thought. That would be sadistic. Then she got a good look at him. Selena had to bite her lip to keep from whistling. He was a specimen, all right. A hunka hunka burning love, muscles rippling, with giant chest muscles, bulging biceps, and a flat belly with washboard abs, just like mama liked 'em!

And he was toting a cannon, all right, with two big dum-dums hanging underneath.

Be damned if he hadn't greased himself down, so with his shaven head he looked like a giant, chocolate replica of the Oscar statue, or one of them bucks on the cover of one of them *Mandingo* books.

For a moment she considered crossing out Ted and Margaret and keeping this one for herself. Business! Keep your mind on the business at hand, Selena dear!

Like a black panther stalking his prey, naked and glistening, Gaddys crawled on the bed until he was over her, supporting himself on his hands. He stared into her eyes for a while, fiercely. She stared back, hungrily. Then he kissed her, lightly, then hard, then light and hard again.

She did nothing at first and then she kissed back, hesitantly, clumsily, and then harder and with feeling, and then their tongues were darting, tangling, rubbing, and she was moaning and sighing and only half acting.

And then he was working down her body, alternating a kiss

and a little nip, kiss and little nip, working on her neck, then down her chest to her breasts, where he nuzzled and kissed her nipples until they were rock hard. Then he was working down her stomach, down to between her legs, alternating a little nip and suck, nip and suck, and then he went to work on her in earnest with his tongue.

Experts had gone down on Selena; on a scale of one through ten she rated this job a one hundred and eleven. He nuzzled and lapped and kissed like he was eating a sweet, tender, ripe piece of fruit; like he savored the taste, now at her clit, now around her labia, now his tongue was inside her until jolts of pure sexual pleasure washed over her in wave after wave.

She felt her control slipping away! That would never do. It was time for the mind trick of Fuck but Not Fuck.

One moment she was lying on the bed, stretched out, moaning in real ecstasy as Gaddys performed expert cunnilingus, and the next she was outside herself, standing beside the bed, looking down on herself and Gaddys.

It was a trick she had learned in a monastery in Tibet, of out-of-body consciousness during intercourse, or Fuck but Not Fuck. It was coming in handy now, because Gaddys was a cunt-lapping freak. He stayed on the oral case for what seemed like hours until orgasms ripped her body like sheet lightning, like a string of 500-pound bombs dropped from a B-52, and she was flipping like a flag in a sexual hurricane.

Only when he had stopped did she rejoin her consciousness to her body, and still the residual afterglow of his love work was almost too much for her.

Oh, he was good!

"Ms. Epperson," he cooed in her ear. "You have been totally forthright with me, haven't you?"

"Yes. Yes, teacher, yes," she gasped.

"You aren't holding anything out on me, are you? No secrets?"

Oh, the man's antennae for danger was marvelous. He could sense something was wrong about her. And what a great time to get a woman to drop a dime on herself. Fucking is the best truth serum there is. If she hadn't pulled her Tibetan mind trick, she would have confessed to the Brinks job if he'd wanted her to.

"Please, teacher, don't torment me this way," she said with a little catch in her voice. "I could never lie to you."

"Good. Good, my pupil," he whispered, stroking her hair.

It was time to flip the script on cuzz. No telling what other tricks he might have up his sleeve. She didn't have his mind right yet.

She breathed deeply, centered herself, and commenced Operation Go Down On Moses!

Part VI

"Oh, master!" Selena cried, ripping her arms loose of the ribbons and sitting up.

"Teacher, Ms. Epperson," he said

"Teacher, master, whatever you say!" she cried, ripping the ribbons off her ankles and rolling on top of him. "Oh, you have given me joy and wisdom as I have never known, for—as you must suspect now—though I have made love to men, I have been . . . frigid!"

"I had suspected as much but—"

"I must—I will repay you! You must let me, or I shall run out of this house and throw myself into the river or in front of a car! I don't want to live anymore if I can't repay you to the fullest, right now!"

"This is highly irregular," he said, getting a little uneasy.

She had to take him down now before he got wise!

In a cave deep in the Arizona desert was found an ancient book, written by the courtesans of the harem of the rulers of ancient Atlantis, that described methods of oral sex so powerful that they actually caused the destruction and sinking of that continent.

Anyway, that's what Selena sometimes told people when she was putting them on. Actually, she had just sucked a whole lot of dick, so she had the science down cold.

Hungrily, desperately, she went down on Gaddys, sucking now hard, now soft, licking at it like it was candy, rolling it, running her tongue around his balls, up and down the bottom of the shaft, and around the head, where it gets so so good to a motherfucker!

At first Gaddys sat up on his elbows and watched her, amused. After all, he'd had many a symphony played on his meat flute, and it took a virtuoso to play the tune that blew him away.

Little did he know, even as he smirked, that his instrument was in the hands—mouth—of the John Coltrane of fellatio!

Slowly the smug look faded, and then he started to breathe a little harder, and then he lay back, and soon he was prone, head grinding into the pillow, eyes shut tight, writhing and groaning and calling on the Lord one minute and his momma the next, and Jesus one time and cussing the next, and before he knew it he had lost all his cool.

Selena put him through some changes, playing his ass like a yo-yo, going on until he was about to come and then stopping and starting all over again and stopping until he was begging for mercy, pleading for her to stop and then not stop, to take him to climax or to shoot him and put him out of his misery!

When it had gone on for what seemed like forever, and when he was screaming like Little Richard, she stuck her middle finger up his ass and the orgasm he had almost blew her head off.

She swallowed his cum, but she needn't have. That little move, which was usually the pièce de résistance and broke 'em all the way down, was wasted 'cuz he didn't see it. He was O-U-T, out! Unconcho! He lay as if dead, with his eyes rolled up in his head, breathing shallowly.

"Was I all right?" she asked him.

She was answered by deep jagged snores.

She snickered. "Guess so."

Part VII

Now will the gander fly the coop, or will he hang around to make love with the little brown goose?

It was later that evening. Selena was at home in her meditation room doing a mental recap.

She had pierced William G. Gaddys' defenses, passed herself off as an innocent ingénue, fresh meat just waiting to be turned out, a tender young morsel of fruit to be plucked from the vine—and probably chewed up and spit out later, when all the juice, the spirit, had been sucked out, when she was turned out, strung out, and used up.

That was the brutal game Gaddys' kind always played. They hated women. The goal was always to hurt and humiliate them in the end.

He'd have never let a hardened veteran of the sex wars like Selena anywhere near him had he but known.

But he hadn't known. She too was a hunter. She too could use camouflage and deception.

His game was tight. Her game was tighter.

Still, was her game tight enough? He was supposed to be leaving for D.C. tomorrow. Would he put the trip on hold?

It all depended on that blowjob. It had been a master blowjob, one of her very best. If it had been a pizza it would have had fifty kinds of cheese, seventy-five kinds of meat, been big as a barn door, and weighed a ton. A 360-degree, 'round-the-world-and-I'm-goin'-again blowjob. No brag. Just fact.

Would ol' swingin' dick want some more o' dat?

Early the next morning he called. Could they get together. Probably wanted to get him a taste.

The nerve!

"Naw, teacher, I really can't," she whined.

There was a long silence on the other end of the line. He was thinking. "That's fine. That's fine," he said brusquely.

"Maybe next Tuesday?" she suggested.

"Not next Tuesday, Ms. Epperson. You know our arrangements. I will call you," he said curtly and then he hung up.

I got your next Tuesday, she thought.

He called back ten minutes later.

"Aww, teacher, really I can't today. I got papers to mark and I gotta clean up my apartment and my hair is really a mess and I smell like a pig."

He hung up this time without saying anything. Was that it?

He called again five minutes later. Desperation was in his voice. He didn't care how she looked or smelled or what she had to do. Could he please maybe just come over just a little while, pretty please?

"Naw, Mr. Gaddys. I got to do my nails and I don't feel good and I got a headache."

There was shock in his voice. She hadn't called him

teacher. His power was slipping. Now, not only his libido was on the line, but also his ego.

Maybe a man can tough it out if you got him by the balls, but a blow to his ego he can't stand—if'n he be a man!

He hung up. Then he called right back. She said no. Then he hung up again.

He called twenty times in a row. She didn't even answer the phone. The twenty-first time, she picked up the receiver.

He had lost all his nuts. He said "please" more times than James Brown. She wished she could have seen his face. He promised her the stars and the moon. The sun. He said he would take her to the Ebony Fashion Fair and the Alvin Ailey Ballet on Super Bowl Sunday.

That one almost got her. Givin' up the Super Bowl! But she had to remember the mission. This was bigger than her. Bigger than him. It was for the sexual health of society that she was working now.

She yawned and hung up on him.

He didn't call again.

Was it over? Would he give up? Would he leave town with his tail between his legs, call somebody else, or get a copy of *Black Tail* magazine, go whack off in the john, and call it a day?

This was the tough part. Knowing how to give ol' dick a little line, like a fisherman trying to reel in a really big one.

I would have made a good fisherman, she thought. Will this be the big one that got away that I'll be telling my sistah-gals about in my old age?

She did her nails and her toes and she thought about something else.

Fifteen minutes and thirty seconds later her door intercom buzzed.

Damn! It's a forty-five-minute drive in light traffic, she thought. Dawg must have broken the speed limit and ran every red light on the way over.

Sometimes I scare myself.

"Yes?" she said into the intercom as though she hadn't the slightest idea of who it could be.

A flood of cryin', babblin', and blubberin' came over the intercom, the sounds of a man with his jones coming down, the sounds of a brotha havin' a seizure.

She let him go on a while and finally buzzed him up.

She waited real good and long before she opened her front door.

When she did, she found Gaddys kneeling in the door-way, wearing his shorts and a T-shirt, and shoes with no socks (hadn't even taken time to dress). He was totally out of it.

Selena sighed, like she was exasperated but too soft-hearted to make him suffer anymore.

All right, she thought. Time to switch from Ms. Epperson, mild-mannered potential sex slave, to Selena, Dominatrix of Steel.

She reached out, took him gently by the nose with her thumb and forefinger, and pulled him inside.

Part VIII

"Repeat after me, Billy," Selena said. "We have been a very bad boy."

"We have been a very bad boy," William G. Gaddys, now "Billy," repeated.

He was on his knees, naked but for a dog collar. His arms were bound behind his back with black leather. Selena had of-fered to use something more comfortable, say silk scarves, but Gaddys had insisted on ropes or leather.

He was almost completely housebroken. Just a little more work and she would get his mind right.

"We have been a liar and a hypocrite," she said. "We have hurt and abused people, but above all, women."

"We have been a liar and a hypocrite, we have hurt and abused people, but above all, women," he repeated.

"We have been selfish. A taker and a user, and not a sharer," she said. "But now we are going to learn better."

He repeated what she said, and looked at her expectantly, hungrily.

Selena was wearing a white terry cloth robe and house slippers. She had considered going the whole leather bitch routine, but she was going to perform some delicate brain surgery here. Too much domination and he would be a useless drone, ready to be abused by anybody, and that wouldn't do anybody any good.

She knew the masters' dirty little secret: that inside each master was a slave!

And she knew an even greater secret: that no slave stays a slave but turns the table on the master at the first opportunity.

It therefore does no good to merely flip the script and make the master a slave, since, sooner or later, the script will be flipped again. The goal is to break up the whole master/slave matrix.

Unless of course they are fully informed, voluntarily participating, consenting adults, in which case that's their bidness!

"We are going to learn our lesson today, Billy," Selena said. "We have been bad. We are going to learn and afterward we are going to be better and we are not going to do bad ever again. Now assume the position."

Gaddys eagerly turned around and bent over, exposing his glistening, naked, muscular buttocks. Selena allowed herself a quick pinch and a couple of feels of the firm juicy rump roast, and then raised her hand to give him a good whack.

"No, no!" Gaddys said. "Rougher."

Sometimes the patient knew best, Dr. Selena thought. She went into the bedroom and came out with a large wooden hairbrush.

"No no!" Gaddys said. "Rougher! Rougher! Really rough!'

"Dis boy in need of some big-time healin'," Selena muttered under her breath.

She got a large, heavy, long, black, plaited leather whip.

"No! No! Really rough!"

She dropped the whip and "thunk" on it for a minute. Then she remembered an heirloom, way down deep in a trunk in her closet; a big, bodacious, leather razor strop that had belonged to her granddaddy!

"Yeah! Yeah! Now we strokin'!" Gaddys giggled when he saw the big ol' thang in her hand.

I'm gonna have to charge Ted and Margaret extra for this one and I'm gonna need a heating pad for this arm when we through, she thought. She rotated her arm a few times to loosen up, then thought of some suitable spank music.

She didn't have to think long. She found a CD of a live, forty-five-minute version of "Lickin' Stick" by James "Butane" Brown, the Godfather of Soul (and Hardest Working Man in Show Bidness), and fired it up on the box.

She snapped the strop. At just the sound of each snap, Gaddys jumped and moaned.

"Don't hold back, give it to me," he begged.

Selena let him have a taste of it. Gaddys jumped and said, "Again."

Selena laid the razor strop hard across his glistening, quivering butt like an ol'-time Loosiana field hand. He jumped. "Again! Harder! Bitch!"

At that, she let herself go, raining blows, snaps, and cracks across his ass. She was an expert. The idea, after all, is not to flay the victim alive but to, as Gaddys said, "walk that fine line between pain and pleasure."

She never broke the skin on his butt, though she did raise some nasty welts. Selena whipped him until she was hot and sweaty. With each blow his dick got harder and harder. Gaddys screamed and wriggled with delight with each blow, more and more.

On and on it went, until her arm felt like lead and she was panting and sweat was running down and she was getting more than a little turned on herself.

Finally, Gaddys screamed and fell over. Cum spurted all over the carpet. He lay there like he was dead.

Thank God, Selena thought as she collapsed exhausted on a couch. I don't think I could have laid one more on him.

They both were silent. Breathing hard for a long while.

Damn, if I wasn't a righteous black woman I could get to like summa dis, Serena thought. I must use this power only for good. Wonder if bruhman got a cigarette on him?

Finally it was Gaddys who spoke.

"I'm sorry, Mommy," he whined.

"I'm not your mommy, William," Selena said. The script was all the way flipped, but she couldn't leave him like a turtle, helpless and on his back with his feet waving in the air.

"I'm yours to do anything you want with," he whispered.

She had taken him all the way down, now she had to bring him up.

"You've done a lot of bad things. Hurt a lot of people, William. And you're going to have to atone for that and make it up to them. That's all I want you to do for me."

She started to get up to untie him. Gaddys got up first,

crawled over to her on his knees, and put his head between her legs.

"I will. But first I want to do more," he said, beginning to flick his tongue between her thighs.

"Actually, William, that's all you have to do," she said.

He kept licking and kissing, higher now.

"Really, William. That's all you have to do," Selena said. She was surprised to find she was getting turned on.

He had his mouth on her cunt, licking and kissing her clit, her labia, all around, nuzzling her hair.

"William—I—well, if you insist—but just for a little while . . ."

She rested both hands on his bald head and leaned back while he worked and ate around.

For a *whole* lot longer than a little while!

Part IX

A week later Selena dropped by Ted and Margaret's office for an end-of-mission wrap-up.

At first they copped a 'tude about her waiting that long, but she told them after all that dancing and cunt-lapping and dick-sucking and ass-lashing she'd had to sleep for a week.

"I ain't Venus or Serena Williams, I'm only a love goddess," she'd sniffed.

After she gave them an oral and written report, she played a videotape that had been shot at the Shalimar Club the night before.

William G. Gaddys was the star of the show. He wore a gold lamé G-string, cowboy hat and boots, and a wild ecstatic smile.

His powerful, rock-hard, lithe, muscular body shined with oils as he did a bump and grind and all kinds of freaky moves with a bevy of beautiful strippers. Women were screaming and stuffing bills into his G-string.

"Thank you, thank you, ladies." He laughed when he finished. "All funds I collect will go to the Society for Sexual Liberation and Freedom and the Home for Retired Exotic Dancers!"

They answered with a chorus of whistles and cheers, by stuffing more bills into his G-string and fondling what was in it.

"Free love! Let it all hang out!" he shouted.

"That oughtta give his old allies, the Housewives Against Pornography, conniption fits," Ted said.

"Who you think was sponsoring the benefit?" Selena said. "You think that congressional committee is still gonna want him to testify?"

They all had a good laugh at that one.

"Selena, you are a wonder worker, a marvel!" Margaret gushed. She was wearing a loose colorful flower-print cotton dress, open, and no bra. She sat on a loveseat next to Ted, who was wearing Bermuda shorts, sandals, and a sexy black silk shirt that was open to the waist. The desk was gone. Plants were everywhere and a large tasteful nude hung on the wall behind them.

"I know I didn't follow your instructions to the letter, but getting dirt on Gaddys just to extort him would have only created a resentful, angry person who might turn on you at any time or slip back into his old ways once your control over him weakened. Now you have a willing ally. You can push somebody down in the mud, but you gotta git down there with him to keep him there. And it's good to see you two now practicing what you preach."

Both of them squeezed hands and nodded almost reverently.

Selena stood up and walked over to them. She gave Ted a lingering, wet, open-mouthed kiss and then did the same to Margaret, and then gently pressed their faces together and left them like that.

A few minutes later she was driving along the interstate in the big pink Mercedes sedan Gaddys had insisted on giving her in gratitude. Ah, the fringe benefits of a job well done!

She punched the CD player and on came Marvin Gaye singing her favorite song, "Sexual Healing."

It was a fine, sunny afternoon. The day was still young.

What to do?

Oh, yeah. That brother who she'd given her number to in the Shalimar Club that night had been calling. Left his number.

He was a fine young thang. Could probably use a little lightweight schooling. Or heavyweight, if need be.

Yeah, she thought. Call him up and see if he can come over. Get in the hot tub. With a friend. Or two. Or six.

She dialed him up as the car glided down the highway, smooth as glass.

Rendezvous

rukiya akua

The day started out like any Wednesday at the office. The receptionist brought in the doughnuts and coffee while the rest of us began to collect money for our weekly lunch out day. A few hours later, I had consumed my veggie sandwich on whole wheat. It was just after twelve when the computer tech arrived. Twice a month, Tonya Stewart came to the ninth floor of the Merritt Building to service the computers for the Millennium Group. Every time she comes, we flirt. Well, I flirt. She just smiles. It had been nearly six months since I first noticed her. I recall that day so vividly. It happened on a Wednesday, of course. We were on the elevator together and I thought her beauty to be striking in a very simple way.

She was tiny at 5'4" next to my 6'6" frame. She had the most perfect skin. It looked silky and I just imagined how wonderful it would be to touch her. Her caramel skin glistened, no doubt from the oil that she wore. It was a very subtle application of frank & myrrh. I thought I was in heaven. I like a woman who wears oils instead of those offensive perfumes. Her eyes were just a tad bit slanted and very clear, a pale brown. Full lips accented what was a very pleasant face and captivating smile. Yep, I remember her on that day as if it were yesterday. For nearly three months, I took every opportunity I could to flirt. At first it seemed as if she were shy, but now I believe it was just her way of trying to keep her visits totally professional. I had to admire her for maintaining a professional decorum. I, on the other hand, decided a little flirting wouldn't hurt anyone. So I never in a million years could have imagined what would happen on this particular day.

I always enjoyed my visits to the Merritt Building. Actually, I looked forward to them. I remember how hesitant I was at first when this site was added to my route. I recall thinking how I would hate dealing with the downtown traffic and how I would probably have to deal with a lot of stuffed shirts, too. But to my surprise, servicing the Millennium Group wasn't anything like that. The best part of my twice a month visit is that I get to look at David Johnson. That brotha is fine! It takes everything I have not to flirt back with him. He's been flirting with me for three months now and I've been kinda brushing him off. But today, today I am going to go for it!

I think she does it on purpose. I know that Tonya wears her company's uniform, but does she have to wear the pants so tight that they show off every curve of her body? But hey, I ain't complaining. I'm just glad that mine is the last computer that she checks out before leaving the office. Sometimes I think she lingers a little just to talk to me. But I've also considered that after nearly three months of flirting and no bite, maybe she has a man or maybe a woman. I don't know, but seems like sistahs are really going there these days.

· · ·

"Hi, Tonya."

"Hey, David, how's it going? Are you having any trouble with this thing?"

Tonya patted the computer and I wished I were spanking her. As she put her equipment down, I could see a little cleavage. Just thinking about it now makes me tremble.

"Nope. Everything is fine, actually. My baby here hasn't given me any trouble. So, how are things going with you?"

"Same ol', same ol'."

"Tonya, why don't you sit down? I really don't think she needs servicing today and if you have a few minutes before your next appointment I could get you some water, coffee, or a snack from the kitchen."

"No thanks, David, I don't want anything to drink, but I will sit down for a few minutes. I have another job to do in forty-five minutes, but it's only a few blocks away so I've got a half hour to spare."

"You know, Tonya, I'm glad that you do have a few minutes. I was wondering if maybe you'd like to go out sometime for dinner, a movie or something? I've looked and I didn't see a wedding ring, so I hope it's safe to ask."

"Well, I have been dating someone, but hey, I'm still a free agent for now. And I would love to go out with you, David. I've noticed you from time to time checking me out so I was wondering if you were going to ask me or not. You just don't know how often guys will grin at me, stare at me, and even sometimes speak to me, but will never step to me honestly and speak their peace. I just don't understand it."

"Oh come on . . . are you saying that every time you find yourself attracted to a brotha you step to him and invite him out on a date?"

"Yes."

"Girl, get outta here."

"Listen, if I am going to put out that much energy to stare, I may as well speak and see how far we can go. I am a very free person and I don't get caught up in that 'demure' lady thing. If I see something, or someone that I want, I go for it."

"Well, alrighty then."

"And since we're on the subject, let me tell you something else. I'm really glad that you asked me out. Like I said, I've seen you for some time now noticing me and I was just wondering if I was going to have to ask you out myself."

"You could have."

"And what would you have said?"

"Baby, you can do whatever you want with me. You can take me anywhere you like, anytime you like."

"Is that right?"

"Hey, it's tight, but it's right!"

"Now, is that right? David, you might wanna be careful what you say. I've been known to take what people say too literally."

"I'm for real. Girl, you know I've been diggin' you. You can. You can do whatever you want to me and I'll let you. You could lean over right now and kiss me and I would just let you."

"Now, don't get yourself into something you can't handle. I don't scare easily. And reverse psychology doesn't work."

"Reverse psychology? Tonya, I'm for real. Look, we're both here. I have this enclosed cubicle and . . ."

"And what?"

"All I'm saying is that you can do whatever you want to me right here, right now."

"Okay, let me see your thighs."

"My thighs? How you gonna see my thighs without me dropping my pants?"

"I dunno, but I really want to see your thighs. I'm a thigh lady and I always find myself looking at men trying to imagine what their bare thighs look like. I like your build, David, and I wanna see your thighs."

"All right."

I couldn't believe it, but here I was, in the middle of the afternoon, at work, in my cubicle, and I was dropping my pants for this woman whom, up until now, I had only flirted with casually. And although I couldn't believe this was happening, I was getting this rush. It was better than anything I had ever rented.

I dropped my pants to my knees, exposing strong, muscular thighs and black silk boxers. To my surprise, I was also exposing my manhood that had grown enormously, as this little game had aroused me. Thank God my cubicle was at the rear and I could see everything around me.

"David, I see you're easily aroused. I like that. I hate when it takes a hundred tricks to get a man up. I bet you cum pretty easily, too."

"Huh?"

Maybe I was a little out of my league with this one. But I was curious. And the way my name rolled off her tongue was inviting. I wanted to kiss her, but somehow I just couldn't bring myself to do it. I think I really wanted her to make the first move.

"I said, I bet you cum pretty easily, too."

"I heard you, Tonya, but I was just surprised to hear you say that. Where did that come from?"

"I see that you've gotten hard already and I just asked . . . so do you?"

"Do I cum easily? Yeah, I guess. But not fast, just easily."

I have to admit that as I sat there, I was getting really hard. I didn't think my dick could grow any larger, but this was really doing something to my ego and my dick. They both were growing out of control.

I noticed that Tonya had started to rub the back of her neck with her hand. Now she was *really* turning me on. And if I didn't know any better, I'd swear she was staring at the bulge in my underwear. Was she licking her lips, too?

"David, do you like oral sex?"

"Yeah. Who doesn't?"

"You'd be surprised. So, do you like to just get it or do you give it, too?"

"Both. Do you?"

"Well, I like to get it, but only if the guy really knows what he's doing. There's nothing worse than being excited and thinking you getting ready to get your pussy licked real good, and the brotha chomping on you like a burger."

"So, you don't give it?"

"Yeah. I love to give head. You know how some women just do it 'cause that's what their men like? I like to do it 'cause I like to do it. I guess I take some kind of pleasure in knowing that I have pleased my man. And I get off on it, too."

"Really? Girl, I wish I had somebody like *you*. You're smart, got a good job, down to earth, fine as hell, *and* you a freak! Damn!"

"Damn what?"

"Nothing. I just wish a brotha could be down."

"Maybe the right brotha can."

"So, what you saying?"

"David, let's cut the shit. We been diggin' each other for a while now and I think we need to just go on and do something about it. What you think?"

"Cool. So, we can go out this week?"

"Yeah, that's cool. What time is it?"

"Uh, it's three-twenty. You gotta go now?"

"Naw, I got ten minutes. Slide your chair over just a little and keep watching for somebody coming."

I moved the chair over and she moved her chair around to face me. The back of my chair was against the wall. Tonya moved between the desk and me. As I looked out at my co-workers, I was in a daze. I couldn't believe that I was about to have sex right there in the office, in the cubicle, while my co-workers were there working. I'd had some fantasies, but this one beat anything that I could have imagined.

As I concentrated on the office, I suddenly felt this surge of pleasure rise from my feet to the temples of my head.

Tonya had placed her hands and mouth around my dick and proceeded to give me head right there in the middle of the day, in my cubicle, in my office, while my co-workers were just a few feet away.

I squealed and she squeezed harder.

The pleasure from the pulse of her tongue and the warmth of her mouth, mixed with adrenaline, moved through my body like a stream of hot oil. It felt good. It took all I had to contain myself. Now I knew I had to have her.

Just when I thought it couldn't get any better she squeezed my dick again while placing my balls into her mouth. Then, she hummed. And I thought I was a damn harmonica. I wanted to call somebody, anybody. But instead I sat in silence as the thrill of ecstasy created orgasms in my mind. I knew the best was sure to follow.

At that moment, she spread my legs just enough to go down low and lick the forbidden. This girl was a freak and as I sat there in the pleasure zone, I thought of whether or not I could hang.

Tonya returned her tongue to my dick and then to my inner thighs as she made wet circles of lust form into streaks of ecstasy. I was in heaven!

As she sucked and teased, I grew more and more restless. The pleasure was growing and I wondered if I could control myself. I wanted to yell, but I couldn't. The sound had gotten lost somewhere between my balls and my dick. It was the first time in my life that I was ever speechless. It felt good.

As Tonya slid her tongue up and down the sides of my dick, I could feel the pressure growing and knew I was about to cum. She knew it, too. Tonya gave one last tug on the balls and a last pull on my head, and suddenly I let it all out. She held my dick so that I would cum all over the floor underneath my desk.

I wondered if she swallowed.

Then she kissed what was left on my penis, licked any evidence off her mouth, and stood up.

Yep, she swallowed.

"Looks like everything down there is okay. I'll see you in two weeks, but don't hesitate to call if you need service before then."

Removing a card from a purple case, she kissed the card, leaving a lipstick print—undoubtedly to tease me with those beautiful lips. Tonya placed the card on my lap, gave me a devilish grin, and left my office.

I tossed the card onto the desk and quickly returned my penis to its place and did the same with my zipper. Taking a napkin from lunch, I attempted to wipe up the cum, but the stain had set in.

Staring at the spot, I didn't know what to think. But quickly my look of confusion gave way to a sly grin.

Picking up Tonya's card, I read it with sheer pleasure and a growing erection.

My Friend, the Pornographer

Robert Edison Sandiford

For the first time in all the years I'd known her—sixteen, since the very first day of high school—Jewel Johnson, my best friend, Jules, had floored me. Knees collapsed, sprawled on my back on the living room carpet, I lay gasping for air, sputtering.

"What?" I said, clutching the receiver, shouting into it.

"You heard me." Jules giggled in that girlish way of hers, meaning you don't stand a chance of refusing her. A former beauty queen with a knockout pair of tits and a kick-butt butt, Jules had been treated like a princess since puberty because of her good looks and adventurous spirit. She had a way of making people—both men and women—do for her feel glad they did.

"You heard me," she repeated. "I want you to tape Jay and me fucking."

Jay was Jules' husband. They had been married for three years. He worked for an investment company but was an accountant by training. He was quiet yet attractive in an aloof way, like a stage actor. I always felt there was another side to him that was sly. But not *bad.* It came out most in his eyes, which narrowed when he smiled as if he was holding back some secret. And he had the body of a long-distance runner, lean and graceful in motion. Besides, what woman didn't wonder about her best friend's husband, especially when he was good looking, had big, loving hands, and she knew what they could do?

Jules was, of course, the kiss an' tell type. It seemed her exhibitionism was taking on new proportions.

"But why?" I said, sitting up, staring at my video bag on the sofa.

"Because you're my Girl Friday. Jay and I discussed it, and we figure A, we can trust you (everyone else we thought of would enjoy it *way* too much); B, you're a professional, sort of, at least you have the equipment and know how to use it; and C, since you're between jobs, we figure you could use the cash. There's a hundred bucks in it for you. If you say yes. Say yes, Rox."

It was true, I was in-between jobs. I had been unemployed for months. I was having trouble landing even a Joe Job. And my unemployment insurance was running out. Like Jay, I was trained for one thing—as a photographer—but could only find work doing other things. (My last stint was as a clerk in a photocopy shop. And that didn't go well. I could probably do with a new line of work altogether.)

"No, Jules," I corrected her, crawling toward my bag. "Not why me, but why do you guys want to tape yourselves?"

"Oh," she said dismissively, "this is something we always talked about doing, since before we were married. But we never felt the urge until now."

"Okay," I said, feeling inside my bag for my purse.

"So you'll do it?"

"I didn't say that."

"Oh, come on, Rox. It'll be fun."

"Fun for you, maybe. We've known each other a long time, Jules, shared a lot of things. But videotaping you and Jay doing the nasty? Just hearing you two in the next room when we were roommates used to make me run for cover."

"Look, Rox, we're deeper than sisters. I'm just asking a favor. But Jay and I really can't do this without you. We could set up a tripod, point the camera. But the final product would probably come out like those sad-looking, poorly edited, dimly lit wedding videos people force you to watch when you visit their house and they've run out of things to say."

"You want a hand-held look?"

"Preferably. But not exclusively. I imagine some positions will be more difficult to tape than others. That'll be up to you."

"I haven't said yes, Jules." My hand stopped rummaging through my bag. I found my purse, opened it. I was down to my last twenty. The rent and electricity were paid, but I had no real food in the apartment. I debated how much more thin soup and weak tea I could stomach again this month.

"You haven't said yes, yet. But you want to—you're about to. I can tell. You know I can tell. Oh, look, Rox, just do it. For *me?* You can stop the camera anytime the action gets too hot for you."

"And Jay's a hundred percent all right with this?"

"Sure."

"And you're absolutely positive you're okay with this?"

"Rox, would I be talking to you about it if I wasn't? You know I don't plan any trip without the intention of taking it."

"When?" I said, replacing my purse, zipping the bag closed.

"Can you come over this afternoon? Jay's off today."

"How about one?" I said, eyeing my tripod by the bedroom door.

• • •

I checked myself in the elevator's mirrors, straightening my beret and matching plaid vest. I shook out my blouse and smoothed my jeans. I noticed, feeling both anxious and proud, that my slim ass stuck out just a little, provocatively. Underneath my clothing, my bra and panties were sheer.

I stopped in mid-modeling. What the hell was I doing?

I wanted to look more than professional for the job— smart, sexy, like some hotshot independent filmmaker. Cool. In control. But all for what? The making of an amateur sex video that no one would see, starring my two best friends? A quick hundred bucks?

The elevator reached the sixth floor. I walked down the corridor to apartment 9A. As soon as Jules opened the door, I had second thoughts. Except for saying, "So here she is—my friend, the pornographer," she greeted me as she always did: with a bright smile, a tight squeeze, a warm, lipsticked kiss on either cheek. And she was dressed in sweats that accentuated her rolling behind and swaying tits. As usual, she wore no underclothes when at home. But the normalcy of all this unnerved me.

"Where's Jay?" I said, searching the room with my eyes. I didn't want to move.

"In the bedroom." Jules was smiling from ear to ear as if she couldn't contain her excitement. "Shall we?"

"Jules," I said, taking a step backward, my back right against the door. "I still don't—"

"Uh-uh, girlfriend," she said, shushing me. "If you've come this far, you can go all the way. I know you can. Now, no back talk. Did you bring the tripod?"

I nodded miserably.

"And whatever else?"

She looked me up and down, considering my bags. Again, I nodded.

"Good," she said. "I don't know if we'll need the tripod . . . but the sooner we get started, the sooner we'll know."

Jules took me by the arm and led me into the bedroom.

Jay was sitting on the bed, naked, reading a dog-eared copy of Errol Flynn's autobiography, *My Wicked, Wicked Ways,* with his right hand. His left hand lay restlessly in his lap, twirling and twirling his semi-erect cock.

"Hey, Rox," he said, looking up, resting the book on the night table, then playing with his cock and balls with both hands. "It's good to see you. I'm glad you agreed to do this for us. I don't know who we would have gotten otherwise. It's kind of like a fantasy come true."

I knew from hours of girl talk with Jules that Jay's cock was eight inches long and nearly as thick. And, from the looks of things, he already had worked it up to three-quarters its size. Yet Jay didn't stop twirling and twirling it, even when his hands became sticky with pre-cum and looked as swollen as his cock.

"Oh, baby," Jules said, staring at him and licking her lips. "You're juicing all over the place."

"Just trying to stay hard."

"But what am I here for?" Jules countered with that girlish giggle of hers. She pulled off her top and dropped her pants in what seemed like one motion.

Jules jumped onto the bed. Her ass, tits, and belly shook as she bounced over to him.

She immediately took his cock in hand.

"Okay, girl, how do you want us first?"

"This was *your* idea, Jules," I said, turning away, pulling out my camera. "You tell me." I quickly put the lens to my eye, focused. But my other eye wandered to her hand, skillfully pumping Jay's cock. I wondered if that was how I looked with a lover: hungry, greedy, even before we had begun to taste each other.

"How about some kissing and sucking before we get to the fucking?"

"I'd like that," Jay said.

"It's your tape, guys. Whatever you want." I stood in front of them at the foot of the bed, off to one side.

"You really mean that?" Jules said, kissing Jay deeply, then turning to give me a cattish grin.

She then wasted no time.

Jules got down on Jay, licking his chin, chest, and nipples until he practically shone with spit. I nearly dropped the camera when she deep-throated his cock in one gulp and sucked on it hard, pulling it out of her mouth repeatedly with a popping sound. "Fuck my boobs," Jules purred. She rolled onto her back, offering them to him like overripe melons. Jay growled back. I hurried around the bed to get a better shot, not too sure if I should ask them to face me. I had always known Jules was rough in the sack, and I could well imagine—to be honest, had on many occasions imagined—how aggressive Jay might be. But they were like animals.

Jay held Jules' tits in his hands. Kneaded them. Squeezed them. Wrapped them around his cock, then rubbed himself in-between so his pre-cum started to go creamy there. I never realized how long his fingers were; his hands were like mitts. Then he jerked himself between Jules' tits, poking through her flesh to her pouty lips. She teased him with her tongue. "You getting all this," he said to me, I assumed, but also to Jules. I nodded and said, "Uh-huh," whipping off my beret and wiping the sweat from my forehead. Then Jay gripped her trembling tits and pulled them to him. He sucked them hard, pinched the fat nipples with the tips of his fingers, gnawed them with his teeth. I glanced from his face to Jules, who was letting out little sighs of pleasure.

"Now eat my pussy," she commanded. "Show Rox how good you are at eating pussy."

"Will you suck my cock the way you should?" he asked with a menace that made me go weak.

As they groped into a sixty-nine, I shucked my vest and tried to decide which perspective to shoot from—his or hers. Since I had already taken her sucking him, I got behind Jay and zoomed in on Jules' smothering ass. If I had any inhibitions, they weren't giving me time to think about them. I taped intently, trembling as Jay first wrapped his tongue then his lips around Jules' clit, causing her to squirm and beg even as his cock bobbed in and out of her mouth.

"Oh, God—don't stop—don't you dare stop. Eat my pussy clean, boy!"

Jay steadied Jules by holding on to her chunky ass-cheeks. He spread them apart to bury his tongue deep inside her, and she humped away on his face, screaming and cursing. I was so close, I could smell them both, a powerfully intoxicating mixture of sweat and cum and pussy juice. I pulled back, catching myself. My underarms and upper lip were drenched, and that wasn't all. I held the camera on Jules and Jay as they untangled themselves.

They sat side by side on the bed, stroking each other, staring at me. "Rox, girl," Jules said, still breathing hard, "come over here."

"What?" I said, lowering the camera. But my breath must have sounded as labored as hers. "Why?"

"I'll tell you why when you get over here," she said, giggling. "Now put the camera on the tripod and come."

I did as I was told. I didn't know what else to do.

Jules patted the space on the bed beside her. She smiled slowly. She wiped the sweat from my forehead with both her hands and gave me a gentle kiss on the lips. She felt up my tits and tweaked the nipples, which were bulging. But I didn't stop her. I felt so weak and scared and shy, as if I had gone too far, done something very wrong and deserved to be punished. Jay looked on, also smiling, stroking his thick cock like before.

"Were we turning you on, Rox?"

"Jules, I . . ."

"Hey, no need to apologize," she said, unbuttoning my blouse. "That's okay. Do you think we invited you into our bedroom just to take pictures of us fucking? If you do, girl, you most definitely have another thing coming. I know you've thought about what Jay would be like between your legs. Oh, don't bother to deny it. You haven't been able to take your eyes off his cock since you stepped in here—not that I blame you. It must be a thrill for you to see it after all the stories I've told you about what it can do. And, as you said, we *have* shared practically everything—even the odd hot shower and sweet caress when we were roomies."

I reddened when she said this. It was supposed to be our secret; I had asked her not to tell even Jay. I should have known better. I was just curious about being with a woman, and Rox offered to show me.

"And Jay and I have thought a lot about you of late," she continued. "About these big boobs of yours." She unhooked my bra, and they came spilling out. "Forty-two-D if I remember correctly. About the same as mine. Do you still shave your pussy?" She kissed me again before I could answer. This time, I tried to pull back but not hard enough. She held me tight, and I gave in.

"Let's see. Come on. We've shown you ours. It's time you showed us yours."

She stood up and pulled me to my feet, her hands caressing my tits. As she lowered her lips to my swollen right nipple, she began to unbutton my jeans.

"Jules," I pleaded and protested in the same breath. "I . . . I . . . I don't know . . . about this. . . ."

She gripped as much of my tits as she could until the nipples were bursting. She gave each just one lick, and I moaned for mercy and for more.

"Of course, you don't," she said, finally answering me. "But you will."

Just then, Jay came up behind me and wrapped his hands around my neck. He kissed me there in a spot only Jules could have told him about. I shuddered. His cock pressed against the full length of my bare ass. Jules had dropped my pants around my ankles, and she already had my panties halfway down my legs.

"Just as I thought—bald as Brynner!"

Instinctively, I backed up, feeling Jay's hot hardness ease between my cheeks, lathering my crack with his generous pre-cum.

Jay held up my head with the tips of his fingers. Jules rose and whispered against my cheek. "Jay and I have wanted you for so long. It was only a question of time. You've always been so dear to us. We love you, Rox." She moved to lick the same spot on my neck Jay had been nibbling.

My knees buckled. Jules held me steady. She guided me back to the bed. I kicked off my pants and panties, along with the last of my inhibitions, as she lay me down. Jay was now behind the camera.

"All set, baby?" Jules purred, glancing up in his direction.

Jay growled in response. He left the camera on the tripod.

Jules lay beside me, stroking my cheek. Then she held up one of her floppy tits and shoved it into my mouth.

"Oh, my," she breathed. I had practically inhaled her. I was hungry for her, greedy.

After repositioning the camera, Jay knelt before me, one hand on my left ankle, the other hand on his cock. I spread my legs, sucked in more of Jules' flesh. I could hear her fingers sloshing in and out of her pussy as she rubbed herself to a climax. Jay buried his cock inside me as Jules fell away, thrashing about the way she did when she was riding the waves of multiple orgasms.

"Fuck me," I said, bucking hard against him. "More— gimme more of that cock!"

Jay pushed into me slowly, pulled out halfway, pushed in a little deeper. He had me clawing the bed, gnawing at the sheets. I shoved my body so high against him I was nearly riding him in mid-air. But I could tell he was about to break. He throbbed inside me, and his balls slapped hot and heavy against my ass.

I was so mad with lust for Jay, at finally having him, I forgot about Jules. She had rushed to their walk-in closet, only to saunter out harnessed with what looked like a ten-inch dong.

"Did someone say, 'more cock'?"

Jules lay down facing me, the dildo resting across the length of her left thigh. She held it up, and Jay spread my legs again, this time for her. Jules rubbed the huge head of the tool against my ready-to-pop clit. The tip was already slick. Instinctively, I remembered the feel of her juices mixed with mine.

I whimpered. "Where did you get that monster? It looks like the real thing."

She pressed a little bit between my lips, easily splitting me open.

"Good," she purred, sliding into me. "Because I intend to use it like the real thing."

Suddenly, I felt Jay knocking against my backdoor. I was so slippery from crack to crack that my ass gave no resistance. I had always dreamed of doubling my pleasure—something else only Jules would have known—but I didn't know if I could take it.

"What are you going to do with me?" I moaned, a bit fearful.

"What do you think, girl?" Jay said, inching up my ass, touching something hot and tingly inside my tail.

Jules kept filling me with endless cock. "What comes naturally," she said, now giggling uncontrollably.

I could feel both their tongues on my neck and, caught between them—wet, fluid, and getting wetter—our bodies merged: Jules' into mine, mine into Jay's. "We love you, Rox," they whispered, over and over again, in my ears. And, screaming my heart out, I loved them, too.

Jay turned off the camera then came back to bed. I was cuddling up to Jules, and he cuddled up to me.

"You think it came out?" Jules said.

"It better have," Jay said.

"Hey, it's not like I don't have more tape," I said.

Jules and Jay stopped talking. They looked at each other then down at me. They started to laugh.

"Rox, you missed your calling," Jules said.

"And what's that? Getting it on with my best friends?"

"No, silly." She brushed my lips with a kiss. Jay gave me a squeeze. "This. Us. What we did. Taping people getting it on. There's money in that, you know. You could start with friends."

"Yeah. Sure, Jules."

She looked over me at Jay again.

"Jay, would you tell this girl I'm serious."

"She's serious, Rox. As a hard-on."

"I can see it now, your name in neon lights, on a sign off Main Street. Intimate Videos Done Here. Satisfaction Guaranteed. Clean. Efficient. Discreet." Jules raised her head, raised it up high. "Roxanne Richards—The Pornographer."

"You really think so?" I said.

"You have to ask?" Jay said. "Take a look at us."

We all laughed, me the loudest.

I rubbed my chin, going "Hmm. Hmmm." It was expected of me, and I never felt more obliging. But I thought about it a little more, then I started to think about it a lot more. Until I found myself—lying naked in bed between my best friend and her husband, a video camera pointed at us, deeply satisfied— I found myself contemplating this whole new line of work.

Josey's Puddy Cat

Jonathan Luckett

My name is Josey and today is my birthday! I'm sitting in this chic new bar on Wisconsin Avenue, three blocks from the Georgetown Mall, with my man of nine months, Damon, and six of my closest homegirls from way back. We are just kicking it, listening to the musical vibe, sipping on these tight sour apple martinis that this cute bartender made extra strong for us, 'cause it's my special day!

Damon just finished toasting me, grinning my way as he raised his glass to those luscious brown lips of his. I replace my glass on the smooth bar surface after taking a swallow and excuse myself for a moment. Damon, with those sensuous eyes sparkling, leans in softly to ask me if I am ready for my surprise.

"Josey," he says, stroking my back in a sensuous kind of way, "my baby's puddy cat ready for some action?"

I feel my face flush and my back tingle with excitement as I nod. Damon and I have been talking about my present for over a month now—he promised that this would be a birthday that I'd never forget. One of the things I love about Damon is that we have the kind of relationship where we can talk about our fantasies without jealousy or uneasiness. And we have spoken at length about what we both desire, sharing delicious visions that float around the ether as we lie in bed after a sweaty session of lovemaking. My thong is moistening with anticipation of things to come. Damon, I know, will not let me down tonight. . . .

I take the hallway toward the ladies' room, my taut nipples and ass brushing against the silky fabric of my dress as I stroll in my fly heels. I can feel the stares from both men and women as I pass them by. The adrenaline rush is powerful. It feels damn good to be noticed tonight!

I take a right turn toward the entrance to the restroom. A tall, dark-skinned sister with short caramel hair and large hoop earrings comes out and puts up her hand.

"Sista—trust me, you don't want to go in there! It is way too foul. Take those stairs," she says, pointing to the end of the darkened hallway. "There's another one on the second floor."

I nod and thank her as I head for the steps.

I climb the narrow stairs slowly as the pulse of acid jazz beats invades my chest. The space darkens and I have to hold on to the railing for support as I come to the landing, and proceed into a fog of smoky incense and near darkness. My fingernails trace a path along the wall slowly as I try to find my way. My heart begins to pound—is this the right way? Perhaps I should turn back. Before I can complete the thought, something brushes against my ass, and before I can react, a hand is thrust between my legs as I am pushed against the wall.

"Let me feel that puddy cat!"

The deep voice coming from behind me is completely unfamiliar, but his tone and the way he speaks those words has me pausing as a tremor runs the length of my spine. I try to turn my head in order to discern shapes, but it is of no use—the hallway is almost completely dark save for sparks of light that, like lightning, seem to come from overhead. I feel something on my backside again—a hand that palms my cheeks and traces the G-string downward toward my core. I shift to the side in protest, alarms going off in my head. Where is Damon? Who is this man? But then that soothing voice returns, and I can feel his breath on my cheeks as he presses himself fully into me from behind. He pins me to the wall, the rock of his manhood pressing into the cleft of my ass as he grinds his hips into me and whispers, "Don't worry, Josey, everything's cool. It's time for your birthday gift."

A part of me wants to scream for Damon. In fact, I feel his name form on the tip of my tongue and lips, but I can't say whether anything emerges at all. The thumping in my chest is overpowering, excitement drowning out everything else.

I am led into a room off the hallway. It too is almost completely dark, but my eyes seem to be getting used to the dimness. I spy a red velvet couch by a dark window. I am led to it and made to sit down. I try to glance upward to see my abductor, desperately needing recognition to flood through my insides so that I can feel okay about what I'm experiencing. The intensity is rising in me like mercury, but the man gently turns my head away and grasps my hair firmly in his powerful hands.

I am blindfolded with a silk sash and commanded to lie down.

I do so, not knowing what else I can do. I feel my thighs begin to quiver, with anticipation or fear, I do not know.

At some point I call out for Damon, sensing him near, but the man with the deep voice is by me in a flash instead, his sweet-smelling breath on my cheek again.

I feel a pair of hands raise my dress and touch my inner

thighs. My legs are gently parted as I feel a second set of hands circle my breasts. I suck in a breath as I feel my nipples tighten and stretch. My G-string is pulled to one side and instantly I sense fingers brushing against the lips of my sex. It is sticky with juice and I am breathing heavy as a mouth covers mine. I taste a warm tongue as someone else's tongue begins to probe my cunt. My back arches as my legs widen. I am in heaven. My mind is racing. Where is Damon? I know this is his doing. I can feel him in the room—don't ask me how I know, but he is close by. I just know he is.

The tongue deep inside me takes my breath away. It is not Damon, I am certain of that. The way this person is working me down there is unlike the way my man does. Don't get me wrong—Damon is an excellent lover and can send me to heaven and back just with his lovely tongue, but he has a rhythm that is all his own. After sleeping with someone for over nine months you get to know their patterns and M.O. This isn't him.

My breasts are freed from the confines of my dress; both nipples are taken hold of, squeezed, and twisted simultaneously. Then a mouth attacks them, first licking across and under my mounds before they are sucked into a mouth, one delicious nipple at a time.

A pair of fingers finds their way into my drenched slit. Before I can moan with pleasure, a tongue is thrust far inside my mouth, glazing over my teeth and fluttering against my own frenzied tongue that quivers like a flame.

"Does that feel nice, Josey?" the low, sexy voice asks me. I try to respond, but I find that I can barely speak. My breasts are being kneaded together, my tits pushed together like twin peaks until my nipples almost touch, and that wonderful tongue—which one I can't tell you; I am losing track of the numerous tongues and appendages—flicks back and forth from one taut nipple to another, glazing my skin and raising gooseflesh. Down below, one of my many unseen lovers has begun to play with my clit, rubbing the engorged piece of flesh between a wet thumb and forefinger before tugging on it in a teasing kind of way. And then just as I spread my legs farther and think I'm gonna lose my mind, those quick fingers are replaced down there by an expert mouth—a mouth that slurps me up whole like an oyster and squishes my hot flesh between its teeth and tongue.

That's when I cry out and come.

My nipples are pulled hard, enhancing the sensation as the waves of my orgasm roll through me.

Oh yeah, ya'll. I come hard!

I attempt to holler again, but a slender finger is inserted into my mouth. As I suck on it longingly, I suddenly feel a long fingernail scraping against the roof of my mouth. The thought of a woman in the midst of this lovefest strikes me like a devastating blow to the face. I had thought about this a million times over, the possibilities of another female joining in, but Damon and I hadn't made any firm plans yet. And now this! It is all happening so quickly that I feel myself grow dizzy. I try to concentrate; attempt to decipher which of my new lovers are male or female as they work their magic on me. Suddenly, the possibility of a woman kissing and licking me down *there* makes my face flush. This isn't happening, I tell myself, but the head moving purposely between my legs says otherwise.

Abruptly I am yanked up to a standing position; my arm is held tightly as I am led out of the room. I can hear muted voices. I protest, yelling for Damon and demanding to know where I am being led next, but no one answers my calls.

Presumably, I am led back into the hallway, my fingernails finding the wall as they scrape across the smoothness of the surface.

Then we stop as quickly as we had begun. My breasts are heaving in front of me, remaining unsheathed from my dress. I try in vain to reposition my G-string, but a hand brushes my fingers away. I am pressed once again to the wall, and the hot breath on my face returns—the silky, sexy bass voice whispering in my ear, "Don't move, birthday girl. Gotta hang here for just a moment more."

I turn my face to the source, open my mouth to protest, but a large hand covers my mouth, preventing me from speaking. A finger slips in and I suck on it as if it were a candy cane.

I sense the back of my dress being raised, my ass cheeks are kneaded and palmed, and I spread my legs in anticipation. In a sudden flurry my G-string is ripped off my body. A stinging pain runs from my waist to inner thigh. I yell out, but the thick hand returns to cover my mouth.

"Sssshh!" a voice whispers forcefully as the full weight of his body presses against my bare flesh. I can feel him coming to life through the fabric of his jeans. My hand snakes down behind me, fingers spreading over the material of his pants as I feel his hardness. I leave my hand there for a moment, feeling him as he becomes engorged. My fingers alight from his pants as if they were on fire. The thumping in my chest has returned and I find that I am out of breath. I try to reconcile everything that has just occurred, attempting to decide what to do next. But it is hard—too many distractions, everything feeling better than it should.

Behind me, my abductor moves away from me for a few moments, and I have time to catch my breath, but barely. Then I feel him reconnect. This time, his sweet member is unencumbered—it is free. It bobs against my ass; without thinking I reach for it and take it in my palm. It is thick and pulsating as if it were alive. I rub my thumb along its latex-covered girth before my hands are removed and placed in front of me on the wall.

He presses into me, his breath tickling my neck as I sense him moving into position. His penis is close to my pussy—dangerously close. He rubs it against my lips, from side to side, and my flesh quivers with every stroke. My face is pressed against the cool wall; my thighs tremble as my eyelids flutter.

I tip my head to the ceiling where flashes and sparkles of light invade my blindfold, and I realize with sudden certainty that the man preparing to take me from behind is without a doubt *not* Damon!

I feel a mix of anguish and total sensual elation. I am in the midst of some public hallway, and with whom, I have no clue.

The weight of that thought is like electricity that courses through my veins.

What should I do???

The thought is fleeting.

He slides his thick member slowly up the crease of my ass and back down toward my cunt. I tremble at the thought of gripping him between my velvety folds. I am offering up my firm ass and lithe hips, daring him to entomb himself in my reservoir.

My breath is weak.

I am near exhaustion.

Perhaps I am about to faint.

I am sliding down. I can feel it.

I try to remain strong, but my willpower is ebbing away, like the tides. Part of me wants this so badly I can taste it. In a moment, I will have no resolve left.

Then he will have his way. . . .

Behind me, my abductor has taken hold of his member and pointed it at my opening. Juices are meandering down both thighs—I am that wet. The air around me is charged. I hear him exhale, slowly and forcefully, as he inches toward my molten core. . . .

A smattering of bombs goes off simultaneously inside of me. The anticipation of things to come is replaced by vivid unfiltered reality. The hardness of his thick strength passes slowly through the opening to my sex as he accelerates toward the end of my womb, filling me up in an instant, a feeling so surreal that for a moment I think that I may be imagining this scene. But the culmination of my expectations has finally taken place. He is *fucking* me now, his manhood seemingly alive inside me. I feel his hot breath on my neck as he pumps me with abandon. And for the first time this evening, I choose to lose myself in this joining, the slapping of flesh against flesh as he takes me from behind, no longer wondering who this lover is or what the consequences will be if he isn't mine. For now, I am enjoying the ride, the way he fills my pussy with his wand, which seems to sparkle inside of my wet folds, energizing me with its rhythm and song.

I am pressed into the wall, my breasts mashed by his powerful body. But I am not complaining. The sensations, which I feel at this moment are localized at my core but expanding outward like a supernova, are indescribable.

Behind me, he is grunting in time with his frenzied thrusts, a hurried cadence not at all unlike techno. His powerful hands are palming my ass cheeks as his fingers squeeze my flesh, dizzying my senses with his spells and incantations. This, my friends, is further evidence that the man behind me is *not* Damon.

Damon doesn't *behave* like this. . . .

Before I have time to fully contemplate this notion he exits me quickly, and like a balloon losing its air, I feel the sudden emptiness, a void where he once existed, and I'm left twitching like a junkie, longing for one more delicious fix, if just for a fleeting moment more.

I find we are moving again, my fingernails scraping against the wall as my captor leads me toward my next surprise. I am calling out Damon's name and yelling for my abductor to slow down, panting as my words catch in my throat, but my shouts go unheeded. We slow, I hear my captor whisper a single word that becomes a command: "Step," and I am climbing once again. Before long, we reach a landing and take a sharp turn to the right. I am breathing heavily from the exertion—both sexual and physical. Then another set of stairs presents itself and I am forced to climb. I choose this moment to pause stubbornly, pulling back on my captor's arm, demanding to know where I'm being led. Simultaneously I reach for my blindfold, but my hand is slapped away.

The nighttime air hits me without warning. We are outside; I can feel a light gentle breeze on my skin. I hear sounds—the din of the distant evening traffic, muted conversations, an occasional honk or blaring of music from a car stereo as someone passes by. And something else—I hear water. Running water. I turn my head toward the source as I'm led forward.

" 'Bout time," a female voice says. "I was beginning to wonder."

The voice is familiar, but I can't place it.

"Just warming her up for ya," the guy with the sexy tenor responds.

"Yeah? Well bring her on over."

The sound of running water is louder as we move farther into the nighttime air.

"Watch yourself," the male voice says, taking my arms and placing them down in front of me on cold concrete. Flecks of water spatter against my face. Instinctively, I straighten up, but he is there behind me, blocking my exit. His hands are tracing slow circular patterns along my dress from the middle of my back to my ass, and his touch is magnetic. I feel a shiver as it traverses my spine. A pair of hands grasp my head and gently pull me forward.

"Come to mama," the female voice intones.

Before I can respond my nose brushes against coarse hair. My face is tilted upward, guided by soft hands, and I inhale the scent of a woman. My heart is racing and my arms are trembling. I place them on the cool cement for support as I feel cool drops of water against my forearms. There are so many thoughts flowing through my head at this moment. Everything is happening so fast. I try to ascertain my surroundings: the sound and feel of running water, cool cement, distant automobile sounds, this female who is hauntingly familiar, but then all of that fades to oblivion as I am guided to this woman's pussy.

Her lips brush against mine. I feel the rise of her flesh. It is warm on my mouth and I slowly, almost imperceptibly, move my head to the right so that I can feel her along the length of my lips. When I lose contact, I retreat the way I came, this time parting my lips as I take in a deep breath, swallowing her womanly scent, and taste a woman for the very first time.

The first thing I notice is that her vulva is soft and smooth. I run my tongue upward along the shaft of her lips; like a flower they part, revealing sweet nectar within. She gasps as I taste her. I take my time, letting her sap coat the tip of my tongue, glazing me with its flavor before it disappears into my mouth as I swallow it down. From behind me, my lover has raised my dress; I part my legs automatically and in one fluid motion he stuffs his beast within me. The movement thrusts me forward. My tongue, which had been darting teasingly between the soft folds of her sex as if playing hide-and-seek, is suddenly thrust deep into her waiting canal. She grips my head tightly as I feel her thighs surround my shoulders. I exhale forcefully and groan against her cunt as I'm being pummeled from behind, my palms pressing into concrete, the sound of rushing water intoxicating, the gentle breeze setting my dress and hair in motion as cool drops splatter against my hot skin.

I reach up for support, my hands gliding along supple thighs to stomach, upward to her tits, which hang defiantly. They are heavy, yet soft to the touch; hard nipples surrounded by waxy areolas that I caress as her whimpers meet my own. As I grit my teeth, I concentrate on squeezing my lover's manhood tight with my own sex, encircling him within my juicy tunnel in an effort to slow him down. But he is unrelenting—a piston that keeps cranking in and out, in and out, with no letup in sight. And so, I give in to the sensations that wash through me—this delicious feeling of receiving and giving love in tandem. A thread of energy passes from this unknown male lover through my body to hers as we unite, three strangers who connect for the express purpose of making passionate love. It's a feeling beyond description—when you gaze upon naked flesh, shivering in anticipation as he enters you for the first time. And I am not ashamed nor do I feel polluted. This force that flows through our bodies is too delectable to ignore.

A sound off to the left startles us in mid-movement. A cough and a voice pierce our reverie.

"Think I've had enough of this."

A voice I know all too well.

Damon's.

"Baby?" I shout.

Behind me, my male lover has slowed his thrusting. He pats my ass as if saying good-bye and then backs away, pausing as the head breaches my engorged pussy lips, allowing both of us one last second of tactile pleasure before he pulls completely out. In front of me, my female friend too has disengaged herself from me, and I am left with her scent and taste on my tongue as it darts between my teeth, searching for more sustenance. Her hand tussles my hair once before she moves away.

"Was wondering when you were gonna join in," my lover says. I straighten up as my dress cascades down my thighs. I use this opportunity to tear the blindfold away from my eyes.

We are outdoors on some kind of rooftop deck. In front of me is a circular fountain. Tables and chairs litter the deck surface. Damon, to the left by the ledge, is sitting back in one of the chairs, fully clothed as he stares unblinkingly at me. On the table nearby is a martini glass and an ashtray that holds a smoldering cigar. He grasps it gingerly between his fingers before placing it to his lips and taking a long puff. All the while, his eyes never leave me. He cocks his head to the side toward my male lover, a tall, dark man, clad only in a tight black T-shirt that shows off his muscles. I can't help but notice he is well endowed. His head is shaved and his eyes are dark. He is unfamiliar to me. He shoots me a smile that I have trouble returning. Next to him stands a curvy nude woman who reaches for Damon's cigar as she eyes me curiously. Her short caramel hair stands out even in the shadows of nightfall, and suddenly I recognize her from downstairs—the woman who spoke to me as I was heading to the ladies' room. That moment seems like a lifetime ago with all that has transpired between us.

I am frozen in place but will myself to move. Damon's voice stops me in my tracks.

"Bitch!"

"What did you say?" I ask, my eyes blinking rapidly.

"You heard me. I see you're having about as much fun as one can have," Damon responds with a hiss.

"What's up, boo?" the woman beside him asks, raking his arm with a fingernail. "Why you tripping? I thought this was your idea."

"It was," Damon quipped, taking a quick drag on the cigar that the woman returns to him. "But I thought girlfriend was at least gonna wait before getting this party started. Guess I was wrong."

"Damon, what are you talking about?" I am standing directly in front of him, glancing downward. He looks so good lying there in the molded plastic seat, his flat stomach and sinewy muscles seemed to come to life when he shifts his weight. "I . . . don't know what you're saying . . . I thought you were down with this . . . I thought you were playing along, waiting—"

"For what?" he interrupts. "Waiting for what, Josey?" Damon eyes me with disdain. My heart is beating fast and I feel a shiver race across my skin. My male lover takes a swig from a wine bottle and hands it to the woman.

"Hey, dude, what's up? I thought everything was cool." He is still semi-hard and makes no attempt to cover himself up. I flick my eyes over his body, shivering with the memory of the way he impaled me with that succulent piece of meat. Quickly, I glance away.

"I'm cool with both of you," Damon says, glancing between the two of them. "It's her I've taken issue with."

"Damon—I don't understand," I say.

"It's simple, really," Damon responds, getting up while downing the rest of his martini. I step back, not out of fear, but because I suddenly feel intensely uncomfortable inside his space. "This whole thing was actually a test, Josey. A test that you failed."

"What?" I implore. "What kind of test?"

"I wanted to see what you would do—given the circumstance—without me—"

"Without you? What are you talking about?" I yell, flailing my arms high. "You've been here the entire time. You set this up, you just admitted that."

"Yes, Josey, but you didn't know that. I wanted to see how far you'd go. In the room downstairs you didn't know if I was there or not, but you didn't let that stop you. You proceeded to get it on, *without* me. Same thing in the hallway. You didn't pause to think about what you were doing, fucking some guy without me being there! No, you just proceeded along as if I didn't exist."

The woman walks behind Damon and wraps her arms around his frame, nuzzling her chin in his neck. Her hand snakes down to fondle him.

"Come on, Damon," she says. "This is getting a bit too serious, don't you think? I thought we were all down for some fun," I hear her remark as she eyes me.

"I was . . ."

I've had about as much as I can stand.

"Let me get this straight, Damon," I say, my eyes laser beams as they stare straight through him. "You set this up—you were willing to have your friend or whoever this guy is over there fuck me, and her, too," I add, pointing to the woman stroking his hardening dick. "As long as I what—asked your permission? Oh, and I see that didn't stop you from partaking in certain pleasures."

Damon is silent as he watches me. I shake my head contemptuously.

I turn to leave as I smooth the wrinkles from my dress. I get about six feet before I twist to face them.

"You know what? Fuck it and fuck you!" I exclaim before I spin on my heels and stroll toward the exit.

"You're just a whore!" Damon yells.

That comment causes me to cease my movement. I stand perfectly still, my back to the three of them, my chest heaving as I'm fuming inside. There are so many things that I want to say, and my eyes dart around for something to throw his way. But then a calm overtakes me as I recall the luscious passion that coursed through my veins earlier. My legs are still wobbly from the intense fucking, and I can feel the stickiness between my thighs. I lick my lips slowly and taste *her*.

I smile to myself as I pivot to Damon one last time.

"You have no idea," I say to my lovers and wink.

And with that I am gone, like a wisp of cigar smoke, into the ether, and out of sight.

Bon Appétit

James E. Cherry

"Please, James."

She wanted me to eat her pussy. But brothers don't do that. Not real brothers, anyway.

"Please, James," she cooed, lying on her back, legs wide open, with me sucking her left breast, the nipple firm against my tongue like a hard piece of candy. "I'm so wet." She took my hand and plunged it toward her crotch, my middle finger making a splash upon entrance. My penis ached with stiffness.

Saliva drooled from the corner of my mouth as I reluctantly came up for exasperated air. We had been through this before.

"Baby, I ain't down with that. Literally ain't down wit it." My hand was now wandering through the wilderness of her thickly tangled bush.

"But you never tell me why."

"Ain't no why."

"Well, how can you complain about something you've never had? I enjoy doing it to you and I ain't complaining."

"Hey." I smiled. "I ain't complaining when you do it either.

Just seems more natural for a woman to do it for a man, though."

"Why? I like to feel good, too. I don't always cum when we have intercourse. I want to feel your mouth on me sometimes." Her voice became heavy with sadness. "Do you not like the way I smell? You have an odor, too, you know."

"What do I smell like?"

"Like dick."

"Look." I was now lying on my back, penis limp as a deflated balloon, hands clasped behind my head, eyes closed, trying to sort and rearrange the many thoughts scattered in my mind. "When I was coming up in the 'hood, if a brother did that the other homeboys would kick him to the curb and call him weak; a chump. You were considered a pussy if you ate pussy. You're my woman and I want to make you happy, please you, but . . . I just need a little more time with that." Suddenly, my mind cleared with a sweeping thought. "Let's do it doggie-style!"

I tried to flip her on all fours but she karate-chopped me to the ribs and sent me flat on my back again. "No." She was atop me like a professional wrestler going for a three count. "Doggie-style hasn't anything to do with it. How many years has it been since you were raised in the 'hood? And not only that, you're not in a relationship with the homeboys. You're in a relationship with me, and if we're going to be and stay in this relationship, we both have to take as well as give. We've been seeing each other for six months and I ain't got no head yet. And you better be careful. The statute of limitations is running out on blowjobs."

"The what?"

Her nose flared slightly, and her soft hazel eyes stared at me from under neatly arched eyebrows. Her black curls spiraled just past her earlobes complementing her polished pearl teeth. Through slightly parted lips, she kissed me as I whispered, "Sharon."

"You like fruit?"

I smiled back at her and stroked her neck with my index finger. "What you talking 'bout, girl? Is the statute of limitations running out on fruit, too?"

"Maybe." She pushed herself up. "Pour yourself another drink."

"Where you going, baby?"

Her firm, brown behind bouncing away from me was her only reply. I really wanted doggie-style now. Instead, I poured a glass of cabernet sauvignon, the sound of the red liquid filling the room. Horace Silver's compact disc was already loaded on the machine and when I punched play, Hank Mobley was soloing. The more wine I sipped, the more I became one with the silk sheets and puffy pillows. The whole room was soft, powdery, and smelled of perfume the way a woman's room should smell. Two scented candles flickered from the nightstands, adding another dimension of sensuousness to the ambiance.

Suddenly, out of the darkness in the room, a thought illuminated my mind. What did Sharon mean, did I like fruit? She knew I ate fruit for breakfast every morning. Hell, the birthmark on my ass is a strawberry. What was that all about?

Lying there with a furrowed brow, my thoughts swirling around imported wine, jazz, and inebriated smells, I could hear light switches flipping off and the sound of bare feet slapping against kitchen linoleum. She entered the room with a bowl of fruit in one hand and a smile playing at the corners of her mouth. She lay beside me, taking a succulent wet strawberry and feeding me until I nibbled gently upon her fingertips. Then she grabbed another berry, slid down in the bed, spread her legs, and pushed the red fruit inside her vagina.

"I like lobster, too," I said. "You think that'll fit in there? Damn. You played me, girl."

Starting deep within the valley between her breasts, my tongue avalanched down her stomach, over her navel, inside the thigh of one leg, around her ten toes and back up to the inside of another thigh, and then I was face-to-face with a fruit cunttail.

"Wait, wait." She rose on one elbow, sipped some wine, and then motioned me to proceed. Like a kid forced to eat brussels sprouts, I held my breath, inhaling deeply the smell of wetness and excitement. As if she were a chocolate ice cream cone, I licked and licked and licked until my tongue was going in circular motions, coming to a rest like a roulette wheel on her clitoris. Sharon began to moan and purr and rotate her hips and stroke my bald head as though it were a penis, all the while murmuring, "Oh, James. You make my pussy feel so good." Then, with her hands still on my head, she began to thrust against my tongue deeper and faster, each thrust punctuated with oohs and ahhs until I sucked the strawberry into my mouth and she screamed and convulsed from orgasmic fury.

I rose to my knees, chewing the fruit meticulously, savoring its taste, licking my lips for any remaining juices, swallowing every morsel. And it was good, too.

Before the night was through, I had devoured five strawberries, half a pound of grapes, two pears, sliced peaches, three plums, a banana, half an apple, two oranges, a kiwi, and something called a kumquat (whatever the hell that is).

"You got any pineapple, baby?" I asked in all seriousness, wiping my mouth with the back of my hand.

Hours passed as we made more love and drank and giggled

and stroked one another and rested. She cuddled in the crook of my arm, both of us basking in ecstasy's afterglow. Thelonious Monk was playing now.

"James." Her voice sounded far away, dripping with sugar.

"Yeah, baby."

"Is there any more fruit left?"

"I think so."

"Can you lick my ass?"

I bolted from the bed, scooped my clothes up in a ball, tossed a hat on my head, and tried to balance the act of running while stepping into my pants simultaneously, but not before stubbing my toe and smacking my forehead against a wall.

"Hell, naw!" I shouted, before closing the front door behind me, stepping out into the cool pink dawn, barefoot, then slowing my gait and reminiscing about the remaining grapes and oranges I had left by the bedside. What a nutritional waste it would be for them to spoil. After all, breakfast is indeed the most important meal of the day.

First Time Blues: A Real-Life Tale of Lost Virginity

Fredric Sellers

Fresh out of boot camp at Parris Island, I was more than ready to face the world as a tried and proven man . . . a U.S. Marine. This was my first time being on my own, away from home. I was nineteen and still had my virginity, not to say that I haven't experienced sex. I've had many near hits, but was headed off at the pass, so to speak.

Believe me, I knew what blue balls were, oh, how many times. The girls in my day allowed you to feel their forbidden parts and even on occasion, to dry fuck . . . but they seldom went further than that. They would send you home harder than times in '29. Thank God for Bayer aspirins and hot water. It wasn't until years later that I found out that the girls were getting their cookies and sending us boys home hurting.

On with my story. Upon graduation from boot camp, I was transferred to Camp Lejeune, North Carolina. After a short time there, I went on my first long weekend leave with my new buddies to Wilmington. We traveled by bus, anticipating having a much-needed sexually fulfilling weekend.

Upon arriving in Wilmington, our first order of the day was to find the train tracks and do the crossover into black land.

The three of us finally found a party that was going on at a house on the main drag. People were out on the porch talking, drinking, and some doing weed. They didn't pay much attention to us as we passed them and entered the house. We walked down a long hallway with rooms on either side. At the end of it, there was a large room where a crowd was dancing to the music from a huge jukebox over in the corner. A few tables and chairs were positioned along the walls.

The room was dark, with the exception of one blue light bulb in the ceiling. You could barely see who you were dancing with, or talking to. We split up to do our own thing, which was all right with me because I've always been a loner anyway. I just stood at a spot close to the wall, which gave me a good vantage point from which I could see at least a little of the crowd. I didn't want to be too quick in making a move on any of the women. I was told once that the people down in these southern towns weren't too cool about strangers hitting on their local women. I definitely wasn't looking for war . . . I was looking for love.

I was in luck. I was approached by a foxy, full-figured woman. I mean, she was filled out nice: full bosomed, big shapely legs, and an ass as tight as a window seal! She was on the dark side and with long straight black hair. She had the prettiest smile I'd seen in a long time and light gray eyes to boot. This combination was strange to me, but she was beautiful in her own odd way.

Her name was Pearlie Mae. I'm serious! Talk about a fitting name! Well anyway, she came on strong to me. We talked for a while, and danced on every slow drag that came on. I was really getting a taste of that southern charm I'd heard so much about. This creature was a real joy to talk to. I felt comfortable with her right away.

It wasn't long before she started turning up the heat on me. I could feel her stomach muscles rippling when she pressed her body into mine as we danced. She buried her face under my chin, breathing deep and hot. The fragrance of her warm body filled my nose, causing me to feel warm and lusty. Damn, this woman was turning me on big time. I got bold and embraced her with both arms, with my hands lightly gripping both of her cheeks. I got no resistance from her. Man, I was in my world. My dick was hard and poked into her big time, and she responded by pressing closer. This was one time I was glad the lights were practically nonexistent. Pearlie Mae was the only person I danced with or talked to that night.

After much talk and belly-rubbing, she asked me if I was staying the weekend and where. I told her I hadn't thought that far ahead yet. She just came out and told me that it wasn't necessary to spend money on a hotel, when I could stay with her. *I couldn't believe I was having that kind of luck!*

She took my hand and led me out of the house and down the sidewalk. We'd only walked a short distance when she stopped and wrapped her arms around me, and kissed me full and deep. Before I could catch my breath, she had placed her warm hands lightly over my crotch and slowly started rubbing me . . . all this in the middle of the sidewalk! I just knew this was going to be a night to remember. We continued walking and talking . . . and stroking. I was relishing every bit of this action.

Now check this out. All of a sudden she stopped short and left me standing alone as she started running up a driveway between two houses . . . pulling up her skirt as she ran. I said to myself, Damn, she just couldn't wait till we got to her place, she wanted to do something now. Shiiiit, I was all for this carrying-on! I followed her up the drive while unbuckling my belt and unzipping my pants.

Pearlie disappeared in the rear of one of the houses, and by the time I caught up with her, my pants were down below my knees and my dick was sticking out of my shorts. I was ready! My jaws dropped to my chest when I saw her. She was in a full squat, and piss was coming out of her like water out of a faucet. I swear! She looked at me in a cute way and said, "A girl got to do what a girl got to do." I felt a little embarrassed as I pulled up my pants and put everything back in order. I thought to myself that I couldn't wait to tell my buddies about this shit! But I knew I wouldn't, because I've always been very closemouthed about my business.

We continued our walk to her place. After a few blocks, we turned up a small dirt street across from some hole-in-the-wall joint. Low-down-and-dirty blues was playing loud. We walked a short ways, passing a row of old small houses, finally reaching hers. I watched her from behind as she climbed the three short steps to her porch. The sensuous way her body moved aroused me again. At first I thought the way she swayed her hips was exaggerated, but I soon realized that it was her natural walk. I still couldn't believe my luck!

She unlocked the door, then grabbed my hand and led me in. I could smell kerosene lamps she used for light . . . there was no electricity. It was a small place. One bedroom, a living room, and a kitchen. Seating me in a sofa chair, she lit one of the lamps. Even though I was amazed at the lack of anything modern, I could deal with it. The only thing I had on my mind was getting next to this pretty thing.

Pearlie sat down on the arm of the chair I was sitting in, and slowly eased down into my lap. She put her arms around me and kissed me, then asked me:

"Fred, have you ever fucked the girl you love?"

I didn't answer her because I didn't understand why she asked me that. Actually, I hadn't fucked anybody yet, and I was too embarrassed to reveal that fact. She leaned back and asked me another question that really shook me.

"Are you a virgin, Fred?" she asked with a little smile on her lips.

"Now, why did you ask me that?" I responded, avoiding her eyes.

"You're a virgin. I can tell." She said this with a broader smile. "My goodness, I have a virgin on my hands."

After saying that, she hugged my embarrassed ass tighter and whispered in my ear, "Don't worry, baby . . . relax. Pearlie going to teach you good tonight."

Then she kissed me again.

Sliding off my lap, she walked over to her icebox, opened it, and took out a half-pint bottle. Getting two glasses off a shelf, she walked back over to me again and sat on my lap, this time straddling me, crushing her warm mound against me. Damn! The heat from her crotch brought my dick to attention.

"Have you ever drank any White Lightning?" she asked as she poured half the bottle in each glass.

"No, I never have," I responded nervously, trying to maintain my cool.

She slowly started moving her hips, grinding down on me, and purred in her soft southern drawl, "Sugar, you're my baby tonight. I'm taking good care of you."

Pearlie took my hand with the glass in it and brought it up to my lips. If a person ever drank White Lightning, they would never forget it. It looked like water, but believe me it didn't taste like water. After a short while my head was spinning. I was feeling good! My crotch was wet with pre-cum. Believe me, I was more then ready to be taught.

Pearlie backed off me, unfastened her tight-fitting skirt, and stepped out of it. God, she had a body on her. I began having doubts whether I would survive this night. She then unbuttoned her blouse and took off her bra, letting them both fall into my lap, baring her full, well-shaped breasts. Pearlie watched my eyes as she took my hands and pulled me to my feet. She unbuckled my belt, then unzipped my pants and let them drop to the floor. I stepped out of them and took off my shirt. She then pulled down my shorts . . . and jerked her head back a little.

"My goodness! Freddie has a nice one, doesn't he?"

Pearlie sank down to her knees and slowly brought her full lips to the head of my dick and kissed it. I never had anyone do that to me before.

She looked up at me and whispered, "And this is just the beginning."

Pearlie stood up and took my hand again and led me over to the bed. She pushed me back on the bed and then peeled her panties down and stepped out of them, leaving her stockings on. Climbing up on the bed, she straddled my chest and leaned over and stretched my arms out to the side.

Pearlie looked me in the eyes and softly said, "I want you to taste my forbidden fruit tonight."

There was no question in my mind of what she meant. I could smell the scent of her sex and it deeply aroused me. I had never been this close to any pussy before.

"Freddie, do you want to taste me? Do you want to know what I taste like?" she said as she scooted up closer to my face.

Her crotch was nestled softly against my chin, and I could feel the wetness of her love juices as she moved her hips, spreading the moisture over my chin and lips. I thought I was going to faint.

"Lick me, Fred, let me feel your tongue. I want you to like it."

Lifting up and lowering herself slowly over my searching tongue, she started oscillating, barely letting her love nest touch my mouth. I was overwhelmed by the fragrance of her sex. At first, I was a little hesitant, but then I said to myself, it wasn't anything that soap and water couldn't clean up.

Pearlie released my hands and placed her hands down to her damp mound and spread herself wide.

"See my rosebud . . . touch it lightly with your tongue," she said as she looked down at me. "You're making me feel good, Freddie."

Without thinking, I cupped both of her full breasts, feeling their softness, soft as cotton. She started moving her hips, sliding her love nest across my face, as I flicked my tongue across her rosebud. I listened to her moan and groan and whimper as an uncontrollable lust built up in her. I couldn't believe that this was me, making love to a woman in this way . . . and liking it.

"Baby, hold up for a second, let me turn around," she said.

She turned her voluptuous body so that her sensual ass was over my face, and placed her mouth in a position directly over my hardness.

"Just relax, baby, and let Pearlie make you feel good."

Believe me, I was in a strange new world, and I was liking it more and more.

I felt her hot breath on my swollen dick, then felt her warm tongue licking it up and down. Her fingernails lightly stroked the bottom of my balls, sending a delightful sensation throughout my trembling body. Wrapping my arms around her ample ass and pulling her wet, hairy love mound down to my seeking mouth, I slid my tongue into her warm tunnel. I was tasting the pussy of a woman for the first time . . . a woman I never knew before tonight. Then it happened. I felt my hardened dick sinking into her warm wet mouth. My whole body shook and trembled as she slowly sucked me in. I felt the rippling of her tongue as she took my whole shaft, nursing it, milking it. My nose was inhaling the scent of her hot pussy as my tongue thrust deeper into her tunnel. I could feel the walls of her pussy snatching at and clinching my probing tongue. This exchange of love lasted for a long while. We were both in our own world . . . nothing else existed. Pearlie released me just when I thought I was going to explode.

"Fred, I want you to fuck me . . . now . . . please," she said as she rolled off me and lay on her back, spreading her full thighs. "Come on, baby, take me," she hissed.

She pulled me on top of her hot moist body, settling me in her waiting nest. With no assistance, my love pole found her and sank deep into her quivering pussy. She hugged me hard as I pressed deeper into her. Burying our heads between the huge pillows, we kissed hungrily, growling and grunting. I felt her gripping my shaft hard with the trembling muscles of her tunnel.

I often fantasized, but never came close to thinking that fucking was like this . . . never dreamed it would suck at your soul. Oh, how I wanted this to last, never wanting it to end. I stroked and gave, she received and nursed. We merged into one, exchanging our energies, our hungers.

"Come, baby, give it up for Pearlie . . . give it up, sugar."

Then I could feel it happening and she knew it, too. She locked her legs around mine as we pressed our bodies hard into each other. Thrusting my swollen dick deep into her, dead-poling . . . mixing our love juices . . . straining and pressing. Then she clamped down on my dick with her quivering pussy, and held me . . . and milked me till there was nothing left to milk . . . then she just nursed me gently . . . ever so gently. We both fell asleep . . . spent . . . satisfied.

Yes, I gave up my virginity and I'm not ashamed to admit it. I'm thankful it happened the way it did, and grateful for Pearlie, the woman who took it.

The Party

Robert Scott Adams

The Further Adventures of Carlotta and Miguel

Southern California, there's nothing like it. More than anything else, the weather combined with the almost limitless scenic variety makes it understandable why thousands of people relocate there every year, and lifelong inhabitants steadfastly commit to spending their lives there even though the area may one day end up as an island.

That's why, when the opportunity arose for Miguel and Carlotta to meet on the coast, specifically Los Angeles, Miguel jumped at the chance.

This trip would require that Miguel interview a trio of mixed-media artists from South America, Brazil, who were about to become the next big thing on the American scene. The trio of two men and one woman were already celebrated in all the major artistic centers in Europe, Canada, and most of South America. And they were recently featured in New York, Washington, D.C., and Chicago. But for all their triumphs they felt the west coast offered what they wanted: ac-

260

cess to everything including movies and television. Their mixed-media collection ranged from architecture and paintings, to sculpture and design.

So as a result they planted the seeds of success all the way across America, planning to end in Los Angeles. In fact, they planned a huge reception in a renovated barn on Highway 101 somewhere between L.A. and San Francisco. This reception would feature paintings, furniture, and other examples of their talents. In fact, Angelo, one of the artists in the group, had redone the barn. This reception would give those in both the entertainment and artistic communities the opportunity to experience this unique trio.

So Miguel was to be one of the interviewers tasked with attending the reception and capturing the essence of this group on paper.

But at this moment Miguel was capturing a different type of essence. He and Carlotta were speeding up the Pacific Coast Highway in a convertible Porsche. The warm ocean breeze circled throughout the open vehicle as it sped up the highway. The ocean crashed against the rocks below as the road narrowed on the way out of Malibu toward the north. The sun was about forty-five minutes from setting so it was still warm and visibility was good, good enough for Miguel to be able to see the road ahead and also see Carlotta's head in his lap as she gave him one of the best blowjobs he'd ever had in his life.

This was one of Miguel's most endearing fantasies, and Carlotta was making it a reality as she sucked loudly and fiercely as they neared their destination.

"Oh shit, baby, damn that's great." Even though he'd gotten blowjobs while driving before, it was never in a Porsche, going over seventy miles an hour.

They'd met in Los Angeles earlier that day. When Miguel came out of the baggage claim area at LAX, there she was in a champagne Porsche convertible. She was dressed in a beautiful black chiffon dress that showed off her beautiful semi-sweet-chocolate-looking skin. She was smiling broadly behind sunglasses. As he approached, she climbed out of the car. The dress was short and showed off her amazing legs. And she was wearing the Charles David shoes, the ones that had the wide strap around the ankle. The ones that made her look like a really expensive L.A. call girl. He was dressed in a black raw silk and linen suit. The sun reflected off his bald head as he slowly walked toward her. He threw his bag in the back and before he could get around to the driver's side to her, she had already come up to him. As she thrust the keys into his hand, she wrapped her arms around him and pressed her lips against his as she thrust her tongue deep into his mouth. Their bodies crushed together as always, making her wet and him hard. It was a patented response that occurred every time they got together; whether they touched or not.

"Welcome to sunny California. Now I got you on *my* side of the world." She pulled him close so she could whisper in his ear. "Damn, not only do you look good you smell good, too. You're in big trouble now. Get in."

"You look great," he said, glancing over at her. As they headed out the Pacific Coast Highway, the smell of the ocean combined with the breeze created the perfect backdrop for the drive. He noticed how her dress had wandered up her thighs, which were encased in black sheer thigh-highs. To accommodate his view, she spread her thighs apart ever so slightly and the dress did its best to provide him with the view she knew he wanted. It was at that point that Carlotta began to play with him. As the car sped up the coast, she leaned over and planted small, yet sensual kisses on his neck, cheek, and lips. If he turned to get a better angle to kiss her, she would playfully slap him.

"Keep your eyes on the road."

So he had to rely on his peripheral vision to see how she was preparing to challenge his driving ability. He didn't have to wonder for long, as he felt her hands unzipping his pants. The zipper easily disengaged and out popped his already rock-hard dick. He had an erection like a church steeple. She looked at it and thought it as sensual as a ripe, thick-veined, dark fruit.

Sex to them was a dance, a romantic, aural, and visual interplay. It combined both love and lust. It came easy, without any active or aggressive prodding or solicitation. It was like when a strong wind approached, and to feel it you only had to turn your face. Yes, they lusted after each other. Their needs stuck out, like a porcupine's needles. At times, his desire for her was almost crippling, as if he'd been solidly smacked in the back of his knees by a baseball bat. When he reached for her she responded with her own level of desire. In describing it to a friend she once said her passion and desire for Miguel "makes me so wild, it's like all I am is liquid, like mercury."

After months of going without each other they would finally meet, and both were as ravenous as sea gulls over a fishing boat.

The last time they met it was in the spring in D.C. Carlotta was there attending a conference. Miguel lived in Philadelphia, so it was easy to get to her. But really, what difference did distance make anyway? This relationship had been going on for as long as Carlotta was married. Yes, she was married. Yet they maintained this long-distance love affair for the past decade. But neither the years nor distance could erode the intense passion they shared. This shared passion escaped in a love battle. It was as if they fought each other to see who would provide the other one with the most immediate amount of pleasure.

This time Carlotta would win, as she lowered her face into Miguel's lap and began to ravage his rigid member. At first she lightly swirled her tongue around the dark swollen head. To Carlotta, it was as tasty as the summer's first fruit, almost like strawberries that were so sweet they didn't need additional sugar. It didn't take long for the intensity of her passion to increase as she began to salivate all over him. At the same time, Miguel was struggling to concentrate on the single-lane road that provided him very little opportunity to lose himself in the pleasure Carlotta was giving him. Yet it was still a thrill.

If he couldn't spend all his time staring at her gorgeous mouth as it engulfed him, he could enjoy the sounds she made as she nearly swallowed him. She gurgled like a content baby who had locked in on its mother's breast. She even made little sounds that demonstrated how enjoyable the entire procedure was.

The sun had nearly set, triggering the onset of the cool California night. Invariably, Miguel's once-sturdy erection began to shrink when the convertible became surrounded by the sudden gusts of ocean-affected air; for some reason water and cool air had that effect on him.

Undaunted, Carlotta increased her sucking as she was determined to bring Miguel to orgasm and fill her mouth with as much cum as she could swallow. So as she increased her attack on him, he began to pump vigorously. His hips strained like a dangerously stretched rubber band as his back became rigid, his stomach knotted up, and he could feel an abrupt rush of semen seeping out, quivering on the head of his cock like a drop of hot wax.

"Umph!" was Carlotta's response. She knew that within

seconds she was going to get what she wanted and that made her even greedier.

But the ride from L.A. to the party wasn't as far as it took for Miguel to come, and as he saw the silhouette of the barn coming up quickly on his left he had to take a sharp turn off the highway into the parking lot, which made Carlotta jerk up from his lap to see what had happened.

"Damnit!" she cursed, anger spreading up through her like a fever, her mouth still glistening from the lather she'd worked up on Miguel's dick. "We almost did it! Damn, I hate that! Why did you have to turn so fast?"

Even with darkness setting in, he could see the rage in her eyes. He slowly navigated the sports car to an open space. "Baby, I didn't mean to. But we were . . . everything happened so fast, and there was this car on my ass. If I'd kept going, we'd have missed the turn, and—"

"If you'd kept going, you would've come. You always could've turned around and circled back . . . shit!"

She was pissed. He parked the car and began to zip his pants.

"What the hell are you doing? You still owe me and I'm not letting you out of this car until you give it to me."

"Darling, I've got a job to do and it would take as long for me to come as it took us to get here. We can do this later."

"Fuck that! I hate that. I haven't seen you for two months. You get me all worked up, thinking I was gonna get some come, and then you pull out on me? It's your fault, now give it here."

She lunged at his zipper. When she felt how wet his pants were, she immediately stopped. A sheepish look came over her face.

"I guess we gotta get you cleaned up, huh? It's a good thing these pants are dark." She had conceded. Miguel pulled his handkerchief from inside his black suit jacket and handed it to Carlotta. As she attempted to make his pants somewhat presentable, Miguel started the car, closed the top, and ran the heater. It was obvious from the way Carlotta cleaned away at his crotch that she was a little embarrassed.

In the middle of her efforts, Miguel stopped her, took her head in his hands, and brought her face close to his. Her lips were red and slightly swollen, perfect for the kiss Miguel planted on her. It was wet and soft, like velvet. The kiss always elicited a rush of emotion between them and in this instance, made Carlotta relax again.

"Don't worry about the pants. That's why they have dry cleaners. You felt great, okay? There's nothing to be embarrassed about. I owe you, okay? As soon as we get out of here, we're going to that hotel up the coast and we can resume this. I apologize, okay?"

This relationship was dependent upon open communication and negotiation. Miguel had just used both of those attributes to diffuse what could've been a contentious situation. That's why she loved him. Even in the heat of passion, he took the time to talk with her and assure her that everything was all right.

They got out of the car and walked toward the barn. Even though neither of them had seen it prior to the renovation, they were both amazed at the sheer magnificence of the structure. What was once a huge shell, empty and desolate, had been transformed into a palace, adorned with wide, glossy, inviting panels of what appeared to be redwood, mixed with great sheath-like glass windows that ran almost the entire length of the three-story building.

Inside, the personality of the structure stood out like the personalities of the people who built it. Like chiffon cakes, it was decorated with soft, pleasant surface colors. The colors, textured furniture, and accompanying artwork of sculptures, paintings and other works were obviously designed to sway the emotions of the attendees. Amid all the modern newness of the decorations was a certain gracefulness the artists had allowed to remain, yet it exuded a peculiar suggestive heaviness, trapping the traditional pride that once housed a family's past, yet still managing to remain pleasing and graceful.

The first floor was filled with twenty-foot-plus sculptures made of every imaginable type of rock, wood, and even synthetic materials. Each artist was responsible for different sections of each floor. Aaron, the leader and organizer of the group, greeted Carlotta and Miguel as they entered. He was a short, medium-built, tanned man in his late thirties. He was dressed in a cranberry ribbed sweater and black gabardine pants. He wore a black beret over his apparently bald head. "Make yourselves comfortable and enjoy the experience. The food and drinks are on the second floor along with some large screens placed around the floor so you can view some of our animated presentations. The other members of our group are upstairs also. The third floor is strictly paintings by Cameron. It's not necessarily open to the public; however, should you desire a private tour, either Cameron or Ciao will be happy to take you. All of the works you see here are for sale, including the platforms and stands, as they have also been designed by our group." With that, Aaron escorted them through the first floor.

Sometimes you can close your eyes, reopen them, and then play "guess what city we're in." In many cases, the answer could be any of the major or medium-sized markets around America.

But the people who live and operate in California, especially Los Angeles, have a different look. First of all, the

women were all beautiful; outstanding beauties like outstanding gifts. They were dressed in Hollywood clothes. The
women wore colors that were as soft as a Mediterranean
dawn, or as clear as freshly cut flowers. The clothes fit as if
they'd been made for the women who wore them. The men
were tailored and frocked like pampered gigolos. And they all
looked comfortable, as if they were sleeping on clouds. The
animated conversations were basically understated leap-
frogging, sparring, and prone to showing off. Yet there was
always a smaller number of conversations flowing like cross-
winds, and they came like grain spilling from a sack, in bursts
of fullness that were shut off in mid-sentence as if someone
had closed the sack abruptly and there was more talk inside.
Yet the guests moved effortlessly and seemingly unattached.

As Miguel and Carlotta were guided to the bottom of the
stairs that led to the second floor, Aaron pointed to a group of
two women and three men and said, "Please focus your attention on that lady in the black dress holding court over there.
That's Ciao, our fabric designer and media specialist. You really should speak with her about our projects, because she is
the pulse of this creation, if you will. She is the one who convinced us to expand this effort to include America; especially
the west coast. She is passionate and full of life and, as you can
see, beautiful."

As they approached Ciao, it was obvious who the dynamo
of the group was. Ciao was a peanut-butter-colored lady with
short black hair. Like most of the women in attendance, she
was also beautiful, actually quite extraordinary, as if she were
painted. And as she spoke, people gathered close to hear her.
They huddled together like dark grapes clustered on a stalk.
Her words tumbled out like coins from a change dispenser
and people clung to her every word with rapt attention.

Aaron stood next to Carlotta and Miguel and beamed like

a proud father after his child had won a spelling bee as Ciao described the artwork and the renovation of the barn, discussed when the impending art sale was to occur, as well as answered questions tossed her way by the partygoers.

"She is powerful, don't you think?" His question sounded almost boastful.

Carlotta, who usually restrained her comments about anybody, leaned over and replied, "Powerful and quite stunning."

Miguel nodded his head in agreement. Rarely did he ever hear Carlotta admire another woman. He didn't have any problem with it; it was just out of the ordinary.

Ciao began to direct the group. "Upstairs, so you can feast your eyes on the wondrous presentations that await you. This is a treat for all your senses."

Aaron made eye contact with Ciao and quickly summoned her to them. He hugged Ciao as she came close and introduced her to Carlotta and Miguel. "This is Miguel. He is the writer whom you spoke with on the phone . . . from the east coast."

Aaron went on to explain that the couple should be allowed to see everything so that Miguel could write a "good article so that we can illicit more excitement about what we are trying to do."

Ciao interrupted him as she moved quickly to Carlotta. "My God, what a lovely, dark lady . . . are you with Miguel?"

Aaron was so intent on getting Miguel and Ciao together, he forgot about introducing Carlotta. But Miguel took the queue. "This is Carlotta. Carlotta, Ciao."

Carlotta extended her hand. Ciao ignored her hand and moved toward her, opened her arms, and moved to hug her as if she were some long-lost relative. "In Brazil there is none of that handshaking thing. We hug and kiss." With that, Ciao smiled at Carlotta like an invitation and hugged her close.

Surprisingly, Carlotta didn't resist. Looking at them hug, the contrast of the two women skin to skin was like looking at a pearl laid against black velvet.

"I will take it from here." Ciao began to lead them upstairs.

"You are now in good hands. So, go, enjoy yourselves. Ciao is at your disposal." And with that Aaron turned to walk away as Ciao, Carlotta, and Miguel began to make their way to the second floor.

The iron staircase was a gunmetal color mixed with an ornamental grating. It sharply contrasted with the warm, polychromatic designs that appeared on the walls as they ascended to the huge openness of the main exhibit area on the second floor. The entire floor was a massive space of oriental rugs that glowed like gardens of exotic flowers. The walls were a soothing orange/brown, and sheaths of multi-colored cloth strategically hung down from various places on them, flowing as if the ocean outside was beckoning them.

Chandeliers, like so many crystal clouds, hung from the ceiling. It was a mix of traditional and modern that defied any comfortable classification. These artists had transformed their reality into a world of imagination and invited all the guests into it. Sculptures of all different sizes and designs, from simple busts of what appeared to be recognizable public figures and celebrities, to abstract designs that defied definition, filled the space, tantalizing and mesmerizing the senses. It was obvious that their art was as irrational as improvisational jazz. It was mad with its own strange loveliness.

"This is something!" Carlotta exclaimed. "I've never seen anything like this in my life." She was as amazed as Miguel.

Although he'd seen videos of their previous presentations, this exhibit stirred the senses to full life. However, the real-life experience was nearly overwhelming. The combination of colors and textures was absorbing like a love affair, as well as enchanting like a meadow full of freshly opened tulips.

Ciao was equally as enchanting. As she guided them through the corridors of the exhibit, she would stop to introduce herself to the guests and answer any questions they had with her neon-like smile and an almost airbrushed softness that complemented the aura surrounding the entire room. Yet even when she had to avert her attention from Miguel, she always seemed to keep Carlotta close enough to touch. And as the evening wore on, Carlotta appeared to enjoy it.

"She's fun. I like her," was Carlotta's simple explanation to Miguel.

"I like her also. She makes you want to go to Brazil. I wonder if all Brazilians are like that," Miguel mused.

"I heard that!" Ciao exclaimed as she turned from yet another group. "We are all fun loving, yet very intense. We enjoy life as if each day is our last." As she stared directly at Carlotta, she said, "That is why we are so hot, so passionate, because the next moment is not promised. That is why we must enjoy all that life has to offer now." She winked at Miguel.

That wink snapped Miguel out of the trance he had been lured into by the exotic aura Ciao emitted. The three of them walked around the exhibition area as Ciao proudly showed off the various creations. This mixture of sight and sound was rare and entertaining. The fact that he was given the opportunity to write about and help promote one of the most unique artistic events of this early decade gave Miguel a wonderful feeling, like the first moments of falling in love. He was full of questions, and unbridled curiosity ran through his head like horses racing at the Kentucky Derby.

At the same moment Carlotta was also captured by both

the aural and sensual menagerie of the moment. She was swept up like the first fallen leaf of autumn. She too was caught up in the magic of being around Ciao. She remained strangely quiet as she observed Miguel questioning Ciao about the exhibit's wondrous treasures. While she watched intently, like a cat watches a swinging ball waiting for the proper moment to grab it, she started thinking about how when Ciao hugged her, she felt a warmness, a closeness like two roots joined together as they expanded into a single flower. Then it was the feeling she had when Ciao made her statement about Brazilians being passionate and living for the moment. For some reason that statement, coupled with the way Ciao looked at her, excited Carlotta and caused her heart to pulsate thru her chest, like some ancient African talking drum sending a message to another tribe about approaching danger. And now, at this moment, a different excitement was deep inside her, like a desert river flowing under the hot, un-forgiving sands.

Ciao's presence actually caused Carlotta to wonder what it would be like to be even closer to Ciao, closer as in naked. The thought of Ciao's honey-colored skin pressing hotly against the sea-bottomed darkness of Carlotta's own skin, as their lips and hands shamelessly introduced themselves to one another, began to warm her body, like large amounts of brandy coursing through the veins.

Yet, at the same time, Carlotta was confused by these feel-ings. She had never experienced any type of intimate connec-tion with another woman. Even though she and Miguel occasionally discussed what it might be like to bring another woman into their erotic forays, it remained a fantasy. Carlotta did admit, however, that when she either read books or viewed movies that involved women engaging in intimacy, she became aroused. But she couldn't conceive of any situation where she might become involved in anything like that, even if Miguel wanted her to.

"You know I would do anything you want me to do sexually. But I just can't see what I would be doing with another woman. I don't want to do anything to another woman. So I guess I would have to let her do stuff to me. But then I don't know if I could handle her doing things to you. I just don't know."

So that's where they left it. As far as Miguel was concerned, her response was perfectly acceptable. On occasion, he had fantasized about a ménage à trois, but like Carlotta, this was simply a fantasy. Miguel had participated in a few small orgies during his sexual campaigns, but only on one occasion did he find it satisfying.

"The problem is that the women have to be really into each other as well as you. They can't have any hang-ups about their bodies or touching each other or any of that."

Miguel theorized that a specific chemistry, an erotic balance, had to exist between each of the parties or the effort would be wasted.

"See, you can't have the women avoiding each other, like they can't be afraid to touch or feel each other's bodies." He would claim, "Sometimes the man had to be just an accessory, almost as if he can't be the main course through the entire sexual meal. It should be natural for the women to kiss, and feel on each other. They don't have to be lesbians or anything like that. They just should be comfortable with their sexuality, whatever the hell that means." To him, the women had to be free.

Ciao finished explaining a sculpture to Miguel. As she did she looked over at Carlotta and flashed a slight, slow smile that clung ever so faintly to the edge of her lips. She extended her arm and drew Carlotta to her. Carlotta didn't resist. The embrace was a side-to-side kind of thing, much as the way friends might do. She gave Carlotta a peck on the cheek, and looked at Miguel.

"All this talk has made me thirsty. Why don't you go to the bar and get us something to drink? You do want something don't you, dear?" She nodded her head at Carlotta.

"I want my usual," replied Carlotta.

"And I will have what she has." Ciao's faint smile had developed into one that widened her lips like spreading oil. "We will be here getting better acquainted, okay?"

Carlotta looked comfortable, cozy, and reassured as Miguel left them to go to get the drinks.

The line for drinks was long. For some reason, Miguel was nervous about leaving Carlotta alone with Ciao. After that remark about how attractive Carlotta was to her, it was obvious Ciao was either bisexual or straight-up lesbian. Why would that make him nervous? Was it the fact that he so coveted Carlotta, her body, her soul, her sex, that he was that insecure about leaving her alone at a party with another woman?

"What the fuck, bro?" he began to reason with himself. "I mean, first of all, it's a party. There are lots of people around, what could they possibly do? Plus she's one of the hosts, so she can't devote all her time to Carlotta. Plus you know Carlotta ain't really into that type of action." Or is she? Miguel had never been filled with so much doubt and distrust. While the line slowly diminished, he noticed the two women standing in front of him. They were arm-in-arm, laughing. One of them had short dark hair just like Carlotta. And the other one had long dirty-blonde hair just like Ciao. They were laughing, and every now and then they would whisper into each other's ear and one or the other or both would laugh loudly. They were thin, but not skinny.

Humph! Models, he surmised. They must be friends or something.

Before the thought could fully develop, the blonde who resembled Ciao moved her face closer to the dark-haired one and kissed her full on the lips. At first it seemed as if the other one was a little resistant. But after a little probing the dark-haired one opened her mouth and their lips met in a brief flurry of eroticism that got an immediate rise out of Miguel.

"Girl, you better stop that!" the dark-haired one said as they broke the kiss. Both of them laughed, but began kissing again. This time the kiss was deeper and it appeared their tongues were really probing each other, like they were excavating for something. Their interplay increased until they reached the bartenders. There they abruptly stopped. As they ordered their drinks, Miguel looked around the room trying to see if anyone else was as intrigued with this exchange as he was. As he quickly scanned the room, he noticed people just milling around doing what people do at parties. It seemed as if they were oblivious to what these two ladies were doing in full view of everyone.

They ordered their drinks, leaving Miguel up next. As he prepared to order, up stepped Carlo, one of the architects of the newly renovated building.

"Hey, Miguel." Carlo had a broad smile on his face and a lovely Latino-looking woman on his arm. Carlo was a tall dark Brazilian with a broad nose and a great wide smile. His friends teased him that he was Pele's illegitimate son, since he bore a slight resemblance to the legendary soccer star. His companion was a chestnut-skinned woman with shiny, thick, black hair piled on top of her head. She wore a dark blue knit dress that hugged her wide hips. Like most of the women at this affair she was also a knockout. "Miguel, this is Clarissa.

Clarissa, this is the writer I told you about earlier. With his help, he's going to make us known to the entire artistic community in America. He's also the boyfriend of Carlotta."

Clarissa's smile grew even wider and her eyes seemed to get big as she said, "Oh, yes, that pretty lady who was with Ciao! You should be happy, Miguel," she went on. "I too would love to be able to have a lady like that to play with like Ciao was doing!"

It must've been the puzzled look on Miguel's face that prompted Carlo to say, "Oh, you must've gotten in line long before they started their antics over there!"

Miguel tried to play it off as the butterflies in his stomach began to flutter and take on a life of their own. "Uh . . . what, er, ah, what do you mean . . . antics?" he stammered.

"Oh, nothing, really," Clarissa chimed in before Carlo had the opportunity to explain. "They were just doing a little kissing and flirting with each other when I met your lady. I'm sure it was all just girls playing around in fun," she concluded.

Miguel was dizzy as he managed a weak "glad to meet you," got his drinks, and proceeded to make a beeline back to Carlotta and Ciao. The room seemed hazy and surrounded by a London fog as Miguel quickly made his way through the party to where he'd left the ladies. In this fog or mist or whatever it was, Miguel almost dropped his drink as he saw Ciao and Carlotta locked in the same face-to-face, tongue-down-each-other's-throat action he'd witnessed with those two models in line just a bit ago. He was again amazed at how everyone else seemed to simply drift in and out of the activity of the party, seemingly unaffected by the lusty exhibition going on in their midst.

The ladies' arms were entangled around each other like ancient serpents in some kind of mythological maze. As he approached, he started asking himself what he was going to do. What could he do? He was almost upon them and he could see it all clearly, his woman and Ciao making out like shameless teenagers in the back of a car in a secluded park. They stopped kissing long enough to look at Miguel and smile.

Carlotta spoke first. "Miguel, Miguel, what's wrong, what do you want?" She reached out her hand to touch him. It seemed like the closer he got to them, the more inaccessible they became. It was if they were dissolving into the fog or mist that seemed to surround Miguel. He got closer and it was at that moment that Carlotta's voice became more pronounced and the mist disappeared.

"Miguel!" she said. "You've been standing here all this time?" It was Carlotta without Ciao. He was still in line. The bartender had an impatient look on his face; Miguel had one drink in his hand. The bartender spoke.

"Is that all you want, sir? I thought you said you wanted three drinks. Will that be all?"

Carlotta reached out her hand, and as she finally touched Miguel it all became clear. He had allowed his imagination to get the better of him. It was all in his head. Carlotta, not knowing what was going on in Miguel's mind, was attempting to communicate with him.

"What's wrong, baby?" she inquired again. "Are you feeling okay? You seemed to take so long coming back, and Ciao had to talk with some potential investors, so I figured I'd just find you."

And then Carlotta added the kicker when she said, "When I couldn't find you at first, I thought you had been captured by one of these hot-assed women." Her eyes began to sparkle. "And I had this overwhelming fit of jealousy that just had me fantasizing all kinds of shit about you and some other woman. So I was really trying to find you."

Even though he hadn't yet returned completely to reality, Miguel was relieved on some level to hear what Carlotta had just said. This synchronized incident of jealous imagination reinforced the desperate situation these two lovers found themselves in. On the surface, they would verbally boast their willingness to allow each other a wide range of freedom.

For example, in Carlotta's case, because she was married and still maintained this long-standing relationship with Miguel, she really believed she allowed him to have all the freedom of a single man while accepting his declaration of allegiance to her.

On the other hand, Miguel would claim he had no problem with Carlotta's marriage. Initially, that might've been true. It was all about providing her with what she wasn't getting at home: attention, romance, and real good loving. She needed to be appreciated and Miguel would do that for her. But as the relationship transitioned from its innocence of emotional irresponsibility to something possessive, controlling, and literally boiling over with lust, it became obvious to them that their hearts were between their legs. At this point their commitment to pleasure outweighed anything else.

It had all been a dream, and Miguel had his Carlotta back as opposed to being caught in some perverse fantasy that had yet to manifest itself. He pulled her close to him and as he ignored the now exasperated bartender, they began a mini-make-out session right in line.

"My goodness, can't you two wait until you get alone?" It was Ciao. "I've been looking for you. And Ms. Carlotta, I'm surprised at you. Here I thought you were going to be *my* little plaything for the evening, and here you are taking up with the likes of *him!*" She then broke out in a high-pitched combination of giggling and cackling.

The two lovers seemed a little embarrassed. They quickly took their drinks and, with Ciao, moved out of line. "I am a frank woman," Ciao began. "I like both of you. But"—she approached Carlotta as she continued, reaching her hand out to stroke Carlotta's bare arm—"I really like you."

At that moment Carlotta surprised herself as well as both Ciao and Miguel as she took Ciao's hand in hers, swiftly raised it to her open mouth, and sensuously licked the tips of Ciao's first two fingers with her tongue. Carlotta's eyes darted to her left where Miguel stood in amazement, mouth agape as he nearly spilled his martini. Ciao's expression mirrored Miguel's as she instinctually tried to withdraw from Carlotta's brazen oral display.

Carlotta became the aggressor, as she refused to give Ciao her hand back. Her eyes gleamed as she took Ciao's index finger deeper into her mouth and sucked it as expertly as she had Miguel's shaft earlier that evening. By this time she was fixated on Ciao's eyes as she amused herself with the reaction she was eliciting from both her lover and the lady.

This exhibition continued for what seemed to be longer than the few seconds it actually took, but it was still long enough for Carlotta to have shifted the delicate balance of sexual power from Ciao to Carlotta.

"See, this is what I like to do . . . I have this oral thing, and I love putting things in my mouth," she said to Ciao. "I get especially oral when I am deprived. See, on the way here, I was able to almost satisfy this urge because I had Miguel deep inside my mouth. As he drove, I sucked him deep . . . he kept getting harder and harder and I loved that. I had total control. I was getting off on him getting off and I almost came. But we got here before I could get what I wanted. So," she continued as she released Ciao's hand and reached to her side where she grasped Miguel and brought him close to her, "I was getting a little antsy. I was getting a little hungry. Do you know what I'm talking about, honey?" And with that she tilted her head toward Miguel and kissed him.

After they kissed, Carlotta again reached over and pulled Ciao over to her and began to whisper in her ear. Miguel noticed how Ciao's eyes lit up at what she was hearing. Ciao's lips parted and she wetted them lightly as Carlotta continued.

"Yes," Ciao replied, "I think that can be arranged. Come with me."

Miguel was completely in the dark. He didn't ask any questions as Carlotta took him by the hand. They both followed Ciao upstairs to the top floor. As they walked, Miguel felt his stomach begin to hatch butterflies, and as they fluttered around down there a strange thing began to happen even farther down . . . he began to get an erection. These stairs led them to the absolute top of the barn. The space was a magnificent maze of divided partitions, each featuring the artwork of Cameron, another one of the members of the art consortium. By this time, Miguel was basically following both women as they walked ahead of him a bit. They were like two high school girls, giggling and talking under their breath.

Ciao took them in and around the front of the art exhibit. None of the guests were allowed on this level as it was for buyers only, and the art sale was scheduled to take place in a few days. So for now the space was empty. As they walked through the area, Miguel noticed the huge windows that ran from the top of the barn to the floor. They were huge panoramic windows that seemed to surround the entire floor. The soft lighting was a calming mix of blue and white. The music wafting from the sound system was much more subdued and sensual than the music playing downstairs. It was an ambient reggae flavor.

"You see this is the place, don't you think?" Ciao asked as she led them. Her black knitted dress took on a different appeal than it had downstairs. In the subdued light, the dress appeared to hug her ample hips as she guided and glided through the labyrinth of artwork. Watching both women walk kept Miguel's erection intact. It wasn't one of those "so hard I got to have it now or I'm going to die" erections. But watching the women walk and interact was a turn-on. It played into the fantasy he'd had earlier that evening while standing in the drink line.

The corridor-like passageway emptied out into an enclosed lounge area, complete with overstuffed couches and chairs. Unlike the hardwood floors that covered most of the gallery, this area boasted soft plush carpet. It was obviously an area where the buyers and non-buyers could relax, have a drink, talk, and probably write out their checks.

"Oooooh, I like it," squealed Carlotta. "You did good. This is perfect." And as she expressed her approval, she reached out and pulled Ciao to her, wrapped her arms around her, and kissed her. She started at her forehead. She gave her small pecking kisses. She descended to her cheeks and ended up with an open-mouthed kiss to Ciao's full lips. Ciao grabbed Carlotta's face and hungrily returned the kiss. As one might expect, the sight of these two women kissing increased the erection Miguel already had. The kiss was real this time.

As Carlotta broke it off, she gently pushed Ciao aside. Pointing to one of the overstuffed chairs, she nodded her head. "Now, you'll get your reward. Make yourself comfortable and watch closely." She turned around and looked at Miguel. She could tell he was hard without even looking down. She reached down and felt the bulge in his pants. "You poor dear, do you feel left out? Or are your intuitive powers working a little overtime? Do you know what we're going to do, baby?"

She moved closer to him and flicked her tongue out, licking the side of his neck and the lobe of his ear as she continued to massage the now rock-hard dick vainly trying to escape from his black linen pants. "We're going to kill two birds with one stone. Sit down."

She pushed him down on the sofa. The huge royal purple pillows seemed to claim him like the crashing waves on the Pacific Coast outside claim anything that dares to attempt to navigate them.

As he settled in, he saw Ciao had pulled down the front zipper to her dress. Her legs were beginning to open as she pulled the dress up until her caramel-colored thighs were all but exposed. "She likes to watch," Carlotta said. "And me, you know I'm still hungry and now I'm thirsty, too. You owe me, remember?"

Carlotta had that look in her eyes: the look of a woman consumed with lust.

"So just relax, we're all going to get off. Right, Ciao?" She turned around to look at the beautiful Brazilian who by now had her hands between her own open legs. "Oh, it looks as if you might need some assistance."

With that, Carlotta imitated a jungle cat as she crawled over to Ciao, who was smiling nervously with one hand between her legs and the other unconsciously massaging her right breast. She wasn't wearing a bra, and her medium-sized breast was peeking out from underneath the dress that she had unzipped to her waist. Carlotta arrived in time to take Ciao's hand from under her dress.

"Hmm, what have we here?" she teased. "We're a little wet. Perhaps you might need me to clean that off those fingers. We wouldn't want to get pussy juice on that fine dress, or better yet, this couch. Here, allow me."

Carlotta moved from in front of Ciao, and while on her knees moved to the side so Miguel could see her put Ciao's fingers in her mouth.

"Mmmm." Her mouth engulfed Ciao's slender fingers past her knuckles, all while Carlotta continued looking at Miguel. Her wet pink tongue slithered under Ciao's fingers as she sucked on them the exact same way she had sucked Miguel earlier that evening.

"Oh, my God." Ciao was squirming around in the chair, her dress riding farther up her thighs. Miguel was watching all this transpire with rapt attention as he became more aroused.

The fact that Carlotta simultaneously had sexual control over two people was somewhat overwhelming. She removed Ciao's finger from her mouth, looked over at Miguel, and smiled.

"I'll be with you in a bit," she whispered as she turned to face Ciao. She bent forward, spread Ciao's legs farther apart, and did a face-first dive in between them.

Miguel saw the expression on Ciao's face go from excitement to almost sheer terror. She threw her head back and screamed. Her arms shot straight down as she tried to brace herself in the soft material of the chair. At the same time Miguel saw Carlotta pull her black chiffon dress up to gather around her waist. And as she continued her assault on Ciao, she slowly rotated her fat ass as her head bobbed up and down, apparently heaping waves of passion on her victim and driving Miguel crazy. By now Miguel's dick had escaped from his unzipped pants and he was stroking it in anticipation of Carlotta finishing with Ciao and returning some of her attention to him.

"Damnit, Carlotta!" he shouted. "Come over here and take care of this!"

Carlotta abruptly took her head from in between Ciao's legs, as if she were anticipating Miguel's demand. Before she made her way over to him, she bent over, looked Ciao in the face, and said, "Here, this is what I tasted. Try some."

All the various juices combined to form sexual foam boiling between their lips. Ciao hungrily attacked Carlotta's mouth as if it were some life-giving substance. But Carlotta didn't allow her to get too comfortable. She said, as she broke away from Ciao, "This is fun but the reason I came up here is for some dick . . . remember?"

And as dramatically as any movie scene might have been, Carlotta slowly slid off Ciao, who was still writhing and clutching at herself, and like a panther crawled back to Miguel. As she got closer, she looked approvingly at him. She nodded her head. "I see you're ready. I didn't even have to tell you what to do with those pants. You *are* a good boy, aren't you?"

The personality of this Carlotta was unfamiliar to Miguel. She was usually lusty, aggressive, and nasty. Now she was spontaneously calm, eerily in control. Miguel was nervous. While they'd often fantasized about the various ways they would engage in threesomes, Carlotta always contended that she could not see herself being comfortable in one.

"Perhaps if I didn't have to know the woman, and she could do me. But I'm not about to do anything to another woman." The thought of another woman performing on Miguel while she watched was a little more intriguing. But regardless, it was usually just talk. Until now, when he sat across from another woman, a woman whom his woman had just brought to the edge of a climax and was sitting there wanting more, but knew she would have to wait and observe someone else being brought to a climax first.

Miguel felt Carlotta's mouth kiss his ankle, first the right one, then the left one. While her mouth slowly traveled up the inside of each muscular calf, her hands performed a deep massage on his bare thighs . . . her thighs. She could feel the muscles in his well-developed thighs start to tense. It was his body's way of letting her know she was turning him on. He loved her warm hands. The more she kneaded his flesh, the more he responded with low groans and muscle spasms of pleasure. It was just starting.

"Mmm, you like this don't you, baby?" she whispered to him as she made her way up between his thighs. Her lips kissed and licked almost every inch of his torso. She teased the area under his balls. While she gently licked and sucked at each firm nut, she began to moan also. At the same time, Miguel was having trouble deciding whether he should instead focus his attention on Ciao, who had inserted three fingers deep into her own sopping wet hole while her other hand manipulated her pointed nipple.

The room seemed to be swirling with lust. As Carlotta was about to surround Miguel's dick with her wet mouth, she placed both hands on his chest. Her nails sank deep into his skin, and as she began to suck him, she got so excited she started jerking her hips and rotating her ass. It was an orgy of sounds, images, and movements. Miguel's dick was as hard as it had ever been as he took Carlotta's head between his hands and forced her mouth farther onto his cock. She obliged by opening her mouth even wider, nearly gagging on this pulsating, vibrating monster deep in her throat.

She'd been wanting this all evening and now she had what she wanted. If she could, she would have consumed the entire thing, but the head of his dick was so fat and delicious, she became fixated on letting her tongue create ice cream-like swirls of saliva around it. Finally the taste of it, coupled with the intense passion of the moment, caused her to plunge her mouth all the way down, gag on it, come back up to admire her handiwork, and repeat the process until the hairs in his crotch, her face, and the soft fabric of the couch were all soaking wet.

There were no words spoken, even when Ciao, who could no longer function as an observer, made her way over to the two lovers. At first she simply sat next to them intently watching as Carlotta maintained her fierce assault on Miguel's cock. Then she replaced Miguel's hand around Carlotta's head with her own, furiously forcing Miguel's turgid rod down Carlotta's throat. Miguel had never seen his dick so wet in all the years he'd been with Carlotta. Ciao was so taken by the exhibition she couldn't help but join in.

"You are so messy, Carlotta!" she exclaimed. "Here, let me help you clean this up."

All of a sudden, Carlotta took Miguel out of her mouth and shook her head from Ciao's grip, took Ciao's head, and forced it down on Miguel.

The sight of this beautiful Brazilian woman's mouth virtually impaled on his love stick drove Miguel almost to the brink of orgasm. If that weren't enough, the sight of his lover's mouth covered with saliva, making it look as if she'd taken two huge loads of cum, did the trick. Carlotta rushed to swap her juices with Miguel. At that exact moment Miguel's hips jerked and bucked. He was on the brink of an earth-shaking orgasm. Carlotta knew it and quickly joined Ciao down on him.

He grabbed both women's heads in time to shoot his load. He watched in awe as both women took all of his cum. It was if they were battling to see who could get the most: two beautiful women drinking his cum and eventually swapping it between them. It was too much and he collapsed. He lapsed into an orgasmic stupor and with his eyes closed all he could do was feel both mouths running all over him. He was too weak to tell them to stop. They wouldn't have listened anyway.

ZANE LAST

I Have Treats for You Tonight

I was so excited. I'd barely gotten through the day at my office. Who cares about crunching numbers for less-than-appreciative clients anyway? I'd made a serious mistake by accepting the job offer from Frasier and Meridian straight out of college. It was time for a change and I planned to make a career move before 2001 rolled around.

First things first, though. I was anxious to get home to my baby. Errin and I were celebrating our fifth anniversary and it was a big day. When I first "came out" to my parents, expressing my undying love for Errin over Thanksgiving dinner, they'd given me less than a year to go back to men.

Truth be known, I never liked men. I just dated boys in high school and men in college because it was expected. Yet, I can still recall the way I used to fantasize about Lorraine, a sister I attended high school with who rarely gave me the time of day. She was gorgeous and had a body that could stop traffic. Unfortunately she was strictly dickly and I didn't stand a chance.

My reluctance to admit my sexual orientation continued well into my college years. That is, until I met Errin. She was completely open about being a lesbian. In fact, she was the president of the African-American Lesbian Association on campus. I met her at a rally on campus. All of the African-American students were protesting the treatment and lack of tenures offered to the few African-American professors on campus.

I'll never forget how cold it was that day. It was the second week of January and everyone had just returned from winter break. I wasn't looking forward to the second semester of my junior year because I had to take Statistics with Professor Isiah Kramer. He was infamous for flunking people and ruining their academic careers if they weren't willing to bend over backward to appease him.

Despite the weather, the courtyard in front of the student union was packed. People were crammed into the space shoulder to shoulder. There was a makeshift stage on the front steps and various students were taking turns yelling into a bull horn. Errin had a tough act to follow as she took her place in front of the rowdy crowd. A militant brother from Queens had just finished delivering a powerful speech entitled "Get a Grip" and half the crowd was chanting it by the time he was finished.

Errin didn't seem the least bit nervous, though. She was quite endearing as she spoke on behalf of the African-American Lesbian Association. I had heard of them but lacked the nerve to actually attend the meetings I'd seen announced on flyers posted around campus. I was still dealing with my overprotective parents who thought my life belonged to them. My mother, especially, felt that I was her chance to live again and make restitution for all the things she never got a chance to do after she'd unexpectedly turned up pregnant with me during her senior year of high school.

Both of my parents had high expectations of me, being that

I'm the oldest of their three kids and the first member of the Madison family ever to attend college. I always cringed when I called home on the weekends, but kissing up to them every seven days was a requirement if I wanted my tuition paid.

It was always the same thing. "Oooh, Paige, we're so proud of you." "Whatever you do, don't let your grades fall down." "Have you met any prospective husband material on campus?"

That last question always came from my mother. She's from the old school and believes that a woman should be on two missions at college: earning a degree and snagging a husband. Preferably, a pre-med or pre-law one. I yearned to tell her that while the degree was on my agenda, a husband wasn't even an option.

I was standing there daydreaming about my parents and how I could break the news to them gently when Errin's voice broke me out of my trance. It was calming, it was sensuous, it was arousing. The fact that she was attractive didn't hurt matters any. Errin is tall, five-ten, with smooth, dark skin that reminds me of an ice cream cone hand-dipped in chocolate sauce. She has large, cat-like, sepia eyes and short auburn hair cut into a cute, easy-to-maintain style.

It had been a lonely three years at college. I dated from time to time, mostly immature fraternity brothers who freaked out when I told them I was still a virgin. Most were very polite about it, even though they still tried to get the drawers to no avail. A few of them were downright rude. One even lashed out at me and accused me of being a lesbian, like the mere words would crush me down to my very soul. Instead, I laughed in his face, not denying a thing. He still didn't figure it out, though. Most men can't deal with the fact that an attractive woman would rather be with one of her own sex than them.

There were quite a few of those immature brothers in attendance that day, making lewd comments while Errin made her speech. A speech that made a hell of a lot of sense and displayed a high degree of intelligence. After the rally was over, I saw Errin walking toward the undergraduate library and followed her, intending only to tell her how much I enjoyed her speech. Things turned out quite differently. We ended up having dinner at Friday's, home of my favorite chicken and mushroom dish. The conversation was fantastic. We talked about everything from music to politics and found that we had a lot in common.

When Errin dropped me back off at my dorm, she asked the question. The one I'm sure had weighed heavily on her mind all evening.

"Paige, are you into women?" she asked me, with one of my feet already firmly placed on the curb.

Like they say, honesty is the best policy. "Yes, I love women but I've never actually been loved by one."

"Meaning?"

"Meaning that I've never been intimate. Not with anyone."

Errin grinned at me. "Oh, so you're a virgin?"

"Something like that," I replied hesitantly.

"Close the door for a second," she said insistently.

I pulled my foot back in and shut the door, the exterior light cutting off as I did.

Errin reached over and started caressing my left cheek. "I had a really nice time tonight, Paige."

Her fingertips felt comforting on my skin and warmed me all over, especially down below.

"I'd like for us to spend some more time together," she continued. "That is, if it's okay with you."

I couldn't contain my blush. "I'd like that."

She leaned over toward me and I remember thinking, *this is it.* And it was. Errin brushed her thick, juicy lips across mine, gently at first, and then she planted a firm kiss on them before sliding her tongue in between them to begin an exploration. It was everything I'd expected it to be. The earth moved, the sun came out at night, and the storm clouds parted, as did my legs, allowing Errin to massage the inside of my thighs.

We remained in Errin's car for a good hour, fogging up the windows of her Honda Accord with our body heat. We didn't go all the way that night. Just a lot of heavy foreplay and she did all of the touching. I was still a bit nervous, afraid that my inexperience would end up being a turn-off if I didn't touch her as creatively as she touched me.

Skilled as she was, the evening culminated with my first orgasm covering the three fingers she'd placed inside of me a mere five minutes before I exploded, bucking in the seat like a bronco because the release I'd waited so many years for came barreling in on me like a ton of bricks.

The better part of a month passed before Errin and I finished the feelings. She rented a room at the Sheraton and had a bottle of chilled zinfandel and rose petals sprinkled across white linen sheets awaiting our arrival. I was flattered that she'd put so much effort into making my first time special.

Errin ran us a bath, overflowing with bubbles from my favorite milk and honey bath gel. She'd spotted a bottle of it in my dorm room and I'd made such a fuss over it that she remembered. We faced each other in the garden tub, surrounded by vanilla-scented candles, and lathered our bodies with loofa sponges.

"Turn around so I can wash your back," Errin suggested.

I did and I could feel her pert nipples pressing into my shoulder blades as she scooted up against me. She scrubbed my back and then dropped the sponge, reaching around to palm my breasts and rub my nipples between her thumbs and forefingers. She nibbled on the nape of my neck and sucked on my earlobe, causing a moan to escape from somewhere deep within me.

One of her hands disappeared beneath the bubbles, eager to slip inside me. I leaned back into her embrace, throwing one of my ankles onto the side of the tub to allow her easier access. "This feels oh so right, baby," Errin whispered into my ear. "I'm going to make you so happy."

"I want to make you happy, too," I responded faintly, lost in the ecstasy.

"You do make me happy, Paige." She feverishly worked her fingers over my clit and I gyrated my hips to their rhythm. "I haven't been able to think of anyone or anything else since we met."

"Me either," I readily admitted.

I turned around and straddled her thighs, showering her with passionate kisses and rubbing my pussy up against her. Errin's mouth went for one of my breasts, drawing it in and suckling on it hungrily. She ran a finely manicured fingertip up and down the crack of my ass, teasing my hole with it a few times before pressing it inside. That was a totally new sensation for me. One I'd often dreamed about. One of the many things I'd dreamed about that Errin made a reality that night.

I rode the fingers of one of her hands while she continued to work my ass over with the other one, grabbing onto the sides of the tub for better leverage. I threw my head back, arching my spine, while Errin moved her mouth from one breast to the other, giving them equal attention. She licked a trail down to my belly button, dipping the tip of her tongue into it, blowing on it like someone was tickling me with a feather, and then dipped her tongue into it again. It was heavenly.

We ended up on the bed, me on my back with the rose petals teasing my wet skin, Errin on her side drying me off carefully with a fluffy towel. We stared into each other's eyes for what seemed like an eternity. No more words were exchanged. There was no need for them.

After drying me off completely, Errin retrieved a bottle of strawberry-flavored massage oil from her overnight bag and gave me a full body massage. Every part of me she caressed, she followed up with her skillful tongue. She gave special attention to my feet, sucking each one of my toes individually and licking my soles.

I couldn't take it anymore. "Errin, please taste me!" I heard myself exclaim. "Please, please taste me!"

"You don't have to beg, baby," she responded, spreading my legs gently.

She lifted one of my thighs, kissed my kneecap, and then positioned my leg over her shoulder, easing her tongue higher and higher until I could feel her hair cascading over the lips of my pussy. Then she tasted me. She tasted me for a very long time and I'd never had such an intense array of feelings in my entire life. I had nothing to compare it to, but Errin was good. Damn good!

She ate me until I came in her mouth for the third time and then she turned around, straddled my face, and I was able to fulfill a dream that I'd had since high school. I felt like my tongue action was clumsy at first but, from the way Errin swirled her pussy on my tongue and moaned, she was obviously enjoying it. I became addicted to the taste of her immediately. I was hooked.

After I ate her out, I spent about an hour sucking on her

full breasts, making long circular strokes around her nipples with the tip of my tongue. She laid back and relished it, running her fingers through my hair. Our lovemaking lasted well into the next afternoon. We called down to the front desk and requested a late checkout. We made use of every available second, too.

That was the first time Errin and I made love but it was far from the last.

When I got home, still hyped up about our fifth anniversary, I was disappointed when I called out Errin's name and got no response. She'd managed to sneak up behind me and suddenly I felt her blowing into my ear.

"Hello, baby," she said seductively. "Don't turn around. I have a surprise for you."

She slipped a black silk scarf around my shoulder and pulled it up to my eyes, tying it around the back of my head.

"Ooh, a blindfold," I cooed. "Feeling kinky tonight, huh?"

"You know it," Errin replied. "It's not every day that I get to celebrate five years of bliss with my sweetheart."

"Can I turn around now?" I asked her. "I want to kiss you."

I could feel her move around me and then she took my face in her hands and slipped her luscious tongue into my eagerly awaiting mouth. We swayed back and forth to imaginary music and felt each other up.

"Are you ready for your surprises, Paige? I have treats for you tonight."

"Treats?"

Errin started squeezing my breasts and nibbling on my left nipple through my clothing. "Yeah, treats. Take my hand."

She led me by the hand into the dining room and the smell of seafood invaded my nostrils. "Ooh, a seafood dinner," I said. "My favorite."

"You can't eat yet," Errin informed me. "I get to eat my dinner first."

I giggled. I heard her loud and clear and knew exactly what she wanted. Errin undressed me slowly and seductively and then pushed me backward until my ass cheeks were resting along the edge of the table.

"Lie back on the table and spread your legs, baby."

"My pleasure," I replied, eager to be her main course.

After I lay back on the table, I spread my legs, holding my thighs open so Errin could get to her meal. She sat down in a chair and licked around the lips of my pussy before sliding her tongue inside and causing me to move my hips to her rhythm. She always knows just how I like it.

I could hear her get up. "I'll be right back."

She returned in less than a minute and I felt something cold and sticky on my skin and the distinct squeaking noise of a bottle being squeezed. "What's that, Errin?"

"Sweets for my sweet. Taste it."

I touched my stomach, gathering some of the goo onto my fingers and tasted it. It was honey. "Um, do I get to lick some of this off you, too?"

"No, not tonight." Errin spread the honey all over me from head to toe and licked every inch of me, including my asshole. I was creaming all over the place.

She later fed me fresh oysters, lobster tails dipped in butter, and spiced, steamed shrimp. It was scrumptious.

She led me to our bedroom and turned on the *Best of Luther Vandross* CD. Another one of my favorites. I was totally relaxed as Errin tied me to the bedposts with silk scarves, first my hands and then my feet with my legs spread-eagle. I trust her completely.

"What are you going to do with me now?" I wondered.

Errin lay on top of me and licked the underside of each

one of my breasts, teasing my nipples with her tongue. They stood at attention, whining for her to take them inside her mouth. "Remember when you said you wanted to try out some sex toys?"

"Yes, I remember." I chuckled.

"Well, like I said, I have treats for you tonight."

"Ooh, what kind of treats?"

"Ones I know you'll like."

I heard it before I felt it, and while I'd never actually seen one, I knew what the buzz was. Errin teased my clit with the cool vibrator and I came immediately. The sisters were right. Vibrators always do their job.

Then came the dildo. Now, I'd never had a dick, real or otherwise, inside of me, so I winced when Errin first stuck it in. I was technically still a virgin in that respect and it hurt like hell when she busted my cherry. Errin fucked me with it and then held it up to my lips so I could suck my own juices off of it. As always, I tasted delicious.

We tried everything that night. Ben wa balls. Anal beads. A strap-on dick. Everything. What an anniversary!

I've already planned out our next anniversary. Even though same-sex marriages are not legal in our state, I am going to ask Errin to marry me. I'm going to propose to her with a big-ass diamond and plan a private ceremony with a few of our closest friends. I might even give her a bachelorette party and hire a stripper to give her a seductive lap dance. She would get a hoot out of that.

Well, my parents were wrong. I am not going back to men because I was never really there in the first place. I love Errin, Errin loves me, and we'll be together until the end of time. She is the only lover I've ever had and the only lover I'll ever need.

The Flood—Part One: Stranger Things Have Happened

The money had truly gone to my head. What the hell was I thinking when I decided to go shopping that Saturday? Everyone had warned me to keep my behind in the house. Everyone from my mother to my best friend Shelly to the sexy brotha on the Weather Channel. The Washington, D.C., area was expecting one of the worst floods in history, but Bailey Banks & Biddle was having an anniversary sale.

The wild part is that I had never been a big fan of jewelry when I was younger. Mostly because I couldn't afford it. Shoot, when I was in college, I was lucky to be able to afford a Happy Meal. When I got out of college, my student loans were so piled up that I was barely able to afford cheap Chinese food. Now that I was thirty-two, things were finally looking up.

My student loans were all paid off, I was living in an apartment in Chevy Chase, Maryland, that all of my friends envied, I was cruising around in a brand-spanking-new Benz, and I had recently received a promotion and raise that guaranteed me two hundred grand a year plus bonuses. Yes, college really does pay off. No one ever believes that when they are suffering through the classes and cramming for exams. It takes a while once you get out to catch up, but once you do, life can truly be a wonderful thing.

Bailey Banks & Biddle was the jewelry store everyone always talked about at the office. In fact, they made those of us who didn't shop there on the regular almost feel like outcasts. Thus, when I saw the ad, not to mention the ten-percent-off coupon, in the paper for their anniversary sale, I just had to see what they were working with. Saturday was the last day of the sale and I had procrastinated all week about getting there. I wasn't about to lose out on the ten-percent-off incentive, so I climbed in my SLK 320 and headed to downtown D.C.

The roads were clear on the way down there and it started drizzling about five minutes before I got to the mall. Nothing major.

The mall was halfway deserted, and that should have been my first clue. Most of the stores had fewer than ten customers and the employees all looked panic-stricken. As I was walking past a small electronics store, I heard two men with accents discussing the weather.

"We need to get out of here now," one of them said.

"Oh, it's not that bad out," the other one countered.

"But the weatherman said it's going to be really, really bad."

"The weatherman's always wrong."

The first one just shook his head in dismay. "Well, you can stay here. I'm going home. You close up."

I could hear their conversation getting heated as I walked

farther away. I was with the one that said the weatherman was always wrong. Half the time I felt like the grocery stores and weathermen were in a conspiracy. I often wondered if the weathermen got kickbacks from grocery store chains when they announced bad weather and the shelves ended up emptied from nervous shopping.

I got to the jewelry store, which was at the end of the first level, and was surprised to see that there were no customers at all and only two sales clerks. The store was decorated with helium balloons and banners announcing the anniversary sale.

An older woman who was standing by the first counter asked, "May I help you?"

"Yes, I wanted to see what kind of diamond tennis bracelets you have," I replied. I reached into my purse and pulled out the ad. "I have my ten-percent-off coupon."

She grinned at me. I was probably her only hope at making a sale that day and I assumed they made some sort of commission. She moved down to the next case and unlocked it. "Let me show you our top-selling bracelets. I think you'll agree that they're lovely."

I took one look at the prices of the two she pulled out and said, "Hmm, I think I'll hold off on those until I find a man to buy them for me." We both laughed. "What do you have that's about half that price?"

About fifteen minutes later, I had purchased a lovely two-karat bracelet, filled out all the warranty information, paid for it, and was walking out the door with it on my arm. I paused when I got to a case containing platinum wedding sets. "Oh my goodness!" I exclaimed. "These are so gorgeous!"

The sales clerk walked up behind me. "Any prospects for a proposal?"

I shook my head. "Not a one. I guess I've been so busy

working that dating has been put on the back burner for a while. Seeing those rings makes me want to go out and find a man right now, though."

"It'll take a rather rich man to afford those rings," she said.

I snickered. "Please, I wouldn't settle for anyone less."

I went back out into the mall and debated about continuing to shop. But there was something about a crowded mall that made the shopping experience more exciting, so I wasn't feeling being there among the few stragglers that were scattered about.

I decided to grab an espresso from Starbucks and head on home.

That idea was short-lived. Once I got within view of the exit doors, I couldn't believe my eyes. There was so much rain coming down that I couldn't even see the cars in the lot. I stopped in my tracks and said, "Shit!"

I continued through the first set of doors and out into the alcove that led outside. I thought it over. I could make it to my car but I would be drenched. I hadn't even brought an umbrella with me, which was a shame. I had at least half a dozen at home that were small enough to fit inside my purse. Even so, getting to the car wasn't the major issue. The amount of water flooding down the street was. A Benz is a great vehicle, but not in bad weather. My previous vehicle was an SUV and I would've given anything for it to have been waiting for me in the parking lot.

"You're not seriously thinking about going out there, are you?" I heard a deep male voice ask behind me. I turned to look into the eyes of a rent-a-cop; a security guard. "You're crazy if you go out there," he added.

"What do you suggest?" I asked. "That I get stranded here all day? The mall closes in a couple of hours and there's no telling how long the rain will last."

He chuckled. "Oh, they say it won't be over until the morning."

"The morning?"

"Yes, and even if you make it to your car, you won't make it out of the parking lot. All the streets are flooded."

He smiled at me and I suddenly noticed that he was attractive. Not fine, but attractive. He was of average height and build with dark eyes, a cinnamon complexion, and a goatee. His hair was closely cropped to his head and he wore an earring in his left ear. I always found a man wearing an earring to be a big turn-off. I could never remember if wearing one in the right ear or left ear supposedly made them gay. Dating was traumatic enough without having to worry about that shit.

"I'm sure the roads surrounding the mall are bad, but once I make it to Route Fifty, I'll be fine."

He chuckled again and folded his arms in front of him. "I admire your determination and I hate to be the bearer of bad news, but they shut Route Fifty down about thirty minutes ago."

"What do you mean? Shut it down?"

"It's like a mini-river. They said there's more than four feet of rain on the highway."

"That's absurd. How can there be that much water on a damn highway?"

"Ma'am, I have no idea, but it's there. In fact, if you go inside any of the stores selling electronics and check out the televisions, you'll see all the madness going on out there with your own eyes."

I smirked. "That bad, huh?"

"Indeed."

I played with the tennis bracelet on my arm. "This shit wasn't even worth it."

"Excuse me?"

"Um, nothing. Just thinking out loud."

"Might I make a suggestion?"

I glared at him and hoped he wasn't going to try to pick me up. "No offense, but you're not my type."

A frown came across his face. "Who said you're *my* type? Men can suggest more than one thing, you know?"

I immediately felt embarrassed. "I'm sorry. I shouldn't have jumped to conclusions."

"What I was going to suggest is that you hurry up and grab one of the few rooms they have left at the hotel adjacent to the mall."

"You really think it's like that?" I asked.

"Well, you can either do that, or case you out a spot on one of the benches throughout the mall. You could possibly make it to your car and sleep in there, but you'll freeze unless you have a lot of gas to burn to use the heat."

"So people are checking into the hotel?"

"Like crazy. I was over there a little while ago and they had a line."

"But the mall isn't even that crowded."

"True, but this is a big mall and there are still plenty of people to fill up the hotel. They had a convention there to start with, so there weren't that many rooms left in the first place."

I contemplated my options for a moment and decided that it was better to be safe than sorry.

"Thanks for the heads up," I told him, before heading back inside the mall. "I really appreciate it, um . . ." I eyed his name badge. "Thanks for your help, Victor."

"You're most welcome."

I kept walking and he followed me.

"Do you have a name, miss?"

"Connie. Connie Wilkes." I held out my hand to shake his. "Thanks again, Victor."

With that, I picked up the pace so I could get to the hotel as quickly as possible. The thought of sitting on a bench, leaning to one side with drool falling out of my mouth was appalling.

I lucked out and got one of the last two rooms available. It was a suite, but you only live once, and it was fly as all get out. The entire hotel was slamming. I would have to recommend it to people from out of town from then on. I went back downstairs. The restaurant was packed and I wasn't that hungry so I decided to have a drink in the lounge and then grab something to eat later.

Pickings were slim at the bar, not that I was trying to get my flirt on. I just wasn't used to sitting at a bar alone. I always ventured out with friends or co-workers; never alone. It felt strange but, at the same time, it gave me some time to think.

Surprisingly, I found myself feeling guilty about the way I'd treated that Victor fellow. He did seem awfully nice and it wasn't his fault that his income for the year was probably less than what I made every month. Everyone is not meant to be successful and people measure success in different ways.

I finished my Blue Hawaiian and made my way back up to Room 1218. I plopped down on the king-sized feather bed and flicked on the television. There was no regular programming on the local stations; all of them were doing extensive coverage of the flood. Flat roofs were caving in on some of the stores and people were stuck on highways and side roads, trying to make it home safely. All I could think was thank heaven I wasn't one of them.

I ran my fingers over my bracelet. "You better last me a long, long time," I said aloud.

There was really nothing on cable. HBO was showing sports highlights and the movie on Lifetime was a repeat of one that I had seen before. I suddenly felt tired and decided to take a nap.

I took off my boots, jeans, and sweater and climbed under the soft comforter. It was always hard for me to take naps during the day. At least, without masturbating first. I started masturbating almost daily during high school and never stopped. I got back up just long enough to get a large bath towel from the bathroom so I could place it between my legs to cause friction on my clit. If I had known that I would be spending the night out, I would've come prepared with at least one of my smaller vibrators. They never fail.

Normally, the men I fantasized about when I was masturbating would be faceless, just dick and tongue. There would usually be two or three of them doing me at the same time. But this time it was strange. My lover had a face: Victor's. His body was Victor's body and his dick was Victor's. I couldn't help but wonder if Victor's dick was as juicy as I imagined it to be.

As I rubbed my hardened nipples and gyrated my hips around the towel, I imagined him eating me out royally and then flipping me over so he could fuck me from behind. My fantasy about him was so good that I came within minutes and it was one hell of an orgasm.

I was lying there, catching my breath, when the loud ringing of the telephone startled me.

I picked it up on the second ring. "Hello?"

"Hello, Connie?"

I recognized the voice immediately and couldn't believe it. "Victor?"

"Yes. I was just making sure you got checked in okay."

"How did you get my room number?" I asked.

"I don't have your room number. I just asked for you by name."

"Oh," I said, feeling like an idiot. Of course he didn't know my room number. "Well, as you can see, I did get checked in. Thanks again for your help."

He was silent for a moment before saying, "You're welcome. Enjoy the rest of your night."

"Hey, hold up!" I practically yelled into the phone.

"Yes?"

"Isn't the mall closed now?"

"Yes."

"So you're off duty?"

"I got off about fifteen minutes ago."

And I got off about two minutes ago, I thought to myself, and grinned.

"You obviously can't go home either, so what are you about to do?"

"The food court in the mall is closed as well so I was just going to get something from the hotel restaurant and then chill out in the security office."

I don't know what came over me but I wanted to know more about Victor. More than that, I wanted to fuck him.

"Victor, I haven't eaten either but the restaurant is crowded. I was down there earlier. Why don't you come up to my room and we can order room service."

"Uh, uh, sure," he said hastily. "That would be nice but . . . are you sure?"

"Absolutely. I'm in Room 1218. Give me about ten minutes and come on up."

"Um, okay."

We hung up and I put my clothes back on, replaced the

towel in the bathroom, and made the bed. I was refreshing my makeup when a knock came at the door.

"Come in, Victor," I said after opening the door and stepping aside. He looked like the cat that had just swallowed the canary. "I guess the last thing you expected was for me to invite you up."

"Yes, that was definitely the last thing I expected, but I appreciate it. I'm not too keen about hanging out with the other security guards when we're not working and I hate eating alone."

"Me, too," I said. "Have a seat and I'll get the room service menu out."

He eyed the bed but decided to sit at the desk chair instead. "So have you called your man to let him know you're stranded and won't be home?"

I laughed. His fishing around for information wasn't exactly subtle.

"I don't have a man. I'm always working." I sat on the edge of the bed, about two feet from where he was sitting. "What about you? Have you called your woman?"

"I got divorced a few months ago," he replied. "She wasn't the one, after all."

"I'm sorry to hear that." I glanced over the menu.

"It's for the best. The only thing I regret is not being able to see my kids every day."

"How many and how old?" I asked, thinking, "Baggage time."

"I have two girls, ages three and seven."

"That's cool." I handed him the menu. "I already know what I want."

"What's that?"

I started to say "the dick" but instead said, "I'm going for the chicken noodle soup and turkey club on wheat."

"Sounds good. I'll take the same."

"I'll call it in," I said. "Hey, want to share a dessert? Something like the key lime pie? I know I can't eat the whole thing."

"Sure, I'll share it with you."

Room service was as quick as lightning. Victor and I had a wonderful conversation while we ate. He actually turned out to be quite interesting. As it turned out, he was only a security guard on the weekends and also worked as a paralegal for one of the largest law firms in the country. That meant he had some intelligence, which impressed me. He'd taken on the second job after his divorce became final to be able to cover his child support and alimony.

I told him that I was the head of development for a large architectural agency. I learned to draw at an early age and became obsessed with it, so becoming an architect was the only thing that seemed logical.

After we ate, we were both full and started yawning. Victor offered to leave but I beckoned him to stay. In fact, I climbed up on the center of the bed and patted the comforter for him to join me.

He took off his shoes and loosened his tie before lying beside me. It was almost time for *The Sopranos* and *OZ* to come on HBO. I never missed an episode of either.

While I sensed that Victor knew I was somewhat interested, I was under the impression that he would be reluctant to make the first move. It would have to be on me, so I started caressing his thigh. He flinched at first and then relaxed.

"Victor, can I ask you something?"

"Ask away."

"Have you had sex since you've been divorced?"

He looked uneasy but finally replied, "A few times, but

that was just to release some tension. Besides, I felt guilty afterward because I didn't have feelings for the women."

"So you think there's something wrong with casual sex?"

"I think it depends on the situation and the parties involved. As long as both people are on the same page, it's definitely not a bad thing. But when one person has higher expectations than the other one, it can be the beginning of a major problem."

"I'm feeling you on that," I said. I moved my hand up higher and started caressing his dick. "I'd like to have casual sex with you tonight, Victor. I have no expectations, no hopes, no nothing. I just want to release some sexual tension myself."

He didn't respond but his dick did. It was getting harder by the second until it filled my palm.

"Are you attracted to me, Victor?" I asked.

"Yes, but I thought you said I wasn't your type?"

"I made a mistake," I said, feeling like an asshole for my earlier comment. "I just have this defense mechanism that I keep in place to ward off men. It just activated a little too quickly this time."

"Well, it's obvious that I'm feeling you. My hard dick speaks for itself, but you're going to have to convince me that you're feeling me."

"Ooh, a challenge. I like that."

I straddled his hips and darted my tongue in and out of his ear before nibbling on his earlobe. I pulled my sweater off and unzipped my jeans. "What if I told you that earlier, right before you called, I was lying up here in this very bed masturbating and fantasizing about you?"

He laughed. "I would say you're full of shit."

"No, really. I was, and guess what? I came really, really hard."

He blushed. "Are you for real?"

I took his left hand and slid it down the front of my jeans, so his fingers could explore my crotch.

"Feel my panties. Feel how wet they are. That's the result of thinking about you doing all sorts of *nasty* things to me."

"What *nasty* things?"

"Um, like tasting me, doing me from behind. Those kinds of *nasty* things."

"Sounds quite interesting but, you know, no fantasy can ever measure up to the real thing."

"No, never," I agreed. "Victor, tell me, do you eat pussy?"

"Not normally, but there are exceptions to every rule. You suck dick?"

"Like a master," I boasted. "Would you like for me to suck yours?"

"Is the sky blue?"

"It wasn't today," I said teasingly.

"Okay." He laughed. "So maybe that was a bad analogy, especially in the middle of a flood."

"It's okay, Victor. I'll forgive you, *this one time,* and suck your dick anyway."

I climbed off him and came out of my jeans, my bra, and panties. One thing about me; I've never had any hang-ups about my body like some women. Lights on or off, I'm willing to show the goods. Shelly and I even went to a nudist colony one summer. It was an unforgettable experience and I looked forward to going back.

Victor sat there like he was scared to take off his clothes.

"It would be a whole lot easier to suck your dick if you don't have any clothes on," I finally said.

He got up and undressed, his mouth hanging open the entire time as I profiled on the bed, making sure he got an eagle-eyed view of everything.

When he was nude, I reached for him and pulled him down on the bed beside me. "Wanna sixty-nine?"

"Sure, why not?"

I climbed on top of him and positioned my pussy over his face. Then I started teasing his dick with the tip of my tongue. He flinched and I loved it. Men who react to touching so quickly generally are very passionate. Some men are so acclimated to sex that you damn near have to choke on their dick before they even moan. Not so with Victor. Before I even had the head in my mouth, he was moaning and his toes were curling up.

"Lovely," I said.

"What's lovely?" he asked.

"The way your toes are curled up." I giggled. "I like it when I make a man's toes curl."

My comment must have truly turned him on because he grabbed the back of my thighs and pulled my pussy down onto his tongue. It was warm and thick and since I had already gotten a head start with an earlier orgasm, my pussy was ready for more action and extremely wet.

We went for it with the oral sex for the next thirty minutes before deciding to get down to business. Instead of climbing off him, I slid down his chest, letting my pussy juice lubricate it, and then sat on his dick facing his ankles. I grabbed his calves and squeezed as I moved up and down on his thick dick. It was even thicker than I had imagined when I fantasized about it.

Victor started slapping me on the ass. At first, I wasn't sure I was feeling it but then realized it was making me more excited. I came for the umpteenth time and the cum trickled down the sides of his thighs onto the sheets.

Victor exploded next and we lay there spent, both grinning in silence.

"So, was that casual enough for you?" he finally asked.

"Yes, it was," I replied. "Thanks for taking a dismal day and turning it into something much more special and memorable."

"Thank you for inviting me up." He chuckled. "I wasn't looking forward to spending the night in the security office with Big Mo and Little Joe."

"Big Mo and Little Joe?" I laughed. "Cute names. I'll have to meet them sometime."

He eyed me suspiciously. "Does that mean you plan to see me again?"

I buried my head in his chest for a moment and then bit his left nipple. "What if I do? Are you down for that?"

"Absolutely."

He drew my face to his and kissed me. "You know, they have very nice showers here. Or so I hear."

"Is that an invitation?" I asked.

"Yes." He palmed my ass. "Will you accept?"

I didn't answer. I just got up and headed toward the bathroom.

Fifteen minutes later, we were going for it again in the shower. I glanced down at the tennis bracelet sparkling on my arm, remembering how the entire chain of events had been set off by a ten-percent-off coupon.

"Stranger things have happened," I whispered as Victor got on his knees and buried his head between my legs.

The Flood—Part Two: Not Me, No Way, Oh Maybe

Shit! I couldn't believe my eyes. The day had been going bad enough already. Instead of hanging out with my sorority sisters, I had to study chemistry before I flunked out of college completely. I got up early in the fucking morning, went over to the science building to make up some lab work, and then it started raining. It wasn't raining cats and dogs. It was raining fucking cows and pigs.

I hadn't heard a damn thing about rain coming that day. Then again, I had partied the night before and rarely listened to the news anyway. I had gone through at least three boom boxes a year during my first two years of college but my television was rarely turned on.

I was never in my room unless I was studying, and my study habits left a lot to be desired. I'll admit that my parents were so strict on me in high school that when I escaped and left Hotlanta for D.C., I was "out there" from day one.

As soon as I got to college, fine-ass men were hanging out in front of the freshmen girls' dorm. While Hotlanta had a lot of brothas, they had played out to some extent. My friends from high school always used to hang out at Morehouse picking up men, but my folks weren't having it. They kept me under lock and key from the time I reached puberty. It was like they could sense boys sniffing my pussy or something.

Hell, I didn't lose my virginity until I got to college and that was just downright sad. My closest friends had been banging up a storm for what seemed like decades, even though it had only been a few years. Let's just say I made up for lost time when I got to college.

I didn't give it up my first night on campus but I gave it up the second night. His name was Bernard but they called him "The Body" and damn, did he have one! Bernard looked like he had been chiseled out of stone. He was light-skinned with dark, bedroom eyes and muscles for days.

I met him at a house party; someplace I had no damn business being since I didn't and still don't know who owned the house. I went to the party with this sister, who lived across the hall from me in the dorm. My roommate turned me off from the second I met her so I wasn't going a damn place with her.

Anyway, Lisa and I arrived at this row house about eight blocks from campus and there were wall-to-wall people up in that joint. I noticed Bernard right away, probably because he was surrounded by hoochie mommas damn near flashing their tits at him. Now, being inexperienced, I was a little *skird* at first, but then I made a life-altering decision.

My parents were a long-ass way from me. My pussy had never been stuck, sucked, or fucked. I was in college, which meant I had some brains. I was an adult, so I said, "Fuck it," out loud and marched right up to him. I was rude and pushed a few of the whores out my way. They weren't happy either.

"My name's Frenchie, what's yours?" I asked him.

"Bernard," he replied in a sexy-ass voice.

I could barely hear him, but luckily the music was concentrated in the basement so we could at least talk.

"You go to school here, Bernard?" I inquired.

"Yeah, I'm a senior. You?"

"I'm a freshman." I pushed my breasts up on him, all 34C of them. "I guess that would make me fresh meat."

He laughed in my face. "I guess it would."

One of the other bitches copped an attitude. "Um, Bernard, I thought we were hooking up tonight," she stated nastily.

He gave her an annoyed look. "Maybe we will; maybe we won't. Let me get to know youngun over here."

"I like the way you talk," I whispered in his ear. "It's sexy."

"You think so?"

"Uh-huh. In fact, why don't we blow this joint?"

Bernard looked me up and down and obviously decided that I was the pick of the evening. Virgin or not, if nothing else, I knew my ass was fine. In fact, next month, I'm going on that reality TV show *Elimidate* just to prove that I'm the shit and can get any man I want. I'm trying to get on *Blind Date* and *The 5th Wheel,* too. I might as well do them all. I want to get on that Blackgentlemen.com show but the waiting list is so damn long, I might be in a rocking chair before I land a spot on that bitch.

Bernard and I ended up back at his apartment. He lived a few miles from campus and drove a fly-ass Corvette. He was originally from the Bronx and I loved his accent. I also loved his dick. Shit, I *adored* his dick.

"The Body" was shocked when I informed him about my virginity. Then this big-ass grin spread across his face.

"Damn, your cherry's still intact?" he asked, moving in closer to me on the sofa.

"Intact and ready to be busted," I replied.

"So why'd you select me to do it?"

"I'll be frank. My parents are—how shall I say it—*strict as shit,* so I've been dick-deprived while all my friends have been living it up like that JaRule song." I reached out and started rubbing his dick through his shorts. "Now it's my turn."

"That still doesn't answer the question. Why me?"

It was obvious that he wanted me to blow up his ego. I decided if that's what it took, so fucking be it.

"Why you? Hmph, well, you're obviously fine, but you know that already. As I said before, I like the way you talk and your accent is the shit. Your ride is slamming and so is your place. If I have to give it up to someone to get the party started, why not you?" I rubbed his dick more aggressively and went in for the kill. "After all, you're damn near perfect!"

He blushed and rubbed his chin. "I just love a woman that recognizes perfection when she sees it." Then he disappointed me. "What's your major?"

I frowned. "Who gives a fuck what my major is? I want to do the nasty with you, not marry you."

"For someone with strict parents, you sure have a filthy mouth."

I got up and started undressing. I was ready to get the first time over with. From what I'd heard, the first time was never all that but it was a necessity. If you never start, you can never excel.

"Okay, fine. My major is fucking with a minor in dick-sucking. How's that?"

"Smart ass!" He pointed at me and rotated his finger. "If you're gonna strip, do it right. Twirl around or something."

"I wasn't exactly trying to strip. I'm just trying to get buck naked." He smirked and it angered me. "How the fuck am I supposed to strip without any damn music?"

He got up, went over to a shelf system and turned on Monifah's "Touch It." Now that shit just did something to a sister. That's one of my all-time faves.

I got into the flow of the music and before I knew it, I was ready to rival a professional.

Bernard eyed me with a smile on his face. "You know, you could make a shitload of money stripping on the side. Lots of girls do it to make it through college."

"My parents have my tuition and shit covered," I said. "They had one of those college funds for me since birth."

"Cool, but money can buy a lot of other things, too."

I got everything off and was ready to stop talking so I said, "Shut the fuck up and get naked with me."

Bernard chuckled and got up off the couch. He stripped and, while I wasn't an expert at that time, his dick looked mighty scrumptious to me.

I'm not going to elaborate too much about the rest of the night. As expected, my first time was just a means to an end. It hurt like hell, Bernard was inconsiderate and just went for his, not giving a shit whether I walked away from the experience with anything or not, and I never fucked his ass again. He was just a dick.

I did take his advice, though. After realizing it was expensive as shit to hang out in D.C. and discovering that fly clothes, liquor, and weed were all necessities to be considered "cool" on campus, I took a gig stripping at Omije. To this day, I don't know what the fuck "Omije" means, but I still work there. I make wheelbarrows full of money, too.

Men are so fucking stupid. You can tell them anything and they believe it. All you have to do is stroke their heads, both of them, and they will give you the lint off their balls if you ask for it.

I don't pull tricks like most of the other dancers. Fuck that. I pick and choose who I am willing to do. Now, eating my pussy is something totally different. If a man is trying to give up the Benjamins to lick my coochie, they are welcome to it. Women, too, for that matter. I've only let a few sisters sample the goods, but tongue action is tongue action, so what the hell.

I love making money for taking off my clothes and shaking my ass. That was one reason I was so mad the day of the fucking flood. There I was, on a Saturday, trying to do the damn thing and study, when those damn cows and pigs started falling from the sky.

There was no way I was going to be able to make it to Omije in weather like that. Water was cascading down the middle of the campus streets like the Nile. I must admit that looking at some of the students trying to walk through that shit was hilarious. Idiots! Common sense should've told them to chill where they were.

My only regret was that I wasn't chilling in my dorm room, instead of the science building. I would've preferred to be stuck anywhere but there. Over one of my sorority sisters' cribs or some damn place.

The building was damn near deserted. I had seen a few peeps earlier but as I went out in the hallway, I didn't hear anything. You could have heard a mouse pissing on a cotton ball up in that bitch.

To make matters worse, I was starving. I didn't bother fixing any instant oatmeal before I left my dorm and my stomach was growling like a muthafucka. I went back into the chemistry lab and searched through my backpack for something, anything, to munch on. The only thing I found was one damn Twizzler and it was stuck to the bottom. It had probably been there for months.

I was startled when I heard someone turning the doorknob. In popped the head of the janitor. He looked just as surprised to see me.

"Sorry, miss, I didn't know anyone was here. I'll come back later and clean up."

Before he could close the door, I yelled out, "Hold up! I'm actually done, but I can't get back to my dorm in the rain."

"That's putting it mildly. They just had to pull one student out of a storm drain over by the business building."

"Out a storm drain? How the hell can someone fall down a storm drain?" I asked.

"It was one of those big ones and the wind gusts and water are so strong, it just dragged her right in."

"Stupid bitch," I muttered under my breath.

"What's that?" he asked, straining an ear to hear.

"Uh, nothing. Is she okay?"

"Yeah, she's fine."

"Cool." I went closer to the door. "Listen, is there anything to eat around here?"

"You mean, other than the dead frogs in the biology lab?"

I eyed the fool like I wanted to rip him a new asshole. He got the point.

"Just joking," he added. "There's a few vending machines in the staff lounge."

Things were looking up. "Where's that?"

"Second floor, behind the bank of elevators."

"Hmph, they have the shit hidden, huh? I never knew it was there."

He grinned. "It keeps the students out, but no one's in there today so feel free."

"Thanks."

I managed to find the staff lounge. "Ain't this a bitch!" I said when I spotted it behind the elevators. I tried the door and it was locked. "Shit!"

As I was stomping away, I heard the door open behind me and a male voice say, "Sorry, we locked it so we could study."

I turned to face the one they called Darwin. There he was in all his nerd glory, with his bifocals on and a pocket protector sticking out of his shirt. Darwin, whose real name I never knew or cared to know, was one of the three campus geniuses whom everyone avoided at all costs. The other two were nicknamed after famous scientists as well: Newton and Einstein.

While I had seen them around campus many times, particularly in the science building where they seemed to live, I had never uttered a word to any of them. To do so would have been considered "questionable" by the other cool people like me.

I assumed when he said *"we* locked it so *we* could study" that he was referring to the rest of his crew. They acted like they were joined at the hip.

"I just wanted to get something from the vending machines," I finally replied.

He opened the door wider. "That's not a problem. Come on in."

Sure enough, when I walked through the door, the other two were sitting there at a table piled up with books. They looked like they were about to pee themselves when I appeared. I didn't care how smart they were, they were still fucking idiots in my book.

The one they called Einstein spoke up. "Hey, Frenchie. What are you doing here?"

I was stunned. "You know my name?"

He blushed and glanced down at the table. "Everyone knows your name, Frenchie. You're like the most popular girl on campus."

I glared at him. "Damn right I am, but I didn't realize nerds kept up with those kinds of things."

Einstein straightened his bow tie and adjusted his suspenders. "Well, we do."

Newton had the nerve to get smart with me. "We're not nerds. We're extremely intelligent and there's nothing wrong with being intelligent. You should try it sometime."

I marched over to the table where they were sitting. "Are you calling me a dummy, you highwater-wearing muthafucka?"

Darwin walked up behind me. "No, he's not doing that. He was simply pointing out that we don't like being called that particular name."

"Which name? Nerds?" I asked. "Well, that's what you are."

Darwin joined the other two at the table. "Define the word 'nerds.'"

"Define it?" I asked.

Newton smirked at me. "Hmph, she probably doesn't even know what 'define' means."

"Kiss my black ass!" I yelled out at him. "You probably don't even know which way the slit on a pussy goes, you faggot!"

"I'm not gay!" he came back at me. "I have a girlfriend. Two of them."

"In your wet dreams," I said nastily. "Who in their right mind would fuck the likes of you?"

Newton smirked again. "You'd be surprised. I go out with some of the hottest women on campus."

I snickered. The fool couldn't be for real. His eyeglasses had a piece of masking tape in the middle holding them together. Then it dawned on me. "Aw, I get it. You prey on the sisters and trade study help for sex, don't you? How pathetic."

"It's not even like that," Darwin said. "Newton has a lot to offer. He's at the top of the class and some day, he's going to run a multi-billion-dollar corporation."

"That must be the same day those damn hairstyles you muthafuckas are sportin' come back in style."

They did have some fucked-up haircuts, too. One was wearing a played-out Afro and the other two were wearing conkalines. Those shits haven't been in style since the early sixties. Afros are coming back, but not the kind Darwin had on his fucking head.

I eyed the vending machines and my mouth started watering. I walked over to them and was disappointed that most of the slots were empty, except for some cheese crackers and one bag of corn chips that looked like it might have been there since the building was first erected.

"Oh, well, beggars can't be choosers," I said aloud. I started digging through my purse for change. The damn machine didn't take dollar bills. How outdated!

Darwin called out to me, "Um, you need some change, Frenchie?"

Einstein said, "If I were you, I wouldn't give her a thing."

I swung around and rolled my eyes in his direction. Now he was trying to get smart with me; the tramp. "I guess it's a good thing for me that you're not him, then." I walked over and handed Darwin two ones. I wanted to get a soda, too. At least they had those.

Darwin stood and dug through the pockets of his highwaters until he found enough quarters. "Here you go," he said, handing them to me.

"Thanks. You're the nice one." I snarled at the other two and walked back over to the machines.

After getting my crackers and soda, I was about to head back out the door. I heard them whispering and giggling behind me so I swung around. "What's so fucking funny?"

Newton eyed me and said, "Frenchie, have you ever been spanked?"

"Spanked? What black child do you know that has never had their ass whooped by their parents? Of course, I've been spanked, idiot."

Einstein stood up and said, "No, not that kind of spanked."

I started laughing. "Are you nerds referring to some S and M bullshit? I can't even picture the three of you fucking, much less spanking someone."

"We don't mean that kind, either," Einstein replied and reached into his pocket. He pulled out a small clear vial that was full of light green powder. "This is the type of spank we mean."

"What the hell is that?" I inquired.

They all looked at each other and Darwin said, "Go ahead, Einie, tell her."

Einstein cleared his throat. "Spank is something we invented. You can snort it or put it in a liquid and drink it."

I shook my head and stomped my foot. "Are you trying to tell me that you three nerds created your own drug?"

Darwin nodded. "Yes, we did. They don't call us smart for nothing. Who do you think creates most drugs? Someone stupid?"

I had to give it to him. That made sense. "I've never thought of it that way, but I guess a person would have to know something about chemistry to make drugs."

Newton snorted. The sound made me sick. "A person has to know *a lot* about chemistry to make drugs."

I was amazed that I had never heard of the shit before. I wasn't a serious druggie, but I worked at a damn strip club and most of the other dancers and the clientele were using one thing or another. "Why haven't I ever heard of it? You sell it?"

They all shook their heads. Darwin said, "No, we don't sell it. That's illegal."

"And making it isn't illegal?" I asked. "What does it do to a person who takes it?"

They started staring at each other again.

"Are you all going to tell me today or not?"

Newton said, "It's a sex drug."

"A sex drug?" I walked back over to them and put my backpack down. "You guys are shittin' me."

"No, we're not," Einstein said. "We've created the ultimate aphrodisiac. If you don't believe us, put a little in your soda and see what happens."

"Hell no!" I lashed out at him. "For all I know, you idiots might be trying to kill a sistah or something."

Einstein laughed and said with disdain, "She's scared. Figures. The girls that always try to pretend like they're the shit never are."

"I ain't scared of shit!" I told him. "Hand it over."

He gave me the vial. I opened it and sniffed it. "There's no odor."

"Of course not. It is undetectable and we can even get away with taking it on the plane when we go home."

"You nerds are lucky I'm bored and probably the most curious sistah on the fucking planet."

Okay, I guess you're wondering why I didn't just break camp when the fools started talking about this Spank shit.

Like I said, I was bored and curious. I put some in my soda and drank it.

At first, I didn't feel a damn thing. Then, about ten minutes later, my pussy started throbbing like it had its own heartbeat.

Normally, I would never, *ever* have sexual relations with men that looked and acted like Newton, Darwin, and Einstein, but Spank made them all suddenly seem like assorted lollipops that I was just dying to lick.

I started with Darwin, since he had been the nicest to me from the beginning. Before I knew it, I had him naked, sitting on a chair, and I was dipping my tongue in and out the slit of his dick like I was on a treasure hunt. His dick was *good,* too. Better than any dick I had ever remembered sucking, and I've sucked many a dick in my day.

Newton got on the floor behind me, lifted up the back of my skirt, pulled down my winter tights and panties, and started eating out my ass. Freak! I must admit it was *good,* too.

I caught a rhythm on Darwin's dick and started rotating my wrist on the bottom part while I waxed the head. "Um, you like that, baby?" I asked, looking up into his eyes, which I could barely see behind his bifocals.

"Yes, I like it. I bet you like it too, don't you?" he replied.

I didn't respond, just kept right on sucking.

Newton wasn't fucking around and started ripping at my tights until he had them in shreds all over my legs. He stuck a finger in my ass and explored it. I was so excited that I came about the same time Darwin exploded within my cheeks.

Newton pulled me up off the floor and spread me on the table stating, "It's my turn."

He didn't waste any time sticking his dick inside me and he hit it so hard that the insides of my thighs were trembling. I couldn't believe a nerd was fucking me so royally. I commented, "Damn, I guess you really can't judge a book by its cover."

He was so deep in me that I could feel his ball sack slapping up against my ass and the table was squeaking and sliding across the floor inch by inch.

Einstein was obviously sick of being the observer so next thing I knew, he was pressing his dick up against my mouth so I could do his ass. I grabbed onto his dick with one hand and started milking it for what it was worth.

Newton lifted my sweater and yanked my bra straps down so he could free my tits. Before he could get one in his mouth, Darwin beat him to the punch. "Let me lick on something," he said, and started in on my right tata.

So there I was, on a Saturday afternoon, in the middle of a flood, in the staff lounge that I never knew existed, having a foursome with the three biggest nerds on campus instead of studying. I guess my major really should have been fucking with a minor in dick-sucking.

I had never had three men work me over at the same time before and damn, it was *good. It was all good!*

That Spank was something, because I sucked all three of their dicks that day and they all tasted like candy. I let all three of them fuck my pussy and they all seemed like they were hung like mules. I even did something that day that I swore I would never do: I let Newton have some of this ass. Now *that* is worth telling about.

By the time it got down to the anal activity, the sun had gone down and the cows and pigs were still falling out the sky. There were clothes (both my fly-ass ones and their nerdy-ass ones) strewn all over the lounge, along with books, and it smelled like straight-up fucking up in that joint.

Ironically, like most sistahs, I always assumed that taking it up the ass would hurt like all hell. Either the Spank helped buffer that shit or Newton was a muthafuckin' expert. When he asked me if he could have it, I took Einstein's dick out of my mouth just long enough to say, "Go for it."

He licked his index finger, toyed with my ass with it, and then placed the head of his dick on my asshole. I must admit that I flinched a little at first but once he stuck the head in, I was craving the rest of it. He took his time and worked up a good pace, going in and out of my ass while I continued to suck Einie's dick. Yes, I was yelling out his nickname before it was all said and done.

We fucked until the wee hours of Sunday morning and it was, and still remains, the most incredible sexual experience of my entire life. All three of them walked me back to my dorm and my nose was so wide open from the "fuckathon" that I actually kissed all three of them in front of the building. I didn't even give a damn who might have seen us—even though the coast appeared to be clear.

I saw them in passing after that but we never fucked again. I was tempted to ask one of them for some Spank but figured it was safer to leave that shit alone. I might have ended up fucking the entire football team, or worse, the entire debate team full of nerds.

I'm still doing the damn thing at the club, making a grip of money. I have started fucking around with the clientele more often. In many ways, that night with Darwin, Einstein, and Newton gave me a newfound sexual freedom. I guess that's why people should never say, "Not me!"

About the Contributors

Robert Scott Adams was born in Rochester, New York. He graduated from Morehouse College in 1975. He is an established poet, jazz critic, and fiction writer. He is currently finishing a novel, *The Further Adventures of Carlotta and Miguel,* which features more erotic escapades from this dynamic duo.

Ife Ayodele resides in Centreville, MD.

Shonell Bacon is the coauthor of *LuvAlwayz: The Opposite Sex & Relationships* and *Draw Me with Your Love.* She is cofounder and chief editor of the AA literary e-zine, *The Nubian Chronicles.* Currently, she is wrapping up a dual masters degree in creative writing and English at McNeese State University in Lake Charles, Louisiana, where she also teaches English Composition and literature courses. She can be reached at *sdb6812@ hotmail.com* and *shonbacon@hotmail.com.*

Geneva Barnes lives a relatively "nondescriptive" life in Brooklyn, New York. She thanks her very special friend for his encouragement, patience, and love, without which she never would've pursued writing. She dedicates her submission to this anthology to him.

blk_man4u resides in Jacksonville, TN.

Deep Bronze, a native of suburban Chicago, has been writing since the age of thirteen. She has won numerous awards and recognitions as a writer of short stories, poetry, and essays. She has worked as a stringer for newspapers in suburban Chicago and San Diego. She has traveled to Ghana and South Africa and looks forward to more international travel. She earned a Bachelor of Arts in speech from Chicago State University and is preparing for graduate work at DePaul University. The thirtysomething mother of two lives in suburban Chicago with her family.

London Brown has been writing literary and erotic fiction for more than a decade. She has completed her first work of full-length fiction and is working on her second. She resides in South Carolina with her husband and two children.

James E. Cherry resides in Jackson, TN.

Victor DeVanardo is a poet, essayist, book reviewer, novelist, playwright Vampyre, and screenwriter who lives in St. Louis, MO.

Bootney Farnsworth resides in Detroit, MI.

Reginald Harris resides in Baltimore, MD.

Ms. B. Haven resides in Brooklyn, NY.

Eileen M. Johnson resides in Louisiana. She enjoys writing in her spare time and is currently at work on her first novel. She is also a contributor to the popular anthology *Blackgentlemen.com*.

Private Joy, aka Rosalyn D, is a very single graduate student working on a doctorate in psychology. She writes poetry,

short stories, and erotic fiction in the few hours she has all to herself. Email any comments to *privatejoy1975@aol.com*.

Marilyn Lee enjoys writing erotic romance or romantica and has developed ardent readers for her Bloodlust erotic vampire romance series. She also writes erotic romances featuring full-figured heroines and has written a number of other multicultural romances. She loves to hear from readers who can email her at *MLee2057@aol.com* or visit her website at *http://members.aol.com/Mlee2057/MLee.htm*.

Jonathan Luckett is the author of the novels, *Jasminium* and *Feeding Frenzy*. A native of Brooklyn, New York, he now makes his home in Washington, D.C., where he is at work on his next book. His work can be found at *www.jonathanluckett.com*.

V. Anthony Rivers is the author of *Daughter by Spirit* and *Everybody Got Issues*. He is also a contributor to the anthology *Sistergirls.com*. He resides in Van Nuys, California, and is currently working on his third novel.

Robert Edison Sandiford is the author of *Winter, Spring, Summer, Fall: Stories* (Empyreal Press/The Independent Press), and two comic collections of erotica, *Attractive Forces* and *Stray Moonbeams* (NBM Publishing).

Fredric Sellers writes under several pen names, depending on the type of writing he's doing. He was born in Akron, Ohio, in 1945 during a time when things were hard. Sellers began writing in grade school, but when he started high school, writing took a backseat when he found out what girls were all about. After high school, he served in the Marine Corps. He attended Kent State University where he studied fine arts. He later served in the U.S. Army as an officer. When his tour was over, he decided to leave the military and became employed by General Tire as an Industrial Photographer. After retirement, Sellers decided to pursue writing again. He has written many short stories, and is currently working on two novels under another name.

Sha'ron currently resides in New York pursuing her masters degree. In her spare time she continues to write poems and short stories.

Sio is originally from Liberia, West Africa. He is a professional currently working in nonprofit management in Washington, D.C. He is married with two children.

Jai Thomas is a thirty-four-year-old female residing in Oakland, California. She has been writing for the past five years and is currently working on her first novel.

reese williams is a writer currently living in Philadelphia, PA. She can be reached at *robbinw831@aol.com.*

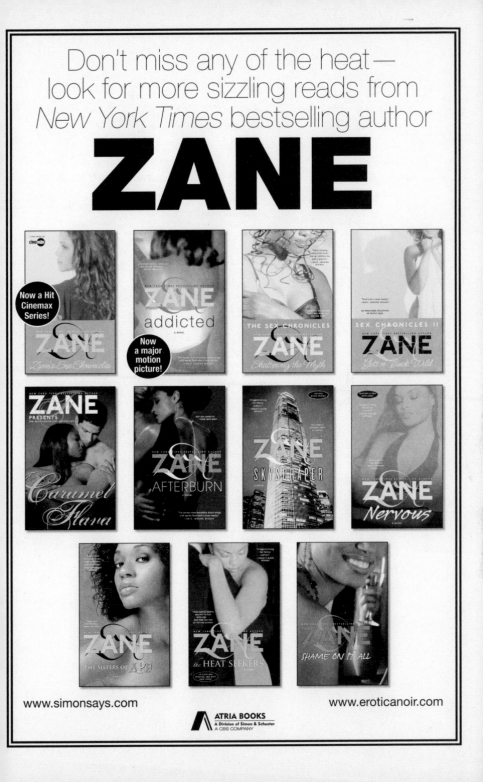